THE SONS AND DAUGHTERS OF HAM

Book I: A Requiem

I found your book to be an exciting and poignant read. This family is not unlike many of the people we know, and you shed light on the atrocities that take place in such a calm, methodical manner: This tragedy could befall anyone. Throughout the book you set the stage for things to come and intricately connected the dots. I especially appreciate the voice in which you write, your judicious use of metaphors, and your decision to take on such a monumental responsibility. This is a story that must be heard since these atrocities continue unabated and only a few get the attention of the powers that be.

LYNN G., AUTHOR OF FREEDOM AND THE CASHEW SEED: A MEMOIR, AND PREVIEW READER FOR *The Sons and Daughters of Ham, Book I: A Requiem*

I read the entire thing on the plane this weekend. Really quite excellent… Your style is very intense but easy to read all at the same time. Your descriptions of people, streets, and situations are right on target, especially having lived in Brooklyn all my life. I thoroughly enjoyed it.

SANDI W., SUCCESSFUL ENTREPRENEUR, CARIBBEAN IMMIGRANT, AND PREVIEW READER FOR *The Sons and Daughters of Ham, Book I: A Requiem*

First, I would like to say my husband and I enjoyed your book. It gave us a better understanding of Trinidadian culture and beliefs. My heart went out to Ophelia for her loss… Even though, I knew Kevin was going to die, I couldn't help but shed tears when it finally happened. A child dying before his parent/parents is a nightmare that no parent wants to be faced with… I love your characters. They were all trying to handle life. In the real world, I have found you can look in a person's face and know what they have been through. A person's eyes are the "windows to their soul," and many a time that's where you can see the things they're carrying in life. I'm an usher at my church and there are times when the room is so full with burdens that you feel like you can't breathe. I feel your characters and the story you told really captured the hidden things that people go through behind closed doors.

MARGARET B., RETIRED GOVERNMENT CONTRACT SPECIALIST ; EDWARD B., RETIRED AIR FORCE CHIEF MASTER SERGEANT, AND PREVIEW READERS FOR *The Sons and Daughters of Ham, Book I: A Requiem*

To see what more REAL READERS are saying, please visit:
HAMNOVELS.COM/READER-TESTIMONIALS/

THE SONS AND DAUGHTERS OF HAM

Book I: A Requiem

PETRA E. LEWIS

BOOKSTAR

Copyright © Petra E. Lewis
Published by BookStar
Printed in the United States

ISBN 978-0-9916136-0-1

Edited by The Threepenny Editor
Proofreading by Bab Griswold
Cover design by Pamela Geismar
Layout & Ornaments by Phillip Gessert
Cover Photo by Shizuka Minami
Author Photo by Kevin Ryan

hamnovels.com

RED

The Lord said, "What have you done?
Listen! Your brother's blood
cries out to me from the ground..."

—GENESIS 4:10

THE AFTERMATH

In the wake of Kevin's death, her mother had become itinerant, but Clarissa knew that it was Linnaeus—not the longings of her own heart muscle—that her mother was following.

Linnaeus, her mother's longtime boyfriend, was a Prince Hall Mason. He and his lodge brothers, along with their wives and girl-friends, took chartered bus rides up and down the Eastern seaboard and through the highways and back roads of the shallow South, sometimes veering north to Canada. But in most of the bus-ride snapshots that Linnaeus took, her mother always looked startled to be wherever she was. As though, numbering among the family's ghosts, she were a specter caught on film.

While the others in their group posed in front of garish roadside attractions, held up bottles of Johnny Walker Red and flimsy plastic cups, or crowded around luncheonette tables with their best, shiny grins, her mother sat there, the flesh beneath her eyes like a rac-coon's—stained black with grief and worry.

Clarissa layered two hand-cut sourdough slices of Amish friend-ship bread with pieces of corncob-smoked Vermont ham, Manchego cheese (which she had recently learned about), and mayonnaise. From her mother's travels she was fed: Upon her mother's return from a Vermont ski trip, Clarissa had first sampled smoked venison. With each new trip, Clarissa found that her own palate became more adventurous. Gone were the days of rum raisin Häagen-Dazs being the most exotic thing she had ever tasted. Her mother and Linnaeus were off again, on another bus ride.

Clarissa turned on the cable, lounging in the den with her hun-gry-man sandwich. She leveled the remote, flipping channels: CNN, Cartoon Network, MTV…Nothing on. After she finished eating, she went upstairs to brush her teeth. She looked at her face in the mirror, at the fine splotches and acne. She picked at one in disgust, but afraid of scarring, stopped.

Leaving the bathroom, Clarissa put her hand on the doorknob to her own room, but turned and stared for what seemed like a very long time at the knob on her brother's door. She knew that her mother snuck into her brother's bedroom at night, a ritual that each woman, in her private chapel of mourning and pride, knew better than to acknowledge. But it had already been four months since Kevin had died, and just as long since Clarissa had seen the door open.

Their mother had marked it as off limits by simply closing it. But she was riding on another bus across some Pennsylvania highway, and Clarissa was sick of putting mayonnaise on her own bread and heating up her own instant dinners. She was raging now, the street, the defiance in her oozing. And this was why she put her hand on the knob and whispered softly, "My turn."

The room was just as she had imagined: immaculate. With help from her parents, her brother's final girlfriend, Ashley, had posted his belongings back from California, and when the boxes arrived in New York, her mother had cut open each one and put everything back in its place.

Clarissa was too afraid to touch anything. The one thing that she knew for certain was missing was Kevin's valedictory suit, because it was the one he had been buried in. But his cap and gown, neatly placed in plastic, still hung from the back of his closet door. Reaching underneath the plastic, she touched the hem of his robe. Then, when she opened the closet door, a strange, life-filled smell leaped out at her as though it had been waiting: a combination of peppermint shampoo, Polo cologne, and the transported surf of Big Sur. Clarissa began to move with authority now, touching the things on Kevin's desk and his bureau. Her mother had given nothing away. Not even to his girlfriend, who had kept no mementos for herself, likely out of respect. And Clarissa's mother had proffered nothing. "That girl has her pictures and her recollection of summer kisses," she had said, as though begrudging Ashley even that. "And memories of whatever it is the two of them used to do whenever no one was looking."

Clarissa began to survey the contents of each bureau drawer, working from bottom to top: shirts, shorts, sweaters, T-shirts, socks, designer briefs. Clarissa asked aloud, "Why is she still holding on to this?" By *this* she meant all of it. In the drawer slotted just beneath the one where he kept his underwear and socks, Clarissa saw her brother's N.O.R.M.L. T-shirt. She retrieved it and shook out its length, then buried her face in its soft, worn cotton. She laughed, even now, at the image of Kevin wearing it standing next to their mother in the kitchen, laughed at the fact that their mother had never known what it meant: National Organization for the Reform of Marijuana Laws.

"Oh, Kevin," Clarissa moaned into its folds, "you are ridiculous." She had spoken in the present tense.

For months after his death Clarissa couldn't speak Kevin's name, nor even refer to him in conversation as "my brother." Instead she called him "my twin," which hermetically sealed their identity from the rest of the world.

And this was what she whispered softly now: "My twin. Sweet twin. Funny twin. Smart twin. High twin…" as she rummaged through his belongings.

She found it—the Indian-head pipe that she had watched her brother lift to his lips so many times. He had bought it on a school trip upstate to an Algonquin reservation. The pipe was pale with sharp, dark lines, like the inside of her mother's hand. She had found it in the back of Kevin's sock drawer. Digging through the drawers' recesses again, she found the pipe's complement, an old bag of weed. It had been there for as many months as Kevin had been dead. How had her mother overlooked this? Clarissa, who knew nothing about getting stoned, wondered if the bag was still good, and she held it up to the light, wanting to laugh that this was the part of her brother that had lived.

Clarissa sat at the edge of Kevin's bed and held the pipe and the weed. Rocking back and forth and closing her eyes, she moaned, a slow, broken, open-mouthed, rattling lament that ended with no sound. Clarissa let her tears dot the tips of her bare feet, then collected the remaining ones in her hands.

"How does it make you feel?" she'd once asked.

"There's nothing like it in the world. All you feel is yourself. All you feel is peace," he'd said.

And, in fact, that was what she wanted to feel. All she wanted to feel. Not this saline distress that she was feeling now and had felt so many nights lying awake in her single bed. Since Kevin's death, although she could not name it, this was the feeling that she desired, the thing that her life had been missing. Peace, at least a morsel of it. And sitting at the edge of her brother's flawlessly made twin bed, Clarissa tried to remember how his hands had moved to form this peace.

Clarissa took a pinch of weed from the bag, packed it into the

Indian head's open skull, then placed the pipe into her waiting mouth. She searched the drawer again and found a lighter.

Stupid, Clarissa told herself. *You can't smoke this in the house.* She went downstairs and found a box of matches in a kitchen drawer. She then went down another set of stairs and opened the basement den door that led out to the garden. The cold air was immediate, but Clarissa liked this coldness, this dampness, that was so much like moss and dew. The day's coolness leeching to her hands and face, she put the pipe to her mouth. Her hand protecting the match flame, she let the warmth marinate her lungs. She waited, and then it came and rested upon her. So this was what Kevin's peace felt like.

Staring out into the darkness with her new confidence, she could make out things in her mother's garden: the evergreen tree, the hibiscus. All the other flowers had run their course, or were underground for the winter. *Underground for the winter.* Clarissa put the pipe to her lips again and took a deep inhale. And suddenly the world came back to her, but differently this time from when she first inhaled. And Clarissa felt as though her eyes were opened as this new knowledge came in.

Everyone mourns, even animals.

Elephants caress their dead with their trunks, carry around the bones, or bury them beneath a mound of branches and grass; others, allegedly, weep. Dogs wait for deceased masters. Burial and mourning are timeless, perhaps preceding the appearance of—but no doubt perfected by—man.

Peruvians, Tainos, Egyptians, Indians, Taoists, Buddhists: They all have their rituals.

But those sitting shiva—ah, yes, *they* know how to mourn. As the corpse is washed and dressed in white linen by volunteers of the Hevrah Kadisha, there is no pretense, no embalming, no transfiguring death to resemble life. As family members enter the funeral home for the viewing, expelling their grief, they tear open their shirts at the place just over their hearts. At the burial site the body is lowered directly in its wooden coffin or straight into the grave in its shroud, expected to decompose simultaneously, returning to the earth as one.

It is we Americans who fumble through mourning. We lack the

tools for grieving. Our dead, once washed and dressed by us, are cared for and handled by strangers. We no longer wear sackcloth, as in Biblical times. We no longer beat our breasts. We no longer fill our mouths with ashes.

But we Americans did once know how to mourn. As families awaited the arrival of a photographer from some far-off town, fresh flowers used to keep the scent of unembalmed bodies from overpowering the guests. *This persists.* Mourners wore black to make themselves inconspicuous, so death would not notice them. *This persists.* The dead were buried six feet deep to keep the smell of decaying flesh from escaping the ground. *This persists.* We know each ritual and relic, but not its history.

For all intents and purposes, Ophelia Ramtahal, mother of Euclin, Clarissa, and Kevin, was now an American. She had buried her son in the manner of the Rio Verde countryside, and had honored his memory by hosting *Nine Nights,* but what now? What next?

Today was a Saturday. She should cook. She and Linnaeus had returned from their trip to Montreal weeks ago, but she felt no urge to make anything.

In the house there were no more rituals. Just six months before, there was chicken soup with dumplings on Saturdays, and heavy-dough bread and salt fish buljol on Sundays. Now she could only make, on any given day, whatever she had the strength to cook. Clarissa—thankfully—ate whatever she could scavenge, and demanded nothing. But now Ophelia decided to make a cookup of beef pelau with pigeon peas. She checked a large, deep circular bin and found a copious supply of rice. She sorted through the rows of glass jars, some empty, others half filled with dry beans. Only the pigeon pea jar was empty. She took some steak from the fridge and placed it on the butcher block to thaw.

She dreaded walking the streets, but would have to go to Church Avenue for the pigeon peas. It would mean seeing at every turn and every corner boys, black boys, many around the age that Kevin would have been. And though she would not know them, she would fear for them. They were all ambulatory corpses to her—their fates sealed and simply an issue of time and luck.

To match her outerwear to the weather, Ophelia surveyed the sky through the living room window. When she had first arrived in America, there were days so cold she broke down in tears in the street before reaching her destination. But today, the weatherman was wrong. She saw no sign of rain. It had been an unnatural spring, almost as warm as summer.

She made her way outside and down the block toward Church Avenue. There were already jerk barbecues on the sidewalk, set against the corner bodegas. *By God, have they no discretion anymore at INS? The quality of some of the people they now let through immigration!* A new breed of people, made of West Indians from every island, seemed to have taken over the neighborhood: the most unpolished, knock-kneed, country-bookie, Island people she had ever seen, with their cheap, tight polyester dresses, broad laughs, Vaselined legs, never-ending domino games, and jerk barbecue drums popping up on every corner. Now men sat on kitchen chairs in front of Latin and West Indian storefronts, playing cards and turning meat on their grills. These men from big and small islands, some leaning on their bikes, harassed every skirt that walked by, from schoolgirls to the women who could be the aunts or mothers of these girls—or even some of these men.

A cock crowed. Ophelia turned, incredulous. *A cock in somebody yard? Keeping roosters in their yards, herding goats into their houses for sacrifice, playing cards and grilling jerk barbecue on every Brooklyn street corner like a race of uncivilized people. Don't they know that they are in America, by God! These people are in America!*

In another era, Ophelia would have been a washerwoman beating laundry against the rocks at the mouth of the Rio Verde River, washing clothes with blue soap until her hands were red with blood. But she was none of these things. It was 1994, and this was America, and she was what she may never have been in the Trinidad of that present day and hour. This was the beauty of America: that she had the chance to be more.

But there was a thing about America: Sometimes it took as much as it gave.

And it came upon her suddenly and inexplicably, this damning, numbing sense of loss—just as it had every day for the past six months.

"How you could go and leave me so, nah Kevin? Eh? How you

could go and leave me?" Ophelia found herself speaking aloud, and she had to grip the gate that led to some unknown family's yard to keep from falling down.

Kevin was murdered in 1993. Now it was 1994. But what is the changing of a year? Years and months are manmade things, ideas to manage life and expectations. Without them, the turmoil, confusion, and hurt of one year bled into the next. In life, there are no solid lines, Ophelia realized, only the imaginary ones that we create.

She still wondered if obeah had been involved.

Obeah, having no boundaries, could follow you over any wide sea. In the hands of the jealous and vindictive, its power could be cruel and frightening. Euclin was so successful, Kevin so smart, Clarissa so pretty. People envied her children. The idea that someone could have *burned a candle* on Kevin's head—took her son's life through obeah—was not beyond the realm of probability.

Ophelia remembered her neighbor, Mrs. Hutchence, trying to barge her way into Kevin's room on the night of the wake. Why not her? It was common, women who wished ill on another's children. Just look at her children, thought Ophelia, one child a thief, the other a cripple. Spoiled fruit. Ophelia shuddered. And Kevin had made that call to the police once, to report that woman's thief of a son after he had broken into a neighborhood storefront. What more incentive did a woman of that kind need?

And that Mouse…Kevin's best friend. They had all gathered together for Kevin's funeral, all the people who knew and loved her son—but where was Mouse? She had a bad feeling about that boy, and at her son's homegoing, Mouse's absence confirmed the only thing Ophelia was sure about: He was the cause of her son's murder. If Mrs. Hutchence had made the decree, then he had somehow led her son to the gallows.

Some people have a pull, an impact so great, that they become little gods, mini orishas, added to the pantheon of those things that people hold near and sacred. The impact of Kevin's death on her parents had been devastating. And in turn, they made her feel inadequate; she had made him fly back to New York, they said. As though she were somehow to blame.

But what nagged Ophelia was how could no one know? A party full of people and a man shoots her son, and then disappears like a phantom because no one seems to know who he was. A backyard full of people in a neighborhood where people must know each other, if not by name, then by face, circumstances, clothing. How could they not know? How could Mouse not know? Somewhere, someone had the answers she sought. *The killer is no phantom; he is flesh and blood just like Kevin was.* Ophelia tormented herself with questions. Was he one of the city's many babies who came into the world at the same time as Kevin? Had he lain in the hospital bassinet next to her son? Had he gone to school with him? Had she passed this young man on the street? And as she walked down the street and saw the shadowy, storm-faced young men: One of them, is that he?

Death, that macabre old friend, was part of being an African in the West: thrown overboard on a transatlantic journey and eaten by sharks, worked to death, whipped to death, shot, stabbed, immolated, lynched, dragged behind a grey Texas pickup. To be black in America meant to have death take up residence, bag and baggage in your home. In Trinidad, death had been so much a part of growing up. The ways in which people died were extraordinary: cuckolded husbands decapitated unfaithful wives with machetes; thousand-pound vaults fell on bank inspectors on the ribbon-cutting day; children slipped into gullies and drowned when it rained. Even murder in Trinidad could not help but be histrionic, magical, or extraordinary in some way.

Back in her own home, returned from her trip to Church Avenue, she cracked open her Bible's black leather spine and lit a white candle. She was an emotional polyglot. One moment her heart spoke the language of faith, the next the language of fear. Yet, seeking the Word, she held on. Turning to the book of Psalms, getting down on her knees, she read:

> *The Lord is my light and my salvation; whom*
> *shall I fear? The Lord is the strength of*
> *my life; of whom shall I be afraid?*

> *When the wicked, even mine enemies and my foes, came*
> *upon me to eat up my flesh, they stumbled and fell.*

*Though a host should encamp against me, my
heart shall not fear: though war should rise
against me, in this I will be confident.*

*One thing I have desired of the LORD, that will
I seek after; that I may dwell in the house
of the LORD all the days of my life...*

Thinking of Mrs. Hutchence as she said her amen, Ophelia stood. "Lord," her voice cracked as she spoke, "they want to see me wriggling on my belly, these people, eh? Like a lowly worm wriggling on the ground." *But she does not know my God.* Ophelia envisioned her neighbor's haggard face. *She does not know my strength, God. She thinks she has swallowed me up.*

Drawing the edge of the sheet to his chest, Mouse sat up on the convex padding of his bed. His sweat had musked the linens, dampened his hair, and formed tributaries behind each of his ears. This was the power of the dream. In it, night after night, things ended differently—he wrestled the gun from Blocker's hand and the bullet went off and entered the sky, harming no one. This was the power of the dream: Blocker left. Kevin lived. The party went on.

But tonight, Mouse wasn't able to wrestle Blocker's hand, and Kevin died all over again. And at the moment of his friend's twin death, Mouse shot up from the pillow with the quickness of a switchblade. And he began to weep, just as he had, standing over Kevin's coffin in the chapel of Linnaeus's parlor.

Linnaeus and Habeas, his mortician's assistant, had just set out the body. The viewing was not until the next day. Linnaeus left on a run to the morgue. It was Habeas who let Mouse in; Mouse made him promise to tell no one of his visit. Then Habeas exited the parlor, leaving him and Kevin alone.

How could he look Ms. Ophelia in the eye at the service when he was responsible? After all, he'd had the fight with Blocker. And he'd made Kevin stay when Kevin wanted to go. So Mouse sat in the chapel in his flimsy all-weather jacket, his hand upon his friend's hand, swollen stiff with embalming fluid. He could not take his eyes from Kevin's broken face.

He had thought about pouring a little tip from a forty in front of the casket as he had seen his friends and their fathers do, but decided not to disrespect Linnaeus's parlor or the next day's service by leaving a stench behind. Instead, Mouse stroked the cold clay flesh of his best friend's hand, remembering the day they met, officially. Mouse had just returned from Cypress Hills Cemetery, where he'd placed a wreath on his grandmother's grave. Six months had lumbered by since she had passed. Slipping out of his good clothes and into his jeans, Mouse hit the streets to loiter, to play, to forget. That's when he saw the sandy-haired boy who always hung out at the funeral parlor. They had never spoken, but Mouse had seen him around.

A thorn from his grandmother's wreath had pricked Mouse's skin, and he was still sucking on the wound. The copper boy stood in front of the funeral parlor, eating cheese doodles from a one-serving bag, and looked at him.

"What you looking at?" Mouse's lip curled like crepe paper.

"What you looking at?" said the boy. He licked the orange powder from his fingers and tried to look tough.

"I hate you," said Mouse. And he did.

"You don't even know me," said the boy.

"I'll kill you."

"You don't even know me."

"I don't have to know you to kill you."

"You want to fight? That what you want?" The boy threw the bag to the floor. "I'll fight. Think I won't...I will kick the living daylights out of you!"

"No," said Mouse.

"Scared now, huh?"

"No," said Mouse.

Then their bodies locked together and crashed against the peeling white paint of the parlor door. In that wrestled embrace, Mouse was shouting, "No, no, no," and collapsed in the strange copper boy's arms. And weeping and fighting, weeping and fighting, then growing still, he held on. It was on this day that Mouse and Kevin first became friends. For it was on this day that Kevin's embrace had saved him.

Kevin hadn't simply died in that Brooklyn backyard, that Labor Day. He—Mouse—through pride, through ignorance, through foolishness, had planted the seeds of his best friend's death one year before it happened. Mouse remembered how it had all started. 1992: the week of Columbus Day.

CHAPTER ONE

1992: Columbus Day week.

Cold air followed Ophelia into her house. Kevin was up, waiting.

"Boy, exactly what it is you doing up so late? Waiting for me?" Ophelia stifled a smile, removing her red wool scarf from her neck.

Kevin helped her as she struggled with the scarf. He draped it onto a hanger, then kissed her hello. He was wearing his black-rimmed reading glasses. The hair on one side of his head was flat. At some point while studying, he had fallen asleep.

He blew into his hands. "Mom—quick—please close that door."

"All-yuh don't have school tomorrow?" She was referring to Clarissa and Kevin.

"Tomorrow's no school, Mom. Columbus Day. Remember?"

Ophelia touched her face before removing her coat. Against the thawing apple of her cheek, Kevin's lips had felt good. Warm.

"Oh, yes, yes. Look at me, how I could forget and I have the day off, too? Papa, when I tell you, and is so I looking forward to tomorrow to finally get some rest."

"You know you won't. You'll probably do laundry all day," Kevin said.

"Well, you know laundry is rest to me." Ophelia was jiggling a pair of plastic flip-flops onto her feet. "Kevin, do me a favor and take up that bag."

Kevin followed her into the kitchen. He was wearing a loose red sweat suit, black flip-flops, and white football socks. "Where you coming from—church? I was wondering where you were."

"Oh, me and this old addled brain, I tell you," Ophelia said ruefully. "I forgot to tell you that the sisters' committee had a meeting tonight." She was passing groceries one item at a time to Kevin, and he was packing them onto the shelf. "Worried?" Ophelia asked.

Kevin said, "A little."

Ophelia replied: "If my brain wasn't already screwed inside of my skull, yes, every day I would forget to put it back in me."

Kevin laughed.

"You tink is joke I making, boy? When I tell you, Kev-vy, is eat that job eating up my old brain. For true."

Kevin bit his lower lip, subduing a grin, and opened up a bag of preserved mangoes. The blood-red dye stained his fingers. He licked it off.

"Let me get a little piece of mango there, nah, please, Kev-vy." Placing the delicacy into her mouth, Ophelia bit away at the flesh, until only a fibrous wedge of mango seed remained. She absently continued to chew on it, the wedge protruding from her lips like a pipe.

"Hey, Mom, is it OK if Clarissa and I meet up with Addie and Mouse for that release party Euclin invited us to? It's tomorrow night."

Their sister Euclin, he explained, had invited the twins, Mouse, and Clarissa's best friend Addie to a party for Blakk Rukus, one of the hip hop acts that Euclin had discovered as an A&R for Amp, the record label her boyfriend's father owned. Blakk Rukus was about to debut their latest album.

"Don't forget that tomorrow is Euclin's birthday, you know."

"I got her the *Sound+Vision* box set by Bowie. When I was at Tower Records I had to choose between that and Ella, Nina, or Joni." Euclin knew all of these artists. Their mother, none. Kevin might as well have been speaking in tongues.

Ophelia extended her leg and flexed her toes. "But, eh-eh, look at how my feet swell up big, big so. What I expect? On my feet, up and down in that nursing home all day. Put on a kettle of water for me nah, please, Kevin. And what happen to that pack of Epsom salts?" Ophelia moved to the kitchen sink and bent down, pulling back the doors of the cabinet below.

With its antiquated pine cupboards, green trimmings, and warm nutmeg smells, the kitchen was the hub of the house. It was the place where Ophelia, Kevin, and Clarissa's lives overlapped. And it was the only place in the house where, for the first time in her life, Ophelia blithely allowed herself to collapse in a chair, any chair, to flex all ten of her toes and stretch out her weary calves.

From the years when Cecil was still with them, and the twins were still little, and Euclin still lived at home, this was what she

2

remembered: being the first to enter the kitchen each morning and the last one to leave; tending the stove; the twins playing musical chairs and spilling the pitcher of evaporated milk all over the embroidered tablecloth; and Euclin, so sweetly ineffective, raging to control them. But Ophelia, in spite of herself, remembered Cecil most of all: *Oh, how neat and straight he always look, even in the midst of that storm.* Perusing the paper with his tie and dress shirt on, his hair unnaturally black and pomaded as brilliantly as a shoeshine, he'd wait for her to come to him with her puffy, seasoned country breakfasts—breakfasts without the taste of which, he proudly told their neighbors and friends, he could not start his day. Cecil. Then, one Mother's Day he was gone.

"Your feet hurting you, Ma?" Kevin said. "You want me to rub them?"

Fatigued and kneading the outer corner of her left eye, Ophelia focused to find Kevin poised on his knees in front of her. "Would you, Kev-vy? Is so they only paining me. Would you? Oh, please." Kevin's initial touch gave her needles and cramps, but in time, the flesh began to feel tender and pliant, and Ophelia closed her eyes. Her body slouched and head leaned backward. "There especially," she mumbled, "Yes, right there so." Ophelia heard her own bones cracking as she drifted toward sleep.

She murmured to Kevin, "You tink that I could ever ask Clarissa to do this kind of ting for me? No, never. Never. Not in a million years…"

In and out, awake, asleep, awake, in between. She heard the whistle of the kettle. Felt the scorching of the hot water and the Epsom salt's saline bounce. Then, there were the Finches. *But why were they there?*

Ophelia was immune to the stench of urine and excrement at the nursing home. She had been living with it for eight years now, six days a week, roughly 3,456 hours a year. But it had been the words of an outsider, or more specifically, those of a child, that had reminded her of how badly her workplace reeked.

"In here smells like when I poo-poo, Mommy," the little Finch boy had said, jerking at his mother's coat sleeve. "And when I wee-wee, too. Right, Mommy? Did someone go poo-poo in his pants? Huh, Mommy? Huh?"

"Oh, Michael, of course not. At least certainly no one in here, I hope." Mrs. Finch gave a small, nervous laugh, casting a knowing look toward her husband and Ophelia, the other two grownups in the room. Stooping down to meet her son at eye level, she fussed with the angle of his Yankees cap, then adjusted the collar of his blue Melton wool jacket until it lay perfectly flat. "Michael Finch the Second, just listen to yourself. Now, do you think that that was a nice thing to say?"

"No," the boy said.

"It wasn't, now was it? It didn't come out sounding very nice at all." As her cashmere shawl sloped down her shoulders, Mrs. Finch tugged at its fringes to keep it from falling completely.

"Here, darling, let me," Mr. Finch said, reaching out to relieve his wife of the shawl.

"It's OK, Michael, really."

"No, Sharon, I said let me." With his left hand outstretched, Mr. Finch stood waiting until she relented.

For the brief moment that Mr. Finch spoke, Ophelia was surprised by the width of his voice, by its strength and boundlessness. For the two hours that the family had been at the home so far, it was Mrs. Finch who had answered all the questions relating to her father-in-law's admission. Where was he born? What was his profession? His medical history? As they moved the elder Finch into his living quarters and the family took another cursory look at the home, it had been Mrs. Finch, moving briskly, who had walked two steps ahead of her husband into every room.

"To answer your question, Michael," Mrs. Finch said, "that smell that you are smelling...it is...it's...Well, as people get older, often they are not as much in control of themselves as they once were. You see how much quicker you've become about making it down the hall to the bathroom to get to your potty? Well, sometimes when people get older, they cannot be as quick as you are. Do you understand now, Michael?"

"Is Grandpa not coming home with us, Mommy?"

"No, Michael. Now, remember how I tried to explain this all to you? Remember how we helped Grandpa move all his things in? Remember that nice room upstairs? Well, that room is Grandpa's *new* room, his own room, and he is taking a nap right now."

"I recall him being wide awake when we left him," Mr. Finch said. "I don't recall at all that he looked sleepy."

"Don't you think it's cold in here?" Mrs. Finch said, turning to Ophelia. She then turned to her husband again. "It's cold. Don't you think so too, dear? I think it's cold. Let me have that back now." She removed the shawl from the nook of his arm and tossed the heavy fabric across her shoulders, then bent down again to her son.

"Michael, do you understand what I am trying to say to you?"

The little boy's legs fidgeted, but otherwise, he made no motion. "Is this where Grandpa's going to live then, forever from now on?"

"Forever. No, no, not exactly forever, Michael, honey. Can't you remember? Remember, I tried to explain this all to you." Her voice started to rise, but she quickly lowered it again. "You'll see Grandpa again—we'll all see Grandpa again. On the days that are very, very special, he'll come back to visit with us and we'll make sure that he has a great time. Now, Michael, do you understand?"

With a steady grip, she forced the boy to look directly back at her, and forced him to be still. Finally, slowly, the little boy nodded.

"Good boy," she said. Pressing down on both of his shoulders, she smiled. "So, so bright." Smoothing out her scarf again, Mrs. Finch turned to Ophelia and laughed a little, in an odd way, as though someone else were laughing for her. "At that age, the things they seem to pick up quickest are the things you don't want them to learn."

Ophelia looked down at the boy, at his very red cheeks and at the tight waves of his sand-colored hair. Its lush curls reminded her of Kevin's. Tweaking his chin, she said to him, "You don't worry at all about your grandpa. He is safe with me and everyone else you see here. It may be even doubly good for him in some ways. Perhaps, in some ways, even nicer, because now it is as though he has *two* families. It is a natural progression," she added, "this moment...for men and women both. Inevitably, we does all reach this moment. Is it not true? Try as we will to stand still. Once a man, twice a child—that is how the saying goes—is it not true?"

But Mr. Finch was regarding her coldly. "He was not asleep when we left him upstairs," he said. He rubbed the base of his hairline, up and down. "He was sitting upright on the bed."

"Yes, Mrs. Ramtahal, it is a natural progression." Mrs. Finch's hands were on her scarf again, smoothing out the fringes. "A natural progression. Exactly as you said."

Her husband lowered his head, and dug through the inner pockets of his coat. For what? Ophelia wondered. For his wallet? For his keys? For nothing?

"Can I walk you back to the entrance?" Ophelia offered.

"Come, Michael," Mrs. Finch said, reaching for her son's arm. "No, Michael, no, do not walk away. Michael, I said give me your hand."

As the Finches walked down the stairs past the guard, along with the urine and the excrement, Ophelia now smelled a new smell, a smell that she had never even recognized as being a smell before. It was the smell of loneliness.

Kevin is rubbing my feet.

Ophelia wondered if and how soon it would be before she would ever see the Finches again. *Kevin is rubbing my feet. Kevin is...rubbing...my feet.* Clarissa: Not in a million years.

"Don't forget tomorrow is your sister's birthday."

"Yes—I know, Mom. So, can we go to the concert?"

"Yes."

And then, Ophelia was asleep.

Mouse pressed his left eye to the splintered circle in his bedroom door, to the hole where a handle and lock had once been. Except for a sheet and a pair of linty red briefs, his father was naked.

In the light of their Harlem kitchen, Sergeant clutched the sheet to his chest and arms. "If God was there, when he took out the knife, did He see?"

It was not the sound of his father's voice in the hall that had first shaken Mouse from sleep: It was the screaming. His weight balanced on one knee, his nocturnal eye probed the darkness and light.

"If God was there, when he took out the knife, did He see? I need to know, Katz. Tell me."

Rachel, Mouse's stepmother, emerged from the room that she and Sergeant shared, rubbing her arms as though she were freezing. "I'm not Katz, and this isn't My Lai. I have no time for your craziness tonight. Just look at what you did to my neck. Just look," she said. "Come on, Porter. Please."

"Don't call me crazy." The sheet began unraveling. Nearly touching the floor, it snaked down the length of Sergeant's back.

Rachel's profile bulged through the open doorway. The sheer fabric of her nightgown clung to her protruding belly, ending in a cascade of blue.

He made her scream, Mouse thought. *That's what I heard. He must have frightened her. Even when he woke up, must have thought he was still dreaming. Sunny… That guy he always talk about. Sunny. His face, it must have come to him again in his sleep.*

"Look at what you did to my neck," Rachel repeated. She stroked her throat with one hand, up and down, up and down, as though putting on and pulling off a rigid choker.

His crouched legs were cramping. Mouse dropped down on both knees, then straightened up again.

"No fire and brimstone when there was a real need," his father was saying. "Just sat back and let it happen." Sergeant looked toward the ceiling, wringing the sheet. "That ain't no God. That's a stone." The bed sheet slid from Sergeant's shoulders. Swishing past his calves, it gathered in a pool of white on the floor.

"Get your crazy behind back to bed!" Rachel yelled, cursing. "Look at the time—look at you."

"I'm not crazy," Sergeant said, snatching the sheet off the floor.

"Crazy, crazy, crazy!" Rachel yelled, her face and shoulders lunging forward.

Sergeant, still wringing the sheet, stretched it taut above his head until the veins and muscles beneath his thin arms showed.

"Crazy, crazy, crazy! Freak, freak, freak! Look at you," Rachel shouted. "I'm sick of all this! I'm sick of you. Look at what you did to my neck. A freak of nature, that's what you are. That's why Charlotte left you." Rachel took a sudden step back, deeper into the threshold, knowing, as Mouse already did, that she had said too much.

Sergeant's disappearance into the kitchen was followed by a sharp clattering of metal and wares. *Charlotte.* The sound of his mother's name. Like the membrane of a jellyfish drifting across a wide sea, Mouse felt his heart pulsing in his chest, in slow electrical jolts—open and closed.

It had been eight years since Mouse had left his mother's house, and since then, he had grown to know two Sergeants—each of them his father, but neither one a man he fully knew. Now, as he waited for his father to emerge from the kitchen, dragging his white sheet across the linoleum floor, Mouse knew it was the second Sergeant he was hiding from.

A heavy plastic bowl, like a discus, shot through the air first, splintering in two when it hit the wall. Rachel gave out a little yelp and backed into the room.

Click. She locked the bedroom door.

Mouse felt a sudden urge to shield his stepmother, and this feeling surprised him. He wanted to open his door—if necessary, to save her—but he did not love her that much. In fact, he did not love her at all, and took comfort in knowing that, behind the protective, closed square of the door, it was all right to be afraid. It was only in choosing to open the door that Mouse would feel forced to be brave. That he would feel forced to be anything.

"Crazy, crazy, crazy! Freak, freak, freak!" she shouted behind the thin door.

The bowl was followed by knives and forks and plates and a set of six glasses; the latter had been given as a grand-opening prize to launch one of the only black-owned banks in Harlem, a bank that the people of Harlem had been sad to see go.

"When he took out the knife, did He see? Did He see?" Sergeant cursed. "Tell me, people, that's all I asked you. You people, answer me."

A yellow plastic tumbler clanked to the floor. Sergeant staggered toward the spot from where Rachel had been, his arms burdened with baking trays, saucepans, and a lone eggbeater, held so tightly it seemed pinned like a very large medallion to his chest.. He stood in front of the door for several minutes, motionless—as though seeing through it—then sighed.

"Come on, baby. Open up. It's me."

Mouse watched as his father abandoned his remaining arsenal of housewares on the floor. His arms collapsed at his sides, and his body took on the stillness of surrender.

"It's me."

Mouse adjusted his own body, soundlessly releasing a crick in his knee.

"He won't let me shake it. No matter how hard I try, he won't let me shake it. I promise to be good, Rachel. Open up and let me in. I'm sleepy." Sergeant stood, exiled at the threshold of his own bedroom door for what seemed like a very long time. "Please." With his index finger, he solemnly scratched at a loose fleck of paint on the door. "Please."

TyQuan rolled over in his crib. The acrylic fuzz of his red sleeper brushed against the plastic mattress cover, and the noise startled Mouse into remembering that he was not alone in the room.

It had been four months since Rachel had ventured to the laundromat down the street, and there was nothing left for them to sleep on. A mucky greyness, like the shadow on the Shroud of Turin, had worked itself into the remaining sheets, forcing everyone in the house to turn their linens inside out or to sleep on bare mattresses. TyQuan slept on plastic, Mouse on inverted sheets. It was the fall now, but in the summer, when the sheets were soiled, Mouse often found himself jolted from sleep by the suctioning sound of TyQuan's sweaty baby skin peeling away from the plastic.

Mouse pressed one palm against the molding and returned his eye to the hole. The door to the room that Rachel and Sergeant shared opened. Even in the room's dimness, Mouse knew that Rachel stood behind the door, holding it open, unseen. Sergeant extended his hand. Grasping onto the knob, he stepped in, joining Rachel through the doorway's triangular darkness.

Mouse went back to his bed. He sunk into his concave and sheetless mattress, his knees too high, his back too low, his body folding into itself like a collapsible chair. His eyes were all stare. No flutter. Mouse rolled over; looked at the alarm clock. Two dot dot forty: 2:40. A half-hour had already passed since Sergeant slipped back into the darkness of his own room. Mouse tried closing his eyes again, but gave up. Pushing away his comforter, he planted his feet against the cold floor.

Barefoot and fearless, Mouse waded into the shards of glass and plastic that littered the hall. Kicking a spoon aside with one toe, he turned on the light in the kitchen then dragged the green plastic garbage can out from its corner. Taking a box of garbage bags down from the top of the fridge, Mouse dropped one into the mouth of the can. Methodically, knife by shard by bowl by spoon, he removed the wreckage from the floor, and what he could not gather by hand, he swept.

The faucet water hit the bottom of the bucket, its weight distending the empty drum. Stretching one arm down along the length of the stick, Mouse moved the mop in wet circles. Suddenly he stopped and stood up straight, surveying the floor. The stain. He had come to the tiles with the stain. Inevitable.

Amorphous, black, and quarantined to a patch of four tiles, the stain stood out on the kitchen's otherwise pristine lime-green floor like a patch of eczema. Long before Mouse had left Oakland, and probably long before Rachel and Sergeant had ever met, the stain had been a part of the floor. But Mouse did not care to know the stain's origins—he simply wanted it gone from his kitchen.

Each time the apartment had received a thorough cleaning, it was Mouse's work. Revolted by the apartment's filthiness and by his stepmother's lack of domesticity, Mouse had taken over her household duties with an air of evangelic disgust. Still, no matter how hard or how long he scrubbed, and even when treated with Clorox and Comet, the stain persisted, shaming the rest of the floor into an illusory dirtiness. Mouse stared down at the stain: He simply wanted it gone.

He must have visited him again in his dreams. But Mouse was still at a loss as to who exactly this man Sunny was, this man who entered his father's dreams and made him afraid—this man who always exited with the same unpredictability with which he came, leaving behind so much chaos and wreckage. But there were only two things Mouse was sure of: Sunny was dead, and his father had caused Sunny's death in some way.

As he rinsed out the mop, he paused. Beads of rain hammered at the window: A storm, newly broken, punctuated the kitchen's quiet dark. He angled the mop again and swept its strands across the blemished floor, thinking of his father and of the plates and knives and Rachel's hand against her neck. He made circle after circle after circle, digging hard into the tiles, uprooting everything—washing over all the places where his father had been, until the kitchen's lime-green floor glowed: almost immaculate.

CHAPTER TWO

Euclin was not considered pretty before she went off to boarding school at Madeira, but she had ceased to be considered ugly.

A thing to know about the beautiful people: They were not always beautiful. There were the *jolie laide*, the ugly-beautiful who were—in their own way—beautiful, too. The secret to transcending ugliness? Half of it was conviction—the other half, material goods.

Another thing to know: Looks did not matter. This was what mattered: how much of it you could buy, beg, borrow, discount, or steal; how well you could gloss up the dull goods that you had to finally make yourself envied and desirable.

As Euclin drifted out and into the throb and flow of those tight, red-bulb spaces packed with vying, shiny bodies, she no longer needed to think about it. She did everything in just the right way, and said just the right things. It was now instinctual—how do you raise your wrist? Cock your head? How do you laugh? Too softly? Too loudly? Do you do it with the proper amount of lethargy? Do you do it with a studied air of detachment both fitting to the frigid enclaves of the Upper East Side and the sybaritic lower sections of New York?

Now, the women at the makeup counters complimented her flawless orchid skin. And the petal-soft fabrics that sheathed her tall and tender body further heightened her beauty—further accentuated an inscrutable, and exotic quality. She was beautiful now, a standout in every crowd, an A&R prodigy, the girl on Brent's arm.

The only girl on Brent's arm.

But then she saw them today. Right in front of the copy machine, near his office, laughing into each other's faces, standing unnaturally close. And from that moment, Euclin knew that she had been right all along. She had to watch him, and watch out when the girl with the cartoon body came around.

"I brought you a crown," Tyler said, as she placed it on top of Euclin's head.

Euclin was celebrating her birthday with Brent and her two best friends, Tyler and Angus.

They were all huddled around a mahogany table edged with crystal flutes and tumblers, Haitian cotton napkins, and silver-plated flatware, in the clubby recesses of the main dining room. It was designed to look like the interior of a ship, down to the portal wall fixtures. Angus and Brent were smoking again, and a veil of white hung around the table, gauzy as mosquito netting.

Euclin removed the Burger King crown, scrutinized it, and then mustered the grace to receive it, a grace that at any other time would have been real. Placing the crown back on her head, she said jauntily, "How fun! Queen for a day!"

Brent embraced her, his body hot and crushing. He licked a boyish circle on her cheek, the width of her face sandwiched between both his hands. "Happy birthday, baby. And on your birthday, queenie, what is your wish? Just say the world, and I'll give it."

Euclin smiled and pried her face from his hands. Still smiling, she looked up at him—the glorious Brent Stein, the man, once nine hundred miles away, whose clove-stained kisses had turned her final years at Yale into an anxious blur of train rides. Euclin searched his eyes, intent on weeding through the treachery that she knew lay buried deep beneath their murk of blue-green innocence. But she found no cartoon girl, no matter how she tried, no copy room, no trail of stolen kisses. Instead, Brent looked at her expectantly, and she began to hate how his face just hung there—marked by eagerness, a stupid and galling innocence that stripped her bare, to rage.

People didn't understand what they had. What drew them together. The beauty of their messiness. That they were more alike than different—having built their life together out of the same kinds of wreckage.

"I already have everything I want," Euclin said. "And you, my dear, are drunk. Couldn't you at least have waited for the rest of us?"

"What is that supposed to mean?" he said, followed by an expletive.

"You know exactly what I mean. You're always on something. Too much, too often. Does moderation mean anything to you? I mean, has it ever?"

"Don't you...Yeah, I had a couple, but haven't we all? This is a freaking celebration, isn't it? And for *you,* no less." Cursing again, Brent reached for his glass of rum.

"Plenty." Euclin tried to stand up, but her knees banged into the edge of the table, and she sat back down. "Hey, Byrd," she said, wagging her head at Tyler. "I'm headed outside for a cigarette and some fresh air. Why don't you join me?"

Tyler looked over at Brent. He was brooding into his rum and coke. Tyler turned back to her. "You're on your own, kid."

Digging through her purse, Euclin snapped it shut, triumphantly clutching a filigreed silver lighter and a pack of Camel Lights in one hand. She had already known she was being unfair, coaxing Tyler to choose between her two best friends. "Suit yourself," she said. "Gus, please excuse me."

Huddled in a corner, her back to the howl of the wind and the rain, Euclin was vainly trying to light a cigarette beneath the restaurant awning when Brent came through the double doors.

He grabbed her shoulders, turning her roughly to face him. "What in god's name was that all about, huh? Huh, Lin?" he said. "Did you think that was cute, making me look...making me look like..." He started to curse, but stopped. "Making me look like that in front of everybody."

Brent's face was flushed the color of canna lilies. Euclin regarded him: his square-shouldered varsity stance; the honey of his hair that dripped past his eyes; the crude halo around him from the glare of the foyer light.

The whole office knows. Everyone knows, don't they? Everyone, but me.

Euclin struck the match on the back of the book until it flared. "It's not my fault that you are what you are," she said.

"And what *am* I?" Brent said, letting her go in a way that made her stumble backward several steps. "Since you seem to know so well, let me know, since you seem to know everything."

Euclin found herself drawn again to the memory of the cartoon girl, her gamine waist and helium breasts. To the fine blond hairs on Brent's arms: gold threads, starting above the joints of his fingers, running up the full length of them. Had he touched that woman in the same way that he touched *her*? She imagined golden hands unhooking a clasp bound by lace and wire, a pink mouth following, pressing toward soft, plum nipples.

"What am I?" Brent said. "Or what am I not to you?"

Tell him, this time. You have to—that this was not the first time. Was not the first girl. That you had every right to suspect, and still do. But a song came into her head just then, an old jazz standard, "The Very Thought of You," the Billie Holiday rendition.

Euclin threw the cigarette butt on the floor and crushed it with her heel, thinking of the final line: *That's everything*. And then she knew. The girl with the cartoon body meant nothing.

"I don't know why I acted so terribly, baby. Maybe it's my birthday, you know, getting older." Euclin shrugged desperately, helplessly, then buried her face in her hands. "I'm sorry. I don't…Brent, I really don't know."

Brent laughed. "Twenty-four is not that old, babe," he said, touching her wrists, this movement quickly unmasking the shabby way that her fingers had covered the salt tracks marring her cheeks. "You're crying. Why, Lin—baby." They looked at each other, remembering clearly the only other time she had cried, then looked away, not mentioning it.

What Euclin had told him, this thing about not knowing, had not been a total lie. Sometimes she liked to think that Brent was secretly seeing someone else, or that he might run off one day with one of the models, dancers, or actresses who daily passed through their lives. It was a game that she played with herself, and this was how the game always began: another new and pretty face to scare her.

Yet, there was something in the offhand, reliable way in which Brent *did* love her that made Euclin wonder if he even saw all those other faces—and even if he did, did any of those women even matter?

No, people didn't understand what they had—their super-supernova love.

"Is everything all right?" Tyler emerged from the restaurant, her red hair swirled back from her face by the tempestuous wind.

"All right?" Brent questioned, laughing. "Does this look all right to you?" Brent's mouth plowed into Euclin's lips, his grasp unyielding. Euclin let out a hoot of surprise, then a tiny giggle, as he dipped her backward. "The Very Thought of You" came into her head again.

Euclin clasped Brent's neck tightly, pressing her body into his as hard as she could and hanging on as though for dear life—in his pink mouth, her coral tongue languishing.

"Aw, come on, kids," Tyler teased, "don't go all saccharine. Break it up and let's go on in and eat something."

Euclin giggled again, blushing. She pushed her hair behind her ears, the kiss now over.

"Listen, you've got Angus prattling on about the gastronomical pleasures of Southern fried 'possum on one end of the table in there, and me about to eat my fist on the other."

"What are we eating anyhow?" Brent said.

"I've set us up for a tasting menu," Tyler said. "Eight courses—beluga-topped gaufrette and glass eel marinated in Thai lime juice, to start with. Fugu—just a little taste apiece—FedExed overnight from Japan. Roasted monkfish. Oh, and mushrooms; roasted shitake caps and some sautéed hen of the woods."

Brent put her in a headlock. "Well la-dee-da, listen to you, Chef Boy-ar-dee!"

"Stop being so freaking provincial, Stein!" Tyler said, laughing as her playful punch to the gut caught him off guard.

"It's cold," Euclin said. "Let's go inside."

Brent put his arm around Euclin's waist and held the door open for Tyler, but a startling gust of wind ripped through them before they had a chance to get fully indoors. Brent shivered. "Yeah, let's go," he said. "I'm starving."

CHAPTER THREE

From her bedroom window, Clarissa watched the wind push Addie across the street, mangling her floral umbrella. Clarissa tugged at the brim of her baseball cap. She did not want to see Addie again, at least not after today, at least not so soon. *Why'd she have to talk all loud like that?* Clarissa thought. *Showing off the whole subway ride home about having the weed.*

Addie's umbrella dipped beneath the awning. The doorbell rang. Again. Then again: four times. When Clarissa reached the foot of the stairs, she glanced down the hall in search of Kevin. Just as she had thought: Still sitting there like a lump, just where she had left him studying in the kitchen. She undid the bolt, then the locks. Addie stood in the cone of the porch light, the bottom of her rayon pants flickering like leaves in the wind.

"You don't ask who it is?" Addie said, shaking her umbrella dry. "What if I was a criminal—some kind of maniac?" She stretched out the wire frame a last time, then laid the open umbrella sideways on the porch's pink terrazzo floor.

"I saw you coming up the walk. I'm not crazy," Clarissa said, reaching for the umbrella.

"That's OK, I don't want it to drip in the hallway. I'll leave it out here." A strong gust blew the umbrella in a half-circle on its side.

Though she had not yet entered the house, Addie's body, damp with rain, released a soft feminine odor that dominated the alcove: pores scrubbed, skin lotioned, breasts lightly talcumed, the intrigue of her own sweat was masked by fragrance and soap.

"I wouldn't leave that out there if I was you. They going up to people's houses now and stealing stuff right off their porch."

Addie squeaked into the hallway, the soles of her shoes grating against the ridged plastic matting spread across the hallway's linoleum floor. Clarissa closed the door. She could hear her mother's heavy walk on the stairs. Emerging from the basement doorway, Ophelia set her laundry basket down with a thud.

"Oh, Adelina, is you," she said, appearing surprised. "I downstairs washing, but I say I only steady hearing something, yes. Was the bell I was hearing in truth."

"How you doing, Tanty Ophelia?" Addie smiled. Ophelia, adjusting her height, stooped down as Addie kissed her.

"I there, I there," she said. "Addie, is you smelling sweet, sweet so like a rose?"

"Oh this?" Addie shyly rubbed the pulse of her neck. "Just some musk from that incense man up on Utica." Clarissa shoved aside a stack of clothes and squeezed Addie's coat into the hall closet. Addie laughed. "Every time I come by, Tanty Ophelia, seems like you have that big straw basket with you. You sure you don't need some help?"

"Oh no, no, Addie, leave it right there so, I going upstairs just now. Is since dayclean I doing laundry, you know?" The rolling cadence of Ophelia Ramtahal's voice, like that of most Trinidadians, exuded a perpetual sense of astonishment and wonder—Clarissa heard it most distinctly when there were guests, and other voices and accents to give it contrast.

"These two children tell me is a sickness I have, yes, but is like a sort of therapy for me, you know? Is a pity it raining tonight, though, yes boy. I doesn't like to use the dryer at all, even when is a little bit cold I does like to hang my wash outside."

"That's a really pretty crucifix," said Addie.

Ophelia peered down at her bosom. The crucifix was slim and smooth. "Is Kevin give me this," she said, patting both silver and skin.

Ophelia Ramtahal, perceived by many to be a large, coarse country woman, had a dark complexion that only seemed to magnify her size. People said that wearing dark clothes helped to lessen one's size, but with dark skin, curiously, the effect was the opposite. In America, Ophelia's darkness was an anomaly: the blue-black of the old, chained Africans had mellowed into browns, reds, yellows, and creams, bleached by the kiss of the South.

As Ophelia and Addie chatted, Clarissa opened the door again and brought in the umbrella. She hesitated before re-entering the house—wanting to stand on the porch in bare feet, as she sometimes did on nights when there was rain. On such nights, sheltered by the green plastic awning, she would close her eyes and pretend to be caught beneath the dry part of a waterfall—the pink of her heels digging into cold terrazzo, inhaling the Brooklyn rain as it came down around her in turbulent, smoke-colored sheets.

Clarissa had never had the pleasure of climbing a real waterfall: traversing green, mossy slopes, gripping slippery rocks with the monkey-toe curve of shoeless feet. Nor had she ever known the startling pleasure of stepping into a warm December sea: this small miracle being chief among the everyday miracles Caribbean nationals longed for in the height of their first Brooklyn winter. This thing that New Yorkers called a beach—their American Atlantic, opaque and frigid, breaking in small, moody waves against stretches of manmade shore—always made the Islanders laugh. Kevin and Euclin laughed. They had been there. Kevin and Euclin both knew how it felt, on a night such as this, to be in Trinidad, in the countryside, in the heart of their grandparents' house as the tap-tap of rain beat like mallets against the curving steel of the galvanized roof. They knew the juice of smashed passion fruits rising like perfume from the yard. Clarissa could only imagine. In all her seventeen years, she had never been to Trinidad, yet Trinidad was everywhere, its presence oppressive and inescapable.

Whenever her grandparents came to visit the States, Trinidad was the strange, green smell that rose from their open suitcases, creeping like an invisible vine through the folds of their flesh and their clothes; on Nostrand Avenue, Trinidad could be tasted at Gloria's roti shop, its essence seared into potatoes, curried chicken, and doughy pleats of dhalpouri; Trinidad, rudely hidden in the double meanings of calypsos, made Clarissa's aunt and mother laugh; Trinidad erupted in her mother's temper, fluttered in Tanty Verlee's singsong voice, dazzled in Euclin's paper-white smile; and its history could be seen, like the markings on a map, stretched along the thin blue veins beneath Clarissa's own pale skin. Euclin was the only one among the children who had taken after Ophelia's complexion; Kevin's hair and skin, in the sunlight, glistened like copper wire, while Clarissa, with her raw cashew undertones, resembled a freckled Creole.

Yet Trinidad defied her imagination and would always continue to be the strange, green-smelling place of her grandparents' suitcases: a place where Clarissa's Americanness was both envied and scorned, in this way exiling her from her parents' country.

Clarissa reentered the house. Her mother was struggling up the stairs now, her face hidden beneath the slant of the full wicker basket. Gazing at her mother's upward shuffle, Clarissa felt the sun's heat peeling at her flesh again, as though she were five, as though it were that summer long ago: that day on the Staten Island Ferry while her father, face flushed, drank in his mother's words. *How could you, Cecil, have married such a thing? She looks like an ox hauling cane.*

Clarissa could still feel the peel of that sun, and could still see her father's weak face. It was one of her earliest memories.

Clarissa pushed back the white, latticed doors of the living room.

The room had its own smell, a permanent and heavy smell that was different from the rest of the house—an efficient and ominous mixture of Old English, Murphy's Oil, and faded potpourri that she and Kevin had always disliked. It was only when company came that the living room's white doors were pulled back, the dull air inside forced to life by the unexpected winds of human movement.

Flanked by a pair of life-sized ceramic Dalmatians, the fireplace served as the living room's centerpiece. An electric log lay dormant in the hearth, but its false embers flickered only once a year, on Christmas. On the piano and mantelpiece was an array of ceramic figurines: French courtiers gliding through imaginary ballrooms, and English peasants reeling in wishing-well buckets and romping through invisible fields. And on the side tables stood two cherubic lamps, as tall as children, topped by velvet tulip shades with tassels the color of mulled wine.

Addie and Clarissa were already seated when Kevin joined them. He placed his chemistry textbook on one of the coffee table's starched doilies and slid onto the sofa with a yawn.

"Jesus, I'm tired," he said, his yawn amplifying into a roar. "So Addie, girl, what the heck have you been up to?"

Addie eyed him. "What you was doing by the kitchen table so long?"

Lacing his fingers behind his head, Kevin rooted himself into the chair. "Orgo exam tomorrow. If I didn't study now, I'd be screwed."

"Is that why you couldn't get up and get the freaking door?" asked Clarissa.

"Listen peanut," Kevin replied, placing his feet on the table, "don't even go there 'cause I'm not in the mood. You got the stuff we talked about?" He turned back to Addie. Addie looked over at the stairs; Kevin followed her gaze, searching for his mother.

"Yeah, I got it right here in my bag." Addie produced a tiny sky-blue Ziploc bag, no wider than a big toe. Its insides were packed tight with leaves. Kevin parted the bag with his fingernail, inhaling.

"Copacetic, copa, copa." Kevin smiled, sealing back the bag with his thumb. "Skunk, huh? You got it from that weed-spot I told you about on Clarkson?"

"Nah, Franklin."

"Franklin?" Kevin asked. "All the way up Franklin? Duh—hello? Anybody home?"

"Yo, chill. I got it, didn't I? We had to try a couple places first, that stuff at Minot's be having mad seeds."

"How would you know?"

"Because I do. We met this guy outside Minot's who told us 'bout this one spot up on Franklin. He said they always have good weed. But we didn't want to go there at first since we only just met this guy today." Addie handed over the second bag of weed.

"Cool, mad cool. No problem then," Kevin said, again pleased.

Clarissa grew spiteful as she watched their exchange. *Was I stupid? What was I on? Why did I go with her in the first place?* She was thinking back to the earlier part of the day and all the time she had blown, accompanying Addie from one dark, understocked variety store to the next, in search of Sensei Skunk and White Owls. *All of Columbus Day wasted. Could have gone and shot some hoops. If not hoops, something—anything else.*

"Every time I'm around you two, I feel like, I feel like…" Clarissa hesitated, thinking of the white, scrolling letters on the back of Kevin's T-shirt. "I feel like I'm at a freaking N.O.R.M.L. convention or something."

"Hey, pretty smart there, peanut-head," Kevin said, poking her in the ribs. "How about a hit? Tonight can be your first time."

Addie laughed. Clarissa grimaced. Addie had left her behind.

Their relationship had reached a point of change that Clarissa was unable to accept. There was a time when Addie was just Addie, and Kevin wasn't just another boy that Addie wanted to sleep with, and that was the time in which Clarissa was stuck. In the last two years,

20

male acknowledgment had become a thing under which Addie flourished. She thrived on the challenge of Kevin's sexual indifference and did everything she could to impress and please him. The time had long passed when Clarissa and Addie could simply hang out and talk about normal things: sports, movies, school. Now everything was clothes and boys and marijuana.

But Addie was her friend, her friend, and with that thought, the old feelings rose up. Clarissa saw herself and Addie as they used to be, tangled on the playroom floor, punching welts into the other's flesh until their arms turned purple.

If only she could still hit her the way she used to, she thought. A real punch. The kind of punches that used to make their parents question exactly what kind of women she and Addie would grow up to be.

"Did I already tell y'all about that new group Euclin just signed?" Clarissa asked.

Kevin leaned forward. "Who you talking about, the Bush Mobb?"

"Oh *yeah*," said Addie excitedly. "They going to be there tonight, too?"

"Supposed to be." Clarissa was glad to be in control again. "But Euclin said Brent's already thinking about dropping them. They too wild. She said the whole gang of them be high as kites every time they come into the studio."

Ophelia creaked down the stairs. Kevin handed Addie back the last bag of weed, and she stashed it away in her pocketbook. Addie looked down at Clarissa's feet, as though seeing her bear-toe slippers for the first time that night.

"Aren't you getting dressed?"

"I am dressed. All I have to do is put on my sneakers."

Addie giggled. "Ever heard of shoes? Girl, this ain't the NBA playoffs. It's a party—lots of people are going to be there."

Lots of men, Clarissa thought. *That's what she means. Lots of men.*

"Where did you tell Mouse to meet us?" Clarissa asked her brother.

"At the coat check downstairs, eight o'clock," Kevin said.

A doily slid down the couch's vinyl backing. Clarissa picked it up, patting it in place on the hump. Sealed in clear vinyl, the stout cushions of the sofa and armchairs rose like packaged cupcakes. The living room furniture was heavy and scrolled, stained in an eggshell veneer. As in most of Brooklyn's Caribbean homes, French Provincial was rampant.

Ophelia entered and sat in a side chair near the window. "Adelina, would you like something to drink or a piece of sweetbread?" she offered.

"Oh that's all right, Tanty Ophelia. We just ate dinner—no thank you."

"But eh-eh, what is this? You mad o' what." Kevin mocked, pretending to be offended by Addie's reply. "What happen to you, gyul? My mother slave and bake up sweetbread and you tun' she down? I never see more...is better Negro belly bus' than for good food to waste I does say, yes."

It was mainly the crude country accent that made them all laugh.

"All right, all right, I'll have some then." Addie giggled, looking in Kevin's direction. "I don't want to offend nobody or nothing—or be a bad guest."

"But this boy does get on schupid when he ready, yes." Ophelia smiled, still amused. "Is Kevin only bugging me for sweetbread all this time. Is so long I ent even bake in this house self." Rising from her armchair, she smoothed the wrinkles of her dress against her thighs. "Come Clarissa, come nah, come and help me pull a little tray together here in the kitchen."

"Why can't Kevin help?" Clarissa said, sucking her teeth. She leaned back in the sofa, all former laughter swallowed. "All he's doing is just sitting on the couch like a lump."

"Clarissa, don't start. Is you I ask, not Kevin."

But Kevin never helps, Clarissa started to say. "It's not like we have real guests," she complained. "What's the big deal? It's just Addie. She can cut a piece of sweetbread herself."

"Clarissa. Watch your manners. I said come help me," her mother said angrily. Then turning to Addie, "When is time for this gyul to marry, I don't know how she expect to find a husband, yes."

"What she needs to watch is her mouth—right mom?" said Kevin.

"Shut up, fool," Clarissa replied.

"You wastrel," Kevin shot back.

"Shut it, you placeholder for sense," Clarissa said, and with her baseball cap she hit her brother on his head and fled after her mother into the kitchen.

22

"Nobody mention anything to me about sweetbread for another month," Kevin groaned, patting his belly. Sugar crystals shone like ground glass on top of the last of the loaf. An air of lazy contentment edged along the emptied saucers, teacups, and dregs of hot chocolate left in the pot.

"Then all the rest is mine," Clarissa said. "Good."

"In your dreams, peanut-head," countered Kevin.

Clarissa snatched up the plate of sweetbread and held it high. "Too late, blockhead. I called it."

Kevin pretended to brandish the knife, grabbing its handle. "You big, greedy horse! Surrender it now!"

"Make me, you pig."

"Oh, I'll make you, girlie. Come, nah. Come. Is knife you want? I'll give you knife."

"Kevin!" Ophelia said. "Put down that ting before someone gets hurt! Clarissa—right now—stop your skylarking and nonsense." Down went the knife, followed by the sweetbread, before some mutual shoving and laughter marked the end of their horseplay.

Ophelia was clustering the teacups and stacking the saucers. Suddenly she broke in admiringly, "But look at Addie outfit nah, Kevin. Matching flare-leg pants and vest and ting—a real saga gyul we have here, oui. I does catch my tail just to get Clarissa to even put on a simple skirt self, Addie."

Clarissa felt an unwelcome prickliness replace the warmth in the room.

"Addie, I does have to beg Clarissa: Oh gosh, nah, man, put on a little rouge, a little lipstick, put on a dress and take off that cap, nah. You see how she gone and chop that whole head of hair off. All that lovely hair gone." Leaning in conspiratorially, Ophelia touched Addie's wrist. "Listen here a minute, nah. Saturday, she wait until she know I gone to the grocery, and she gone and tell the barber to chop it off—chop it *clean* off."

I am not your dolly, Clarissa thought, fingers poking under her cap, fondling a soft lock of hair.

"I think it looks nice, though," Addie said, weakly.

Clarissa huffed, tucking a lock beneath the brim. "I just don't like long hair."

"Listen, nah, Addie, you know what Clarissa does tell me?" Ophelia continued, as though, for the entire time, she had been the only one speaking. "She does tell me I too old. That's right, papa—I too old. She does say, 'Ma, this ain't the old days. This ain't Trinidad. Women don't have to wear dresses no more.' I might be old, but one ting I know for sure, is a lady is a lady anywhere you go. That's right. When I was growing up, you see me..."

I was a proper lady, Clarissa thought, rolling her eyes.

"I was a proper lady," Ophelia continued. "In those days, you couldn't leave your house and go to Princes Town without putting on your hat and your gloves. When you run around the house and the yard you could put on any old buss-up old thing, sure, but when is time to step out..." she paused dramatically, "papayo, is zest for so, oui! People used to come alllll the way outside they gallery just to see Miss Joycie daughter when she walking down the road. That's right."

Clarissa cut in, "Mom, it's almost seven o'clock. Can we get a move on."

"We used to have a cousin who used to send us barrels full of clothes from America. Talk about pretty, pretty things."

"Mom, I think Addie's heard this story a million times before—OK?"

"You see what I telling you, Addie, you see how rude this gyul is? You see Euclin, Euclin never give me any problems, yes. Is only when Euclin gone away to that school that she start to give me headache. Euclin turn White Woman now, yes, oui. Yes, yes, that is right. Euclin come back from boarding school and Yale full of airs, thinking she too high, high up and good for all of we. Euclin have she white man and she friends and she career, and that is all she need. I couldn't even reach Euclin in person to wish she happy birthday self today. Imagine that—I have to leave a message." Ophelia shook her head scornfully. "But you see this Clarissa, you see this one here? Not me atall, I can't even self begin to deal with this one here."

"Oh, Clarissa's just giving you a hard time, Tanty Ophelia. She don't mean no harm—you know that." And the tension diffused as Addie, lips parted, smiled her killer smile of perfect, white teeth.

"Well," Ophelia, sighed, slapping her hands on her thighs, "I don't want all-yuh to be late. I guess it's time for the three of you to go. Kevin, just make sure that Euclin call a cab to send all-yuh home."

"Did Kevin tell you he apply for early admission to Stanford?" Ophelia said proudly, holding open the door. "But I tell him he should of try early though for Columbia instead, or NYU since both are right here in New York."

Clarissa stood up from tying her laces. Addie and Kevin were already outside on the porch.

"This boy will be the next prime minister," Ophelia predicted. "Mark my words, another Williams we have here."

"Kevin was always a brain," Addie said, and giggled.

And what will I be? Clarissa thought. What would she be in her mother's eyes, other than somebody's wife? Clarissa kissed Ophelia goodbye and stepped out onto the porch. Pulling on her hood, Clarissa looked up at the sky. She suddenly thought, *How strange: Rain does not fall at the same time in every single part of the world.* She had never considered the thought before. All three stepped off the porch, as the rain paled into a drizzle.

CHAPTER FOUR

It had started with Columbus, the blow on Mouse's cheek. It had started with Columbus, and the hard rain that kept him and his father and Rachel inside all day, on each other's nerves. His father had been drinking. Wary of the way that things appeared to be headed, Mouse extended his hand.

"Let me take you to bed, Sergeant."

Sergeant thrust the outstretched hand back with greater force than Mouse would have expected from a drifting, inebriated man. His father pushed past him, headed to the other end of the hall. On his knees, he began to feel around the closet's dark, junk-laden floor, hands searching, fingernails scratching. At last he stood up, Jack Daniels in hand. He wedged the bottle into the crook of one arm and lumbered past. Mouse followed, guardedly.

The kitchen. The table. More drinking. One final taste of the glass. Eyes shutting, eyes shutting, eyes shut. All leaden, except a buoyant head and a dribble of spittle on his lip.

Eight months ago, there'd only been one Sergeant, when he still had his night watchman job: the same one that greeted Mouse and TyQuan with a smile and gentle ribbing in the mornings; and in the evenings, lay down next to Rachel again. That watchman's job of three years—a hook-up from an old running buddy down at the VA, with decent pay and good benefits—had staved off his alcohol cravings, miraculously. Then, the only time he'd fallen asleep, he came home with his thermos and a pink slip. "The racist crackers. Bet they wouldn't do that to a white boy." Within a week of getting fired, his father doubled again, all pretense of sobriety gone. The only money coming into the house was from Rachel, who was collecting disability, pending litigation against the MTA and the City. The three of them, Rachel, Sergeant, and Mouse, had nowhere to be on a day like this.

Hoisting his father up by the pits of his arms, Mouse slowly dragged him to bed.

"Come on, Sarge. Easy now," he said.

When he turned the bedroom knob, he found Rachel in the corner, undressing.

"Goodness, can't you knock!"

"Sorry." Mouse looked away. Rachel had been about to pull her T-shirt up over her arms and shoulders when he had entered.

"Why are you standing there like some gaping ape?" she said. "Obviously, I'm changing. You'll have to leave."

But Mouse knew exactly what she would do to Sergeant, saw the whole scenario clearly: put on her own clothes then leave him folded onto the bed, halfie-like, his street clothes still on him. It just wasn't right.

"Undress him."

Rachel bristled. She came over, her hands and shoulders already calcified by gruffness. Mouse made a motion to leave, and she stopped.

"By yourself," he said. "Don't ask me to help you."

Not up to the task of disrobing him alone, Rachel didn't say anything, just bundled her clothes and left for the bathroom.

Mouse took his father's arm from around his own shoulders and laid him flat on the bed. He unlaced his father's Florescheim Nubucks, fanning the air as he peeled each Gold Toe sock off. Unbuttoning his father's shirt, Mouse inhaled the scents that made him, that marked him as Sergeant: the Duke hair pomade, the Brut aftershave, the Swisher Sweet cigars, the whiff of Jack Daniels, clinging to his body like cologne.

Mouse tried to raise his father's shoulders higher up on the pillow. He thought of how easily Linnaeus, Ophelia's boyfriend, had pulled a corpse up by its neck, adjusting it in its coffin. Mouse and Kevin often worked odd jobs at Linnaeus's parlor to make some extra money.

Mouse's hand lingered on his father's jawbone. Just above his brow, there was an inch-long scar that glowed in sunlight like a quick, silver fish. Mouse had always been drawn to that scar, found it dangerous, thrilling; but his father had never told him how it got there, and Mouse never asked. But now, he scrutinized Sergeant's face as if it were a stranger's. Mouse remembered having been surprised, when he first got to New York, to learn that his father was not a tall man. He had always imagined that he was, and his mother hadn't once mentioned it, this just-average height. And he wished that she would have said. It would have explained so much, told so much about who he was and would be, if he grew up like his father.

Still holding Sergeant's face, Mouse decided that his father was a handsome man—then released him.

By seven o'clock the rain had eased to speckled drops against the living room window. TyQuan had toddled into the living room a half-hour before and fallen asleep, his small body splayed out on the couch's middle cushion. They had gathered in the living room, in front of the TV, Mouse and Rachel, to eat their supper and watch the evening news.

"What about Sergeant?" Mouse had said, settling into the easy chair.

"What about him?"

"I was just wondering, you think he'll get up in time to eat? Or should I put the food in the fridge?"

"Who cares," Rachel said, stabbing her lasagna again and swallowing hard. "Who cares, and who knows."

Sergeant appeared in the doorway just then, eyes half-mast and face befuddled. Rachel, instead of appearing startled or even angry, regarded him with a weary tenderness. The dim living room light stained her mouth and eyes.

"What's there to eat?" Sergeant's weight creaked down in the other side chair. "See the party's started without me."

"Sit tight," Mouse said. "I'll fix you a plate."

When Mouse returned, Sergeant tasted the food and began complaining.

"This thing ain't even cooked right. How you expect me to eat this kind of hot-outside-cold-inside garbage?" He cursed. "Take it. Here." He made a small, gaseous noise into his fist, something between a cough and a burp, and shooed the plate away.

Mouse took it from him. *Like it's my fault the stove don't work. Did he ever stop for a moment to think. Did he ever?* He walked into the kitchen and dropped it, hard, into the sink.

By then the evening news had come on.

Already covered, the requisites: local politics, the week's white-collar crime, and a panorama of urban violence, dark faces looming as perpetrators. Now came a rainbow of protestors marching down Columbus Avenue, re-stenciled Genocide Avenue: First, the words "Columbus Get Lost (Again)" dripped in red on a sprawling white banner, preceding a confederacy of Mohawks, Pequots, and Iroquois. Next, a skinny, militant lesbian with green Dep-gelled hair and nose ring, mouth an angry O, spewed soundbites, blaming Columbus on this, the five hundredth anniversary of his arrival, for ushering patriarchy into the Western world. The protest was capped by Hispanics and Blacks, some pelting eggs, others chanting as they looped a noose over the neck of a Genoan effigy.

Like a footnote, a brief clip of the traditional Columbus Day Parade closed the coverage: up Fifth Avenue sailed the *Niña*, the *Pinta*, the *Santa Maria*, followed by movie stars, politicians, mothers with babies, smiling, milling, pacing as they had been doing for so many decades. In the absence of the protestors, they trod along in a uniform calm.

"Did you see that?" Rachel said. "Did you see that whole big doo-dah? I don't even see what these people've been making this whole big, doggone doo-dah about—for weeks and for weeks and for weeks." She hunched over and rapped one knuckle on the TV screen. "See here, there they go again. There they go again, this whole Columbus thing, trying to make us colored folks look bad."

"What's so bad?" Mouse said.

"Tell me, did you see any white folks pelting eggs and hanging dolls on up there?"

"No," Sergeant said. "But back home in Mississippi I've seen 'em hang people."

"But Columbus killed the Indians," Mouse said. "Your mama's half-Indian. Why aren't you mad? The Indians, in the Caribbean, didn't do nothing to Columbus when he landed except treat him well, and he took their gold and planted his cross and worked them and worked them—and killed them."

"So what?" Rachel said, "Who cares. I'm alive. You're alive, ain't you? Columbus is dead. You hear me, dead, dead, dead. Now I don't know about you, but there ain't a *doggone* thing that any *dead* white man can do to make me get up on TV like that and act the fool."

"That's because you're ignorant. You're black and you're ignorant," Sergeant said. Gripping the arms of the chair, he stood up.

"Well, well, you seem to have some pret-*ty* strong opinions there for *half* a man," she said. "Drink yourself to death, got no job, can't even buy your eldest boy a decent pair of sneakers, you social cripple, but there you go, wanting to talk. Look at his feet. *Look*—look at that sorry pile of trash he's got on."

Watching Rachel and Sergeant train their eyes, like lasers, on the small fissure in his Jordans where the sole and body had begun to hang apart, Mouse found himself in the middle.

That's when he remembered the paper in his jeans pocket. He'd gotten so caught up in the argument, in the evening news, he'd forgotten all about Shimmer and the earlier part of the day. Shimmer—a.k.a., Lucent DuBois—small-time numbers runner, sidewalk-teddy-bear hustler during the holidays, sometimes-janitor at the Harlem Y, and the closest thing, as far as Mouse could see, that his father had to a best friend, had come by earlier that evening with talk of a gig, working security at the MoMA. "Tell him all he got to do is stand there and guard the pictures while white folks walk by. Easy, real easy, man. Just keep 'em behind the ropes when they get too curious. Make sure nobody reaches out and touches anything."

Mouse had remembered, as Shimmer spoke, the first time his mother had taken him to the Fine Arts Museum, across the Bay in San Francisco. He had been very little, but he recalled her energy. It was in abundance that day, passing from her hand to his like juice from a jumper cable, as she pointed up, excitedly, past the ropes, telling him things she seemed to have wanted him to remember, but Mouse now found that he no longer could.

Shimmer had handed Mouse the information, scribbled on a face from a brown paper bag. "Angel—you ever met Angel on the stoop?—that's my wife's new brother-in-law," Shimmer said. "He's real tight with the guy who does the hiring. Tell Sarge they got two positions open right now. And, if he's interested, tell him Shimmer says that one of em's got his name on it." Shimmer was the kind of man that his mother would have held nothing against, but to whom, outside of hello and goodbye, she would have had little to say. "Most of them don't even notice you," Shimmer was saying. "Or, at least they pretend not to, at least that's what Angel said, like you're the part of the tour they can skip. They'll just ask you a question from time to time. Sarge can pretty much keep to himself that way."

"What about you? You thinking 'bout one of those jobs?" Mouse had asked.

He laughed. "Me? Naw. That ain't my style." He laughed again. "Naw, man, I'm a *born* hustler."

Reaching into the pocket of his jeans now, Mouse retrieved the paper from the narrow strait of lining. Balled up, it felt warm, solid in his hands.

"Imagine, that boy's got a party to go to downtown," Rachel was saying, "looking like that. Got some big-time, civilized folks gonna be there, and he's got to wear some beat-up, old sneakers like that— all because his daddy's half a man." Rachel's Tennessee drawl, in the heat of the argument, had thickened like lard.

Mouse approached his father now, the paper burning his hand. His father was shriveling like a slug in salt, and Mouse, coming to him, figured he could hand him the paper—a chance at his old life, and the way things used to be for all of them. Then the argument would fizzle. He'd forget all about Rachel then.

"You useless, old fart!" she was shouting. "You half a man! Both your boys, the big and the small, can see what you are. You social cripple...You old crazy! Even Mouse, at his age, knows what you are."

Mouse was remembering the night watchman years. He was re-membering Oakland. He was remembering the spiraling, spiraling eaves of the gingerbread cottage that he and his mother once called home, and he knew things would get better, of this he had always been sure. Already, things were happening. He stepped forward, the paper burning his hand as Rachel shouted, "I've heard him on the phone with his friends! Yes I have. I've heard him say so..."

And then, there he was. Close enough to watch his father's face flatten, his mouth narrow into a thin, fierce line. And without a word between, Mouse found himself falling.

Looking up at his father, he cradled his face with the flat of his hand. Mouse had hit the couch with a thud, stunned and sinking, his father's fury packed knuckle-deep in his jaw. It happened so quickly, Mouse thought—how his fist had extended and retracted with a switchblade's gleam and precision. *Why hadn't he seen? Why hadn't he seen?*

"You little..." His father cursed him. "Tell me, don't I take care of my own?" He slapped Mouse and cursed him again. "Tell me—huh—don't Sarge always take care of his?"

His mouth as dry as cotton, Mouse rubbed the swelling on his jaw. His father looked gargantuan then. *Sidewalks tearing into my feet, like they got teeth, these soles so thin. But I never asked you.* Mouse probed the cut in his mouth with his tongue. *Not one day, I never did. Because I trusted that you would, when you could. And that's why I never asked.* Then the blood flooded his mouth like water from a burst dam.

Mouse felt his father grab his collar, but instead of pulling him up to him, he bore his own weight down. "Don't old Sarge take care of his own? Don't he?" he said.

His face veiled by a thin gauze of fright, his body melting into the sofa's wilting springs, Mouse responded in the way that he thought he ought to. "Yeah…yeah, yes, sir."

"Yes sir, who?"

"Yes, sir, Sergeant," Mouse said, looking up at his father, not wanting, at that moment, to be frightened. Wanting, at that moment, to be more.

Rachel, disgusted, packed a small blue gym bag and fled with TyQuan for her mother's apartment in Coop City. Sergeant returned to the kitchen, and, unscrewing the bottle, picked up where he left off. And Mouse had hidden beneath the dirty laundry in the tub, as he had done in troubled times before.

Mouse raised his head timidly—wondering where his father was now and what the time was. Everything was quiet, even the rain. Hearing a heavy movement, Mouse covered himself again with the clothes and pressed his face against the bathtub's pocked enamel. Its coolness quelled the swelling on his cheekbone.

He got up. He felt down. He felt dirty. Mouse wished that he had fought back. Peering into the mirror, he touched the bruise on his cheek. *One day, I'm gonna…* Mouse flinched. Frightened by his own thoughts, he covered his eyes, ran both hands down the length of his face and stood still, shivering, afraid of the picture he had just seen in his mind. Afraid of what he was capable of. Instead, he palmed some Blue Magic hair treatment into his scalp, and raising his T-shirt, doused his neck and chest with Brut cologne. He worked stealthily, briskly. Sergeant was still sleeping. If the old man woke up before tomorrow morning, Mouse wanted to be gone before then, down at the Blakk Rukus party—none of this on his mind.

Mouse crept out of the bathroom and into his room to retrieve his windbreaker. In the kitchen, he checked the knobs on the stove—no gas escaping, good—then shut the kitchen window. The rain had stopped, but beneath the sill, a puddle of silver water had collected on the tiles in an ominous pool. Some had also hit the table. A large stack of bright napkins was sodden, and he reluctantly scraped it all into the trashcan.

The last thing he did before leaving was to go to the doorway of his father's room. Sergeant still slept, bundled tightly in a white sheet. His ribcage rose and fell, and Mouse thought how easy it would be, at that moment, to kill him.

He bolted the apartment door closed—still trying to make sense of his father and the two men he was. One, full of jokes and gentle. The other, vicious and fleeting. But, creeping down the tenement stairs now, Mouse thought instead of Clarissa, Kevin, Addie, Blakk Rukus, the music, the celebrities, the girls, the liquor, the weed, the club, all waiting…All waiting downtown, as he made his way through the front door, onto the glistening streets, and into the world of the living.

CHAPTER FIVE

"Come on now, baby, wake up." Euclin tapped Buddha's face. "We got a show to put on here tonight. Come on, now." *Tap, tap.* The sound on his cheek was like applause.

Buddha lay against the black marble shower tiles, passed out and stripped to his underwear. Miko had called her during dinner, just as the roasted monkfish arrived: Buddha was knocked out, she'd said—cold. How soon could she get there? Brent implored Euclin to let Miko handle everything, to stay here with him and her friends. But Euclin whispered a whisper she knew would assuage him: There was more food to come; Tyler had made such an effort; Angus was there; and he should enjoy the quiet before things got stressful again. She'd kissed his forehead gently and said, "Baby, stay. We'll meet up later."

Brent said, angry, "That's it—no third chances. This is the last time. I told you not to use them again. I just hope they get that lighting sequence right before the opening."

"Don't worry. I'll set them straight." Euclin winked and gathered her things, not knowing why she had lied to him.

It was Slammah who spoke now. "That n$gga ain't stopped drinking since last night. I told him, man, to ease up on that Tanqueray, but that n$gga don't listen…"

Euclin stooped down and pulled up Buddha's sagging weight by one arm. She steadied him as though he were a recalcitrant man-nequin. She noticed, for the first time, that his chest was hairless—muscular, smooth—and that his nearly naked body was the color of flan. Euclin tried peeling Buddha's eyelids back with her fingertips, but they would not stay open. *Like a dead man's,* Euclin thought, even though she had no idea how a dead man's eyes would look or feel. Touching his eyelids again, she wondered if Buddha were dreaming, and if so, of what?

"Has he been doing anything else?" she asked Slammah.

"Yo, I don't know, man. You know I ain't down with that mess no more, can't even stand to look at the stuff. Hey, that nsgga's his own man. He his own responsibility. He ain't want to listen. Can't nobody tell him nothing."

"But you three are like brothers—you are your brother's keeper. You should have tried to stop him. You *knew* we had a show tonight. He is *your* responsibility, you are *his* responsibility."

"Buddha responsible, now that's a good one." Slammah laughed. "Yo, why I always got to be the responsible one? Huh? Why? Cause I carry the Bible? I'm tired, too, Miss Ram. Listen, man, I'm tired, too."

"You should have stopped him," she said again.

Slammah made a disgusted sound with his teeth and left the bathroom.

Euclin stroked the stubble on Buddha's head, trying to draw him to consciousness. She was beginning to feel convinced it was all a sham—their association with Blakk Rukus: Buddha held the weed, Skizzah held the liquor, and Slammah held the Bible. The Bushwick trinity she called them—the bane of her existence.

The Bush Mobb were protégés of Blakk Rukus—one of the first acts Euclin had signed to Amp in her new role as its A&R. They were also the first hip hop group signed to the label—ever. Two years ago, Black Ruckus' frontman Lucky Dogg nearly had to have his leg amputated after a motorcycle accident in Key Biscayne. He came out from his coma and said he'd seen Jesus. Brent was skeptical. Euclin was skeptical. But it was true; Blakk Rukus had changed. They were serious now, easier to work with. They put God in most of their songs. The Bush Mobb—which consisted of Slammah, who was Lucky Dogg's cousin, and Buddha and Skizzah, their childhood friends—was Lucky Dogg's baby.

Twice already Brent had threatened to nullify their contract, but each time Euclin had stopped him; whatever power she lacked in the office, she exercised on him at home. Change seemed inevitable, yet Euclin continued to feel a certain inexplicable tenderness toward all three that, even in her angriest moments, made her more magnanimous than she ever realized she could be.

"You got any idea yet, Ms. Ram, on what you wanna do?"

"Big Mike. God, I'm glad to see you."

Big Mike stood in the arch of the bathroom door, his monstrous hands pressed against the molding. Strands of his reddish-blonde hair were stuck to his forehead from sweat.

"Who called?" Euclin asked.

"Miko did. She said that Slammah rang her cellular."

Euclin paused. "That was good of him. It's good that you're here."

"No problem, man, I was on my way over here, anyways." As he stepped into the bathroom, it was as though he were not composed of muscle or bone. Beneath his rayon suit, Big Mike's body swayed like gelatin.

"You working security?"

"Yep."

"We could have used you at that Irving Plaza gig last month."

"Yep, I heard about that. You got plenty on your hands to deal with, Miss Ram. I mean *plenty.*"

In another part of the country, Big Mike would be called a redneck. Here, most of the other black bouncers and performers treated him as though he were black. They spoke in their natural voices around him, and said things that they deleted from their conversations with other white people. Around them, Big Mike could use the word n$gga as a term of affection, or in a joke when he felt like it, and did so with impunity. Only a few of the bouncers and performers were uncomfortable with this arrangement, this talking to a white man as though he were another black man, but those who trusted him would say, "Big Mike, man, he all right. Leave that n$gga alone, man. He cool. Big Mike, he all right by me."

After checking Buddha's irises and pulse, they decided on an elementary plan: keep dousing him with cold water and ice until he regained consciousness. As Big Mike hoisted Buddha's limp form over one shoulder and took him to the shower, Euclin summoned Slammah and Skizzah to follow them. Once inside, she turned to face them.

"You guys aren't going on tonight," she told them.

"I knew it. I knew it. Aw, man," Skizzah whined, yanking his cap off. He had on a quilted banana-yellow jacket, wrapped fat around him like pudding. "But I'm saying, yo, I'm all dressed up. Got my girl out there. She got her peeps out there. They expecting to see us blow this mess *up*. Yo, I mean…Never fails—never. Seem like *every* time we 'bout to come on, *some* kinda mess be going down."

"Now, whose fault is that?"

"I know, I know…Next time." Skizzah massaged the silk of his jacket. "Next time."

Euclin sighed, laying Buddha's head back against the tiles.

"You three get your act together, and maybe there might actually be a next time. You haven't even finished cutting the album yet. Consider this practice. And if you can't get practice right, then what can you?"

Euclin glanced at Slammah, but still he said nothing.

"What we supposed to do then?" Skizzah asked.

"Just go out. Mingle with the crowd."

"I'ma go find my cousin then, go find my peeps." Saying this, Skizzah looked at Euclin one more time, as though still hoping she would change her mind.

"I don't care, just…Just find something to do with yourselves," she said, positioning Buddha in place so Big Mike could turn on the shower.

CHAPTER SIX

The storm had returned. Mouse drew the hood of the windbreaker tightly over his head, but the rain soaked through the flimsy blue nylon. Drops slapped against brick and concrete, silver and heavy as nickels. Even as the lightning folded back into the sky and the thunder ceased to roll, the storm clouds grew even more agitated, assembling like predators: grey, terrible, menacing. Mouse looked up at the sky. It was a night to be inside. It was a night to be home.

Pinching through the fabric of the windbreaker, he stretched the clammy cotton of his Blakk Rukus T-shirt away from his chest. The dampness oozed across his body, and he shivered. The rain dragged at his jeans, making walking difficult. The slickened streets were empty, and the only movement was that of the livery cabs gunning by, myopic and murderous: dropping off, picking up, dropping off, picking up the last marooned, umbrella-less souls.

But here he was. Mouse eyed the murky gutter water rushing just below his feet. Potato chip bags, soda cans, cigarette butts, and other urban flotsam scraped against the curbs, whirling down the asphalt tongue of Lenox Avenue. Mouse moved faster, suddenly sure that he was running late.

The squat, sandy brown of the Schomburg Center and the brooding blue of Harlem Hospital loomed above the subway entrances on either side of Lenox. Standing at the crosswalk, Mouse felt the blood again. It mixed with his saliva, coiling around his teeth and his gums. Sticking his finger into his mouth, he pressed against the open wound, then spat. There was something about the taste of blood that always reminded him of the sea, and of food. Walking quickly through the rain, he headed across the street to the open station.

The storm's scent descended the stairs, hanging coldly in the station. Wads of blackened gum were embedded in the subway floor. Within the compressed square of the token booth an aging clerk moved about, his blue shirt alert with starch, his argent hair precisely trimmed. Transferring unsorted sacks of tokens to the front counter, he was engaged in a violent, solitary discourse.

Approaching the booth, Mouse pushed his hand into the pockets of his windbreaker, then stopped, frantically searching his clothes. In his haste to leave the house, he had forgotten to transfer his wallet from the pocket of his black jeans. He fingered the fabric all the way into the corners of his windbreaker pocket: a single dollar. Its weightlessness depressed him. He was one quarter short of a token.

Mouse looked around the station.

Mouse saw no one.

He decided to jump.

Yet, for reasons not clear—feet still planted—he remained where he was, hesitating to hop the turnstile, even though he did it all the time when short of money or bored. But, trying to pinpoint the source of his sudden apprehension, Mouse found no logical reasoning to which he could attach his fears. The token clerks were generally apathetic, powerless, or too terrified to move beyond the Plexiglas cocoon of their booths. *Cut the bull and jump then. Just cut the bull and jump.* But Mouse couldn't. And smelling danger, Mouse followed his instincts.

Waited.

Saw the plaid swatch.

Mouse wondered why he had not noticed the man before. Dressed in work boots and a padded flannel outer shirt, a raven-haired construction worker stood on the other side of the booth, reading that day's *Post*. There had been no commuters visible on the platform or on the wooden benches when Mouse had entered, and up until that point, besides the token clerk, he had considered himself alone. A white man in Harlem was not an unusual sight—but rarely at this hour. Still, Mouse wondered whether the man was really a construction worker lingering past the end of his shift, or an undercover cop, waiting, hawk-eyed, for a single act of stupidity.

Definitely undercover 5-0, Mouse reasoned. *Those boots look too new. Maybe he's for real though: could of just bought 'em for work. But why he ain't waiting on the platform, though? No, 5-0, 5-0, definitely. He expects* *you to jump. They think that n$ggas always be jumping. Cool now, cool, look natural. No need to start tripping just yet.* But Mouse had already grown nervous, and wondered how he would make it downtown if this man were really a cop. He wished he was already at the club with Kevin, Clarissa, and Addie, over and done with the worst parts of this night.

Mouse looked over at the construction worker again. The man coughed, evened out the pages of his newspaper, continued reading. All of these moments, totaled, told Mouse nothing. There was a frantic, unsure part of him that wanted to confront the man, just for the certainty of knowing. Then he remembered J. C. from 4-F two summers before, who had been too bold or foolish enough to ask a plainclothes subway loiterer whether or not he was undercover, 5-0. Amused, the man had simply smiled and replied, "Well, why don't you try jumping and see," which J. C. did, and not long after, was carried away in tight handcuffs. *Grinning J. C.*, Mouse thought, wondering what had ever happened to him since he moved to Mount Vernon. *Never had too much upstairs.*

"I wonder where that n$gga at, man," Mouse said aloud, sucking his teeth. *A dollar, a dollar*, he thought, fingering the crumpled edge of the bill: one quarter short of legitimacy. He went to the token booth once more and asked for change, shoving the balled-up bill into the coin slot. He heard the sound of metal as four quarters appeared in exchange. Mouse shook the coins in his hand, feeling their weight. *Either this will work, or it won't*, he told himself, deciding. *Either way, I got nothing to lose.*

He dropped the coin into the payphone slot, punched the touch-tone numerals, cradled the receiver between his ear and shoulder, and waited, speaking into the void of a phone that he knew was dead. "Yeah, hello…Yeah, Clarissa? Mouse. He broke out already? Word? How long ago? Nah. Still in the subway." Mouse continued speaking into the emptiness of the broken phone. Then he heard it: the grumble of a distant train approaching the station. "Nah, freak it, I ain't waiting…Probably chill out at the crib, watch some TV, you know." Mouse tried to judge the direction by the sound—*downtown? Uptown?* Couldn't be sure. The train was still too far away for him to tell. "I-ight, bet. You still going? Let me know how it went." A flash of silver whizzed past. *Downtown train.* "Talk to you later then…I-ight…Peace." Mouse replaced the receiver.

Hands in his pockets, Mouse walked toward the stairs. The man's paper dropped slightly, and the construction worker's eyes tailed him. The train braked into the station. In a minute the motorman would open the doors. A man and woman, not bothering to close the umbrella they shared, hustled past Mouse down the stairs. *Forget it, man, it's not worth it, too risky,* but Mouse's body had already turned, defying his instincts. He vaulted over the turnstile. *I'm going, oh no. Crap, this is crazy.* His feet had brains of their own. *Oh god don't let me trip, oh god don't let me trip*—his mantra in the air. His right foot landed solidly.

"Hey, you. Hey, you!" the man in plaid yelled. "I said, hold it right there." The cop threw down his newspaper and nodded to the clerk as he ran toward the turnstile. He reached out with a thrust of his fist, missing Mouse. Stuck, he moved from side to side, hands menacing, body unsure.

The train had stopped. The doors opened. Both feet on the ground, Mouse grinned. *Idiot. Must be a rookie.*

"Release the turnstile, you moron! " yelled the cop.

"What the heck you want me to do, it's stuck!" the clerk replied.

"Then open up the service gate!" the cop roared back, cursing, pulling at the wrought iron bars. By this time several passengers were peeping through the silver car doors, and the motorman had advanced his head through the side window.

Clumsily heaving over the turnstile, the cop yelled at the motorman, "Shut it down! Now! I said, now!" Confused, Mouse ran back and forth, wanting to jump on the train, but no longer sure what to do. Mouse looked at the motorman, and the motorman at him, hesitating. Mouse felt as though the motorman were sizing him up, weighing the potential seriousness of the crime—was he a fare-beater or a murderer? Why should he shut his train down? Shutting the train down would cause a night's worth of delays. Mouse wondered what the rules were, if the motorman would have to. The cop was on the platform now. Mouse began to sprint again. He had not gotten far when a throbbing exploded in his head; he felt his body arch backward, then pitch and barrel into the wall.

Mouse winced as his face slid down the tiled wall, hitting the ground. He then felt the cop on top of his back, yanking his neck into a chokehold.

"I got him, close the doors. Don't worry, I got him," yelled the cop.

His voice was high and sure. The motorman pulled his head back inside, closed the car doors. The train's motor creaked, emitting a gassy exhale.

In that instant, the steel of the handcuffs minced at Mouse's wrist, at his arm—clip, clip—each time failing to fully encircle him. The cop's body felt neutral, neither hot nor cold, but his weight was frightening, formidable as a jungle cat's. Mouse reached down until he felt the cop's scrotum, and gripped it just hard enough to make the cop dismount. He stumbled and cursed and writhed, clapping his hands over his fly. "When I get a hold of you," he screamed, "I'm gonna kill you! You black bastard…When I…Just wait! When I— when I…I'm gonna tear your monkey hide!"

Mouse turned to face the wheezing silver train. It reared back, pulling from the station, on the brink of movement. Either he had to run past the angry, staggering cop, or run home. If his father were still drunk…Any direction meant murder, but he had to choose.

Mouse sprang, feet pushing off the platform, his black and red high-tops ascending like doves. Then he felt himself falling, and he reached out: for the black rubber ropes, for the bright silver chains, for the bobbing metal platform, for someplace—anyplace—between the now creeping cars, that might be strong enough and steady enough to catch him when he landed.

CHAPTER SEVEN

Lucky Dogg was being held aloft by the audience, passed from hand to hand, while Jethro scaled one of the massive stage speakers and snapped a long bullwhip, letting it crack just above the heads in the crowd. The audience reacted to the sting of the whip with a mixture of terror and thrill.

Euclin released the heavy black curtain and returned to where Brent stood waiting. He had just arrived and handed her the envelope. When Euclin opened it she gasped, then turned to Brent and smiled. Two tickets to Barbados lay nestled inside.

They had gone down twice before, Christmas of junior year, and the summer after college graduation. Brent's parents had a sprawling winter home there—cabana, servants' quarters, guest bungalow, everything—that overlooked a cove on Sandy Lane Beach.

Tracing the stripes on the sleeve of Brent's tracksuit, she laid her head against his chest.

"Floored. I'm absolutely floored, Brent. I really don't know what to say."

"Say something. Just *something*, baby," he said. "Quickly, before it's all gone from us. All gone and smashed to pieces."

Euclin lifted her head from his chest, regarding him strangely, her pupils pierced by the sharp glare of the overhead lights. There was something deeply wrong in the slurred way he spoke and in the way he had jumped at her touch.

"Brent, stop talking trash and make sense." She didn't mean for the words to come out so angrily.

Brent laughed, though there was nothing to laugh at. His hands errant, like pigeons, he laughed and laughed and laughed. A thin wisp of sweat hung over his lip like a translucent mustache. He laughed some more, then dipped his head down and licked the exposed triangle of flesh where Euclin's Lycra top plunged in a V.

"Your sweat tastes like candy." he said. "I want more."

Euclin backed away.

Brent, it dawned on her, was completely coked up and flying straight out of

his head.

She wanted to claw straight into him, right there and then. To cleave into him, purely, righteously, deeply. But, she moved away from him, drawing her breath, and returned to the curtain, peering out at the stage and beyond.

It was the summer following the end of sophomore year, the year they had met. She and Brent had gone to visit Spence Rawlings at his summer sublet on 66th and Central Park West. He welcomed them in, saying, "Where were you? I couldn't get in touch with you for nothing, dude. You missed a stellar party, man."

"My machine's broken," Brent had replied. "Euclin and I were out in East Hampton. I wanted to show her around. Just for the day, she'd never been. We missed the Jitney, and ended up crashing at Eden's. Euclin, Spence. Spence, Euclin."

"Hi."

Spence nodded. "Have a seat." He expelled two batik cushions and the Sunday *Times* from the sofa to the floor. "Lots of leftovers— that's the good news."

"Really," said Brent.

"Really," said Spence. "I'm game. How about you, Stein?"

Brent nodded. "Sure."

"Good man." Spence, grinning, thumped his back. "Good man. Be right back in a sec." He disappeared into another room and reappeared, clutching a small ball of tinfoil.

"But it seems so very little," Euclin said. The words had just come out.

Spence guffawed and eyed her, amazed. "Dude! Have you been holding out on me? Exactly how much can she pack away?"

Brent, clamping a hand on Spence's shoulder, whispered something in his ear. That was her inkling that the leftovers he and Brent were about to consume had nothing whatsoever to do with food.

"Oh. Uh-huh." Spence said, tentatively clutching the foil. He spoke to Euclin now. "Do you mind if we...?"

Was that a question? "Do I mind what? Pardon me, but I must have missed something."

Brent patted Spence on the back. "Pardon me." Spence laughed. "Where did you say you were from again?" Euclin felt as though Brent and Spence were ganging up on her.

"I never said where I was from." Her words were clipped, abrasive. "I was born in Trinidad, but I grew up in the US."

"Trinidad and Tobago. Home of the Mighty Sparrow. My father loves calypso." Then Spence, to buttress his point, broke into an egregious rendition of "The Banana Boat Song," bellowing: "*Day, me say day, me say day, me say day. Me say day, me say day-ay-ay-o...*"

"Harry Belafonte is Jamaican," Euclin said.

"Then how about this." Without missing a beat, Spence segued into "Rum and Coca-Cola."

Drinkin' rum and Coca-Cola
Go down Point Cumana
Both mother and daughter
Workin' for the Yankee dollar

"You see," he said. "How was that? I wasn't bullcrapping you. I bet you thought that 'The Banana Boat Song' is the only calypso I know."

"That last one was by the Andrews Sisters—they're American. Still, most people have never even heard of Trinidad."

"They plagiarized it," Spence corrected. "The original was sung by some dude from Trinidad called Lord Invader." Spence moved on to "Jean and Dinah," the third in what was to become a sprawling medley of calypsos. Placing the ball of foil on the table and singing merrily, he spread the metal out around the pile of white powder, like the fanning fronds of a palm. "Error of errors, I forgot to bring out the spoon. *The* spoon." He yanked up the waist of his Duck pants to cover his love handles and left the room.

"Hold up," Brent said to Spence. He placed his hand, like a shield, above the flattened foil. "This isn't right. I don't think she knows what it is, what we're about to do here."

"Yes, I do. Stop being such a prig," Euclin said. "Go ahead, Spence."

"You didn't even know what that was," Brent hissed as soon as Spence was out of earshot. "I know you, Euclin, and you didn't, did you? I bet you thought that was food."

"Yes, I knew what it was," she lied. Euclin felt her chicken heart leap up, flap, flap, flap, warm and plump with feathers.

"As if," Brent snorted. "Sure."

Spence returned with the tiny spoon, gold-plated, made in Berlin, its handle opalescent mother-of-pearl.

"Pass it here," Euclin said. "I want first dibs." Spence looked first at Brent, then at Euclin. Shrugging, he gave her the spoon.

Brent rose and snatched it out of her hand. "What in god's name are you trying to prove?"

"Don't you tell me what to do," she said. "You always treat me like I'm an infant, or some West Indian schoolmarm in sensible shoes."

"Oh, please, Lin, you think that coke comes with a stripe on the can and black bubbles inside. Even pot makes you swoon. You've never done this stuff a day in your entire life, so what are you trying to prove?"

"Isn't there a first time for everything, Brent? Look, you righteous little buttwipe, I said give it here." She lunged for the spoon, and he held it high out of her reach. "I can make my own decisions. I said, give it here."

"Lin," he said. "Don't. I don't care if you don't. And Spence doesn't care, either. You don't have to prove anything to anyone here."

But in the end she got the spoon.

Her left knee trembled as she leaned over.

And with no one to emulate, she hedged about with the spoonful of powder. She finally settled on sticking the spoon, from tip to mid-handle, straight up her nose.

"No, no! Not like that!" said Brent and Spence in unison.

Too late though, and done *good enough*. Euclin had smoked pot enough times in her life to need more than ten fingers to count her transgressions, but her body remained uncorrupted, making the coke's impact immediate, pure. Euclin felt a swirling rush of warmth, and the feathers of her chicken heart molted.

"I was afraid you'd do that," Brent said.

She tried to stand, then fell back on the sofa giggling, her arms and legs spread-eagled in a socialite's sprawl. She rose up on her elbows to find Spence and Brent both staring straight up the crotch of her underwear. And for once in her life Euclin Ramtahal did not care.

Spence wiped off the spoon on his shirtsleeve, and was heartily dipping in when Brent came over and sank down on the cushion beside her. He reached out, stroking her forehead.

"You OK?" he asked.

She nodded.

"How does it feel?"

"Good. But really warm."

"What else?"

"I can't feel my tongue. Is that normal?"

"Yeah." He laughed. "Sometimes, yeah. What else? You seem really mellow."

"*Te quiero*," she lisped.

"What?"

"*Te quiero.*"

"I took Hebrew," Brent said.

"I want you," she said.

"I could see your underwear."

"I know."

He rubbed her knee. "Bad girl." Grinning, he pulled down the hem of her skirt with a dexterous tug, so Spence, who sat Indian-style on the floor with his foil and his spoon, could no longer see even the lines on her knees.

On the other side of the curtain, the crowd was cheering.

"You promised that you wouldn't," Euclin said.

"Wouldn't what?"

Palms open, she held up both of her hands. "Don't play dumb, Brent. Just don't do it. Don't even."

"Really, I've forgotten. Remind me."

"Kiss mine," she said, walking away.

Lips mocking, puckered, he grabbed at her arm. "Normally, I'd love to. But right now, your yawning trap's wide open, you nag."

"For your sake, I hope that was the coke talking."

"And what if it wasn't? Then what're you going to do?"

Euclin repossessed her forearm with a sharp pull. "You bloody oaf. Why is moderation such an arcane concept for you?"

"Moderation-botheration. Botheration-moderation, designated—" he slapped his hands together—"for the weak." He pointed one finger to the crown of his head, in a gesture of thinking. "I know how to handle myself, mama. Just you sit tight and don't worry."

"And you're doing such a fine job now."

The cartoon girl bobbed up in Euclin's mind, like the decoy that she was. Then all the other pretty girls. She felt an impasse. Again. It was not the cartoon girl that had upset her at dinner, but this— this implacable feeling. There was something in the road that had to move, that had to move for both of them.

"Talk, talk, talk, talk, talk." Brent threw up his hands. "You look like you want to, Lin. Do you want to, Lin? Lately, all you want to do is talk—so, let's."

But, already, there was too much talk inside Euclin's head. *They didn't even show up at the studio. Their money, that's what I tell them all the time. Well, of course, Slammah showed. But Buddha, the little monster—well at least now he's standing. Twelve thousand just on the open bar and hors d'oeuvres. God. Brent is going to kill me. All coked up like an imbecile, he is—but maybe that's good—Buddha won't even cross his mind. I thought we agreed…What is he trying to prove? Please let this night be over. Please let it be over. Clarissa and Kevin, oh, Jesus, that's right.*

She couldn't remember where she said to meet—the stage or the bar? What had she said to Clarissa? How stupid, Euclin thought, not to type it into my Palm.

Brent stood quietly with his hands in his pockets, coming down from his high, disheveled, waiting. *Let him wait*, Euclin thought. She turned again to the stage, tracing her fingers over the outline of the envelope, inside the tickets. *Let him wait. I have been waiting also.* She stared out at the heads of the cheering audience, wishing she could find her siblings in the crowd. *This should have been over a long time ago.*

A crow hovered above the lip of the stage, a wicked monstrosity. Its beak alone was as large as three men's heads, and its iridescent black feathers were dull from years of dust. Two silver chains pierced its back and were locked deep into its stuffing: Though the portentous wings seemed about to swoop up through the skylight, through the club's ornate ceiling, and into the night, the crow could not and did not move. Amid the human hustle on the dance floor, it seemed infinitely aware of its own deadness and the pull of the chains that confined it.

Mouse had made it. He rubbed his hands together—they still stung. He'd used his palms to break his fall when the cop had grabbed him.

At the launch party, Mouse had taken a wrong turn at the door. He had ended up in the belly of the club instead of at the coat check where he and Kevin had agreed to meet. He observed a large and disorderly assemblage of people—*Got mad heads up over there. Must be something free.* Afraid that he might be missing out, Mouse pulled aside a lanky boy in a hooded sweatshirt and asked what was going on.

"Drinks is free till ten p.m., son. Yo, you besta go get yours." The boy moved on before Mouse could ask anything else.

Mouse's throat was dry, and he decided that he wanted a drink, especially one that was free. He moved close enough to the bar to observe the tongues and teeth inside of black, brown, and beige mouths that never seemed to stop moving, and the black, brown, and beige hands that grabbed up each drink from the bar. He watched the frantic motions of the two blonde bartenders, and wanted to laugh. They reminded him of grasshoppers, with their two arms moving, with their four arms moving—the grasshoppers in the yard of his old house in Oakland, grasshoppers that he used to watch being eaten by ants.

Mouse decided to wait until the crowd thinned. Instead he drank in his surroundings: the room, the stage, the crow, the VIPs moving high above like shadows behind the iron balustrades. Mouse also felt and heard the heat and commotion of the dance floor, individual bodies seeming to lock and melt into one large mass of writhing, perspiring flesh. But Mouse's own body felt none of this warmth. His rain-soaked clothes were still on him, and his mind was still plagued by thoughts of Sergeant, of the cop, of the train. Baked in this furnace of flesh, his garments felt even colder, and he reeked of the subways and streets.

Wish I was warm or naked. Wish I had new clothes to put on me. The chilled shirt and jeans made him shiver.

Mouse tried not to think of the coldness, or what had come before, to keep moving. There was so much to see. Mouse smiled. *Mad honeys, chronic floating freely. Nsggas feeling nice, yo.* He looked around him, feeling bolder, more at ease. *Just like one of them pictures at the back of the Source, just like one of them parties.* But seeing no one familiar—no one famous—Mouse felt a sting of disappointment. All he saw were everyday faces, common faces—faces just like his own. Was this what he had come down from Harlem to see? But groomed and pressed beneath those everyday faces were the brands and styles of clothing that Mouse had always envied. *Nsggas geared up head-to-toe in DKNY, Polo, and Tommy, nuff music. Still they are all nobodies. Dressed up nsggas, but nobodies.* Mouse ran his hands down his jeans. He decided that he wanted that drink now.

As he waited in line, somebody careened into his shoulders, shoving him forward.

"Yo, man, shoot, watch who you pushing, man," Mouse said to everyone, to no one. Black, brown, and beige shoulders, elbows, and arms tangled thick as mangrove roots around him. As he pushed his way forward, he began to sense a strangeness in the air, the distinct and unmistakable aura of celebrity. Some people deserted the line at the bar, straining for a better view. The aura emanated from a man in round sunglasses and a black Nehru jacket—medium stature, coffee-bean skin. This was the source of all the upheaval.

Volney Cox. Oh sweat, there go Volney.

Flanked by six bodyguards, he strode, encircling the waist of a farina-skinned woman in a small, shiny yellow dress. This was *the* man. The man that his father might have been. The man that his father could have been. His father had told him (so many times, that Mouse had lost count), that in the late sixties he had once been part of Volney Cox & The Chasers. The original group, just as the band was forming, all of them newly in their twenties—just before they hit it big.

Then his father got himself kicked out of the band. This was before "Sweat." Before "Tingle" and "On My Knees" hit the airwaves. Before VCC (as they came to be known) came to dominate the R&B charts, then the pop charts. Before Volney left for a solo career, then founded his own record label. A man seemingly impermeable to failure. This was the Volney Cox his father talked of weekly (sometimes daily) when he spoke of another time, a life stillborn, and the millions lost.

The crowd hovered around Volney Cox's perimeter, his entourage, his enigmatic energy, as though by proximity they too would become sublime. He stopped to sign an autograph. More came for autographs, and Volney Cox signed these as well. When a third wave of seekers approached, his bodyguards moved in without being told and reestablished distance. Volney Cox encircled the waist of the woman at his side, and she giggled. A bouncer unclasped a blood-velvet rope and Volney Cox and his companions ascended the stairs and disappeared: head, shoulders, thighs, calves, the polished heels of his shoes. The atmosphere lost its charge.

Mouse had intended to join the third wave of seekers, but had been too slow in finding a pen. He gazed up at the rows of tables—votive candles flickering in their centers, back and forth like greedy tongues—trying to see if he could still see Volney Cox, but he was too deep in the interior.

But what if Volney Cox saw him? What if Volney Cox looked down, and somehow saw who he was? What if, standing high up in the balcony, gazing down into the crowd below, he saw the face of Sergeant in Mouse's own face and remembered his old friend and this was how things began? Would he send down two of his bodyguards and make them bring him up? Would he make them part the ropes for the son of his old friend, Sergeant?

Mouse envisioned himself being summoned to stand in front of a Volney Cox who loomed as big as a billboard—glowing, superhuman, untouchable.

"You're Sergeant's boy, aren't you?"

"Yes sir, Mr. Cox." Mouse would not ask him how he knew who he was.

"I thought so. I can see it in your face. Anybody ever tell you that—that you got your father in your face?"

"Plenty of people tell me that, I mean, yeah…Yes sir, I guess so."

"I can see that old crazy bastard's face right inside of your face. Make you feel like you don't have a face of your own, don't it? You look scared. I didn't mean to scare you. You old enough to drink? Careful now, the answer's always yes when you're around me. Even when you're short on age.""

"Yes sir, Mr. Cox, I could take a little something."

"Come over here then, there's some people I'd like you to meet. Sergeant, man…What he up to now? That old n$gga still crazy? Still with the same old lady, still living in Harlem, still on that same old street?"

Now that he had actually seen him in the flesh, Mouse now

wondered, were the stories even true—all those stories that his father had told him about Volney Cox? For so long, Mouse had treated these stories as though they were just that—stories—no different from the fairytales and bedtime stories that his mother had once read to him each night in Oakland. But it wasn't the stories that Mouse felt conscious of when his father spoke to him, as much as the fact that the telling of these stories marked moments of true peace between him and Sergeant, moments when all that was required of Mouse was to listen.

But here he was, for real; here was Volney Cox. Mouse thought again: If Volney saw his father's face in his face, would he insist that the ropes be parted? Would he summon him up? For the rest of the night, would he take him under his wing? Would he treat him like his own son? If the light reflected down on him, Mouse thought, at just the right angle, and in this light his face became visible, what would happen then?

"Stupid n$gga, look where you going, man—you just spilt that mess all over my sneaker!"

Rum and coke in hand, Mouse stepped from the bar and found himself jammed up against a large, angry man. The alcohol's warmth lumped in Mouse's throat.

"Sorry, man," he mumbled.

"Sorry—that all you gonna say? Sorry? I should punch your sorry face in for that mess. Look at it—all over my brand new Jordans." The black liquid shimmered at the tip of the angry man's sneaker, a small body of water whose meaning and reach, at that moment, were far larger than its actual size, far more treacherous and immeasurable.

"Yo, no need to trip, I said I was sorry, man," Mouse repeated, wishing he were bigger and taller. Fear pinned him in place like a second spine, and Mouse grew ashamed of his own cowardice.

"Watch me put my foot up in it," the man said, cursing him. "*Then* you'll be sorry!"

"Yo, man, leave that punk n$gga alone, man," said the angry man's friend. The friend was distracted, focused on two women sitting on a red sofa to the right of the bar—one of them swept a veil of shiny brown hair away from her face, and the other peered out from behind her friend's shoulder and smiled. "Come on," said the friend. "Let's just go *conversate* with these females, man."

"Don't be riling me about no chicks," growled the angry man.

"Don't you see me dealing with this little baby anus over here?" He turned his full attention to Mouse. "Let me tell you something: I just bought these sneakers last week. Know how much they cost? One hundred and fifty dollars—and you don't look like the kind of n$gga that got no hundred and fifty dollars. I should make you kneel down and eat the rubber for being so dumb."

"Not tonight. Come on, Stack, you know I came here to kick back and socialize, have a couple drinks. Yo, just shake that mess off your shoe and let's go. Leave that little punk n$gga alone. He ain't worth damaging."

Stack. The angry man now had a name, and with the pronouncement of this name, he looked even angrier.

"I'm here in the middle of some bull, and all you can think and talk about is hitting the skins."

"Look, I said, chill. Just dead it, man, and let's go."

Stack gave Mouse one hard, final look, then headed toward the two women.

Mouse was glad to see them go, but a heavy feeling had slipped into the void that the two men had left behind. *The heavy thing*, this was what Mouse had started to call it. He could not articulate exactly what the heavy thing was: like a shadow or a specter, but saddled with weight, burdened by substance. He only felt the heavy thing's presence in moments of danger—earlier in the evening on the train, for instance. And though he could not be sure, he felt convinced that it was also the heavy thing that had spared him, and the evening, from his father's waking.

Still, Mouse had not made up his mind as to whether it was the presence of the heavy thing that drew him into trouble, or if it was the presence of the heavy thing that took trouble away. *Three times in one night. Hell! What…what…*Mouse shook his head as though shaking off the entire night. He put the red Sweetheart cup of rum and coke to his lips and drank, and kept drinking until he saw the round white eye, the empty bottom. *But trouble's gone, trouble's gone,* he told himself. His head already swooning, he wandered over to the bar and stood in line for more.

CHAPTER EIGHT

A grainy, black and white projection of the album cover loomed above the stage: Amerikan Nightmarz. Dressed in leather jackets and army fatigues, members of Blakk Rukus sneered down at the partygoers dancing and drinking below. Standing and squatting in tight-lipped masculine stances on the cover, they bore hatchets, re-strained lunging Rottweilers, and held firmly coiled pieces of rope. In the background, on a chain-link fence, an out-of-focus American flag perished in flames as a ghostly, Christlike figure rose from the conflagration.

It was not until Addie placed the cup of orange juice in Clarissa's hand that she stopped looking at the screen.

"What you looking at?" Addie said.

"Up there. Rukus."

"Oh, them. Please. I stopped listening to them since they started singing all that crap about Jesus."

"Then why'd you come?"

"Cause it's a party. Came to hang out, look good, get high…What else, stupid?"

"Don't call me stupid," Clarissa said. "I told you not to call me that."

"God, chill out. I'm just joking." Addie had taken off her flo-ral pantsuit. She was wedged into a dark blue spandex mini-dress. Sparkles shone like exposed diamonds in the fabric. *She must have stuffed it into her knapsack before she left the house. One day she'll get caught doing that. One day her mother's gonna see her.* Clarissa won-dered if Addie's parents had any idea where Addie really was.

Too much smoke, too much noise, too many drunken people. Already, Clarissa was bored. She had come for Addie's sake, but not for Addie's pleasure. The artists usually showed up hours late to per-form. There was always a fight or a brawl. And she wanted Addie to see things her way, to see what she saw: lots of people, lots of noise, all adding up to nothing. Clarissa thought: *These parties are really no big deal.*

"I forgot to tell you, that guy from Mystique is here. This girl just told me in the bathroom."

"Which one?" Clarissa asked.

Addie pressed the upper part of Clarissa's arm. "The cute one—you know, with the pretty green eyes."

"Not me. I like Marlo better. All the one with the green eyes be doing is acting cute—he don't even sing."

"You like Marlo?" Addie made a face. "He mad ugly."

"No, he's not. You just don't like him cause he's dark."

"Anyway, they said they seen a whole bunch of other people up in here, too. Volney Cox, a whole bunch of other people. I cannot wait to see Shantay tomorrow in French. She gonna be mad, mad jealous."

"You weren't even at the coat check." It was Kevin, head to toe in Polo, his copper curls glowing in the club's subdued light, his confidence owning the room. To his right was Mouse, still saturated in rainwater, his jeans sagging off his backside from the added, liquid weight.

Kevin said, "What you think, Negro, I'm some kind of psychic?"

"Don't look now," Clarissa said, "here come morons incorporated."

"Man, stop jocking me." Mouse stepped back and made an angry gesticulation, raising the red cup in his hand. "I told you I was headed for the coat check. I got lost, that's all."

"Man, your butt is always getting lost. Buy a map."

"Hey, you want me to go home? I could go home right now. I'm serious. I'ma go. You know I will."

"You're getting on my last one, man." Kevin squinted. "And what happened to your face?"

"You ask too many questions," Mouse replied.

"Will you two just quit it?" said Clarissa.

"Well, well, if it ain't the Beast from the East, code name: Clarissa." Slyly sipping from his cup, Mouse awaited her wrath.

"Don't even start with me tonight, Mouse. I swear to god."

"The one you should be swearing at is the guy who gave you that busted haircut." Mouse laughed.

"You shouldn't even be talking, Mr. Please Pass the Peas. At least my hair knows what a comb and scissors look like."

"Look, all of y'all just need to shut up and chill," Addie said, pushing Mouse away from Clarissa. "I'm sick of y'all. All that picking and pecking—act like a bunch of old chickens." Addie pushed her hand into her knapsack and pulled out the bag of weed from her purse.

"Yes, yes, it's time for the lovely stuff," Kevin half-commanded, half-sang, as he took the packet from her. "Addie, pass me those White Owls. Yes, yes girls and boys, its time for the lovely stuff, come and get some right here and right now." Kevin crouched down in a corner, slitting open a cigar on his knee with a pocketknife.

"Hey, Candyman," Mouse said in a child's voice, "don't forget about me." Addie stood over Kevin, watching the knife and his hands. This was as much of the ritual that Clarissa could stand to watch before walking away.

Mouse continued sucking in, inhaling deeper and deeper. Swaddled in smoke, he felt the heat in his mouth.

Kevin grabbed for the cigar. "Lighten up, dude. Pretty soon you'll be inhaling your finger. Doggone it, man, give it here, you don't even have enough money to chip in for the dime."

Reluctantly, Mouse passed it to Kevin, Kevin to Addie, Addie back to Kevin.

"Wait, where's mine?"

"You already had plenty," said Addie.

"We'll give it in a minute," Kevin said. Addie and Kevin held out for a while. Mouse watched them smoke, yet in his mind, he was shipping off to far-off places. Did anybody know that he was disappearing? *Did anybody see? Someone must have noticed. Someone must have.* Mouse felt his inner core becoming smaller, shaved away in tiny slivers, smaller, smaller, small—all his former self whittled down now to essence—the heavy thing gone. In this swirl of white smoke, he had become a black ornament.

Mary-J was somehow more pervasive, more powerful than crack.

Mary was a sexy and understated thing, a shy girl with stage presence. All who desired her welcomed her bitter acid taste—like the stink of a lover's morning saliva. In Mary's sexy, stupefying arms, mistrust and fear were forgotten. And, as they savored and inhaled, in this atmosphere of bliss, the communal love and grandiose chatter the previous generation had abandoned and forgotten to pass on pleasantly tripped and arose.

Mouse was losing himself. *Too many freaking people—why don't they all go home? Why that guy laughing? Why he looking at me? Why you laughing n$gga? Why? You don't know me. You don't know what I could do. I could kill. I could kill you.* Mouse stood feet from the stage, in the thick of things, desperately wanting to sit down. There were no chairs. *I could kill you, and then fall asleep.*

Mouse watched as a guy he did not know—warmup suit, about seventeen—pressed his lips close to Clarissa's right ear.

"I said leave me alone," Clarissa said, wrestling to free her arm. "Do you understand English? You bought me some juice. It was nice. Now leave me alone."

"Hey, she said to leave her alone. Now leave her alone." It was Kevin.

"Hey, me and the lady are having a righteous *A–B* conversation here, so *C* your way out of this, my brother."

"You're not talking to a lady, my friend. You are talking to my sister."

"She look like a big girl to me. Ain't you a big girl—what was your name again—Clarissa? Pretty hair, pretty skin, yeah, you look like a Clarissa." Clarissa, who met his height exactly, raised her cup and tipped it. A cascade of yellow poured down his face. "You bought me juice, now I've returned the favor. It tasted good to me. How does it taste to you? Good?"

The orange juice—like sunrays—glistened in the dark.

The guy in the warmup suit smiled, wiping juice from his face with his forearm. "I know you didn't just do that." He laughed. "No, I know you didn't, cause I don't care if you a girl. I will kick the living daylights out of you!" He started to curse her.

The heavy thing had returned. Mouse stepped forward, then forward again—so close to the guy that their breath mingled. "Touch her and the only person getting anything kicked out of them tonight, n$gga, is you!"

"Who let this little punk out the nursery, man?" The guy in the warmup suit laughed again. "Does your preschool teacher know where you are?"

Mouse felt a muscle jerk in his shoulder.

"Hey, hey, cool it, man." Kevin wedged his body between them.

"Let's just kill this thing right here." Three more strangers appeared. Mouse concluded that these were friends of the guy in the warmup suit.

"What's going on, LayQuan? You got beef with any of them?"

"Couple punks jumped up to get beat down. But you know what? I ain't even gonna sweat it. I'ma be a man and walk away."

Fidgeting, the three new guys seemed indecisive about their role.

"Yo, let's just go," said the bigger of the three. He was large and teak-skinned, a gentle giant or a menace. But in all of their faces, Mouse saw the face of the angry man, of the cop, of his father, and something grew and hardened in him, as though he were now the bearer of two spines. At that moment, the heavy thing descended.

"See you later," the guy in the warmup suit said. He laughed and called Mouse and Kevin a bi—. Then repeated the word again. And again. A total of three times.

Euclin emerged from the smoke and dark. "There you are! I couldn't find you—"

The word echoed in Mouse's head, and he felt his right fist harden. His body felt driven by two fists, by two spines. He swung.

As the stranger in the warmup suit went down, Mouse towered over him.

"Your mother's a bi—"

He cursed as he punched.

"Your grandma's a bi—"

Over and over Mouse repeated the word that had transformed and ignited him into flames. "Who you calling a bi—?"

The stranger in the warmup suit writhed on the floor like a fish.

"How does it taste? Does it taste good?"

The stranger pulled down the zip on his jacket and began to reach in. Mouse jumped on him again, still cursing, the throbbing in his temple keeping time to the pulse of his exquisite rage.

Kevin was yelling. "What are you, crazy? Are you trying to get us killed? Do you want to get us killed?" He pulled Mouse up from the floor by his arm.

"Skizz!" Euclin said, grabbing the sleeve of his yellow jacket. "What's going on here? Who—? What—?"

"That's my cousin, man," Skizzah said. "That's my cousin, LayQuan, that that little punk just tried to beat down."

Euclin tightly squeezed the sleeve of Skizzah's jacket.

"Buddha, Slammah," she yelled at both, Buddha in the mix of the fight, Slammah on the sidelines. "Get over here. Both of you, now!"

CHAPTER NINE

For the fourth time in two weeks, Ophelia dreamt of a black crow. Two days before that, she had dreamt of a massive snake that had opened its jaws and swallowed her. These were portentous dreams—death dreams.

Upon waking, Ophelia sat straight up in her bed, fretful and surrounded by shadows.

In the last letter that Mam had posted to Ophelia's brother, she had written in her tight, precise cursive that Pa's health was failing: his diabetes, his hypertension, his heart. Such were the machinations of growing old, but Ophelia clung to her parcel of nightmares gingerly, awaiting what, exactly, she did not know.

Ophelia stared through the pane of glass, one of eight in the French door that led out to the yard. It was spring and already things were thawing, melting quickly. The tulips were already emerging from beneath the winter mulch, their pale baby heads peeking through. She studied the layered ribbons of white-upon-blue sky, and thought of home, of airplanes, of leaving.

Imagine that. More than two decades had passed since she had left Trinidad, and TELCO's telephone wires still had not touched the second half of Tamarind Road, where her parents' house stood. When they had last spoken, Mam had announced, "Who can't afford to, take phone. And we on the main street can't get phone. You ever see such a ting as that? Bambye you go see am. Soon. God willing—what is meant to be ours go come along soon."

Ophelia had long relied on the Pooransinghs, who had a telephone, to pass the word along. Over the span of decades, the process had grown formulaically smooth: Ophelia to Mrs. Pooransingh; Mrs.

Pooransingh to an elder child, more than likely Jimmy; Jimmy to Miss Joycie, as Mam was called; Mam to Pa. Both of them headed down the road to the Pooransingh's house, well in advance of the designated time. Mrs. Pooransingh offered up chilled glasses of sorrel on a bamboo coaster—juice on which Mam and Pa would patiently sip, sitting in the gallery, awaiting Feelie's overseas call.

Ophelia had offered to pay for her parents' passage to New York, urging that they settle down for good. In fact, she'd offered so many times that she stopped counting. But the uprooting of old bones and old ways was frightening to Mam, and Mam would give a simple, knowing laugh, or some sharp retort. "When young chick look out at the yard, he only see fence, but when old rooster look out, he see plenty." And the pall of her mother's words would dull the prospect of some imagined new beginning.

Ophelia rued her own uprooting, and this equipped her with infinite empathy. On the days when New York became too hard or too cold or too large, and she found herself missing the Trinidad countryside, Mam's trepidation and Ophelia's own longing met——offshoots of fear grafting together. Then there were days when Ophelia remembered the backward parts of the Caribbean, and felt a raw and open disgust for Trinidad: the brownouts and blackouts, with or without storms, no running hot water, all those years and still no telephone. *Imagine that, in such an educated country.*

Ophelia could not envision a return to such aggravation, to such instability, to so much unknown. *Every minute Verlee there say she only running and running to Trinidad, but not me, yes. No, papa. No, sir. What is the sense? Spending all that money. What is the sense? America, for better or for worse, is where I will lay down my bones.*

On this spring morning, Ophelia was already worrying about the squirrels who came in the spring to eat the heads of her tulips, then again in the summer to behead her marigolds and make off with voracious bites of green tomato.

There were only inklings of the life to come in that garden, but Ophelia saw it full-blown: the slugs, the pale earthworm farmers churning into the dirt, then wriggling out when it rained to keep from drowning. She followed the curved, woody husk of the grapevine, stunted in its final phase of growth from the previous year, still twined around the posts of the makeshift arbor that she and Linnaeus had built. Standing there, Ophelia already saw the vibrant green of its leaves, and the rich, tart, burgundy fruit that the vine would bow down and bear.

The grapes made her think of the Ali family, the prosperous Syrians who owned several shops in the Rio Verde junction when she was growing up. In Trinidad, all Middle Eastern people were referred to as Syrians—but in the case of the Alis, they were indeed from Damascus. They had a handsome split-level home with a lily pond in the back and a grape arbor in the front yard, from which passing schoolchildren would sometimes climb up and steal. To put a stop to the pilfering, the Alis introduce a German shepherd named after their home city. But Damascus—no trained assassin—quickly became the darling of schoolchildren, and small groups of them would distract him with affectionate pats and lunch scraps while the others stole grapes on tiptoe.

According to the rum shop rumors, in 1944, the elder Ali emigrated from Syria with only three items of clothing: an Egyptian cotton shirt, a pair of flour-sack trousers, and a pair of secondhand briefs. The only money he had, five pounds, he kept secured around his neck in a small sack, like an amulet. His first night in Port of Spain, he slept on the street, then found a job the next day. Signing on with a plantation recruiter, he hopped a train south and worked the cane fields of Caroni alongside indentured East Indians. Within two years, he saved enough to open a rum and grocery shop; within three, a haberdashery. Decades later, after his two eldest sons graduated from university in England, they elbowed their way into boom-time construction and oil, where they both made a killing. There were doctors in the family now, lawyers, mid-level managers, shop owners (of course), and even one or two ne'er-do-wells who, thanks to family money, were lazily thriving.

Nothing, thought Ophelia. Mr. Ali came from nothing. And thinking of this nothingness, she thought of Mam, and the business, and the small fortune lost.

In her twilight years, Mam had been given a blessing. She had received a contract for a school lunch program, copiously underwritten by government money, and she eventually expanded the basement of the house into an industrial kitchen. It was as though God were making amends to the Abels and Johns for so many generations of uneven fortune and poverty.

Mam began the operation modestly enough, cooking school lunches for the children of St. Agnes' Preparatory. Other schools soon approached her independently, then the government took over, subsidizing the meals for nearly all Rio Verde's schools, and in time she was awarded contracts for schools as far as two towns over. There were delivery vans to buy. Payroll accounts to manage. Checks to write. Creditors to pay. Management began to outweigh cooking. Grown slightly jealous, Pa retired to his garden. It was too much for Mam to oversee alone. Verlee, Ophelia's sister, quit her job and went down to manage indefinitely, but her poor head for figures made a deeper mess of things and she flew back up to New York just as quickly.

Once Verlee had gone, Mam called in outsiders. Local girls she treated like daughters. Local boys she treated like sons. It took a while, but she began to notice eventually: pots, pans, sacks of rice, whole sides of beef disappeared. Lunch deliveries failed to arrive on time. There were squabbles about overtime. Accounts lapsed. The bank discovered check forgeries. Five years later, up for evaluation, the contract was not renewed. Instead, it was given to Mrs. Singh, a neighbor five houses down on the other side of the road, who had long been known to covet the business.

Niles, Ophelia's brother, flew down to help Mam file for what amounted to bankruptcy. Ophelia and Verlee flew down to take inventory and help organize the liquidation sale. Pa returned from his garden. Life went on.

As always.

Lord, Ophelia sighed. *God, what is the matter with black people? While we dwell at the bottom, everyone climbs. All over the world, the same.*

Sometimes when she read her Bible, she wondered if it was true what they said—if there was really a curse....

The sons of Noah who came out of the ark were Shem, Ham and Japheth. (Ham was the father of Canaan.) These were the three sons of Noah, and from them came the people who were scattered over the whole earth.

Noah, a man of the soil, proceeded to plant a vineyard. When he drank some of its wine, he became drunk and lay uncovered inside his tent. *Ham, the father of Canaan, saw his father naked and told his two brothers outside. But Shem and Japheth took a garment and laid it across their shoulders; then they walked in backward and covered their father's naked body. Their faces were turned the other way so that they would not see their father naked.*

When Noah awoke from his wine and found out what his youngest son had done to him, he said, "Cursed be Canaan! The lowest of slaves will he be to his brothers."

He also said, "Praise be to the Lord, the God of Shem! May Canaan be the slave of Shem. May God extend Japheth's territory; may Japheth live in the tents of Shem, and may Canaan be the slave of Japheth."

Were Black people *really* cursed? Trouble, yes she knew trouble— but Ophelia refused to believe this. But sometimes on other days— against her will—Ophelia found herself believing the exact opposite.

Ophelia undid the metal latches securing the door's head and foot and then pulled back the bolt in the middle. Moving around on the small wrought-iron porch, she removed a long terracotta flowerpot from the window ledge. Placing the pot on the floor, she broke off the porous slat of wood that once composed the bulk of the ledge, surprised that it had rotted in the middle of winter. Ophelia made a mental note of this, adding it to a growing to-do list for Linnaeus— the short circuit in the den's overhead lighting, the peeling porch rails, the boiler's incessant dripping. Others might just call it luck, but Ophelia was aware that she was blessed. Linnaeus rarely taxed her spirit, never complained, and never seemed to tire of doing the things she asked of him.

But, it was so queer how we met, she thought, stroking the wood. Walter's death had been their blessing.

Walter was an orderly at the nursing home who died at thirty-three. While peering over the ledge for an arriving subway train in Times Square, he'd lost his footing. The buzz about the office was that the train had sliced him in half. The service, which had taken place four years before, had been held at the McBride Funeral Home, Linnaeus's parlor, just before the Easter weekend.

As the mourners queued up for the final viewing, Ophelia had looked up to find Linnaeus staring in her direction. She glanced around, not sure he was studying her or Mrs. DiFranco behind her. She recognized *the look*, being older and wiser than when she had met Cecil. But Ophelia, refusing to meet his gaze head-on, had girlishly tucked in her head, and Linnaeus, recognizing her recognition, had looked away out of decency.

He pulled her aside just as she was exiting. She remembered how softly, how tentatively he had touched her arm with his white-gloved hand. She had been walking with Margot, her lunch buddy from work. Margot gave Ophelia and Linnaeus the once-over, as though sizing them up as a couple, and bounced her car keys ever so lightly in her palm.

"Felia, should I wait?"

"No, you go ahead," Ophelia said. "I'll be along."

The remaining mourners were filing through the parlor door. She knew it must have looked tacky, flirting at a funeral, and Ophelia felt the blush of chagrin. But there he stood, all six-foot-two of him stretching before her, all salt-and-peppercorn hair and supple, butterscotch skin. Ophelia resuscitated her boldness, her sense of rightness. He was a grown man, and she a grown woman.

"How did you know Walter?"

"Coworker," answered Ophelia. "Such a shame. Really—*such* a shame. I can't believe it. He was so good at handling the residents. Such a wonderful, decent young man."

"Funerals are not for the dead," responded Linnaeus. "Actually, they're for the living."

"What an odd thing to say."

Linnaeus laughed. "You look so appalled," he said. Ophelia felt embarrassed. She'd forgotten how expressive her face could be. "No, really," he continued, "the living, not the dead, are the central focus of this industry. As a ritual, funerals—they provide a sense of finality, a sense of transition that helps those left behind get on with their own existence. Don't get me wrong now, grief takes time, to be sure, but this is the place where things first seem to register. Without the flesh as a vessel—a thing that people can *touch* and *see*—the spirit becomes too abstract for most people."

Looking Linnaeus over again, Ophelia nodded her head, already beginning to make up her mind from that moment. *You mad o' what? A funeral parlor director? You done lose your mind? Gyul, just listen to that crazy talk he talking.* She wasn't that desperate.

"So, young lady," said Linnaeus, "what do you like to do for fun?"

"I should be asking *you* that," she said. Her tone held no sunshine.

He laughed again. "That face of yours. I threw you a curve ball, I see. I guess I thought you could handle it," he said. "Few people can truly handle what I do. I guess that's why I've tended to date nurses. At least there's some common ground between us."

"Wait, how did you know?" Ophelia said, her guard dissolving.

"Your shoes."

Looking down at her nurse's shoes, Ophelia found herself laughing. "Oh, dear, this old, addled brain of mine—of late, I've become so forgetful. But, I could of swear I remember taking them off when I changed into my black suit. I could of swear…"

"I must say, those are some of *the* whitest shoes that I've ever seen in my life."

"So, then, is my *shoes* that you want?" asked Ophelia, emboldened.

Linnaeus stopped smiling, grown serious. He pulled out his handkerchief, wiping an invisible speck from the tip of his nose. "What I want cannot be grasped so easily. Only a woman who's in it for the long haul can understand the things that push and pull me."

Ophelia fell silent and Linnaeus reached out, gently touching her arm.

"Do you understand?" he said.

She nodded quickly, dumbly, caught off guard by the swiftness of things.

"I must say that your accent struck me immediately."

"I'm from Trinidad. Trinidad and Tobago." Ophelia tucked in her chin. "Rio Verde. Deep in the country."

"Oh-ho, a Trini, I see! I thought so!" he exclaimed. "Eh-eh—give me some roti and curry nah, man."

"What *don't* you know?" she asked. "I see you're just full of surprises."

"One of my good running buddies was a Trini. Selwyn Harry—God rest his soul. Lovely, lovely people, those Trinis." Then he whispered, "And crazy, too. I remember—oh my goodness—no one can beat those Trinidadians for parties and songs."

"They like to fête too blasted much," Ophelia scolded, then caught herself. "Please do excuse my rudeness. Have you been down there?"

"No, but just looking at you, I feel like I'm already going, Ophelia." He smiled. "I feel like I'm already gone."

Soon it would be planting season again, and Ophelia would be glad to be down on her knees. She bent down and touched the damp earth. She would put a rhododendron here, perhaps a large patch of pink peonies. She looked at the naked hibiscus shrub that, in the summer, would be laden with red blossoms. It all took time to figure out, to plan one's garden. But a garden could not be planned in a single summer; it took many summers. It took years. Things could never come together in the right way if one made decisions hastily.

The wind blew, colder this time, and she thought of Kevin. He had propped open his bedroom window the night before, and then fallen down exhausted on top of his goose-down comforter.

Sometimes in the mornings she would stand at the entrance to his room, sometimes for a very long time, just to watch him sleeping, the outline of his body lit by the moon. Only then would she move to close the window. And after that, she would wrap Kevin, with a sheet or heavy comforter, from shoulder to toe. Through the dark, Ophelia would then feel her way back, past Clarissa's door, to her own king-size bed.

Ophelia buttoned her cardigan to deflect the wind. *They seem to fear nothing*, she thought, not even the cold. These American children, they saw the world so differently. Theirs was a world of plastic gadgets, mesmerizing blue TV screens, bigness and abundance everywhere they looked—and this abundance consumed them, even as it was being consumed. Because of this abundance, these children would never fully know the soil as she or her mother, or her mother's mother did, and a great, black chasm would always yawn between them and the earth.

She pitied these American children, who did not know what it was like to plant, to dig their hands deep down into the soil, or to raise those same hands over a pit and sprinkle seed. These American children, who did not know what it was like to take hold of a plant that came from somewhere else, from someone else, and have it thrive in a tiny strip of backyard soil. If asked to feed themselves without a fridge or a marketplace, surely, these children would starve.

No. They had absolutely no idea, these children, of exactly how lucky they were.

Ophelia left her garden and entered the house. As she closed the door, behind her back a crow appeared, alighting in a branch of the tree that overshadowed her yard.

CHAPTER TEN

Papermate correction fluid smells like guava. Euclin could not remember when she had happened upon this fact, but she felt glad that she had. It had grown into a secret habit, unscrewing the cover when things at work became stressful, drawing its acute and fruity scent in. The smell of guava in the middle of a Manhattan high-rise grounded her.

It was six months after Blakk Rukus' record release party. Inhaling this time, Euclin thought of the trip that she and Brent had taken to Barbados the autumn before. They walked the beach together, and wherever she went, the sun tracked her mercilessly, no matter how hard she had tried to hide from it. The second day of the trip she looked in the guesthouse mirror and touched her face, disappointed that its former ashy dullness had split into an opulent plum-blue.

After only two days, Brent had grown restless around the house, around his parents, and they had packed a basket and their swimsuits; she and Brent escaped to the other side of the island. Jumping into their rented moke, they had taken the Tom Adams highway down to the Crane Beach Hotel.

Smelling the guava now, Euclin remembered sitting upstairs on the hotel's wraparound verandah, outside the bar and main dining room. The beach's waters were located at a juncture where the Atlantic met the Caribbean Sea, causing the white of the waves to unfurl with roughness and tenacity. Surfers paddled belly-down out to sea. Coconut trees and sea almond bushes lined the beach, and foreigners parked themselves on an embankment of sand piled high against the shore, roasting themselves into mulattos. They occupied, Euclin noticed, three-quarters of the beach, while the locals—ones not selling trinkets to foreigners—held down the southern corner. And here in the hotel, behind the sliding doors, maids set down cutlery for the evening meal, while the bartender garnished rum punches and piña coladas with umbrellas and ubiquitous maraschinos.

"God's country, isn't it?" Euclin said.

Through the smoke of a Cohiba, Brent said, "I know."

A small bird plucked at a forgotten maraschino on the verandah ledge. Euclin held out a crust of bread from her flying fish sandwich, and tamely, the bird hopped toward her.

The bird struggled with the bread, dragging it away.

"How can you stand her?" Brent said.

"Your parents are much better people than you think," Euclin said. The bird gave up and flew away. Slipping off her Prada sandals, Euclin pressed her feet against the verandah's pink terrazzo. A dark, slender hand took up her empty rum punch and replaced it with a fresh one.

Shading her eyes, Euclin, looked up and smiled. "Thank you."

She and Brent had had to climb a high, steep staircase of weathered wood to get up to the hotel, which had been built on top of a mammoth scarp of black coral. At the far end of the sand, they saw a rough assemblage of rocks and another stretch of beach that lay beyond, beckoning. A local man with thick, sun-bleached dreadlocks commented cryptically, "Not worth the venture. Much, much better over here."

Since that encounter, Euclin had spotted the sun-bleached dread combing the beach. She'd watched him plop down in the sand next to what looked like the wildest or the loneliest of the foreign women.

"There goes our friend," Brent said.

"I see."

"Do you think he's going to score?"

"Slim pickings, looks like. Most of the women down there seem to be with someone."

"These guys," Brent said, and took another puff of Cohiba. "Do you remember Grantley, our old groundskeeper?"

"Sure. Nice old man. He used to bring me stalks of sugarcane, once he learned that I liked it."

"He's retired now, in case you haven't noticed. Dealing with the old lady, I suspect, probably drove him to it. Anyway, Grantley'd tell me stories all the time about these guys, about these women. Once they've hooked them, he said, these women pay for everything: every meal, entertainment, cash for sex, pocket money, put them up at hotels. But a lot of times it doesn't just end there. That's the part I found fascinating—the way it stretches beyond sex. Some of these girls actually fall in love with these guys. And when they go home, some of them even wire down tickets so these guys can come up and meet them wherever they are—Paris, Munich, Amsterdam, whatever. Some of them even lay out money to underwrite the guys' businesses. Can you believe it?" Brent held his glass up in a toast, tipped his chin at the sun-bleached dread in salute. "The life of Riley, these guys."

Euclin looked down at the dread, who sat behind a very thin, freckled girl. The girl looked underage and shapeless, flat on all sides like a board. The dread was pouring suntan lotion into his hands, talking all the while as he rubbed lotion onto the girl's back and shoulders. Watching him work, Euclin thought of the small, friendly bird that had hopped up beside her on the ledge.

There were many small birds like that, always perched along the perimeters, consuming the things that tourists dropped or fed them. Euclin started to feel as though she were somehow judging the dread and the way he chose to live, and she tried not to; but she realized that she really wasn't judging him at all. She was simply trying to understand. They were all part of an ecosystem: the dread, the freckled girl, the foreigners, the bartender, the maids, the trinket sellers, the bird, the sea, an ecosystem of nature and human relationships, but one in which there were no hosts or parasites, just a balance, just a circle, like a leech, she thought, like a leech whose mouth was suctioned on its own hind quarters, turning and turning around.

It began to drizzle. Then the rain came down harder, suddenly, falling into the ocean in big, grey plops, and Euclin watched as the swimmers emerged from the sea, huddling beneath bright umbrellas on the embankment of sand, like fugitives.

"Maybe we should go," Euclin said, one hand over her rum punch.

"No," Brent said calmly. He looked up at the sky. "It will pass."

And it did. The rainclouds dried up and retreated just as quickly as they had appeared.

Euclin was on the telephone when Miko popped her head through the door.

"Listen, Starsky, someone's at the door. I have to go. Yes, boo, I have crazy love for you, too. Of course I'll be there! All right then, all right. Ciao." She looked at Miko. "What's up?"

"Brent called an emergency meeting. Looks serious. His dad's flown in."

"Oh, crap, a meeting. Not now—just look at all these demos!" Euclin held up her call sheet. "Look at all this freaking work I have to do!"

"Don't shoot the messenger." Miko shrugged. "I'll see you down there."

"Yeah, I'll see you." Euclin was not perturbed by the meeting as much as by Brent's not having warned her. They had woken up on opposite sides of the bed that morning, shared a sink, grabbed scones and a latte at Bubby's before hopping in a cab, and he hadn't told her a thing.

Miko was right: It must be serious. There was very little that would get his father off that yacht.

She entered the conference room to find what looked like the entire company there. "Hey there, Linny," Mr. Stein said. His reading glasses were flipped up on his head, and he patted her hard on the back. "What's cooking, beautiful?"

"Hey, Pops. How are you doing?" Euclin kissed him on both cheeks. "How's fishing?"

"Great, just great."

Euclin walked over to Miko; she had saved her a seat. Brent entered the room just then, and Euclin thought about reaching out and grabbing his arm. He walked past her and took a seat at the other end of the table, next to his father.

Gripping the head of the table, the elder Stein stood up. He slapped his hands together and gave them a campfire rub, flipped his glasses down to the bridge of his nose, and began.

"Well, it looks like everyone's here. First, let's cover the good news: You are all being laid off...Just kidding, people." He rubbed his hands together again as nervous laughter filled the room. "I can promise you now that it's not *that* bad, but things are not pretty."

Euclin kept looking at Brent, but he avoided her gaze.

"First up, the major news is that we are terminating The Blakk Rukus." Euclin felt her head jerk. Expectant eyes, all around. She felt them train in her direction. She had become the focus of the room. *How could...But it isn't fair. It just isn't fair. They worked so hard; we worked so hard on this.* She was careful, though. She would not react.

Her mini bottle of Evian was in front of her and she took a swig. Slowly, the eyes fell away.

But where was Brent in all of this? She looked at him again, desperate for him to look back. *He kept this whole thing from me. Bastard. Now he can't even look?*

"The whole industry is in a slump," the elder Stein continued, "but The Blakk Rukus, compared to their triple-platinum debut…Their sophomore album has moved less than 100,000 units in what's fast approaching six months. Taking this, and a number of other priorities into consideration, we're shifting the focus of Amp.

"As many of you know, when I founded Amp thirty years ago, our stable of artists was all rock acts. Over the years, we increased our portfolio of R&B, and when my son started actively interning here during his college years, we added more and more rap acts to our roster—The Blakk Rukus being our biggest-selling act, by far."

"Blakk Rukus—*just* Blakk Rukus," Brent said.

"Why thank you, Brent. It's so nice to have a son with an agile mind, who can correct you. After spending…As I was saying, after spending time evaluating the overall industry, I've decided to take Amp in a new direction, or some might say an old one. After looking at the success of acts like Pearl Jam and Nirvana, I've decided to take Amp back to its roots. I've decided that we'll be pushing more heavily toward an alternative format, *grunge* as some call it. I consider this to be a very wise choice, and executed at a plum time.

"As for our R&B acts, they are among some of the strongest in the business, but, for future dealings, we'll be highly circumspect about the number of rap acts we recruit, and we'll be reassessing the ones we currently have in our roster." He stopped and sipped from a glass of water. His throat made a chafing sound. "I spoke to Lucky Dogg and other members of Blakk Rukus—did I get that right, Brent, Blakk Rukus?"

Brent clicked his pen with his thumb.

"We spoke privately, and after negotiating for some time, we could not reach an amicable, win–win situation for all involved. That said, the group has officially brought its relationship with Amp to a close. But I do wish them the best of luck, and I'm sure that a number of other labels will approach them quickly." He flipped his glasses back up on his head. "Are there any questions?"

The room was silent, everyone knowing that there should, and would, be none.

"You'll be getting additional follow-ups," he ended, "via memos and a series of e-mails. Meeting adjourned."

Sneakers and shoes cut across the carpet as the staff slowly exited. Before she left, Miko squeezed Euclin's shoulder. Euclin sank back in her chair. *They cut me out, completely. Those bastards cut me out from everything.* All she had left was the Bush Mobb. A shadow moved across her face. Mr. Stein stood over her.

"It could only be done privately," he said.

"David." Euclin started to rise. "You know that wasn't fair."

"It's my company, Linny." Mr. Stein smiled sharply. "It's not about fair."

Eyes closed, sinking down to her knees, Euclin pressed her hands and face against the office window. The visible heat of her breath flowered against the glass, then shrank back into itself, like a touched anemone. At last, she was alone.

She turned, stared at the phone on her desk. Rico. Yes. She wanted to call Rico.

Two years already? Has it been?

He would greet her: "Hey there. Why the long face? Come here, you. Give me a hug." And he would call her princess. His girl. And he would go to the back room and return with a foil packet, saying, "You are gonna looooove what I have for you today, princess. Here. I want you to taste." He would hold out his finger, whitened, tempting as a donut. On the inside of her thigh, a nerve would jump with anticipation. He would call her his family, and give her the rest at no charge. And she would close her eyes and grin, and say, "Rico, it's heaven…"

When she almost got expelled from Madeira the first time she smoked pot, her mother had said, *I give my best to raise you. Euclin, I give my all.*

But I'm trying. Can't you see I'm trying?

Trying? Not good enough. Is shame, Euclin—is shame you gone and shame me.

Suddenly Euclin felt weak, vulnerable, youthful. She did not like this low feeling. Those days were past, long over. She faced the window, stood tall, shoulders stiff. Looked out at the pale sky. Cleared her mind of Rico.

Twelve floors below, people were walking on the pavement, their bright spring jackets like flowers. Euclin wondered where they were going. Most, she suspected, were headed off to places where bosses, lovers, family, friends, awaited them, but where they had no desire to be. Why coddle desire? Why disturb the equilibrium? Showing up demands so little energy. Move forward, forward, forward, never stopping to look. Euclin understood them perfectly.

The phone rang. Three times.

Euclin crossed the room, picked up the receiver.

"Oh, hi, Mum. Yes, Mum...I'm so sorry. I was going to—yes, yes, I was going to give you a call....Exactly what is that supposed to mean?...Look, Mum, I can't talk at the moment, really. There's someone in my—there's someone in my office, Mum. But I promise, when I get home later...Yes, yes, I promise that I'll call."

Hung up the phone. Embryonic in her swivel chair, head tilted back, Euclin stared down the empty length of her office. Her thoughts shifted—back to the meeting, her mother's voice evaporating. Why had she not stood up to David? Why had she not tracked Brent down afterward, and confronted him? She couldn't bring herself to call Lucky Dogg—still. She felt as though she had failed him. Pushed before the face of tumult, she despised her own paralysis. But what else could she do? This was not an ordinary situation. A lover, his father. These were not strangers. She wasn't just an employee. Maybe paralysis was acceptable—respectable, almost.

After all, *David was David. But Brent...There* was the question. *Linny, it's not about fair.* How could she have backed down so quietly? How could she have let them get off, scot-free?

She imagined David, likely en route to his yacht by now, or holed up around the corner at at Trader Vic's, downing a Mai Tai. David was not the problem. It was Brent that she would have to deal with every day. He had switched his alliances with such unsettling ease. Euclin tried to imagine climbing into the same bed with him that evening. She tried to imagine them lying down together: staring at the pores on his back, feeling the heat of his body.

She didn't have to go home. Angus had a small spare room; Tyler had a foldout. She had options.

But he's the one who was wrong.

So why was she the one running?

Euclin returned to the window. Rico. Again. Her mind had settled on Rico.

People didn't understand how it was back then. It was more than an exchange of money. There were words in between, things that he said. He was like a bartender or hairdresser, turned de facto shrink—always seeming to know what she needed. *Had it already been two years?* She had sworn to leave, and leave she did. Checking out, she had exited. But she missed that crescent of her life, the way youth had endowed her with arrogant certainty. She'd known more in those days of pale lines and uptown journeys to Rico. She'd known more about herself, about Brent, about everything, and since then, she'd watched her wisdom and sureness wither—rather than bloom—with each passing year.

Now here she stood, confused, trivial, vain, and fumbling, turning around and around, retracing her steps, like a woman who had lost a favorite lipstick.

Nearly every weekend, from sophomore to senior year, Euclin would ride the Amtrak train down from New Haven. Hailing a cab at Penn Station, she would head uptown to the main Columbia campus on 116th. In his dorm room, Brent would be waiting. Covetous of their first moments alone, they would sequester themselves in the room on Friday nights, trying to intensify through taste, touch, talk, whatever it was that had first drawn them together.

The next morning, guided by the day's first tangerine light, Euclin would stir him awake with one long, plum leg draped over his torso. Branding small puppy bites into his neck, she would mark him as hers. On lazy days, they would shuffle over to John Jay dining hall for a clinical brunch of powdered eggs, cheeseburgers, and soggy French toast sticks, and on sunny days, they would venture down to La Rosita on 108th for café con leche and oily, satisfying plates of arepas and huevos rancheros. In the evening they would shower, then arrange to meet the entire gang—Tyler, Caleb, Mercer, Francis, Josh—at the College Walk sundial. Bundled in their pea coats, vintage suede jackets, English-boarding-school scarves, and Doc Martens, they spilled out onto Broadway, noisily hogging the sidewalk, forcing other pedestrians to the side. Euclin and Tyler, enamored of each other, arms linked, would sing "And I Ran" by A Flock of Seagullsor some other awful new-wave high school song, at the top of their lungs, or mumble through the words of some Husker Dü song they had never fully committed to memory.

Huddled at a lacquered table at the Broadway Cottage restaurant, they hunkered down and ordered pot stickers, followed by Chicken Lo Mein, Happy Family, and General Tsos, the Chinese waiters constantly replenishing their free carafes of bad wine—which were the only reason the students went there. Next they'd go to Augie's to get drunker—ordering a round of Coronas and Rolling Rock—and to listen to jazz. And at some point, Brent would say, "What do you say we ditch 'em?" As spring's temperate weather tiptoed into their routine, they would break off alone, and on the way home, pit-stop at St. John the Divine, sitting and talking on the stone bleachers that rose up like an amphitheater around the Peace Fountain. Here in the darkness they would huddle, hidden beneath the low-hung stars and the cathedral's long shadow.

Or when they grew tired of nesting, they would venture out to the Hungarian Pastry Shop. They would share a plate of baklava and hot cups of Viennese coffee or a pot of orange spice tea. The café was a place to fall in love in. The cake display near the entrance bore pink, white, and electric-green confections adorned with nuts, sprinkles, cream, sugar piping, cross hatching, and elaborate swirls. It was like a childhood fantasy gone awry—ending with an unforgettable tummy ache and an adult finger wagging.

Having placed their order at the counter, they would tramp over the pastry shop's dull wooden floor, past the clusters of mismatched chairs and compact, brown Formica tables. Brent would point to a free table. Ten minutes later a waitress, holding their order on a tray, would wander down the narrow aisles, calling their names as she searched for them.

In the spring of their senior year, they were sitting at a crowded table on a cement perch outside the cafe, watching passing Dominican Catholic schoolgirls (a few with kilts hiked questionably high) and West Indian nannies with strollers pushing their American wards. Brent was cutting the baklava into tidy fours.

"I don't know," he said. "I guess I'm just frightened."

Euclin laughed disdainfully. "Honey, you're a white American male. The thing that can scare you hasn't been made or born yet."

Brent raised his iced coffee to his mouth, staring off toward the cathedral.

"I hate it when you joke like that."

She adjusted her sunglasses. "That's all it is, babe—a joke."

"When you start blubbering about something your mom did, do I blow you off?"

"Blubbering?"

"All right—poor choice of words." He tapped the knife against the table. "Look, let's not get into it."

"Fine." Euclin shrugged. "So, you're frightened. I'm listening." Brent continued tapping the knife. She touched his free hand, made him stop. "I said I'm listening."

"My father said he's selling the company."

"What? When did this happen?"

"It's been happening. He's been talking about getting out of the business for years."

"But I thought he was grooming you to take over."

"It's his company. It's bleeding money. No buts. If the old man says he's tired, he's tired. Me? Whatever. What does he care?"

Euclin reached across the table, stroking his cheek with the back of her hand. "Baby, I'm so sorry. Really. Love."

"Lin, come here." Pulling her closer, he buried his face in the dark of her shoulder and bosom. Euclin stroked his hair, not knowing what else to do. She was thinking about the first few times that Brent had stopped her in the street and tried to kiss her. Never understanding why she had tensed, he had squeezed her shoulders until she relaxed and yielded. She had never told him why. She had heard about so many terrible incidents with couples like them, but he could never have understood.

That next summer, after graduation, they moved in together: a shabby walkup on Amsterdam, just above a little botanica. It was there, listening to Chet Baker and maxing their credit cards by ordering out, that they plotted their scheme for saving Amp before his father put it up for sale.

"Definitely more hip hop," said Euclin. She bit into her falafel, and wiped tahini from the crease of her mouth.

"Mercer sent a couple guys by the office—god. What a pack of jokers, man. They totally sucked. Who you got?" Brent peered over her shoulder at the paper on which she was scribbling.

"That friend of mine—the one I used to deejay with at the college station—said he could turn me on to a couple good acts from Queens and New Haven. The one from Queens is called…." Euclin scanned the paper: "Blakk Rukus."

Brent slid a clove cigarette out from the pack. "What am I thinking? No way. My dad won't go for it. He hates rap. He hates anything new. He hates the groups we have now."

Euclin winked. "I'll talk to him."

"Yeah, you talk to him. He *loves* you. Oh, dat Euclin—she is such a nice, nice West Indian girl."

"Don't mock me. Yes, I'm charming. Hey—turn that up." Chet Baker was crooning "Forgetful."

While Brent turned up the volume, Euclin searched around the floor for the Blue Nile incense. She lit a stick with the Zippo and blew. She was wearing an Indian-print tank top, flip-flops, and cutoffs. Recently she had started weaving her hair—which she loved and Brent hated. The weave was long and straight and black like a Cherokee's. Underneath, her scalp was sweating. Slipping out of the tank top, Euclin switched on the fan and smoothed her hair against her shoulders.

"He's such a silly, silly boy," she said about Chet Baker. "I keep wondering how many times he's going to fall in love."

"And every time he does, it's like a Mack truck hit him."

They both laughed.

"Yes," said Euclin, drawing her hands to her mouth. "Yes, that's it exactly." She sat back on the futon. "OK, where were we? So more hip hop acts—definitely."

"I mean, yeah. I mean…I like NWA and PE and Tribe and all that, but, yo, what is it with you and hip hop?"

"Baby." Euclin clicked her pen with her thumb. "Trust me."

Brent's father was stubborn, entrenched in his antiquated maneuvers and deeply suspicious of popular culture. With no serious buyers in his ballpark, however, he finally OK'd the experimental chance that Brent had begged him for. From their graduation on, one multi-platinum album at a time—starting with Blakk Rukus—she and Brent rebuilt the family empire on the antics of controversial, menace-to-society rappers, unctuous New Jack swingers, and celestial R&B divas.

A slender, pretty English major turned fast-track A&R, one year out of college, Euclin had spun Blakk Rukus into a triple-platinum juggernaut. She and Brent rose in the ranks fast, joining the stellar ones to know: young, connected, moneyed, beautiful.

If this world were fair, this would be my company.

But what did she know about anything?

Again, she was thinking of Rico.

Someone had knocked on the door. Euclin stirred from her chair, but did not get up. Miko poked her head in. "I just wanted to pop in and say g'night."

Euclin rubbed her eyes. "Oh. Yeah, goodnight." Her voice came out weary and low. She twisted the watch on her wrist. *God.* Already 8:30.

Miko stepped past the threshold. "I won't be in on Monday. I'm taking a long weekend."

"Where you headed?"

"Aspen."

"Nice. Still seeing that broker?"

"Nah, history. Ancient. Just a conference, nothing sexy."

"Have fun."

"They're accountants. I'll try." Both of them laughed. Miko touched the back of the reception chair, as though she were about to sit. She started, "Lin…"

Euclin shook her head. "Miko—look. Have fun. I'll see you come Tuesday."

Miko squeezed the neck of the chair. "Tuesday. Yeah." She turned to leave, then turned around. "Lin, be well—OK?"

"Yeah."

The pleasure one derives from badness in childhood seems to make badness an end unto itself—a goal. But as an adult, Euclin had come to realize that badness in and of itself wasn't a goal. It was, in fact, a testing of boundaries.

Even at her most decadent, when she was making visits to Rico five times a week, she had always maintained a level of control. It had been a wild phase. She had been a kid then. Fresh out of college with all her wet-behind-the-ear, utopian ideals, she had pursued badness with the ardor of a spurned lover, just because she loved the challenge.

Liar.

She was scared to death of failing. She knew that she was in way over her head, and the Ricos of the world had been a part of that transition, the bridge between college and adulthood that had kept her dry and safe above rough waters. It was a nasty little habit, begun with Spence Rawlings, that she still feared might be with her forever. This was what scared her the most.

But now it was over, wasn't it? Let it be gone. Euclin began to hum.

Every need has got an ego to feed. She likes to party...

Or had she reversed the lyrics?

She likes to party...Every need has got an ego to feed.

Upon hearing the song, she had al ways imagined a pretty, slender, brown-skinned girl in a shiny, sequined halter dress, dancing with an open bottle in one hand.

She knew she had been lucky. She knew that she couldn't keep jumping from peak to peak, forever. Waiting below were valleys, hard, flat, and barren—and one day, inevitably, she would fall. But what was the answer to her question: Would she forever be addicted to the Ricos of the world, forever running to them to keep from falling?

Head tilted back, still sitting in the swivel chair in her office, Euclin had an epiphany: No, not if there was understanding. True understanding. This was what she had been missing. It was just like that day at the beach. She hadn't thought about it before, but it was. There was an ecosystem. An ecosystem of human relationships that she couldn't treat as a simple aside, couldn't crush like some overly ambitious brute with her heel.

She was trying to understand, trying to figure out the territory that had been carved and partitioned without her. She wasn't willing to walk away so easily, to leave behind the things she had built. She could defer to the father, the son, yes, but she wasn't invisible. Try as they might, she could not be rendered invisible. To David's liking, or not.

Yes. It was an ecosystem. An ecosystem of human relations, and she was trying to get some understanding.

And—she—understood...

He wasn't shutting her out. He wasn't. She could imagine his divided allegiances, the tugging that he must have felt, between warning her and betraying his blood.

She understood now.

Since her arrival at Amp, she had stagnated, had been lazy in expanding her knowledge. Being Brent's girlfriend was not understanding. It was a brutish, uninformed sense of entitlement—stupid and cretinous. Cronyism in its most nauseating form. She had been lazy, and, as a result, she had been missing the signs. Blakk Rukus had hit triple platinum on their first try. So what? There was always more to do. More, more, more. There would be other openings, other ways to grab a small fistful of power and pocket it. Things were changing fast, but she would have to find some way, a new way, to survive. It wasn't the end of the world.

She remembered Brent's face, his agitation in the meeting. He had seemed uncomfortable—the faint antagonism between him and his father, visible only to her. Maybe he had shut her out for the sake of their own relationship, knowing that, one day, the old man would permanently set sail on his yacht and never come to shore again. Yes. He needed to appear flexible in the meantime, make occasional sacrifices to his father. How could that be selfish? It was a brave thing that he had done, for *them,* to ensure their future, relinquishing breath— just for a moment—in order to breathe. All things were forgiven, all things understood. She would ask him nothing, because nothing more needed to be said.

CHAPTER ELEVEN

The spectacle of Carnival was unfolding in their living room.

Tanty Verlee, fresh from her extended Trinidad sojourn, had come by to divide with Ophelia and the children the delicacies that she had smuggled from home, and to teach them the latest dances. This was the first stop on a circuit that would end in South Orange, New Jersey, with their brother Niles and his family.

Every year, in all her Bacchanalian glory and with the energy of a monsoon, Verlee returned to the States and pranced through Ophelia's living room as though it were her own personal stage, shoving her self-filmed footage of the Panorama finals into their VCR. Year after year, the latest dance was some lewd variation on wining. The living room mirror, meant to create the illusion of larger space, spanned the breadth of one wall from ceiling to floor, and it was there she demonstrated the moves. The entire display was accompanied by bootleg compilations of that year's top calypsos, and Kevin and Clarissa demanded that Verlee play them over and over again until they had memorized the words.

Verlee's annual exploits were not unlike that of the snub-nosed fashion cognoscenti, newly returned from the European collections. The *mas*—the costumes and the masquerades—that Verlee saw in Trinidad in February or March were to be the ones that would play in carnivals for months to come, all over the world.

This year, 1993, they were dancing to the road march, "Bacchanal Time," by Super Blue.

"No. Is not so you do it, Rissa." Verlee stopped and repositioned Clarissa's hands from her waist to farther down on her hips, then returned to the starting position and gave three sharp jabs of her pelvis toward the mirror. "Right—is so."

Next, dragging Mouse and Kevin from where they were holding up the wall, Verlee positioned their hands and their legs, placing them in her lineup. Clarissa continued to practice, trying to exorcise Mouse of his American stiffness.

"But, Feelie—look! Look, look." Verlee summoned her sister. Verlee clapped her hands and let out a scandalous laugh. "Look the Yankee gyul—oh, god, nah! But, gyul, how you could wine like a Trini so? I wonder if Euclin self could even remember how to wine."

"*Euclin* can wine?" Clarissa stopped dancing.

"But of course, Euclin born in Trinidad. Euclin? When she was little—Euclin love to dance too bad. Kevin, Rissa, Mouse, when I tell you, from the time we put the radio on, you should see how Euclin, with she little self, used to jook up she waist and wine."

"Yes, is you who used to encourage her," said Ophelia. She was consuming a plate of pelau, a one-pot dish of rice, pigeon peas, chicken, and coconut milk that she had cooked in honor of Verlee's return. "I had to break Euclin out of that nasty habit. Anywhere we go—church, department store, grocery—if Euclin hear music, Euclin used to put down a stink piece of wine and embarrass me."

Everybody laughed.

Kevin lowered the volume on the stereo. "I think I hear the door."

Ophelia poked her eyes and nose through a chink in the curtain. Linnaeus stood on the porch. Wiping the tip of his nose with his handkerchief, he moved to knock again. "When will that man," she announced, overjoyed, "ever learn to use a bell?"

She opened the door, and Linnaeus entered along with a gust of lukewarm spring air. He gave Ophelia a brief kiss in the foyer, then moved to join the others.

"But, eh-eh, look who's back," said Linnaeus, as he entered the living room. Verlee, wining all the while, inched her way across the room toward him.

Why must she always do that? Ophelia frowned. She would not be outdone.

And Linnaeus suddenly found himself the ham in a sandwich, one sister in the back, and the other in front of him.

"Look at Miss Ophelia!" shouted Mouse. "Copper. Clarissa. Hold up—look at your moms! She's wining up on Mr. McBride." Mouse squinted, then opened his eyes far wider than normal. "Your moms, yooooo! Your moms looks like one of those...like one of those half-naked women your aunt showed us in that video!"

Crazy things can occur when calypso enters the blood—enflamed by jealousy. Ophelia found that her pelvis and waist taking her all the way down to the ground, as they once had light-years before as a mini-skirted teenager.

Verlee stood still.

Kevin moved in closer. "Mom?"

Ophelia, startled, found herself frozen in a squat in front of her family, Linnaeus, and Mouse. *But, oh Lord, what do me?* she thought. No decent, upstanding Christian woman should be wining that way, like a heathen. Standing up in shame, she smoothed the wrinkles of her dress against her large, muscular thighs. "Wow, Miss Ophelia," said Mouse, "did Aunt Verlee teach you that?"

"No." Verlee winked, drawing him near. "Is Ophelia who teach me."

"Linnaeus," Ophelia said, patting her hair into place, and maintaining an air of forced cool, "you've come a long way. Why don't I go into the kitchen and fix you a nice, hot plate of pelau."

The tumbling sound was the storm door opening. They had just finished eating. The mail slat creaked, followed by the heavy landing of mail. Kevin went to retrieve it.

His slippered footsteps suckety-sucked through the hall, followed by a pause.

"Stanford!" he shouted from the foyer. "The letter. It's here!"

Linnaeus peered over Kevin's shoulder. Verlee, Clarissa, and Mouse all gathered around.

Ophelia's heart sank, a red stone. "Stanford you say—eh?"

"Aren't you going to open it?" asked Clarissa.

"Good thing I slept over," said Mouse, excited.

Verlee, grinning, slapped at his hand. "Oh, come on nah boy, and open it!"

Kevin held it over his heart, pressing it to his chest with both hands. Then he held the envelope up to the light, squinting. He hadn't gotten in early admission. This was his last chance.

He wedged a fingernail into an ungummed part of the flap and jimmied the envelope open. Clarissa fidgeted and covered her mouth, giggling. Ophelia moved in closer, drawn against her will.

Kevin slid the letter out. Silently, quickly he mouthed the words.

"Read it!" yelled Verlee. "Don't be selfish. Read it to all of us."

"I got in!" screamed Kevin. "Oh, thank you, Lord, Jesus. I—got—in!"

A passionate, beautiful bedlam struck. There was a lot of whooping after that, rocking, elongated hugs, and sloppy kisses. Kevin, forgetting that he was no longer a boy, jumped into Linnaeus's arms, and the elder man lifted him up and swung him around as though he were his own child.

Kevin threw his arms about Ophelia's neck. "Mom. Did you hear? I got in!"

Ophelia's heart was a rock hitting water, and now it had reached the muddy bottom, stirring up decaying leaves and brown dust.

Kevin sensed her reservation—she felt the instant that it happened—and the joy left his body.

"You're not happy for me, are you?" Kevin's face grew red. His clenched teeth became a hard, white block. "You're not happy for me, and you can't even be because it's not what *you* wanted."

"Kevin, no. That's not it."

"Well, what about what *I* want?" he said.

She wanted him not to be angry. She wanted him to understand. A child's grief, even if she is the cause of it, becomes a mother's pain. She wanted him to understand. But it would take words, and words would take time, but the timetable for her desire was now. Right now, right here, where they stood, at that moment, she wanted how she felt to be comprehended. She had never planned on letting him go—she had hoped he would grow out of the idea.

"Kevin," Ophelia's voice was a murmur, "it is too far."

One time, maybe two, she had rehearsed how she would deal with this undesirable situation, but clearly, she should have practiced more. She had let him apply for sport, as a measure to quell him, and his early-admission rejection had lowered her guard. Getting his hopes up that way…She should not have humored him at all.

"What the two of all-yuh only shoo-shoo-ing about over here in the corner?" asked Verlee. She made a wild, scattering motion with her hands, as though she were breaking up a convention of hens.

"Mom won't let me go."

"But Feelie—no!" Verlee grabbed her sister's dress sleeve. "How you does only like to latch on to these children like a tick so?"

"You ever know what is like to have morning sickness?" responded

86

Ophelia. She didn't want Verlee in the middle of this. "Then why you only pushing up your mouth in here?"

"This is *my* nephew, Feelie. And this boy work hard. Of course I go talk."

"What's this, Ophelia?" asked Linnaeus.

"All I said, and I have every right to, is that Stanford too far." This was *her* child. All she wanted was a moment with her son, and for them all to leave her alone.

"But so was Trinidad," said Linnaeus. "And for two years."

"Home was different."

"You let Euclin go away," said Clarissa.

"That was different. Euclin? You know how long I had to struggle with letting Euclin go to boarding school, with letting Euclin go to Yale. And look at Euclin now—White Woman. Euclin hardly have time for we."

"But didn't you go away? Didn't you take a journey a long, long time ago, too?" said Kevin.

"But that was different. That was a whole different time, a whole different country. Where I was, there was no future for me at that time. I had to make my own way."

"Well, I have to make *my* own way. Why do you refuse to get that part of it, Mom? I have to make my own way, too."

"Let me have the letter," she said.

After she had finished reading it, Ophelia folded the letter lengthwise, maintaining the sharp creases of its original lines.

"We will see, Kevin. We will see," she said. "After one time there is another, I suppose."

CHAPTER TWELVE

Euclin stood in front of the mirror. Strands of black hair cut against the gaunt slope of her cheeks. She looked like a douglah with that straight hair, not her own—like a mixture of black and East Indian with her dark skin and small features.

Brent lay on the edge of the bed. His back and neck were pressed into the duvet and two propped pillows, but his feet were still flat against the floor; one half of him was ready for anything. He leveled the remote, flipping past the higher channels.

"Stop there," Euclin said. She grasped the handle of her black paddle brush, turned around to face the TV. Josephine Baker was dancing, and Euclin flipped through the Rolodex of memory—Film Forum, Olubade, 1986. "*Princess Tam Tam*," Euclin announced, voice distant.

While buying their popcorn, before the lights had dimmed, she and her boyfriend at that time, Olubade, had actually imagined that they would be seeing a princess—some cinematic incarnation of Josephine Baker walking her pet leopard down the Champs Elysees. But the film's opening scene is a marital spat between a reputedly famous French pulp fiction writer and his wife. "Failure! Cretin!" screams the wife, as the viewer learns that the author is plagued by writer's block. His literary agent conveniently drops by their flat, just as the wife goes into the adjoining room. The agent and the writer conspire to travel abroad to seek inspiration for his new novel. "Let's go among the savages," says the agent, "the real savages. Yes. To Africa!"

Olubade, her fine black-velvet beau, regal as a Dinka, had set his tub of popcorn on his lap and stopped chewing. And Euclin knew right away that they were both waiting for the same thing: Josephine Baker—enchantress of Paris, wearer of Christian Dior, deed holder to a French chateau, mistress to a leopard in a diamond collar. Her beauty would redeem both herself and them, the only two black people in the whole audience, from that awful feeling of being *less than* that had sprung from the awful scene that had just played.

Finally Ms. Baker appeared: not a princess, but a vagabond, barefoot and garbed in a soiled and dusty caftan stealing oranges from a stall in an outdoor bazaar. Afterward she is chased by the police and an Our Gang ensemble of local children.

"That's nature," says Max, the writer, delightedly observing the scene.

"I prefer the perfumed chicks of the Rue de la Paix," says Coton, the agent.

"But nature smells much better!" exclaims Max.

"Manure is nature!" says Coton.

"Well?" retorts Max. "Lovely roses grow in manure."

Olubade heckled and hissed at this, throwing two popcorn puffs at the screen. Euclin had to grip his arm to keep him from leaving. She whispered, leaning close to his ear, "Let's stay." In her mind: *Maybe it will get better.* In reality, it never did—all that shucking and jiving, shimmying, cartwheeling, tree climbing, and couscous eating with bare hands. Later she and Olubade would argue at Café Reggio about whether or not the agent's name—Coton—was slap-in-the-face symbolism to people of the African diaspora. "Coton—cotton. I mean, come on, can't you see it?" said Olubade, his face cloudy with anger. "They're calling us all slaves." Euclin, downing her espresso, accused Olubade of seeing a Pan-African conspiracy in everything.

What was jumping on the TV—now, before her and Brent—was the primitive and charming Alwina, Baker's character, offering to take the writer, his agent, and their two female companions to some Tunisian ruins.

"You wouldn't subject us to that savage's company!" says the French blonde.

"Ugh!" says the brunette. "A Bedouin."

"Smelling musk," agrees the agent, "makes me lose my appetite!"

"What is musk?" Alwina asks softly.

"The smell of wild animals," Max replies.

"So, I'm a wild animal?" replies Alwina, offended.

"Maybe you're wild, but you're no animal," Max says.

They sit down to a picnic among the ruins, and Alwina secretly replaces the salt with desert sand. After generously seasoning their plates, each member of the party takes a bite and spits out his or her food in succession. The writer, laughing, is charmed; he has found his African muse.

This was the only part at which Olubade had laughed, all those years ago. But what Euclin remembered most of all about the film was its lack of geographic reality. Baker's Alwina, in her conflated exoticism, is at once African, Tunisian, Oriental, and later declared in Paris to be Princess Tam Tam, the (fictional) Princess of Parador and daughter of "the King of Central Indian Tribes." It was the same brand of sloppy cartography, thought Euclin, that had once made people mistake Caribs, Arawaks, and Tainos for Indians—who were still called so to this day.

To Olubade, Josephine Baker's being cast in the movie made no sense. Hadn't she, along with decades of other black expats like Baldwin, Wright, and Simone, fled from America to Europe to escape this very same death-dispensing narrow-mindedness, this *less-than* feeling, this spiritual abortionist view, this killer of black and brown souls? In the movie, this *less-than, lower-than* feeling never lets up. Even after Alwina's *Pygmalion*-esque transformation, when she has learned, like a child, to read and multiply, shots of her are immediately followed by shots of painted monkeys. Only the most open-minded among the movie's Parisians are able to open their eyes and their mouths to concede that Alwina is beautiful: but Alwina, being Josephine Baker, is nonetheless astonishing.

Black and beautiful—hah, hah, hah—that timeworn oxymoron.

Over tiramisu and espresso at Café Reggio, she and Olubade had finally made peace by agreeing that the film had not been about a black princess, but about a black girl who enters a realm in which she isn't supposed to be, and somehow ends up succeeding there. Except, in this film, it turned out to be only a dream.

The hair that Euclin is hiding beneath the wig is damaged and thin. As a little girl, she used to sport beautiful plaits that were thick and woven like holiday challah. She had convinced her mother to perm it just before she left for boarding school. It was through COP, a program aimed at expanding the worlds of *gifted minority youth,* that Euclin had earned a scholarship to Madeira. As she left the beauty salon that last day before school, excited to be headed to her own *expanded world*, there were scabs on her head that would last a week. Those four hours in the chair had changed her hair forever.

In her new dorm, her mother gave her one caveat following another as she unpacked the blue American Tourister. "Be sure to wear your slippers. That is how you catch cold. Be sure to tie your hair down with the green silk scarf I gave you. Don't forget. Every night before you go to bed. And don't eat oranges for breakfast before you go to church on Sunday," the latter on account of the citrusy smell. Out of habit, Euclin nodded at every word. She rolled her knee-highs into colorful, nylon balls and arranged them in the left-hand corner of her sock drawer.

"Mummy, it's getting dark," she said. "You'll soon have to head down the road."

Christina Spencer, her first-year roommate, had already taken the bed nearest the window. Nearly all of Christina's clothes were sheathed in dry cleaner's plastic or wrapped in pink tissue paper, lifted from white cardboard boxes fastened with fancy string.

"Christina. I am walking my mother back to the car. Can you keep an eye on the stuff on my side of the room, please?"

Christina rolled her eyes. "Like who would take it?" At the time, Euclin did not know if she had meant that Downy-scented clothes from a Brooklyn Maytag were not worth stealing, or if Madeira was not that kind of school. Years later, she still would not be sure. In the catalogue, all the girls smiled the same bright smile, but in real life, of course there were differences.

Euclin watched her mother disappear down the winding drive, past the stables, past the indoor riding facilities, past the tennis courts, headed toward Georgetown, then home. Sucking on a Dinner Mint, Euclin returned to her room to unpack. Carefully, she separated her wardrobe into color-coded piles.

"What are you sucking on?" Christina asked.

Euclin turned to answer. A cigarette, like a stunted conductor's baton, wagged off Christina's bottom lip. Euclin covered her mouth, a small Vaselined O, with her hands; then smiled a tight, stunned smile and tried to relax.

"They're Dinner Mints."

"Where did you come from?" Christina exhaled, a giddy stream of smoke escaping her lips. Christina would later confess that she found Euclin's self-conscious stiffness to be freakishly fascinating.

Euclin responded, "New York."

"I drove through Harlem once," Christina said. "We were lost."

"But we don't live in Harlem. In fact, I've never been. Did I not mention that? Did I not mention that our house is in Brooklyn?"

"Did I not mention," Christina muttered to herself. "In *fact*, did I not mention…" She stuck her hand in the sock drawer and held up a red nylon ball, squeezing it in her left hand, as though she were sizing tomatoes. "Where did you get these?" She ashed on the floor. Euclin was in awe.

White people are craaaazy.

"Ground control. Hello? Come in, Major Tom. I said where did you get these?"

"Oh, at Mays department store, downtown—in Brooklyn, I mean. They have all kinds of colors, not just this kind, all kinds, blue and green and red. All sorts of colors."

"Knee-highs, what a riot. My grandma wears these, but in a nude French. It matches her skin tone exactly." Euclin felt a sudden, unexpected shame. Ever since her mother had allowed her to wear grown-up stockings, Euclin had tried to find the right flesh-toned shade. But there was none to be found. And right now, Euclin felt grateful for the umbrage, the cover, of her dark skin. Christina could not see her blushing. Christina took out her pack of Marlboros. She flopped down in a chair near her desk. She sat spread-eagled, yawning, dark hair tumbling.

"Cigarette," she offered, tilting the pack. Euclin quickly shook her head, *No.*

"What's that?" she said.

"What's what?"

"That," she said again, pointing with the tip of her cigarette.

"My grandmother made it." It was a macramé sweater.

"It's actually kinda cool. Madonna has one just like it."

"She does?" Eulin felt pride replace shame, a card deck shifting.

"Oh, Euclin," laughed Christina, "you're so gullible." Christina blew smoke through the window. "Look at the campus—our campus. How pretty." She grinned. "I hate the winter, though. Soon it's going to be bloody cold." Christina, who had spent the summer in England, had starting adding bloody to everything. "Anyway, why do you talk so funny?"

"Funny? I do not talk funny."

"Yes, you do. Where are you from?"

"Brooklyn. Didn't I say Brooklyn?"

"Testy, aren't we."

Euclin didn't know what testy meant, but she knew that it was bad, or at least impolite.

"I'm sorry."

Christina waved her off. "No biggie. But really, you have *the weirdest* accent. Where are you *really* from?"

"Trinidad," confessed Euclin.

"Oh, our old houskeeper, Clemence, was from Trinidad." Euclin felt a faint inkling of pride at this utterance, a feeling, again, of almost gratefulness. She had actually heard of it. Someone here actually knew of her small island.

Euclin ended up popular. She told stories people loved, stories about obeah, Soucouyant, and La Diablesse. "Oh, Euclin, please tell us one of your wacky stories!" their group requests often began. There was nothing wacky about the tales—after all, this was her life, her mother's life, her grandmother's life, her great-grandmother's life—but Euclin never disappointed. Classmates were eager to hear, and she was eager to please. She told them about a prosperous Indian family's fortune and the gossip of black magic that trailed it: Every time the family opened a new business, someone was killed on or near the premises. To keep them wealthy, her mother had said, the devil needed new souls.

"Oh isn't she a scream! She's just the best," Gussie Ferguson squealed, shooting Euclin an admiring glance. Augusta "Gussie" Ferguson and Christina had quickly become best friends, and shared a fascination with Euclin.

"Tell them about your Aunt Verlee," piped Cass Ahlgren, "and that time when your mother got chased by that ghost."

"A ghost, you've so got to be kidding," countered some incredulous newcomer.

"No, really, you've got to hear this," Christina would say.

"I wish I grew up like that," Gussie would say. "That must have been so fun, running all wild in the sun and the countryside."

In three of her care packages, Euclin had her mother send calypso compilations, and after study hall and on weekends, all the girls would crowd into the room that she and Christina shared for dancing lessons. Euclin, lining them up, would teach them to swivel their hips and go down to the ground, wining and whooping like Trinidadians.

Euclin's primary role, at first, was entertainment; this was how she entered their circle. But slowly this dynamic began to dissolve. The novelty of Euclin's few recycled stories wore thin, and even she grew tired of being an Uncle Remus with pigtails.

It was her intelligence and steadfastness as a friend that eventually prevailed, allowing her to ditch her raconteur's kickstand—allowing her to be just their friend, not the entertainment. Throughout that fall, Euclin was in deep with the South Dorm clique. Then, a quarter of the way into the spring semester, during the Easter holiday, Gussie Ferguson held her first sleepover—her parents lived in Chevy Chase. On the eve of that appointed day, Euclin watched her friends pile into Christina's white Saab and Gussie's red BMW and drive away without her. No one had spoken a word to her about their leaving. With her knee-highs, granny sweaters, and wacky Caribbean tales, Euclin realized she was good for a laugh—but little else outside of that.

That weekend, Euclin decided to work in the kitchen. Make some extra money, why not? Madeira, mandating equality, suggested that the parents of all girls at the school—whether poor or rich—stick to a forty-dollar-per-month allowance. Some of the wealthier girls, at least the coolest and most grounded among them, carried this egalitarian campaign one step further and took on jobs washing dishes in the kitchen for pay.

Euclin sat in a corner of the commissary kitchen on a milkmaid's stool, hand-drying industrial plates. There was only one other person on duty that weekend, a chunky redhead in combat boots, once black, whose toes had been scuffed down to grey leather. The head cook introduced them.

"Tyler, this is Euclin Ramtahal. Euclin, this is Tyler Byrd." And with that, the cook put on a parka, and stepped into the meat locker.

"Are you the one with the stories?" Tyler whispered. She seemed in awe.

"What stories?"

"The ones about the ghosts, and the women with goat's hooves."

"Oh, that." Euclin laughed.

"You're already a legend," Tyler said.

Euclin felt at home at once, sensing no pretense between them. Instantly she knew: This girl would be her friend.

"Are you a frosh also?" said Euclin. She had never even heard of the word before coming to Madeira. People say that one can't hear oneself talk—can't hear one's true voice—but this is not always the case. Euclin could hear herself quite clearly; she could hear her own voice changing. Each passing day she sounded more and more like Christina and less like herself. Her mother had pointed it out first, followed by Kanifa, her best friend from junior high, with whom she now spoke less and less. The lilt in her voice, once someone else's, was slowly becoming her own. And new words had been added to her vocabulary, things like trundle bed, cotillion, duvet, Weejuns, mudroom.

She and Tyler began to talk about their old lives in Boston and in Brooklyn, their families, the way that some Irish superstitions mimicked those in the Caribbean, and the shared raucousness of Irish and West Indian wakes—the liquor, dancing, and songs. They had both tasted milkshakes made from seaweed, milk, and spices. Euclin, like other Trinidadians, called it sea moss, and the Jamaicans had dubbed it Irish moss. She now understood the latter's etymology.

Euclin and Tyler sponged and dried dishes all afternoon, poking ruthless fun at Christina and Gussie. Feeling neither allegiance nor alliance, Euclin made no move to defend either of them. The moment they drove off in their shiny sports cars without her, they had ceased to be her friends. But beneath the cover of the bitter laughter that she and Tyler shared, Euclin's longing and hurt lay raveled deep inside her.

Euclin asked, "How did you get here?" Tyler picked up on what she meant immediately. Tyler—everything about her—clashed with the other Madeira girls and their fleeting, is-he-looking-at-me? she-said-what-about-me? teenage identities. Tyler, like a golden Buddha, had settled fatly into herself. She had a rebel's vapor, that girl. And over the years, always at odds with the narrow-minded, she would change little.

"My Laura Ashley antibodies keep me immune from this place. They inoculate freaks like me from annoying Wasps and Southern belles long enough for me to get an education. But after six months in South Dorm, I think I'm due for a booster shot," Tyler said. She bit into the fat end of an unwashed carrot. The head cook registered her disapproval by dredging up her nastiest scowl, which Euclin saw, but to which Tyler remained oblivious. "Actually, my mother forced me to come. Some crazy old spinster lady philanthropist that she used to clean house for on weekends, Miss Brooks is her name, is on the board of trustees. I met her a couple of times when I went to meet my mom. She said something about my being smart, and that she may look like a lady now, but as a girl, she had also been a wild seed. What I remember is how she kept touching my face. Her hands were so old and cold. Next thing I know, I had a private tutor prepping me for the SSATs, and Miss Brooks had talked to the head-mistress and written me a rec. Presto change-o, here I am, gone from pumpkin to coach." Tyler had reached the thin end of her stolen carrot. "Anyway, that's me. And what's *your* story?"

Euclin reached for a carrot as well, but the head cook scowled again, raising her spatula, and Euclin dropped it.

"COP—Children of Promise. It picks out minority kids and sends us to places like this one. I guess it's supposed to civilize us."

It was this last, sarcastic phrase that captivated Tyler and cement-ed their friendship. In the utterance Tyler saw Euclin as the loos-ey-goosey best friend that she would grow to love, the sardonic and highly corruptible girl who one day would peel off her knee-high stockings and walk down Georgetown's Wisconsin Avenue barefoot.

Returning to Tyler's origins, Euclin said, "Boston is a long ways away."

"New York is also."

Like drying cement, their bond took on a permanence that night, a sidewalk into which they had etched arrow-pierced hearts and their names. Their imperfection was what made their friendship perfect, the very core of their affections. Madeira, its people, its unwritten rules and etiquette, was vastly different from their worlds. Each girl had yet to fit in, but of the pair, Euclin had and would always come closest.

Oh, Euclin, you're so gullible. Oh, Euclin, you're so earnest.

That's how people saw her when she first came to Madeira. But Euclin grew out of it. Yet being brought up to be proper and pleasing came in handy: She was able to walk a fine line between everybody, even when the fine line wasn't always fun to walk.

When she returned home to Brooklyn, everyone noticed right away that she'd become more polished. The first thing to go had been those knee-highs, thanks to school mixers. Euclin refined the manner in which she dressed, gauging her attractiveness by other people's reactions—the laughs, the acid stares. Rushing to the bathroom mirror, she would stare at herself until she found out what was wrong. A change of lipstick, a different Forenza sweater; this was her armory.

When Euclin returned home one spring break, as they got ready to head to church, her mother stopped what she was doing and stared down at the her daughter's bare legs.

"Where are your stockings?"

"Those knee-highs? Oh, I don't wear those anymore." Euclin waved her hand.

Then came her mother's great-oak stare, solid and wooden.

"Euclin—straighten!"

"But what did I do?"

"You hear me? Right now—straighten. We're not leaving this house until you put on your stockings."

Euclin stood still for what felt like minutes—feet between two worlds.

"Euclin!"

Shoulders slumped, Euclin went up to her room and slipped on a pair of knee-highs she'd left behind in a drawer. Off they went to church, her mother beaming.

When she returned to school after the break, Euclin took all the stockings that she'd left at her mother's house with her, wrapped them in a bag, and threw them into a dumpster the cleaning staff used on the school grounds.

The next time Euclin returned home for break, her mother angrily insisted once more that she put on her stockings.

This time Euclin said no.

Euclin held her black paddle brush, looking in the mirror yet again, so many years later. She took off her wig. Her own hair was pulled back in a sparse knot. Without the wig, she no longer felt beautiful.

Looking in the mirror, Euclin was wishing for that twelve-year-old girl with the thick, challah-bread braids. She was wishing that the girl would come and sit beside her. Euclin wanted that girl to speak to her. She wanted that girl to tell those Caribbean stories once again. Euclin wanted that girl to refresh the memories of her origins; for like family photos on a sunlit windowsill, they were fading.

Euclin put the brush down, put on the wig.

"I'm going to see Angus," she said.

Brent stuck his hand into a bag of terra chips, crunching out a reply. "Have fun." He stuck the same hand down the front of his shorts and continued surfing channels.

Euclin was standing in front of the free-range poultry stand, waiting to meet Angus. It was Friday. The farmer's market at Union Square was teeming with seekers of the fresh, the crunchy, the pretty, the healthy, the new. She sipped from a cup of fresh-squeezed carrot-apple-ginger juice, and nibbled on a bald pumpernickel bagel.

An old man stood a short distance away. He was handsomely dressed in a tan spring jacket, a Fair Isle sweater, and olive corduroy pants. The man looked up as a woman approached him. His wife, Euclin presumed. The approaching woman's hair was a solid mercury, no black or white strands laced through it. Her rain jacket was a lovely, pale daffodil yellow. Underneath it, she wore a ribbed sweater, robin's egg-blue, and a calf-length skirt with a sensible floral pattern that matched the blue of her sweater. They both wore low, molded, practical shoes. Just as his wife reached him, the man bent to the pavement on one knee, and began to retie the laces of her shoes.

By this time she had finished her bagel. In Euclin's head: *Wow.* She lowered her juice in deference to her amazement.

Someone goosed her. Euclin spun around, protectively cupping her jeans' back pockets. "Gus! You fool." She grabbed one of his shoulders, and tiptoeing a little, kissed Angus on both cheeks. "Now what if I had slapped the person who did that?"

"Then I'm sure I would have enjoyed it," he purred. "As I do everything with you."

Euclin slid her arm under his, and they walked together that way: bound, fraternally Siamese. They stopped at a stall with fresh-cut flowers. Euclin eyed a rainbow of anemones. "You think they'll hold up at the bottom of the locker?" she said.

Angus scooped up a bunch from the barrel, surveying it. "I can't see why not," he said. Euclin paid the vendor, and a moment later, they caught a cab to the Tenth Street Baths.

Inside, they sweated silver beads. The "radiance room" was what Euclin and Angus colloquially called the Russian Room, which had dry heat.

"No, he wasn't bad the last time we hung out," Angus admitted. "For your birthday dinner, he was on his best behavior." They were talking about Brent, whom Angus fell just short of despising, despite Euclin's never-ending PR campaign.

"*My* birthday dinner? Has it been that long?"

"No, you're right. I almost forgot about Tyler's party. Have you heard from her yet?" Angus asked, referring to the bon voyage party Euclin and Brent had held for Tyler at their Tribeca loft two months prior, before she took off for her culinary internship in the South of France.

Euclin replied, "The last time we spoke, she said that Biarritz is breathtaking, she's headed to Marseille, and that when she returns, she is certain that she won't be the same person she was."

"Change is good," said Angus. "Whatever it is, let it come."

"Well, I'm just glad that she's happy. It's getting really hot in here. How about you?" said Euclin. Sweat freckled her face like rain.

"Why don't we plunge into the little pool," said Angus, "have a short swim?"

"Let's," she said.

A small oven heated the entire radiance room. Stacked along the room's tiered seating were urban nations: Afrocentrists with dreadlocks, corpulent Russians, and flirty twenty-somethings looking to score. Shielding soft skin from the Arizona-hot of the harsh concrete slabs, Bath-issued towels were spread out over the tiers. A woman, completely nude, was having a platza done by one of the masseurs, who was vigorously rubbing the length of her back with wet oak leaves. A man walked to the communal bucket, and using a plastic cup as a ladle, doused himself with arctic water.

Euclin and Angus emerged from the room, steam rushing out behind them. A man was waiting to enter; he was tall and well built, Asian, with smooth, rice-white skin. He stared at Euclin, paused. Their eyes locked. She smiled, bound her towel tighter around her narrow torso. The wig that she wore was a match tip, and igniting her scalp, but still, she wedged the hair behind one ear for effect and walked past him.

It felt good to be wanted.

Angus dove into the cooling pool headfirst. Euclin calmly stepped in behind him. The wig—though pinned—made her self-aware. She imagined it floating to the other side of the pool, a black and rootless lily pad. Keeping her head just above water, Euclin clung to the shallow end.

Kevin and Mouse were lolling all over themselves at Ophelia's table. They were in the kitchen, in the back of the house where it was most quiet. Dogs barked on the backyard neighbor's property, but otherwise their whole street was a quiet block— in between thoroughfares. The hour was early, the time of morning when the sky transfixed one's eyes, like ink dropped in water—darkness diffused by rising light.

Ophelia was setting out the things she needed: milk, chives, onions, bacon, eggs. Linnaeus would be by to pick Kevin and Mouse up any minute. They were going to work in the parlor. The body of a drowning victim had been flown into JFK from South Carolina on Friday; the family wanted to hold the service that upcoming Monday.

There was also a family of six that had died when a building collapsed, and their viewing was on Wednesday. It was going to be a busy day.

Ophelia dug through one of the lower cabinets. A set of metal mixing bowls made a clankety-clang as she pulled them out. Kevin made a lemon face. She placed one bowl on the countertop as quietly as she could.

"Sorry to disturb you," she said.

Kevin rolled to one side, closing his eyes again.

She had been their human alarm clock, dragging them out of their beds, polite urgings giving way to the tender grabbing of ankles, the yanking of covers, the final flipping on of the overhead light.

Soporific mutiny, looks that could kill, soundtrack of grumbling—but they rose.

Next door, Clarissa tossed about in bed. "Stop making so much noise!" Her voice carried through the vent. Ophelia knew the routine: Clarissa's protests, then the tough sound of a pillow being pulled over her head.

Ophelia cracked an egg, then another. She looked from Mouse to Kevin. The dogs had ceased their barking.

The original Catskills camping trip that Linnaeus had planned, and for which Mouse had slept over, had been canceled when the body was flown in, replaced by a daylong fishing trip on a rented yacht in Sheepshead Bay. The boys were still tuckered from the wind and sun. Ophelia watched them, their stone-heavy slump, bodies caving. They reminded her of the smallest of children, in that moment in the night when sleep takes over completely, and a four-year-old becomes as heavy as an anchor.

The decibel of her movements rose with the morning light. Chives into onions into milk into eggs. Silver beater—beat, beat, beat—into everything. The dogs started up again. The sun was a yolk, half hidden.

"Mmmmmm, what time is it Miss Ophelia?" Mouse's question was both an inquiry and a yawn.

"Time to get up." The batter sizzled and splatted in the frying pan.

"Is that for us?"

"If you can keep your eyes open," she said. "How about some juice with that?"

Without waiting for a reply, Ophelia opened the dishwasher and fridge, pouring out the juice in two glasses. "You need your Vitamin

C. Never mind that it's warm today. The seasons are changing—some days still feel like winter."

Ophelia pulled out two gingham placemats, two porcelain plates, two knives, two forks, two napkins. Hand-cut pieces of West Indian heavy-dough bread browned in the toaster. She placed the entire meal in the center. Mouse moved in for his share immediately.

"Kevin." Oil glistened on the spatula she was holding. "Will you be having any of this?"

He touched his stomach. "No, thank you."

Things had not been the same since the letter had come. Kevin was there but not present, and Ophelia missed him as though he had already left.

"I should have made more eggs," she said. Mouse had eaten far more than his share. She was a generous woman, but sometimes it bothered her that he lacked self-awareness—that this boy did not seem to know how to stop. She began to gather fresh ingredients. Things were scattered, out of place. *Where did I rest that extra half onion?*

Kevin opened the fridge. He piddled. He handed her milk, chives, onions, eggs, one at a time. "You'll need more bacon, too," he said, handing that over. He dropped his empty glass in the sink.

"Thank you," she said. Balancing a box of Honeycomb cereal, milk, a bowl, and a spoon, he returned to his place at the table.

So, he won't eat my food.

She wanted the whole human being. Not just the grudging respect, the caricature of the good son. Outright impudence would have been far more satisfying, far more considerate.

At least she would have had the right to be angry then.

There was a knock at the door.

"Linnaeus," Mouse said.

"You left some of your stuff in the bathroom." Kevin shook more cereal into the bowl.

Mouse reached for the ketchup. "T-shirt?"

"Yeah, and sweatpants, I think."

More knocking.

Mouse said, "I'll get that."

The sound of a bolt being pulled back; the injection of street noises. Linnaeus's dress shoes clackety-clacked down the hall. Mouse bounded up the staircase, rubber chafing wood.

"Good day, folks." Linnaeus removed his dress hat as he entered the kitchen. He rubbed his nose against Ophelia's cheek in greeting.

"Hi," said Kevin.

"Where's your shadow?" said Linnaeus.

"Upstairs." There were droplets of milk on his mouth.

Upstairs, Mouse was packing his final possessions. He foraged for his wardrobe, locating each piece and investigating the spots where more might be hidden. He backed into the spider plant, nearly breaking off a cluster of tiny white flowers, knocked the talcum powder onto the floor, which he cleaned with dampened toilet tissue, did clumsy morning things in the process of looking. He laid hands on his pants. He had forgotten them on the edge of the tub. Next, he spotted his shirt on the floor.

When Ophelia permed her hair yesterday—which she had always insisted on doing herself—she had placed her silver crucifix necklace on the radiator ledge. Mouse's shirt was pooled on the floor beneath. In the tumble-rumble of his search, the necklace had slithered from its perch, nestling into his shirt's folds like a serpent. Not seeing it, Mouse shoved his shirt in his bag.

It could have happened to anyone. But it had happened to him, carving the shape of things to come in his life, forever.

From the foot of the stairs, Kevin called up. "Come finish your breakfast, slowpoke. We have to get out of here…Yo, you'd better get down here before it gets cold."

"I'm coming." Mouse pulled the zipper closed on his knapsack.

Downstairs, Linnaeus helped himself to a piece of bacon. He looked from Ophelia to Kevin. "Is this a house or the morgue? I can't tell. I need some information."

"I am handling my business as best as I can," Ophelia said.

Reaching into the plate, Linnaeus pilfered another strip of bacon.

"Wash your hands," said Ophelia. "You just came from the street."

"My hands. My mouth. Why wash? What street?"

Close, but not perfect. Ophelia said, "Show me a man who isn't difficult."

Show me a man who isn't difficult.

Kevin. Linnaeus. Cecil. Even her brother Niles, with his demands that their parents build a bicycle shack in the yard. Her parents had ripped up her beloved anthurium lilies, her girlhood garden, flinging them to rot in the compost heap at the back of the house. *Anything for she darling Niles. No matter that we didn't have that sort of money. Look at how they just gone and dig them up so, eh. Just look at the kind of wickedness they gone and do me.*

More and more, after they had torn up her garden, Ophelia, on the pretext of doing laundry, began to journey down to the river. She looked forward to these journeys alone. The monotony of beating the clothes against the rocks and the cool wash of the Rio Verde over her hands brought her a great and indescribable calm. Ophelia remembered the pleasure of laying the family's scrubbed alabaster Sunday clothes out on the rocks to dry in the sun.

This was how she first met Cecil. August 1, 1966: Independence Day.

Ophelia had worn a wide azure scarf, tightly wrapped about her serpent's nest of thick plaits, a buffer between her scalp and the bamboo-reed laundry basket that she toted African-style; and it was the purr and clink of the spokes and the chain slowing down that had made her turn her head to see who was coming.

It was an unfamiliar young man, dark-haired and cinnamon-fleck-ed. He nodded his chin hello, coasting alongside her on his bike. "Why, on such a glorious day, are you carrying around all that load? Why are you not in Mayaro?"

She noticed that along the bridge of his otherwise aquiline nose, a small crick made him look like a douglah, a mixture of black and Indian. But his skin was lighter, his dark green eyes hinting at drops of Spanish blood, or French Creole. Later she would learn that he was all of these things, and more.

"I have too much to do," she said.

"Too much to do? Listen to this word carefully: *holiday.* It sounds a lot like hold the day, doesn't it? I think that is the intention. Hold-the-day. That's what they want us to do. And exactly why a lovely girl such as yourself wants to haul around an old basket of clothes when it's such a beautiful day for a swim is beyond me!"

The word pressed into Ophelia like a finger against a pulse, even though it had been said only once and gone so quickly. Lovely. He said, lovely.

"Look at that cloud." He pointed.

"Where?"

"There. It looks like an aeroplane—don't you find? See—there is the tail, the nose. There—see?—right over there are the wings."

"I see. Yes, yes…I see. Have you ever been in an aeroplane? I've never been, unfortunately."

"No. But one day I will. One day soon, I'll be leaving for America."

"For good?"

"For good."

"Do you already have a ticket?"

"Well, no, not just yet." He spun the bike pedal around and around with the toe of his sneaker.

"Where in America? Is such a big country."

"New York." He brightened. "Of course New York—that's my final destination. It's where all the West Indians go. I have ideas—clever ideas—that will make me a fortune in a place as big as New York. I intend to die a rich man there." He looked up into the sky as though it were something edible, something he could reach and break off a piece of.

But his eagerness saddened Ophelia, for his talk of New York made her feel as though he had already left. But an unexpected laugh followed this thought, and Ophelia, acknowledging her own silliness, smiled tightly to stifle it. She did not even know this boy, this man, this…Yet here she was—silly, silly, silly—already feeling as though she were missing him. But many years later, when Cecil had left, Ophelia would recall this as her first, bitter taste of his power to sway. But Cecil was equally vulnerable to persuasion, and this became a problem, too.

But this first day, Ophelia found it hard to continue looking up under the weight of the basket. It dug into her scalp, despite the azure scarf's padding, and Ophelia longed to remove it. To rest. To have a better view of the sky. But the bending down and picking up of a full basket was a tedious art that she felt loath to replicate.

"Too much to do?" he scoffed. "On a holiday, one should have absolutely nothing to do."

"Well, I do have something to do. Important things to do."

"Well, I have to go then," he said. Ophelia winced at the tone of his voice, as though she had somehow goaded him to leave. She felt silly again. He was so handsome, so fun to be around, and she, with her silly laundry basket, must have seemed like a bore.

Resting his crepe-sole sneaker on one of the pedals, as though about to shove off, he coasted again and balanced with one foot on the road. "Do you often go down to the river to wash?"

"More than most. More than I should, I suppose. I love to be by the river."

"The river." He savored the word like a dab of ice cream in the crease of his tongue. "Everyone has something they love," he said. "Me, my thing is swimming. I like to swim until my arms are heavy as lead. I like to swim as far out as I can get from the shore. Well, I imagine that there must be some kind of solace in tedious things— I've found so myself, but I prefer pleasure to drudgery."

"No one likes a bore," Ophelia said, stopping quickly.

"Do you think you're boring? Is that what it is?" With his thumb and forefinger, he rubbed the creases on either side of his mouth, laughing mischievously. "I've talked to you for no more than five minutes, and I've had the most pleasant time. How could you be boring? You're so easy to be around, so easy to talk to. And while everyone else is doing the same exact thing—like a bunch of mindless sheep—in the exact same places, here you are, headed off with your big basket." He winked. "I find you courageous, not boring. You're the most interesting girl that I've run across since I've been in this town."

Ophelia tucked her head, staring down at the ground. Too much. It was all too much. Jesus.

He surveyed the sky. "But it is a beautiful day, and the sea is waiting, and back at the house, they must be wondering where I am."

Ophelia looked up again and shaded her eyes with her hand. "But you don't find is late?" She felt a hollow rumble in her throat, but she tried her best to talk coolly. "How it is you only heading out now?"

"The car shut down for a while. We couldn't get it to start. They're repacking the food in the trunk as we speak, and I'm riding down to Mr. Choi's to pick up some extra bottles of Solo and Peardrax." He laughed. "How much farther is Mr. Choi's? Before this whole conversation began, that is was what I had slowed down to ask of you."

"Not much farther." She pointed. "Right there so. Just over that dip in the road."

"Well, I suppose I should be going now," he said.

Stay. Please stay. Maybe she should put the basket down, make more conversation. If only it were not so difficult.

He extended his hand. "Well, it was nice to meet you."

Reluctantly, Ophelia relinquished her own hand, sandy and calloused from washing. "Ophelia. Ophelia Abel. And you?"

"Cecil Ramtahal."

She watched him mount the pedals of his bike, shoving off. He turned around once to wave and thank her again for the directions. Then over the hump. And he was gone.

Monday, exactly one week later, he reappeared.

"Well, well, hello there. Still with that laundry basket on top of your head I see, eh. If I didn't know better, I would say that time has stood still on this road."

Ophelia, startled by the sound of his voice, had to grab for her basket to keep it from falling. She had recognized his voice instantly, without turning around. *No more silly things.* She adjusted her face into a sure smile and turned around. "Maybe it has."

"You with your laundry basket and me with my bicycle. That is a thought, eh. Maybe you are right. Maybe time actually has."

Hopping off and rolling his bike, he walked alongside her. "Do you live far from the river?"

"Right here on Tamarind, about one mile back down the road."

"Well, I live...What I mean is, I'm staying on Tamarind also."

"On the main road? In truth? But I never saw you before."

"I just got here about a week and a half ago, that's why. I'm staying with my Tanty Junie."

"Junie. You mean Miss Fernandes, the junior sec science teacher?"

"You are screwing up your face. Why are you screwing up your face? What is it that you are thinking about?"

"Nothing," said Ophelia, turning away.

"You are." He held onto her arm, but in a good-natured, curious way. "What is it that you are thinking?"

Ophelia stopped, sighed, grew quiet.

"Well, what?" Cecil stopped rolling his bike, and Ophelia was forced to stop, too. "Why don't you give me that basket," he said. "Give it here. Maybe less weight will help you to think better."

Ophelia bent down, feeling put on the spot, but she handed the basket over to him. "Miss Fernandes—she isn't, well, held in the highest regard by all of the people here in Rio Verde. By this, I don't mean to say every single person, but many."

"And why might that be?"

"She looks down on people, your aunt. If you are not of a certain kind—by this, I mean a certain kind of person, she is sure to look down on you. Do you understand what I mean?"

"Maybe I do, but why don't you tell me."

"Color, money, breeding, these are things that concern her deeply, or so I've been told, and if you aren't…Well, if you aren't of a certain kind, she'll have nothing to do with you; or, if she does, she'll be sure to make you feel small."

"Has she ever made you feel small? Has she ever done this to you?"

"No. I am just a child to her. I am not on her level. But stories spread. You know the kind of talk the old people does talk when they meet."

"Tanty Junie needs a man," he said. "That's what my mother always says about her. She said that in her youth, Tanty Junie picked over every man that came calling and dug out his flaws—even if he didn't have any—then one day she woke up a spinster, and angry. That's the key to Tanty Junie. Making other people feel small just makes her feel better. That way, she doesn't have to focus on her own reality."

"Really? Is that what you tink that it is?" Ophelia twisted her hair. "Really?"

"Yes, really. That is all that it is."

Ophelia suddenly felt small and terrible. "Oh, I hope that you don't think that I'm a gossip. It's just that when you mentioned the name of your aunt, that was the first thing that came into my head."

"I understand." He rubbed her back. "No need to worry."

"Cecil?"

He lifted the laundry basket from the seat of his bike and gently laid it in a patch of weeds at the side of the road.

"Cecil…"

"I must be going now," he said, then hopped on his bike. "I have to get some biscuits and ice from Mr. Choi's. I guess I'll see you around."

She watched him pedal up the hill, slowly, methodically, then disappear over the hump. Squatting beside the laundry basket, Ophelia bent down and touched the dry earth, which bordered a breadfruit tree. She covered her eyes with her hands. *You silly, silly girl. Look what you've gone and done. Why are you so silly?*

But the next week he returned. And the week after that, and the week following, but on Saturdays now, since school had started. He walked farther with her than usual. She stopped him at the mouth of the ragged path that spun down to the river. It was her private place, and she could not let him come. But by the sixth time, she asked. She asked, and Cecil, removing her basket from the seat of his bike, agreed to journey down to the river with her on the following week.

She had been catching him in snatches, like a nap, alongside the road in prior weeks, and Ophelia now looked forward to their sitting by the river, alone, free from donkey carts, cars, and passersby. She looked forward to reaching the river, where they could sit and speak in one long, unabridged spell, perhaps share a bag of tamarind balls and a bottle of Peardrax kept cool in the river.

The next week came. Ophelia waited. Cecil did not show. Another week passed. It had been a trick, and she had had her suspicions all along. *Why would he be talking to me? Surely there is some trick to this.* But three weeks later, Ophelia was on the road when behind her car tires pressed softly into the hot asphalt and he called her name.

Ophelia spun around.

"How are you?"

Cecil, driving one-handed, sat behind the convertible's wheel.

"You scared me," she said.

"I'm sorry." Lord Kitchener's "Sock It To Me Kitch" was playing on the radio. Cecil tapped his fingers happily against the wheel. "Well?"

"Well what?"

"What do you think?" He opened the driver's side door, rising out of his seat. "Sharp, eh? You like it?"

The car was a sea-blue Zephyr from England.

"Is it yours?"

"I should hope so. I spent a week in Port of Spain waiting for its arrival." He wiped a speck from the windshield with his thumb. "I'll have to wipe this down again later. Tanty Junie calls me obsessed, sick, crazy. But this is my baby." He touched the hood. "My car." He walked over and rubbed his finger, the same one that he had used on the speck, against the apple of her cheek. "Did you grieve for me?"

Ophelia, too startled to answer, blushed beneath her veil of dark skin.

"I hope that means yes. I thought of you while I was away. Many times, I did."

She was angry. That was what she was. She wanted to ask why

he had made no mention of leaving. It was the civil thing to do, the decent thing to do. If he spent a week in Port of Spain, then what about the other two? Not a week, not a fortnight, but three weeks had passed. But here he was. That was the important thing. The most important thing. That was all she wanted.

"You are grace, Ophelia," he said, "kindness itself. I'm sorry that I was gone so long. Can you please forgive me?" Saying this, he grasped her right hand and unclenched it, kissing the palm. He stood and took the basket from her head. He opened the back door and slid the basket onto the seat. He escorted her around to the passenger's side, held the door open. Ophelia, easing in, looked around her. She pressed down on the safety latch, locking it. The new car smell was rich with possibilities.

Until she noticed.

People were staring. People she knew. Waving, then walking, then turning, turning again, reminding Ophelia suddenly, cruelly, of the girl that she was. Large, plum-colored, coarse-haired, callous-handed, dry-footed, country; a girl who, if things were going at that moment the way they were meant to go in the world, should not have been sitting here in this bright new car next to Cecil.

Cecil turned the ignition. The engine roared. The car began to move.

He would notice in the stillness. Here in the car, he would see her better, she feared—really see her for what she was. He would see everything: the ash on her knees, the cracked flesh on her heels, protruding from the backs of her cheap Bata sandals, and the unseemly curves of her large backside, which now threatened to spill over the edges of the calf-skin seat like boiling milk in a pot.

Ophelia had seen cars like the Zephyr before, in the print advertisements of British magazines tucked into care packages, sent over by English cousins; and she had seen their American equivalents, Oldsmobiles and Buicks, in Yankee magazines. She had also seen cars like the Zephyr at the Crown Cinema, zooming through movie reels, transporting elegant, beautiful women, both American and European, down long stretches of road. Limber, striking, exquisite women like Grace Kelly, Bette Davis, and Sophia Loren, their hair lifting behind them like the wings of cherubim. This was why people had turned to stare: Ophelia was not one of these women, and would never be.

Feeling gargantuan, Ophelia longed to stand up again. If she could stand in one straight line, she thought, her spine as straight as a ramrod, with the heavy basket gracefully balancing over her, surely she would seem smaller, more dainty, more poised. The girl, the woman standing up—not the one sitting down—was the one that Cecil must have seen that first day. The one that he had been taken with. But the myriad stares fatigued her, and she laid her head back and closed her eyes.

She awakened to Cecil's fingers lightly drumming on her knee. She opened one eye, smiled wanly, then shot him a look of chastisement and slid his hand off. Had he noticed? Had he noticed her heels, her knees, the state of her hair, the staring? She regarded him furtively for a very long time, but his eyes were focused on the road, and he never once let on if he had.

By their own choosing, he was here, and she was here. Who were people to judge? They had chosen one another. Didn't that mean something?

"What are you thinking about?" Cecil smiled.

"Nothing. I'm just glad to be here," she said. The dark, shady leaves of the baobab trees sprang up from either side of the valley, crowding in around them.

"Good," he said. "So am I." He leaned over and kissed her once on the mouth.

Under this fleeting touch, Ophelia's body shuddered, the uncorrupted scent of new leather filling her nostrils with thoughts, her head with possibilities. She stared straight ahead. Climbing over the hump in the road, the Zephyr's body rose and fell.

Ophelia had no time for nonsense anymore. Cecil was her first and last mistake. She poured more Dove into the water. It was noon and the day was a stain in the sky. She agitated the soap with a swish of her hands; submerged the breakfast dishes and pans beneath the suds. She pulled out a sponge from the mouth of a blue ceramic fish, and then circled the backs and fronts of each plate. She set them aside, thinking of difficult men, journeys, and letting go.

Distance was a thing that frightened her, not the starting point nor the destination, but the spaces that lay in between. It was distance that hid the mutations in her children's character that she could neither prevent nor anticipate. Hydroponically bountiful, distance like water grew things: She'd sent Euclin to Madeira, and Euclin had become a stranger. She'd sent Kevin to Trinidad and he had returned as the child she had hoped that he would become, in some ways even better. But send Kevin to Stanford, and who or what would he become? This part of it she had told no one: She had a very bad feeling about the whole thing.

The absolute nerve of that Verlee. She had circled back to this again.

Hopping from carnival to carnival, man to man, dragging debt behind her like a red wagon: and at the age of thirty-nine, Verlee fancied herself Dr. Spock, an authority on child development. *As there is a living God—never. I know how to raise my children just fine.* Ophelia frowned. *Who Verlee can raise? Verlee can barely pay rent. She need to raise sheself first.*

But maybe, just maybe, Verlee was right. Maybe her love was too stifling.

She lived for her children. She worked and lived to attend their needs: tuition money stashed away in savings bonds and Education IRAs, the earliest of which had been funneled away before each had a first tooth, karate lessons, piano lessons, swimming, algebra tutoring, Polo and Nautica jackets, Tommy Hilfiger jeans, Timberland boots, Nike sneakers, Sega Genesis, Nintendo and more than one hundred games, a TV and a VCR in each of their rooms.

The purchases she made for herself were always planned in advance. Neatly arranged in her closet were four pairs of slacks (all season), two good blouses (in neutral colors), two skirts (one floral, one neutral) five good church dresses, a pair of sneakers, a pair of pumps, a pair of comfortable flats, boots for the winter, one overcoat, and a short jacket for the days the overcoat would drag through the snow. There was more space in her closet than clothing.

She began to put away the dry dishes, making room for the wet. She was doing everything backwards that day. She thought of Kevin, of how far he had come, of the new boy, of the new young man that he was. Didn't he deserve this moment? It was his, not hers. He had worked for it. Independent of her desires, didn't he deserve to shine?

It was the chew of the chainsaw that drew her attention. A redheaded man in work pants had sidled up the side of the giant Norway maple in her neighbor's backyard, and was now suspended from its trunk by a thick strip of leather that hung about his waist. She watched as he thrust and parried the chainsaw, lopping off one part of a snaking branch, then another.

She set down the towel and went outside, shading her eyes against the afternoon sun.

On the porch in the yard diagonally across from Ophelia's, a portly, oatmeal-colored woman stood. The hem of her caftan lifted and curled in the wind. Ophelia had never, in all her years on the block, seen her before. For many, many years an elderly Jewish couple lived in the house, and would stand on the porch where the woman stood now. Summers, the husband would hand her plum tomatoes over the fence, and, in return, she would hand him fistfuls of green beans and tea roses. The wife always smiled and waved. When Ophelia had last spoken to them, they said that they were still seeking a buyer, and once they sold it, they'd be headed to Orlando. *Gone. Imagine that.* She had seen them just the summer before. And she had not even had a chance to learn their names or say goodbye.

This new oatmeal-colored woman had a bristling air of ownership, and the house, like all the houses on the opposite side of the fence, loomed like some foreign country. The woman remained on the porch with a longhaired chihuahua under her arm, directing the red-haired workman and his partner. The Norway maple dwarfed them all. Its branches spanned across four yards, and in the summer Ophelia found its ample shade pleasant—she'd lie easy and unhurried on a sun chair in the yard, while all the neighbors around her were shackled to their air conditioners and the indoors, grumbling bitterly about the heat.

Off went another branch, revealing more clouds, an airplane contrail. Ophelia hoped that he knew what he was doing, and felt a familiar grief.

Spring always seemed to end just as soon as it had come: carcasses of color in the yard, rotting petals and stems, tulips, crocuses, and daffodils ready for their yearly beheading. And each year it reminded her of losing that long-gone garden in Trinidad: every square inch of open land, to the front, back, and side of the house, crowded with thin-stemmed anthurium lilies, hibiscus, and jump-up-and-kiss-me. She had wept when her parents tore up those lilies, those towering hibiscus shrubs, first in the back to add a new wing to the house, and next in the front to build an ugly concrete bike shack for Niles.

Ophelia looked up at the man in the tree and found something amiss. There was far too much sky. Then it dawned on her, how foolish of her not to realize it. They weren't just trimming branches. They were cutting down the whole tree.

Ophelia watched, mute, as another hacked limb met the ground. She thought of the old couple whose names she had not learned. They must have thought that they had left their home and yard in good care, in good hands. But that was the point of selling it—the house and the tree no longer belonged to them. The woman stood like a foreman, watching with satisfaction as another limb fell. She owned the house, she owned the tree. But to cut it down when it was in bloom seemed particularly cruel. Each ring meant one year of life. Did that not mean anything? And the cutters, did they not feel anything, either?

"We do as much as we can. The rest we leave to God," Ophelia said aloud. It did not completely connect with what she was watching, yet somehow the sentiment felt right. Another tree branch fell, and a flock of crows ascended from their former home.

She raised her hand to her neck to stroke her crucifix, disturbed.

And that was how she discovered that her silver necklace—the one with the crucifix, the one that Kevin had given her as a birthday present, the one that she had shown off to Addie on Columbus Day—was gone. She tried to remember where she had put it. Alone in the house, she would search and search, but the necklace would never be found that day.

CHAPTER THIRTEEN

Weed, semen, and hope. That was what the studio smelled like. But the only things that Euclin wanted to smell were progress and work.

The heels of Euclin's boots went slush-slush against the sound-proofed length of the hallway, then came to a stop as she put her hand on the recording studio door.

She caught Buddha by surprise. His eyes were red. "What you doing here, Miss Ram?" he sputtered. She often felt herself the butt of their humor, as though there were some smug, secret knowledge between them. She was the teacher, the mammy, the nun.

The first thing that she did was ask the girls to leave. Chickenheads. They were the ones who brought the reek of hope into the studio— to all studios, hotel rooms, tour buses, and trailers. Hope: that things would last longer than they always did, that they would one day actually lead to a ring, perhaps. That they wouldn't be tossed out, sometimes not even fully dressed, to do the walk of shame. When would these girls learn?

Along with Buddha, Slammah, and Skizzah, there were also two young men—one of whom Euclin recognized: LayQuan. He was the kid that Mouse had gotten into a fight with at the Blakk Rukus release party on Columbus Day. Sitting next to him on a chair in the studio was another young man—whom Euclin did not like the looks of. She looked at both with thinly veiled contempt. *Nothing but trouble.* She told them to leave.

When she and Buddha were alone, she said, "The question is what are *you* doing here, besides wasting your own time and money and bringing down my good name." Euclin said this to the whole Bush Mobb collective, the entire vexing, sorry lot as she cut a path through their tense silence.

For no good reason, pressing her hand against the couch outside the engineering console, she tested the springs.

"You don't get it, do you," she said. "Maybe you didn't hear me the first time, or the fifth. It's *your* money. Every dime and minute you squander here is yours. Not mine—*yours.* But the *name*—the name is mine. This is the name I was given, and I will never allow any two-bit rappers to put their dirty boot prints all over it.

"And didn't I *tell* you," Euclin said, pounding Skizzah's thigh with her fist, "to put that junk away when we're in the studio!"

For Skizzah, it was business as usual—his third blunt of the day.

"Get up! Boy, I said get up!"

Skizzah stood.

Euclin tried to confiscate the blunt, but Skizzah stood on the arm of the sofa and held it from her, high in the air. "Yo, chill out, Ms. Ram. I'm up. But what's up with *you,* the way you came busting in here like Charles Bronson? Can't you see I need to relax?"

A minor play for power ensued, a mini tussle for possession of the Philly. Euclin won, of course.

"Hey, could you get off the couch!" Phil, the engineer, came out from behind the console, where he had been listening to the day's tracks on the monitor. "Could we *try* to keep it professional here?"

Euclin clapped her hands and walked toward him. "Bravo! I didn't know—is it Oscar season already, Phil?" The rubber band finally snapped. She jabbed a finger into Phil's flabby chest. "I haven't even started with you." Then she mocked, "Let's add some bass. Put a little more middle on this sample. Why don't we play around with this track? You know that stuff costs money, Phil—their money—but you encourage them, because at the end of the day you are getting paid—and you're getting paid lovely. You know why I'm here? Several people passed through here from the label this week, but only one—only *one*—had the guts to tell me about the free-for-all that you had going on down here."

Skizzah sing-songed loudly behind her back, "Miko…" He spat out a hangnail that he'd bitten off. "Miko, she a squealer."

"Yo, shut it," said Buddha.

Euclin gave him her great-oak stare.

Immediately Skizzah straightened.

"I mean, here you all are, smoking blunts and screwing around with the tracks for hours when they're already behind schedule and there's lots of *real* work to be done. What *do* you think this is? Grown men and I have to come down and play mammy…"

Phil seemed to be enjoying the tongue-lashing. The way she that she was calling him *out of his name.* He had a look, as she talked to him, like she was giving him the kind of thing that some men might pay good money for—and buy themselves special equipment.

But behind her back they called her Eunuch. The way she acted, they said, as though she wished that she were Brent or old man Stein himself, as though coveting the very things that endowed them as men. But the best she could be still sexy—a dime—and still woman, they whispered behind her back, was *a counterfeit man without ba...* Yeah, she was tough all right. Perfectly playing the part. If only, to them, she weren't so doggone sexy, it would be easy for all the boys, in whose faces she spat, not to feel shaken.

Then it happened.

"What you tink this is?" Euclin screamed. "A pappy show, o' what? What—I must be look like Ma Mary backside to you. Is play? You tink I playing with you? You tink you could give me a six for a nine!" And Euclin railed on. When she chose to become an A&R, she didn't know that she would also become a nanny. She had not signed up for this.

This was the point at which she lost them—the point at which she *always* lost them, those lovestruck men and boys. The part where, much to their horror, Euclin transmogrified from her take-no-prisoners, bad mother (shut your mouth!) Cleopatra Jones, big-booty archetype into someone's bitter, bearded West Indian Aunt, minus the perks of rice and peas and curry chicken. This was the part where all longing for her crashed and burned.

Slammah, Buddha and Skizzah—not knowing what the heck she was talking about—simply looked at each other. Phil looked at them. The look they gave back: *Yo—don't ask us, either.* Skizzah spat out the remainder of his hangnail and shrugged.

"And me? What about me? Can't you see that *I* need to relax, too?" Euclin ranted. "Making you guys appear to have skills isn't easy, you talentless fu—" She stopped herself just before it came out.

Three days. Eight tracks. All of them awful. Every. Single. One. Sucked.

Euclin wanted to cry, but couldn't in front of them—didn't dare. Not in this business.

But she *had* heard potential on the demo. That's why she had signed them. Now everything was going wrong. What was *she* doing wrong? Why couldn't she bring it out of them, what she *knew* was there? Euclin wished that Lucky Dogg were there. Or even Angus. Brent. Some strong biceps on which to lean, to make her feel better.

The Bush Mobb was all she had left. Turning them into stars was her lone remaining act of consequence—her only counterweight to the elder Stein. She owed this final, muscular act to Lucky Dogg—and to herself.

Euclin cursed the "S" tattooed on her chest, and on that of all black women.

The world just kept on taking, and taking, and taking, never thinking or stopping to ask what it was *she* needed.

Three weeks later Euclin and Brent were sitting in the label's conference room listening to the first tracks.

People tell me shut up with that music, but it be the realest.

Jesus died so you can live. You god, can you feel this?

You gods, can you feel this?

Brent pressed his thumb down, hard, on the recorder's STOP button.

"Euclin, what year are we in?"

No answer. Euclin's shoulders slumped.

"This is not a rhetorical question, Lin. I said what year are we in?"

"Nineteen ninety-three," she said defensively. "What about it?"

"You know what this makes me think of?" Brent tapped the STOP button with his fingernail. "This makes me think of P. E., and KRS-1. The good old days. The conscious days. What—four hundred years ago? P. E. and KRS didn't even take it this far. And know what? That's played, sugar." Brent stood. "No one wants to hear that crap no more."

Brent cursed, then sat back down again.

"Bootcamp Clique, Biggie, Wutang, Dre—that's what they're snatching off the shelves. Nobody wants to be preached to. Everybody, black, white, purple—whatever—wants to be an O. G. or a ho these days—have you noticed? Everybody wants to be a thug, living the life. And if that's what they're snatching and why they're snatching it, then that's exactly what Amp's gonna throw their way. They say they want cake, well, tell them that we've got their lemon, coconut,

Red Velvet, and angel's and devil's food right here—nice and moist.

"We're taking a new route from this point on—you hear me, baby? We're no longer going to go around the Cape of Good Hope. What we're building is a Suez Canal—straight from us to the masses." Brent toyed with the tape recorder. "We need to start handling our business like the informed and enlightened people we are. Amp built this house on rock, but, truth be told, R&B and hip hop paid the mortgage. You know that, and I know that, but the old man just doesn't get it." Brent got up for the table and began to pace the room.

"Hip hop does a little banana-peel slip on SoundScan and he's ready to toss the whole thing overboard. Believe me, Lin, this grunge thing is next year's disco. But as long as the old man takes the time to dock that yacht, walk off, and come here, we give him an audience. We let him spin his wheels and pretend to hang on his every word." Bret sat back down and leaned towards her, "But you know what you do while he's spinning his wheels? Underneath the conference table—in your lap—you keep scripting your own agenda, keep that memo pad and pen jumping, baby, scripting out your very own master plan. Waiting—you hear me, Lin?—just waiting for the very *second* that the old man pulls that anchor back up again and sails away. And then you can put that pen and paper back on top of the table—where it belongs." Brent stroked her face.

I was right, she thought. He had done it for *them.*

"Talk it to me straight," said Euclin.

"Gangsta. O. G. Hydraulics and hos."

"But gangsta's primarily West Coast," said Euclin.

Brent said, "We'll make it East, with a touch of the mob. Give Lucky Dogg back his tired ream of lyrics. We're delaying the rollout, completely changing course. Tell Buddha, Skizzah, and Slammah to put pen to paper, quit the preaching, keep it real, scribble quick."

Euclin watched the flame rise in his eyes. It was the same flame they both had only three years ago, when they declared their intentions, made it plain, then made it happen.

"It's a new day at Amp, baby. And Blakk Rukus? Their monuments have been toppled, their libraries burned. Part one of the master plan that I've been scribbling under the table: The Bush Mobb are Amp's new emperors. The age of Blakk Rukus is over. This is a whole new dynasty—our dynasty." Brent laid his hand on top of hers. "Not his."

Realizing that she knew even less than she had thought, Euclin felt excited, afraid.

Just as she had thought: He had done it for them.

But what about *her* master plan, though? Would she continue to follow—or one day would she lead?

CHAPTER FOURTEEN

Mouse was on his way to Central Park. He was thinking of a dream he had the night before. In the dream, which was really a nightmare, his face was his own, but his body was that of a deer. His father was tracking him through the crosshairs of a Bushmaster. He hunted Mouse down, and shot him. But before Mouse knew for sure if he was dead, he woke up.

The phone was ringing.

"It's me—Copper. Sorry to call so early."

Mouse yawned. "Yo, what up, son?"

"How you living? What's popping?"

"What's popping…" It was the first time Mouse had ever heard the phrase; and he smiled, making a mental note of it. "Everything is everything." Briefly, Mouse considered sharing the dream, but didn't know where to begin.

"I was wondering," Kevin began, "if, the last time you were here, you saw something of my mom's that's been missing? It's a chain, that silver chain—the one with the crucifix—that I gave my moms on her last birthday. Do you know what I'm talking about?"

Mouse answered truthfully, plainly. "It's here." He didn't feel fully purged, as he had hoped, but this truth-telling had given him a sub-tle relief. Mouse remembered the day of discovery: savagely picking his knapsack up from the floor after TyQuan, acting up badly, had goaded him almost to rage. Mouse had spilled the backpack's con-tents across the bare mattress—then, along with the dingy hill of greyish-white and faded black cotton that he called his clothes, a silver necklace came slithering out.

Slowly things registered: a silver chain, a crucifix, plum skin the color of display velvet, Miss Ophelia—Miss Ophelia's.

Slowly, Mouse also recognized that moment for what it was. If he tried to return it, they'd think he was a thief. A saint Mouse was not.

He had stolen before. But Mouse instantly felt like a thief although he'd done nothing. Sometimes simply being interrogated like this made Mouse feel guilty.

A saint he was not, but then again, neither was Kevin.

"When did you plan on giving it back?" Kevin said.

"I didn't take it," Mouse said. "But it's here." Mouse clung to the talismans of simplicity and forthrightness, hoping that the truth would set him free.

Kevin sighed, then his voice bent at a new angle. He re-approached the conversation. "I'd like to meet up," he said. "Get the chain. How much more sleep do you think that you'll need?"

Mouse was thinking of the year when his grandmother fell ill and they used to visit her at Harlem Hospital. His friend's sudden neutrality reminded him of the business-as-usual tone he'd often heard when the orderlies greeted deranged patients.

"I told you that I didn't take it," Mouse said. "It fell into my bag, then it fell out again once I got home."

"Let's link up at one o'clock," said Kevin. The words had come out slowly. "Meet me at the entrance to my job."

Mouse took the local train to Columbus Circle, then walked east. Horse-drawn carriages and the occasional flower vendor lined the streets, and the cool spring air was thick with manure and roses. After confirming the direction of Wollman rink from a peanut vendor, Mouse descended a flight of stairs into Central Park.

Kevin worked as a skate clerk at Wollman, which converted from ice to in-line skating as the weather warmed. It was the final week for winter skating. At the turnstile entryway, Kevin was already waiting. He handed a guest pass to the entry booth clerk and ushered Mouse inside.

"You're late," Kevin scolded.

"Yo, man—chill. Five minutes," said Mouse.

"I get a half hour break," said Kevin. "Learn to be on time and stop messing around."

"My day just started, and you're not my moms—so cut it," said Mouse.

"It's always the same with you, isn't it."

Mouse, no dummy, began to realize that the issue at hand wasn't time. "Here, Model Worker," he said, starting to hand over the necklace to Kevin before they had a chance to sit down. "Use that extra twenty-five minutes to screw around." (He had wanted to use another word.) "As for me, I'm out."

"Where you going? What'd you do that for?" said Kevin, refusing to take the necklace.

"I want to know something," said Mouse, still clasping the silver crucifix in his hand.

"What?"

"Do you believe it, Copper?"

"Believe what?"

"Do you believe what I told you?"

"What," said Kevin, "that it fell into your bag?"

Mouse looked through the long stretch of glass at the skaters traversing the oval outside.

Kevin sighed. "Let's go to the back." Inside, he opened up his combination locker while Mouse waited on the bench. Kevin slammed the locker with his elbow, peeled away the red and gold label from a Tunnock's candy bar, and took a bite. Mouse watched him chew: some strange chocolate brand they ate in Trinidad, he figured.

"As long as you give it back, man," said Kevin, still chewing, "I don't care how it got in there. I'm not even going to say anything. Where or how it got in there, I'm not concerned."

But Mouse knew exactly what must have been Ferris-wheeling around in Kevin's mind as he said this: the time they heisted new kicks from dumb little kids at Brooklyn's Kings Plaza Mall. Cheated the dollar-van drivers from Brooklyn to Queens. That day at the Wiz. Four months on the Barge. All their antics that led to Kevin's two years in Trinidad.

"Why am I gonna steal a cross?" Mouse said. "You think I don't got more respect than that? Your moms is more like a mom to me than my stepmoms will ever be. You know I ain't like that, man. And if I was gonna steal—and I'm not saying that I would—you think I'd steal a cross? N$gga, come on. If I was gonna steal...Yo, come on, you know me, man. You know me better than anybody."

"Why you trippin' over our friendship? I said I don't care how," said Kevin. "Just give it back." So Mouse did.

"That ain't even where my head is at," said Kevin. "Everywhere you go, got some grimy, insecure fool trying to pop some junk to impress his friends or his girl. I gotta get outta this city, son. Word is bond. This place is getting hectic, man. This city is chewing my head. Negroes need to chill it with all that aggression.

"A day from now, a month from now, whatever's eating them won't even matter anyway. Every morning when I roll out of bed, to me it means a new day."

"That ain't where my head is at, either," Mouse said. Mouse reached out his hand, and Kevin broke off a piece of his Tunnock's. Mouse tasted it and nodded his approval.

"Son, did I tell you? I got in."

Kevin's eyes widened. "You got *what?* You mean the restaurant school?"

Tongue roving teeth, finding the last bits of caramel and wafer, Mouse nodded again. Kevin's jostling embrace swept him off the bench, bringing him to his feet.

He cracked a shy grin when Kevin let go. "Yeah." Mouse sat down again. "But those happy bubbles didn't last long. I mean, what was I thinking—I don't have that kind of money. Rachel just got word of her settlement, but right now she's still on disability, and my pops, he's unemployed again. Rachel said that when the time comes for school, she'll give me some money, but I'm not betting the ranch. I still have the admission letter, but, man, what am I supposed to do with that? Right now, given how I'm living—no cheddar in the bank—that letter's just a step above toilet paper. The same time you apply, the school makes you map out a financial plan." Mouse scratched behind his right ear. "I *thought* I had a plan. Now I don't know."

"Can't you get any scholarship money?" asked Kevin.

"Some," said Mouse. "But not enough to go around. Mostly, people get student loans and some kind of grant. Tap and Pell. Still, if you ain't got bank to fall back on, what you left with is a big, old donut hole to fill."

Between the generous package that Kevin had been offered, the money that his mother had saved, and the scholarships that he had won, he had a full ride at Stanford—to the point of excess, to the point of money to squirrel away in savings. Someone—or something—it seemed, was always looking out for Kevin. Staying out of juvie, Mouse thought, was just about the only piece of luck he'd ever had.

"You should talk to my sister's friend, Tyler. She used to work at a bank, and now she's training to be a chef."

"The redhead?"

"Yeah."

"Cool. See if she'd be willing to talk to me."

Kevin nodded, indicating that he'd take care of it. "More Tunnock's?" He proffered the last of his candy bar, a one-inch stump surrounded by too much foil wrapping.

Mouse waved it away, still thinking. "Nah, no thanks."

Kevin took the last bite. He held the silver chain up to the light. "I'm going to put this in some corner of the bathroom," said Kevin. "Make her think that she found it. No questions asked. And don't you worry about any of it. We been through too much together, Negro, for me to turn on you. We like two halves of a heartbeat," he said.

Mouse was on the subway, riding back to Harlem, remembering how things used to be between him and Kevin. They once threw a floor-model TV off a tenement roof.

Why?

Just for the heck of it.

They waited until the man that they'd been eyeballing, some random stranger, had walked five feet ahead of the square of sidewalk that they had chosen.

X marks the spot.

Hitting the cement, the Zenith's plywood body, with its faux mahogany grain, had splintered and scattered like a row of uprooted piano keys. The man had stopped. The man looked up. Then the man began running. The man ran down the remaining length of the block. The man turned the corner, the rubber of his sneakers hugging the curb like the tires of a fast car. Even when they could no longer see his head or his body, they could still hear that man's feet running. It seemed as though that man was so scared he would never stop.

The only thing that lasted longer was their laughter.

Mouse and Kevin continued giggling, squatting over the roof's hot tar.

"Did you see that n$gga's face, man?" Kevin made a face when Mouse used that word now, but it was a word that he used to use then, too. They peered over the edge of the roof, surveying the TV's tube, which lay wasted like a grey eye dug out from its socket.

They used to steal back then, too. They used to steal plenty.

What made them stop?

The time they boosted eight cassettes from the Wiz—fiending for that new L.L. Cool J, MC Shan, Eric B., and Rakim—and Kevin got locked up in juvie. He spent four months on the Barge, a juvie that floats. After that, Kevin went away.

When the consequences began to get between them, *that* was when they stopped.

For all the store items he'd boosted, for all the things that he'd done wrong, Mouse had never spent a single day locked down in juvie. But, clearly, it was just a matter of time before he lost his Harlem lucky charm, and that angry rabbit called payback came searching for its severed foot.

"The dinner was good." Ophelia stood up, yawned. "Clarissa, you are to wash the dishes." Kevin stayed where he was.

Clarissa gathered the glasses, plates, and flatware without a word, even though so much was heavy on her tongue. In her heart, she wished that Kevin were still a thief. Many times, in anger, she had thought about unmasking him for the pathetic little pothead that he still was. Kevin had returned from his exile in Trinidad changed: He hit the books hard, and there was no more stealing. She watched her mother dole out love like gravy, grateful for her answered prayers. Kevin, golden boy, golden calf. In her mother's eyes he gleamed, infallible—all else and everyone else amounted to naught.

And so she wished he was still a thief, sucking up all their mother's hate instead. Either way, he took all that was meant for them both, leaving her with almost nothing. Clarissa rubbed the blue sponge against the red plates. Her brother read his green textbook. Her mother flipped through the bright, white pages of the latest home catalogue.

"I want to get a new TV and VCR for the family room, but, Lord, I can't find my glasses. Kevin, calculate the shipping and tax on these tings here for me, nah."

Kevin looked up. "You putting that on credit card?"

"Maybe. Perhaps," said Ophelia.

"Would you pay it off right away?"

"Maybe. I not tinking that far ahead."

"Then I should calculate the APR," Kevin said, "and factor that in."

Clarissa shook the soap from her wrists and fingertips. "Let me do it," she said.

"No, not you. Not you at all. Kevin, move your head out from under that book and do it now for me please, nah. You know Clarissa have no head for numbers and them sort of ting. And that Verlee, that Verlee just the same way—always want to push up she mouth in tings she don't even self understand."

Always just Clarissa—Clarissa the dummy.

Clarissa whirled around in her place at the sink. "What makes you so special?" she demanded of Kevin.

"What *did* you say?"

"I said: *What—makes—you—so—freaking—special?*"

"But, Clarissa…What is this I hearing, Clarissa? I say to hush your mouth right now! Better yet, step out of this house with that type of language." Her mother's rough hands shoved, and Clarissa barreled ahead of them. "I say you better step out this house and cool it, before I teach you how it's done."

"Why are you pushing me outside?"

"Not in my house—I will not tolerate that nasty, filthy kind of talk in my house."

"But I didn't say anything. All I said was freak!" Her mother's detention-hall grip bunched her collar. "I said to take…I said, take your hands off me! You've cursed at us before. Did you think we'd forget: when Daddy left and you were mad. How you used to use those words and scream at us way worse than that."

But Ophelia kept on pushing. Clarissa found herself out on the porch. The air was mild, but under her bare feet the pink terrazzo was cold.

"When I curse you? Never. I never curse all-yuh."

Clarissa tried to elbow her way back into the house, but her mother's massive mahogany form blockaded the entryway.

"Yes, you did. You did curse us. When you used to get drunk, when Daddy first left."

The memory deepened her furrowed brow, seeming to hint at shame.

"What I here talking about is *your* behavior. Is talk I talking to you. We not talking about no past now."

"Well I am. And you did. First, you cursed Euclin. Then, one day, you cursed us, too. We *all* heard you."

"What it is you talking, Clarissa? Child, I say to hush up your mouth." She sounded as though she were choking. "Is hush I say to hush. You hear me, child? I am your mother. And is hush I say to hush."

"And what kind of mother says the kind of things you said to us?" Upon this declaration, Clarissa took a sudden step back, away from the threshold, already knowing that she had said too much. Her mother's rough hands delivered the final shove. And then the door closed.

Stooping down to yell through the mail slot, Clarissa bellowed: "You're nothing but a big hypocrite." Her granite exterior began to crack beneath the jackhammer of tears. "You are nothing but a big, old hypocrite! You've cursed us before. You have. Ask Kevin. Ask Euclin. Ask God." But shoeless and trapped, Clarissa remained where she was.

No one answered her knocks. When her mother finally did open the door, hours later, she had on her nightgown. As she watched her mother make her way up the stairs, Clarissa shivered with rage. Clarissa did not immediately go to bed. Instead, she pushed back the living room's accordion doors, and knelt before Jesus, who hung on the wall. The Jesus of the Ramtahal household had Mediterranean eyes and hair that was yellow and thin, like manger straw. Clarissa had seen other Jesuses who looked different, but not that different, from theirs. Their Jesus was a lenticular motion card that hung above the Sony floor-model TV, and He had a gaze that followed you: When you stood up, his eyes sealed shut, and a slanted crown of thorns rested on his brow. When you dropped to your knees, his eyelids flew open, and the thorns vanished.

Clarissa stayed on her knees and He kept watching.

She folded her hands in reverence, and tried to think clear, clean thoughts. That was the way she had seen her mother do it, the way it seemed as though it ought to be done. She didn't drink. She didn't smoke. Sometimes she swore—a little. What was He thinking? What did He think of a girl like her? Was she good? Was she worthy?

"What are you doing?"

Clarissa was on her feet. "Nothing."

"That didn't look like nothing to me," Kevin said. "That sure seemed like a whole lot of something. Were you praying?"

"Leave me alone," Clarissa said.

"What were you praying for?"

"None of your business."

"It's OK," he said. "Sometimes I pray, too." His voice was gentle. This made her suspicious. Their mother said she had been able to feel them, when she was pregnant, tangled like pretzels in her belly. She said that they never seemed to stop kicking, fighting for space since the womb.

"What do you have to pray about that Jesus would actually want to hear?" she said.

"That the things I hope for will come true," he said.

"Things like what?" she said.

"That I'll have enough time," he said.

"Time?" she said.

"That I'll be able do all the things that I want to do."

The small hairs on Clarissa's body stood: goose bumps. She rubbed her arms briskly, trying to flatten the skin. Twins were supposed to have a secret language between them. Clarissa had understood nothing. *Sometimes Kevin is so weird.* She brushed past her brother, intending to bound up the stairs, headed to her own room. Kevin stopped her.

"I'm sorry about what happened to you tonight," he said. "Mom isn't mad at you—she's mad at me. She's not happy that I haven't backed down about Stanford."

"Then raise your hand next time," Clarissa said, "so she can see where you are. I'm tired of her taking everything out on me."

It was warm enough for Ophelia to hang laundry outside wearing just a sheer housedress and slippers. She moved on to the next line and separated the two sets of clothes, Clarissa's on one and Kevin's on the other. The stars in the heavens were visible now that the big tree was gone.

Ophelia was thinking of an odd dream she'd had the night before. In the dream, an old neighbor, Mr. Syril, had come to her complaining about a toothache. She had sat him under the Immortelle tree in her parents' front yard, and one by one she had pulled all the teeth, both good and bad, from his mouth.

She had another one the night before that. In the dream, she was standing in front of the old shack that had once served as her grandparents' house. Upon entering, she had found Clarissa wearing a white dress and standing in a pool of urine. Ophelia knew that pulling teeth—just like dreaming of black crows—meant death. As for the dream with Clarissa, she did not know. But Ophelia was certain of one thing: neither dream meant good.

Even standing on the back porch, she felt the whole house vibrate as the front door slammed shut. Then she heard four things: the sound of two sets of feet; the opening of the refrigerator door; the banging of dishes; and the clinking of glasses. Then the dining room light flipped on.

"Look, Mom's outside, C. Hey, Ma," said Kevin. He came outside on the porch with two baloney sandwiches, and Clarissa followed with a mug of Welch's grape soda. Kevin rooted himself into one of the aluminum chairs. Even during the winter they kept the entire patio set outdoors.

Ophelia glanced at Clarissa without making it apparent that she was observing her: *My stiff-necked, mule-headed child.* Ophelia smiled. She knew a sorry wasn't coming from their previous disagreement. Nor did there need to be. This was what it meant to be a Ramtahal.

Kevin drew a long slurp from his straw. "It's really nice tonight. It's gotten so warm. Weird."

"I know, and spring just started," said Clarissa. She stole a sandwich from Kevin, who at first pretended to fend her off, then laughed. She tore off the crust, and bit the edges of naked bread.

Ophelia shook out the creases from a pair of khaki pants and clipped them to the line. "How was the dance?"

"Mad fun," said Clarissa. "Carlton hired a DJ." Ophelia laid a heavy hand across the line. "It was always Verlee who was biggest on parties, but I remember when we used to go to fête back home in Rio, how lovely it would be—new dress, new shoes, your hair pressed and shined up with castor oil. But you had to be in bed by eleven p.m.—eyes shut tight. When I tell you is strict your Mam and Pa was strict back then.

"Growing up, ballroom music was big, big ting down in Trinidad back then—oh, yes. I was being courted at that time," she said, avoiding mentioning Cecil by name, "and we used to go to balls at the Princess Building in Port of Spain." Ophelia, sorting through her clothespins, found several broken ones—and placed them to the side on the ledge. "I'll never forget those days, the way we used to dance the Castillian, the Mambo, the Samba, the Bolero, the Fox Trot, the Bounce, the Waltz, and so many more. Those big dancehall days were so grand." Ophelia reached for Kevin's arm and shoulder. Kevin stood up and they began to glide through an imaginary ballroom, giggling together like old school chums.

"Me, I was never a real big party gyul," she repeated. Kevin smiled as he released her. "But when I went to fête, I sure was a stepper back then." Clarissa smiled up at her mom. "Oh, how could I forget. I have big news." Ophelia touched her cheek. Soon, I will finally be an American."

"What do you mean you're *finally* going to be an American?"

"She means she finally applied for her citizenship, moron," said Kevin.

Clarissa struck him hard on the shoulder. "Don't call me that."

"That's not the way I meant it," Kevin replied, cradling his bruise.

Clarissa went back to the sandwich she'd stolen from Kevin—a goppy thing with mayonnaise and baloney on Home Pride bread.

"The other day," Ophelia continued, "I tell myself, it's time to start putting down roots, yes. I've been in this country too long." Returned to her laundry, she pulled more clothespins out of the bucket. "Oh, and let me tell you...Mr. and Mrs. Lamb start up with one set of bacchanal again today. Next ting, you see two squad cars pull up in front of the house. I bet my last dime is that nosy Mrs. Hutchence who call them—her own son is a thief, but she there calling police on people. And even with the cops in plain sight, even then it didn't look like those two wanted to cool it down and stop with their nonsense."

Clarissa's eyes widened. "Remember the time Mrs. Lamb threw that tire at him, and she knocked out three of his front teeth?"

"Yeah, I remember *that,*" said Kevin. "Poor man was in the drive-way just fixing his car, then up she came. Whole thing went down right in front the Mr. Softee truck. I remember the Mr. Softee guy was *pissed*. Nobody wanted to buy any more ice cream after seeing that much blood."

"Strange you mention that story," said Ophelia. "Is teeth I keep dreaming recently. I dream about it again the night before."

"That's not a good dream," said Kevin. "Mam told me that when you dream of teeth, it means death." For all his education, Kevin, an acolyte of Mam and Pa, shared his mother's and grandparents' superstitions.

Ophelia replied soberly, "Yes. That's what they say."

Kevin laughed. "I was just thinking—how does that story about Pa and his dentures go again?"

"You mean the time he wouldn't let me go to fête and I hide his false teeth?" Ophelia laughed. "All-yuh ent tired hear that story?"

"No," Kevin and Clarissa said in unison, then they began to tell the story themselves.

"Remember how he woke up and came outside in his Jockey shorts…" said Kevin.

"Just as you were talking to that boy from school you had a crush on…" Clarissa said.

"You went to fetch water down by the standpipe…" said Kevin.

"And," said Ophelia, "your grandfather walk in search of me all the way down Tamarind Road in his Jockey shorts and sandals alone."

"Cussing the whole time about his teeth," said Kevin.

"And you know your pa is a man who doesn't cuss," Ophelia said.

"That's when he picked up that cutlass," said Clarissa, "the one that the albino man who sold coconuts had set down at the side of the road."

"Yes, Mr. Halsey, the *beke negre*," said Ophelia. "And when I do so, and I see your grandfather raise up that cutlass—and he start to wave it in the air—man, I take off!"

"What did that guy you had a crush on do?" Kevin asked, as though hearing the outcome for the first time.

"Godfrey?" Ophelia sucked her teeth. "What he go do but run. I say I looking for Godfrey, that time Godfrey jump over high, high fence—and gone."

"Then *you* ran and hid in the mango estate," said Clarissa.

"The banana estate," corrected Ophelia. "And I couldn't bring myself to leave till after nightfall. Man, when I tell you is run we run. *Run!* You never see run so."

Clarissa and Kevin laughed, contented. Clarissa laid her head on Kevin's lap. Absently, he toyed with her hair, softly pulling down on one of her curls.

"Leave me alone, nah, boy," she said, swatting Kevin's hand away. But neither of them really moved. Up until that evening, ever since that day when Ophelia had pushed her out the door, Clarissa had been cool towards both her and Kevin. Now here they lay two weeks later, lackadaisical as cats, neither moving nor at war. Clarissa reached up, feeling for the mug. "Hey give me some," she said, her fingers brushing against her brother's lips. He did, and she took a little drink of what was left, then passed it back to him. He drained it.

Ophelia was happy to see Clarissa that way, her head slack in her brother's lap. It reminded her of when they were entwined in her own belly.

All three sat there in the Brooklyn moonlight, the mediocrity of their daily living made transcendent by that moment. Ophelia picked up the wicker basket and went inside. Kevin and Clarissa followed, but much later.

The next day, Ophelia got up early. She stepped out onto the back porch, to test and see if the night breeze had been strong enough to dry all the clothes, or if the morning sun was needed. The arch of her foot rolled over something hard as she walked. It was only by grabbing the rail that she had kept from falling. On the outside, the object on the ground was tubular, colored a deep golden brass, and on the inside, grey and filmed with ash. There was a dent in the back of the empty cylinder. Ophelia bent to pick up this small, dark, curious thing, but it was hot—so hot she dropped it. Using the edge of her robe, she retrieved and inspected it.

It was a shell casing lying on her back porch. Never having seen—much less handled—a gun, she did not know what it was. She decided that she would show it to Linnaeus. Once the small, dark, curious thing had cooled, Ophelia massaged the tube between her palm and fingertips, turning it over and over again. Then, turning her head, she looked up at the sky, as if this were the place it had come from.

CHAPTER FIFTEEN

Soon the sun would be rising. Brent had fallen into her arms like a baby at midnight. Euclin let him lie where he fell. She wore a long silk nightgown the color of champagne, and he, his head in her lap, lay sleeping in his street clothes.

You are my baby, yet you are not. How many times had he fallen onto some part of her—her arm, her leg, her lap—and that part of her was forced to hold him up?

The night before had been his birthday, and Tyler had helped Euclin cook a dinner. Tyler had just returned from Biarritz and Marseilles, and was still carrot-topped but newly and stunningly thin. She had suggested a meal of bouillabaisse, bread, good wine, a mixed-greens salad with tangerine and sesame dressing, finished off by crème fraîche crowning a sweet and simple fig tart. So, off she and Euclin went to the Fulton Fish Market, Gourmet Garage, and Dean and Deluca. They congratulated themselves upon finishing their errands, and returned home to cook. They sat on high stools in the kitchen, sharing a bottle of Pinot Noir, waiting for Brent to come home from work.

But hours passed.

Tyler tried to break up the time with gossip.

"Are you going to the fundraiser?" she asked, meaning an upcoming event at Madeira.

"Probably. You?"

Tyler laughed. "Not unless they send wild horses my way."

"I think they were talking about them dragging you away from someplace—not to it. But I understand. There's nothing for you to return to."

"But you know who I am curious about?" said Tyler. "Miranda Stone."

Euclin laughed, then she said sarcastically, "I wonder why?"

"She was such a total skank!"

"Beyond belief."

"But guys just loved her," said Tyler. "I wonder if she will be there."

"*I* wonder," said Euclin, "if Stoner the Boner is married yet, or still slutting around."

"Married?" Tyler laughed. "It isn't even our tenth-year reunion yet. And it's only the eager beavers who go to anything before the tenth year, anyway—former student council members, the kids of trustees. You should wait another five or ten years—but don't wait up for me."

"Still, I might just go," said Euclin. "I'm curious. Besides, things were different for me. Things were never so bad. And anyway," Euclin said as she poured herself another glass, "she of the pomegranate tresses, who is this Marcel?"

"Marcel?" Tyler laughed, remembering suddenly. "Ah, Marcel. What I needed was a man like Marcel. It's been so long and I've forgotten what it's *like*, and he reminded me that most penises—French or otherwise—aren't worth pursuing."

Euclin pursed her lips, screwed her face into an expression between an admonishment, a guffaw, and a smile. "Woman, you're like walking repellant!"

"Always been," said Tyler, flexing one sculpted calf, like bait.

"That must be good for something at least," Euclin said.

"Lovers?" Tyler said, "Honesty makes the losers wither and die. It's the strong ones, the ones worth knowing, who stay."

Euclin raised her glass. "Here, here. To honesty—and more of it."

"Make that plenty of it."

They clinked glass against glass. "You look radiant," said Euclin. She brushed a curtain of red hair over Tyler's right shoulder, away from her face. "Biarritz was really good to you. Beyond wonderful. So how does it feel?"

"What do you mean?"

"You're so thin now."

"You're more experienced at being thin than I'll ever be," Tyler replied. "Shouldn't I be asking you?"

Euclin waved her off, remembering the shrinking woman she'd become upon entering Madeira.

"Honestly?" said Tyler, "it's strange. There are certain pots in the kitchen—at the restaurant—that I used to be able to pick up by myself, but now I can't. I have to call the busboys for help. The whole thing feels weird sometimes, like I'm weak, you know? Sometimes I forget I'm not that other girl." Tyler pinched the skin on her arm, admiring the economical way in which it hugged her muscles. She did a little chant after this, her tongue taking on a grammar-school dexterity: "Marseille—Marcel. Marcel—Marseille…" But just as quickly, she stopped. "Now it's back to work, school, a big, bright, empty studio. Loneliness is going to kill me someday, I swear."

Tyler sloshed her wine around in the glass, then like a good girl washed it all down. Nine o'clock. Brent still wasn't back. They'd exhausted another bottle of Pinot Noir. It was not the first time, nor the last. Euclin had simply outgrown it. Or had she grown with it, giving these things their own space? No: There were definitely times when she became angry. That she could not deny.

Tyler finally left—she had to be at the kitchen early. Euclin continued waiting for Brent and fell asleep in the bed alone. She dozed off and woke up, and toddled into the kitchen to stare into the depths of her eight-quart All-Clad Master Chef stockpot. The bouillabaisse had developed a slime. Euclin dismantled the entire meal, pressing down hard on each blue airtight cap to seal it away, and then pushed the containers to the back of the fridge.

Now Brent stirred, more sober. He opened one eye and reached for her wig.

"Take it off. We're alone," he said. "You know how much I hate to see that thing on you."

Euclin held the edges of the wig down in protest. "Brent, please stop. Just leave it be."

"I said to take it off—now off!" Brent absently rubbed the ginger hairs on his chest, waiting for the wig's removal. Finally she did. "Yes," he said. "Look at how much prettier you are." Touching her chin, he tilted her face to the side table light. "At least you've finally ditched that nasty weave. Used to snag my fingers like a mink trap."

At least twice, Euclin had tried leaving on the wig when they made love, but Brent told her flatly that it turned him off. He let his abhorrence be known by ritualizing its expulsion, making her sit at the edge of the bed while he peeled back the wig's elastic edges. When they made love, Brent liked to hold fast to her head, stroking the cornrows, at once fuzzy and coarse, that lay underneath. He would ram away happily, sighing and cradling her skull. Underneath him she would do her part, undulating her magic hips (as he called them).

The wig's removal was a signal, a lever to open the floodgates of sex.

Not tonight, though. Not if she could help it.

She was angry again. Angry that Brent hadn't arrived when he was supposed to arrive, and at the condition in which he had arrived when he did. Euclin grabbed for the wig, motioning to stop the ritual, to avoid Brent being inside her after she had given so much and he had given so little, and taken so much for granted in the process. But Brent, doing a jig, stood tall on the mattress and held it from her, high in the air, out of reach.

"It's mine. Give it to me." Euclin said, circling her arms about his calves to topple him. "Give me what's mine."

Brent just laughed, jigged some more, snapped his fingers. Her hands tree-hugging his calves, Euclin closed her eyes tight, squinting stars: *Is everything a joke to you?*

Still happy, Brent sang:

I'm the ice man, baby, I sell the coldest stuff in town

I'm the ice man, baby, yes I sell the coldest stuff in town

Any time you get hot baby, call up your
ice man and I'll cool you down

"Now please me, mama, please," he sing-songed in his littlest, blondest, little-boy voice.

Euclin, still struggling with him, had stood up on the mattress, too. The bed, a padded trampoline, bounced beneath their weight and commotion. Finally she dropped down on the bed again and gave Brent her back. She lay on her side, drawing her knees to her chest.

Brent knelt, still on the bed, and reached for the straps of her gown. "Haven't I always been good to you?" he said. "Let poppa in."

Euclin buried her face in her hands, rolling closer to the edge of the bed.

Brent sank his knees deeper into the mattress and gently turned her over, forcing Euclin to face him. He kissed her navel through the fabric of her gown, then rested his head against her belly. He traced the peach fuzz that formed a trail down her stomach, and laid his palm flat against the flat of her tummy.

"Hasn't poppa always been good to you?" he said. "You can't tell me otherwise." Euclin refused to respond. It was like the night of the Blakk Rukus release party all over again, she thought: *Listen to him babble.* Euclin shifted her body until both his head and hand slipped off her abdomen.

"Hasn't poppa always been good to you? I want you to say it," Brent commanded; he balled the fabric of her gown in his fist. "Say it now. Just once. I need to hear you say it, mama—please."

She wanted him. She wanted him more, perhaps, than at any other time in their relationship. Euclin wanted to feel whole again, instead of like jetsam floating downstream. But what it was, truly, that she wanted beyond that—the very thought left her icy and bewildered.

"No," she said.

Brent said, "I asked nicely."

"No," she repeated.

"Say it," he insisted. "The night is moving, baby, and papa's patience is wearing thin."

"No."

"Say it."

"Yes, then!" she said.

"Not like that: "Yes, papa. When you say it, say it good: 'You have always, always been good to me, papa.' These are the kinds of things, baby, that a man needs to hear."

Euclin shook her head in defiance.

Brent grabbed her wrists. "Be nice, mama. Remember, I was born on this day. I need you to be nice today, mama. I need for you to treat me well."

"Let go of me," she said. But he wouldn't. Euclin shot upright. "Yes, papa—yes! There, I've said it." The moment she said it, he let go. Euclin had still been in the midst of struggling, and her wrists, newly sprung, were caught by surprise, both her arms flew up in the air. Nursing her wrists, Euclin hissed, "You are so pathetic. I'm not sleeping here tonight."

One leg was out the bed already, on the floor.

Brent covered her mouth. "Shhhh…Hush now." If Euclin had

stuck her tongue out, she could have tasted the soft inside of his palm. Finally he took his hand away. "I only want what's good tonight. I don't want any trouble. Does my love repulse you?" he said. "Do I disgust you?"

"You—are—a freak," she said.

"Is that what I am to you?" he asked. "Some kind of stumbling-jumbling, drunken white boy freak, to the point where you can't stand my presence?" Brent crossed his arms, gave her his back. "If that's what you think, then don't tell me."

"This is crazy. You're crazy. And I'm leaving," she said.

But she couldn't. Both legs out the bed and on the floor, Euclin hid her face in her hands and slowly began to weep. She looked up. "Why are you doing this to me, Brent? Why do you keep doing this over and over again, when you know how much it hurts me?" She rubbed beneath her nose to keep the mucus from dripping. It was only the third time he had seen her cry. "You come stumbling in here every other night, barely able to walk or open your eyes. I don't deserve this, Brent. I'm at a point in my life where I want…" Euclin paused. "Where I want things that I can rely on.

"If you don't stop this…this craziness, Brent, I will leave. Do you hear me, Brent? I will leave."

She attempted to stand. Brent grabbed a handful of fabric from the back of her nightgown to keep her from going.

"Remember that flat on Amsterdam?" he said. "Remember what we said we were going to do, and how we were going to do it? Remember how, one day, we said we were going to live? We're here," he said. "Don't you recognize that we're here?"

"This isn't living." Euclin said. "And this has always been your present. Me, I'm just trying on someone else's clothes, hoping that one day maybe they'll fit. But so many years have passed, and I'm still not sure. I'm still not sure of anything."

Brent laughed again.

Euclin sighed. *Funny. Always funny. Like some kid.*

"You'll never leave me," Brent said, bunching more fabric from her gown in his fist, reeling her closer, roping her in. "You'll never leave me, Lin, because I love you. And no matter how far you look, you'll never find a love like what I give you, mama. You will never find a love this pure." He gave a final pull of her gown, and Euclin found herself, against her will, seated on the edge of the bed beside him.

Brent, turning her around, took both of her hands again, pressing his lips against the palms. "Purity, purity, pure. Let's do it on the floor," he said. Stepping off the bed, he took her hand and tried to draw her down with him. Euclin's body went stiff.

"Down here. I'm here, waiting. Come on, mama," Brent said. He was crouched on his haunches. "Come on down to papa, please."

"No." Her thin lips curled. "You disgust me when you act like this. Brent, just stop it. Please."

She turned her head away and would not look at him, but Brent rose again, encircling her wrists, gripping them tight in his hands.

"Come to papa, down here. Be a good girl, Lin. Please. Come to papa...do."

He pulled at her arms until Euclin, yielding, met him where he was.

Brent slept beside her, and she was thinking of being in Paris—of the streets, and what it would be like to move there, and stay. She saw Paris and Europe in flashes, the cafes, the bakeries, the Metro, the Africans sweeping the streets. The pickled vagina and buttocks, and the stored bones of the *Hottentot Venus* (better known to her captors as Saartjie Baartman) warehoused in the exhibition rooms of the Musee de l'Homme, preserved so far from South Africa's Eastern Cape where they should be. The punks and punk rock of London. Late night dancing and tapas in Barcelona. So many beautiful boys in Italy. So many beautiful boys. She remembered thinking that Europe had not only sent its poorest, but its ugliest, landless younger brothers to America. She met Brent the summer after, back in New York. He reminded her of those hunky, blonde, blue-eyed towers of Northern Italy.

His mother was Armenian and German, he said (as though explaining his tawny blondeness, his looks). His father, the record mogul, was American, Jewish, religious when the spirit moved him. To be reckless with her chicken heart—this was what Euclin had always wanted. This was the thing she found in Brent. There was a time when she and Brent had no thresholds, no self-control, when they couldn't wait to profane the conventional, signaling some change in space, in place; new opportunities to laugh and make a public cavalcade of their lack of fear and discipline. Then, when the world was slipping behind them, they would search out new and concealed spaces, new places in which to devour each other.

Now here she was, asking for reliability from the very man who had liberated her from the reliable. A part of her was still that awkward immigrant girl, ever-practical. She needed markers in her life, things that could be measured and understood. Sometimes it pained her to think that daily she carried a wallet that cost more than most working-class rents. There had to be far more to life than princess heels, monograms, sycophant sales help, champagne flutes, pavé diamonds, and calfskin leather.

There were people in her life—her mother, Angus—who could only make sense of the shortcomings of her relationship with Brent through the prism and prison of race. But both her parents were black (albeit one Creole) and hadn't their union failed miserably? At some point it goes beyond pigment, she insisted. At some point it goes beyond race. The things that she and Brent were facing applied across the board, to lovers universally.

In college, Brent was the front man for a band called Lime. One night, she and Tyler filled in for their band's backup singers, who were stuck in traffic on the LIE. As a mosh pit formed in front of the stage, Euclin felt the urge to jump, so she did.

Isn't there a first time for everything?

Being passed from hand to hand, surrendering to the lawless pit, Euclin had felt an electric thrill. The feathers of her chicken heart rose up, touching the sky. Brent, extending a hand, had helped her get back to the stage. They had not yet become lovers—they'd only met a couple times before, through Tyler. But being pulled back on stage, Euclin could feel the electricity being transferred to her hand from Brent's. His palpitating touch zinged with the life and innate freedom that boys like him seemed to have, that girls like her—black, Caribbean, square—could never have, not in lives of inherited propriety. Reckless kids like Tyler and Brent had been born into their skins, into their experiences, but Euclin had to sip her freedom through a thin straw. But soon it was as though, every time he touched her, Brent was also touching himself. By taking off a piece of himself and sewing it onto her, and by making her whole, Brent had made her want to touch herself in new and strange places, doing things that were impractical, illegal, inane, and insane. Making her want to do things that would surely give her mother an aneurysm, or at the very least a mild seizure.

"Want to hear something funny?" Angus once warned. "White kids know that they can sever themselves from their parents and later return to that same spot, picking up where their parents left off. We sever ourselves from our parents and we can never return. You hear me, girl? We're gone."

But she'd seen free black boys and free black girls at Columbia, Yale, and Madeira. Black boys and girls just as reckless as Tyler and Brent—as though they didn't have a care in the world. But black skin had always looked so alien on those free boys, on those free girls. They wore their skin like a wetsuit, a thing that one could unzip and take off, even though in reality it had been *sewn* onto them, sown into them. But this impossibility didn't matter to these black boys, to these black girls; in their heart of hearts they were liberated. Beneath their black rubber skins they roamed, free.

Euclin had awakened to Brent on top of her. He called her the Black Madonna of his lust, and slid his tongue deep into the gully of her back. A moment later, tunneling deep inside of her, he said, "It feels like rushing through sky. Night sky, not blue."

Euclin stared at the ceiling, waiting for the time to pass. With each rhythmic thrust, she thought of the Rio Verde sky, the Caribbean sky, of its convex, oval quality, which made it seem endlessly panoramic, spilling out stars. Her grandparents' sky seemed infinite, while the sky of New York—so unlike New York itself—had always struck her as square and limited.

Euclin had never noticed before, how much alike they moved, she and Brent, after so many years together—like liquid, so secretive and smooth. He pressed his fingers into her as though she were clay, ardently kneading her flesh. His hand groped toward some wet nirvana. And she felt him falling, headfirst, into her abyss.

Euclin felt a white gulf rushing inside of her, and gasping and heaving, she swallowed him whole. She crumpled in exhaustion, the neutral air resisting her lungs.

Brent stroked her face, sweat glistening on the side of his neck. He laughed.

"Look at you, all laid out, mama." Viewing her sweaty exhaustion, Brent laughed again. "I know you're not mad at me now."

Kevin held up a black Hugo Boss.

"A black suit is too somber, Kevin. Get something with a little more life, a little more zest. Try a lighter color," Ophelia suggested.

Ophelia, Clarissa, and Kevin had taken the B46 Utica Avenue bus to the end of its line, Brooklyn's Kings Plaza shopping mall—KP for short. They were in the men's department at Macy's.

Kevin and Ophelia compromised on a double-breasted Calvin Klein with a coal-grey herringbone pattern. But leafing through the racks in the women's department, they couldn't find the right dress for Clarissa, and Ophelia refused to buy the white, tropical wool Esprit pants suit that Clarissa had fallen crazy in love with.

Before breaking for lunch they cruised the mall, and bought greeting cards and wrapping paper from Hallmark. Then Kevin purchased a pair of #8 Jordans, white with grey suede on the toes, sides, and ankle from Foot Locker, with money he'd saved up from his job at Wollman Rink, and odd jobs he'd done at Linnaeus parlor. He wore them out of the store.

They were the kind of sneakers people could step on, dirty easily. They were the kind of sneakers for which people were being shot—either for wearing them (the sneakers heisted off the feet of the dead or dying) or in retaliation for stepping on the foot of someone proudly sporting them. Ophelia had furrowed her brow as she watched Kevin try them on. She wasn't quite sure if those were the same sneakers she'd seen featured in stories on the evening news. But she had asked no questions.

While Ophelia stocked up on white pantyhose for work from Parklane Hosiery, Clarissa and Kevin wasted time at Spencer Gifts, playing with the toys and gags. Kevin surreptitiously ogled the girlie and soft-porn novelties.

They reconvened in front of Alexander's department store. Next stop was Sbarro's. Kevin and Clarissa ordered two pepperoni slices apiece, Ophelia the baked ziti platter, which came with a side salad and roll. Kevin was showering garlic and hot pepper flakes onto his slices when a boy bumped into him at the condiment stand.

"Yo, man what's your problem?" Kevin asked, a smattering of garlic now marring the rust color of his rugby.

"You're standing in my way," said the boy. The boy was roughly Kevin's height and age.

"What way?" Kevin spread his arms. "There's enough room here for everybody."

"No there ain't. There's only room for me," said the boy. The boy had a scar that cut from the corner of his left eye to the bottom of his left cheek. He was the kind of kid who lived, and would die, for trouble.

Kevin said, "You crazy, man."

"What'd you call me?" The boy leaned in closer. "Don't think for a minute—pretty n$gga—that I won't floor you right here."

"Don't you touch my son." It was Ophelia. She and Clarissa had been sitting at a nearby table. At her approach, the boy began walking away, smile on his face, hands in his pockets, his eyes still stuck on Kevin's. "Ho. Ho. Ho!" he said, chucking his chin, a not-so-subtle stab at The Dozens. Translation: *Your moms look like the Jolly Green Giant*. He took a final, covetous look at Kevin's suede Jordans, and then he was gone.

"What that was about, Kevin?"

"Nothing, Mom." Kevin licked the pizza grease off his fingers, took his slices to the table, sat down next to his sister, then began eating as though nothing had happened, as though this sort of exchange transpired every day. Unbeknownst to Ophelia, it practically did.

Scanning the crowd in the mall for the boy, who was long gone, Ophelia's thoughts returned to a Sunday more than a decade before. Kevin and Clarissa were toddlers then. They had traveled to the flower show at the Macy's flagship store in Herald Square directly after church. Euclin and Cecil had not been along, but Ophelia could no longer remember why not. Clarissa wore a bright yellow sunflower dress lined in crinoline, and Kevin wore a blue three-piece suit the color of broken-off sky. They were on a crosstown bus after leaving Macy's, one errand left. A teenager sat across from them the entire length of the ride. The boy wore dirty jeans with deep, faded seams ironed down the front of each leg and a cheap patchwork leather jacket the color of liver. Ophelia remembered how jealously the boy, openly staring, had looked at Kevin, as though wishing to snatch the very breath from him. Such terrible envy in the eyes of such a young man, and toward a wee toddler. What could this little boy do to this big boy? What could such a little boy do? Her children were well dressed and well kept because she worked hard, and loved and cared for them. That it seemed as if this boy's family did not do the same for him on the one hand made Ophelia pity him. On the other hand his sense of entitlement galled her—and even worse, this boy seemed willing to take what he felt he deserved, by any means necessary, from her or somebody else.

After Sbarro's, they scoured the mall for Clarissa's graduation dress. She implored them to travel to the Macy's flagship in Manhattan, but Ophelia's impatience was growing.

"Miss Clarissa," she said, hands akimbo, "I am very sorry, but Manhattan is out of the question at this juncture in time. You had a right was to look earlier, but your blame head too hardened. You children are too backwards—dawdle and wait too late for every-ting." She pronounced the last word as though it were really two.

It was true: Clarissa, unlike Kevin, had ignored her mother's advice to find a few dresses she liked beforehand. Kevin had done his reconnaissance, and that's how they ended up at Macy's. Declaring the value of her time—*and to think I turn down overtime for this!*—Ophelia almost succeeded in forcing Clarissa to settle on what Clarissa called the disco grape: a gaudy purple sateen halter-back dress loaded with lavender sequins.

Desperate, Clarissa cried out, "The Gap!" And it was there that they finally found exactly the type of thing they were looking for: a white, empire-waist dress in a modest eyelet pattern, something pleasing to mother and daughter both.

Homeward bound on the B46, the trio tore through a paper satchel crammed with Old Fashioned, peanut butter, and oatmeal raisin cookies from the Cookie House, their final group treat before leaving KP.

At the crossroads of Utica and Church, the police halted their side of traffic for a large religious procession that was migrating across the intersection. Everyone in the processional—men, women, and children—wore head-to-toe white and were either jubilantly twirling in the streets, carrying placards and banners, singing hymns, or all three. Clarissa and Kevin, who had switched their seating for a better view, pressed their faces forward, just short of touching the glass. Leviathan speakers were perched atop the moving flatbed truck that led the procession, blaring gospel accompaniment. Off the side of the truck hung a banner that read: THE LORD IS COMING… REPENT!

Ophelia leaned closer to her front-seat window, sponging up the familiar hymn:

> *Jesus walked this lonesome valley.*
> *He had to walk it by Himself;*
> *O, nobody else could walk it for Him,*
> *He had to walk it by Himself.*
>
> *We must walk this lonesome valley,*
> *We have to walk it by ourselves;*
> *O, nobody else can walk it for us,*
> *We have to walk it by ourselves.*
>
> *You must go and stand your trial,*
> *You have to stand it by yourself;*
> *O, nobody else can stand it for you,*
> *You have to stand it by yourself.*

Singing in the missionary summer camp choir in Trinidad, Ophelia had always thought of the hymn as a dirge, but these worshipers, injecting their joy into everything, had transfigured it into a work of rapture.

"I don't know why you want some dead Korean woman's hair in yours."

"They're alive, these women. When they cut off their hair, they're alive. So never you mind what I like. I like what I like," reprimanded Ophelia. "You just keep on sewing." Ophelia was seated in the kitchen. Clarissa was stitching a wet-and-wavy-textured weave into her mother's head the night before Kevin's graduation.

"Do you really think you need another woman's hair to make you look beautiful? Now really, Ma." Clarissa pulled the thread, her own graduation one week away.

The front bell beckoned. Clarissa put the needle and thread on the counter and went to open the door.

It was Verlee. "But Clarissa! When you go get tut-tuts for real instead of them two spider bite you have there for breasts?"

Sighing, Clarissa protectively crossed her arms over her chest. "Aw, Tanty V, leave me alone."

Verlee winked. "I keep telling you, gyul. The right man will help them to grow. The right man is like water." Then she yelled out in her fishmonger's greeting, "Feelie, gyul—woi!"

"Why is only yell you yelling through my house, like some kind of low-class market woman," said Ophelia, "like you have live crab to sell."

Verlee sucked her teeth. "But I never see more. What do you?" Chiding was a fundamental part of their ritual, and when Verlee reached the kitchen she and Ophelia exchanged sisterly kisses. Surveying the half-done weave, Verlee touched the natural part of Ophelia's hair. She circled the chair, taking in the terrain of her sister's scalp, and exclaimed, "But look how that hair looking natural in truth!"

"Is since morning we start this, you know," Ophelia said. "Start and stop. Start and stop. In this house, that is how it goes."

"Yeah, but I'm not the one who always has to do laundry, then go out on the porch to *catch some breeze* while I hang the laundry, then talk to the neighbors for a half hour while I'm at it, when my weave's only a quarter way done."

Ophelia made a complaining noise, even though she was not truly perturbed. "But, Verlee, you don't find this gyul is too fast? Completely out of order. You never mind that, Clarissa. Is sew I say to keep sewing."

Bee-lining for the fridge, Verlee asked, "What all-yuh have to eat?" Sticking her head into the icebox, she didn't wait for an answer. A rapid shuffling of cardboard, crunching of cling wrap, and clinking of glass quickly followed.

"I tell Clarissa that she need to find a good man to help plump up them two spider bite on she chest she there play she calling tut-tuts. You ever notice how those young gyuls does fill out—breasts, hips, bottom, and everything—when they start to take man?"

"Who say my daughter have any time to study man?" Ophelia's pride and contempt toward the subject bordered on arrogance. Reaching one hand behind her head, Ophelia patted Clarissa's elbow. "Not my child. Them young gyuls today will tell you plain that they want no part of school. All them young gyuls want is man. Like they too pudding-headed to know, first come the man, then baby follow."

"You need to bless your stars," said Verlee, "that Clarissa different."

"Why don't you wear your hair out more often?" Ophelia said, meaning Verlee's thick, creeping tresses that she had caged in a bun. It was not unusual for people, mostly women, to physically stop Verlee when they were out on the street to quiz her about her massive, healthy locks. Most mistook Verlee's black haystack of hair for a fourteen-ounce undertaking of an Italian Yaki–style weave. Vainly trying to ascertain the name and directions of the store that carried this shiny and exceptional Yaki grade, most continued to look doubtful when Verlee corrected them that it was hers.

Verlee scrunched several weighty handfuls of bun, as though weighing the idea of unleashing it. Waving off the suggestion, she sucked her teeth again. "Nah, man. Is too much trouble."

"You should have hair like mine to deal with," Ophelia said, cutting her eyes at Verlee's mane. "*This* is what you call too much trouble."

Slippered feet approached the kitchen. "Hey, Tanty V," Kevin said, "I *thought* I heard you."

While he kissed his aunt's cheek, Verlee knuckled him in the ribs. "Boy, I want to hear that speech."

Kevin shook his head vigorously. "I told you nope, Tanty V. I'm not budging."

"But boy, how you could be so selfish, and with such a clear head? I want to hear that valedictory speech." Her face broadcast her displeasure. "And why it is that you are not letting us hear it, hmmm? Speak nah, boy." With one arm, she lassoed him tight by the waist, reeling him in next to her by the fridge.

"Because I want you all to hear it fresh tomorrow, that's why— same as everyone else. I'm keeping those words cool and crisp like lettuce."

"Cool and crisp like lettuce," Clarissa mocked.

"But I never see more," responded Verlee, letting him go. "Kevin there say he reading the speech to this friend, and he reading the speech to that friend, but he can't read it to we." Verlee sucked her teeth. "Like that lettuce done wilt already."

"Us," corrected Ophelia. "But he cannot read it to us."

Brow furrowed, Verlee peered around the fridge door. "Feelie, hush up, nah. You just leave me alone with meh Trini slang. You ever notice," Verlee said, directing her observation to Clarissa and Kevin, "how one minute your mother there talking broad, broad Trini, next minute, she there playing like she Diana, Princess of Wales." Verlee, displaying Exhibit A, stuck out one mocking pinky. "Dear Duchess Clarissa, would you care for a spot of Earl Grey tea with me, so soothing to the palate, you know." Then she turned to Ophelia, "Don't forget you born and bred in Rio Verde—just like all of we!"

Ophelia seemed to redden beneath her veil of dark skin. "Yes," she snarled. "Yes, and that is why you failed all your common entrance examinations twice, before you gave up. Didn't know a neutron from a noun—not to save your born life."

"Well, Mam gave Niles the brains, and Pa gave me the beauty. What did you get?" With that, she dropped the matter and resumed digging in the fridge, whistling the calypso melody to Scrunter's "La La."

Ophelia bristled, her cheeks and chest plumping like a puffer fish. "Verlee there say she selling Shaklee; Verlee selling Amway; Verle selling Mary Kay; yet Verlee never have money. That is why she always bringing her fast, greedy tail into my house to dig through my fridge for my hard-earned food. If you cannot pay your rent *before,* then why in God's name do you travel down to Trinidad for so many months at a time, year after year, if you know that you could barely afford to pay your rent afterwards?"

Verlee emerged from the fridge with one cold stewed chicken leg in one hand, an apple and a bottle of pepper sauce in the other. "Like pepper burning the seat of your mother pants today, o' what?" Verlee, the perpetual carnival chaser, set the apples and pepper down on the table, then steupsed again—a hard sucking of her teeth. She waved Ophelia off with her right hand, which now held the salt from the pantry. "Your mother like to lug around a set of old grip and baggage, but you see me, I know your mother so well, I don't even pay she no mind half the time. Especially not today. I came to see my niece and my nephew. Is Feelie self who pack up them bags full of bitterness and is she who going to have to unpack them for sheself." The rumbling in Ophelia's throat already evident, Verlee closed the matter by rubbing her hands together, then spreading her arms.

"You see that, I done. You hear me, Feelie? Not—another—word."

Tufts of copper curls toppled from the crown of Kevin's head onto the linoleum, under Verlee's shearing hands. The growing mound radiated out from Kevin's feet and around his chair.

Kevin gazed into the large handheld mirror Verlee had given him. He brushed his palm over his scalp several times, displacing the last stray strands, and nodded his approval. Verlee took the towel from his shoulders, dusted him off. Kevin stood, beaming and poised for his next XY adventure—whatever Brooklyn boy shenanigans next came his way.

"But, boy, where you tink you going? The broom is back that way," said Verlee, pointing behind Kevin.

"But, Tanty V," he whined, "I'm supposed to be meeting my friend Raheem at the basketball court in ten minutes. Then me and Etienne are headed to KP for the movies."

"Who Etienne—that Haitian gyul you seeing?"

Kevin rubbed his chin, smiled, then lowered his head. "Yo, that cute little Haitian girl is wearing me out! Since we're going off to different schools in the fall, come summer, we're going to break up and stay friends. Now she's trying to see me as much as possible. Every day if she can."

"What school she going to?" Clarissa asked.

"Howard," Kevin said. Then turning back to his aunt: "Since we're breaking up—plus she's headed to Haiti for the summer—she wants to meet up all the time, you know, trying to get as much mileage out of me now as she can. That's why I got to break out, Tanty V, otherwise I'll barely have time with Raheem before I meet up with Etienne."

"It took you more time for that cock and bull story than to sweep. Plus, I didn't ask you all that. But I never see more," Verlee said, incredulously. "Is hair that come off the boy own head and is say he saying he don't want to stay and pick it up, yes."

Ophelia waved him forward. "Don't worry, Kev-vy, we will tend to it."

"You mean *I'll* tend to it," said Clarissa, "just as soon as I'm done slaving away at your head."

"Feelie," Verlee reprimanded, "you have that boy too blame spoil. Is the same blasted thing that Mammy used to do with Niles. Niles never wash a spoon a day in he life."

"Don't worry, Mom," said Kevin, "I'll stay and do it."

Verlee, always firm, wielded a strange power over Kevin that made Ophelia uncomfortable. He swept and gathered the hair, disposed of it, and in less than two minutes, was on his way out the door.

"Look at that, Feelie," remarked a beaming Verlee. "Absolutely spotless!" She goosed Kevin. "You not too old to get a pinch on your bamcee, you know. Well done! If you marry some woman and give she headache, is we to blame. Now gone!"

Verlee washed her hands in the sink and returned to savor her mock-tropical concoction of sliced Granny Smith apple dipped into a chunky homemade mixture of hot pepper sauce, water, and salt. The tart, almost pickled taste of a Granny Smith apple in particular made it an able substitute for salt-and-pepper-friendly West Indian fruits like unripe plums, mangoes, and pommecythere.

"When I gone down for Carnival this time that just pass, all I live on was pepper mango and pepper plums," Verlee remarked, relishing the sting on her tongue from her apple. "When I tell you, I eat so much pepper plum and mango, I only have Mildred there experimenting with all sort of sorcery, full of questions and simidimee. She there telling me to open up meh eye big, big so, trying to look in it to see if I pregnant in secret and not letting she know—is so I only craving pepper and salt.

"And *guess* who gone to church for midnight mass Ash Wednesday self this year, as soon as Carnival done."

"A big pagan like you went to church?" Ophelia teased. "When you walk in, I sure the service stop and everybody turn around to look. I sure even Christ raise up he head from the cross, and only doing so to see." Theatrically, Ophelia slumped her head, then lifted it against an imaginary crucifix, craning for a better view.

"Well is Ash Wednesday, so I have to get my ashes." Verlee winked and poked Clarissa in the ribs.

"Well then," Ophelia said, "you need to preach to that one back there." She was referring to Clarissa. "That one tell me recently she don't believe in God."

"Eh!" said a wide-eyed Verlee. "Pa*pa*—what!"

"I didn't say I don't believe. What I said...I mean..." Clarissa stayed her needle in mid-stitch. "What I mean is just that it's hard to..."

"But all you have to do is believe, child," said Verlee. "What is so hard about that?"

Clarissa sighed, dismayed by her own lack of language and scope, her small puddle of little-girl thoughts hemmed in by sentiment.

"Pay no attention to those who say that faith is what you wear and what you eat," said Verlee. "None of that matters, though I once used to tink so. Don't listen to them atall, gyul. All you have to do—all that matters—is that you believe, and that you love, and you love unconditionally."

But Clarissa's head shook in defiance, even though her hands had resumed their obedient sewing. "But it isn't that simple."

Verlee bit another bite of her apple and smiled. "Yes it is, oui."

"No it isn't! What people... What *I* need first is evidence—proof."

Verlee interrupted, "Proof of what?"

Clarissa took a moment, then said thoughtfully, "That God's in control, and that he answers prayers, like the Seventh Day Adventists say in Addie's church." Clarissa felt her small puddle of thoughts ripple, its kelp-green-colored surface shimmering, suddenly brilliant and beaded with light.

But Verlee, with her caged hair and her uncaged breasts and her simple faith, remained adamant. "Just believe. Is that simple. And you know what, Rissa, one day when you're ready to believe, you *will*—and it will take no thought, child, no effort. People so accustomed to work, they don't want to believe that believing is a light and easy ting. No work, no worries, you hear?"

"But you're not *listening*," said Clarissa. "All you're doing is repeating the same old thing."

Verlee bit another bite of her apple, still smiling. "Yes, I am. I hear *every* word."

"And what about you, Tanty V? *You* don't act like no believer," Clarissa challenged, the street, the defiance in her oozing.

"Oh, but I do." Verlee pulled down the hem of her dress, which, like hosiery, expressed each brown mound of her body. "Remember, Clarissa..." She stopped, then started again. "Man does judge by external appearances, always looking for contradictions, but God, he does simply judge your heart."

But Clarissa's head still shook in defiance, even as her hands, in obedience, continued to sew. "I don't care what you say," she began.

"Clarissa!" her mother started, moving beneath her, the needle shifting.

Verlee dismissed the ruckus with her hand, still smiling, still chewing green. "Hush, nah, Feelie! Let the gyul have she say."

"I've already seen my evidence," said Clarissa. "I see it every day. On the front-page news, or six o'clock on TV, same thing, whether it cost you a quarter, or you get it for free: nothing out there but bad news, people crying, dying, getting high, getting robbed, getting shot, lots of people, everywhere, all over, trouble.

"That's what *I* see. I don't care what nobody say. What I see every day with my eyes, *that's* my evidence." Clarissa laughed a laugh of the street. "I don't know why you acting so sure, Tanty V. When these people needed God, he *gave* them no evidence. The way I see it, in this world, things just happen, God or no God, believe, don't believe—it don't matter. That's what I see." Clarissa shook her head. "Tanty V, *people* choose. *People* do what they want. It's people who make things happen. That's what I see, Tanty V. God has lost control. That is—if God ever existed."

Verlee and Ophelia sat in the kitchen way into the night. They drank Creole coffee that Verlee had smuggled into the country; Pa had grown and dried it himself, and his seasonal workers had polished the beans by dancing on the harvest, rubbing them with their bare feet. They had drunk their coffee mixed with heavy cream and brown sugar. It was a little past two o'clock when Verlee bid Ophelia goodnight, and slipped into Clarissa's room, where the extra twin bed was newly dressed and waiting. Tomorrow was Kevin's graduation, and they would all travel there together in the morning.

Her nocturnal ritual begun at last, Ophelia went to close the window in Kevin's bedroom. She stooped to cover Kevin, but Kevin had already covered himself. Something told her to sit for a while, so she did. Ophelia drew a chair out from Kevin's desk. Resting, she watched him, recollecting Kevin's bad years. He hadn't yet been eleven when he first began dangling off the precipice of criminality, Ophelia knowing that if he fell, the place he would land was prison. America had become dangerous, and so had her own son.

"I am not one of your friends, you better get that straight, and quickly," she'd said during one of their many outbursts. She would pick up words like street glass, trying to defend her territory, herself, trying to reestablish the line between mother and son—quickly, before his little-man stature grew too big for her to cut down. "I am a woman, but you are not a man. You understand me? *You* are not a man!" Her only son had one foot over a cliff. This country to which she had lugged so much hope and ambition had turned on her. America had betrayed her, gnashing her son and eating him up with its Dixie-white teeth. She was afraid that those teeth would spit out the bones, that one day she would have to wear black. She was afraid of what her son, this boy she once knew, had become, and still was becoming.

She remembered the bravado of that punkish young boy who once stood in the middle of her kitchen, his menacing words, his very demeanor a threat, speaking to her in a voice she did not recognize, wearing clothes that she had not bought him. More vividly than any other, she remembered the day when she decided to send Kevin away to Trinidad. It was exactly one week after he had returned home from the Barge. In her housedress and slippers, she had stood in the foyer, yelling: "You get a little hair on your privates, and now you name man? I telling you, Kevin, I am the only man in this house. There is no other man in this house. *I* am the woman, and *I* am the man!"

A vein in her temple did not stop throbbing for hours afterward, and Ophelia feared it would pop. There were forces outside of her home over which she had no control, and the pull of the streets was like a magnet.

"If you don't tame him, you will lose him," Verlee once said. "That is what go happen in the end."

Ophelia took the next day off from work. She called the Poorasingh's and waited for the word to reach Mam and Pa. She didn't ask her parents if Kevin could come and stay with them; she told them that he would be there at the end of the week. She charged a one-way ticket to Trinidad from Ah Wee Travel, and picked it up that same day. By Friday, even though his scent lingered in parts of the house, her only son was gone.

Clarissa yelled, "What are you doing in there, getting a makeover? Putting on your girdle?" She rapped her knuckles against the door. "Kevin! Kevin did you hear me?"

Kevin mocked her exasperation from behind the closed door with gibberish. "Clarissa heard. I did not heard. I do be speaking proper good English."

"Always got to take so flipping long to bathe!"

Ophelia stomped her foot, arms rigid at her sides. "Clarissa!"

"What—what? All I said flipping. Flipping isn't a curse. And I'm not the one you should be yelling at."

Kevin cracked the door open and stuck out his head, steam unfurling around him. "Read my lips, meathead: It's *my* graduation." And then he retreated.

"Buttmunch!" Clarissa struck the door with her palm.

Ophelia was still secretly peeved at Clarissa's use of the "f" word—though not really the "f" word, but close enough—and they got into another verbal scuffle twenty minutes later, not only over Clarissa's refusal to put on pantyhose, but her insistence that she go to the graduation with her legs West-Indian style, the fine hairs unshaven.

"I can't get this tie," Kevin huffed. He and Clarissa, now both out of the shower, were getting dressed. Kevin's knot was too fat, and the skinny end dangled well below the wide section. Clarissa came over and tied a pretty knot for him.

"I didn't know you know how to tie a tie," said Kevin.

"Dad taught me. I still remember." Clarissa patted the knot. "There."

Ophelia stood in the doorway. With his brilliantly pomaded hair, and buttoned so neatly into his valedictory suit, Kevin looked like his father. Pumping her fist in the air, her boy moved, and she smiled a smile of victory. "My boy, my boy, my boy. But, boy, yuh looking sweet too bad, yes!" In her eyes there resided a mixture of pleasure and astonishment at the child that she had created. Her son had evolved into this intelligent, tall and handsome young man, and he was splitting with promise.

Kevin headed to the phone to call a cab. He had to leave early to review all the pomp-and-circumstance minutiae of his speech with the assistant principal of English and the coordinator of student affairs. Clarissa, Verlee, and Ophelia continued hustling to be ready on time.

"But, Clarissa, what happen to your hair?" Ophelia chided, referring to Clarissa's drooping, ungroomed curls. "You and a dog have a fight, o' what?" Squeezed into her girdle, Ophelia's dark flesh spilled out like rum-soaked fruit from a black cake baked for a Caribbean Christmas. She heaved herself next into her bullet bra and skirted her waist with a lace-hemmed half-slip.

Kevin still had his hand on the receiver when Verlee caught up with him. She took Kevin by the shoulders and spun him around. "But, eh, eh look at you, doux doux! Look at how sweet you looking, child. You have it!" she exclaimed. "Boy, you have *it!*"

"Can't you see that Verlee is just mamaguying you," said Ophelia. "She still looking to get an advance on that speech you know." Jokingly, she pointed to Verlee with her mouth, in that strange way that West Indians sometimes do. "Verlee, eh, don't pump up that one full of any more air. Is so he tink he looking too good already. See that fat head ballooning—he head go float away, you know."

The phone rang. Verlee cupped the receiver. "Is Lin."

Ophelia took the phone. "Euclin, is nearly eight o'clock. What time you intend on getting down here?"

"That's why I was calling you, Mum. I just got in from LA about an hour ago. I'm sorry, I can't make it. A whole stack of new work just came in. This place is already a zoo."

"Why don't you tell Kevin yourself," Ophelia said, not interested in hearing the remainder.

"Mum, let's not start, please," Euclin said.

"Clarissa, Kevin—please! Stop it nah, man! Can't you hear I'm on the phone? And Kevin, what you still doing here? Shouldn't you already be in a cab?" Ophelia returned to a normal speaking voice and said to Euclin, "Anyway, how what-he-name doing?"

"Mum, why must you always do this? Brent, Mum. He has a name. And Brent's fine."

"Is he the reason why you cannot come? Is that who you choose today?"

"Choose? What is there to choose? Mum, look. This has nothing whatsoever to do with Brent, so don't drag him into this. Listen, I'm taking Kevin out to celebrate for his graduation. Since I didn't even get to see you for Mother's Day, why don't we celebrate both at the same time? What do you say?"

Ophelia said nothing.

"Look, this place is a zoo. Let's map out plans tomorrow for dinner. I'll have some time free two weeks from now. Tomorrow. I'll call you. I promise."

Ophelia, replacing the receiver, turned to Kevin. "I want you to mark my words carefully, Kevin: Clarissa, your Aunt Verlee, and I will be the only ones clapping for you in that audience. White Woman just call and inform me that she cannot come. Apparently there are far more important matters in the world."

Kevin was saying, "I'm not the same person that I was yesterday, nor am I the same person that I was on the day preceding. The one consistent thing throughout my life is that I answer to the same name. But, I'm no longer a toddler. My body has stretched in length and girth, and I stand before you like so many other males in our graduating class, on the cusp between boy and man, or on the female half, between girl and woman…"

Ophelia fingered the graduation program bill, nervous but enamored with this moment: the sound of her son's rich voice filling up the giant auditorium. Kevin was the family's second valedictorian and—hope against hope—he had fought for and earned the right to stand at that podium. She was oblivious to everyone else in the audience, and to the grand Art Nouveau auditorium. She was thinking that in this room only she, Clarissa, and Verlee knew Kevin's journey from orange prison overalls to grey herringbone suit.

What she *had* noticed was a beach ball, traveling around the audience, from the hand of one graduate to the next, finally yanked away by a be-suited and scowling member of the faculty. She turned forward and pressed her full attention to Kevin.

He said:

"Change came for me by crossing physical boundaries. In order to molt off my old skin and become a new creature, a new boy, a new man, I had to leave New York—and I did not do so willingly. But you, members of the Class of 1993, and members of the audience, do not need a plane ticket, nor even physical movement of any kind in order to experience transformation.

"Regardless of the limitations of our circumstances, our economics, where we were born—and to whom—we can still be transformed through the renewing of our minds. Or, more specifically, by choosing to change, to be different men and women today than we were yesterday, and to be different men and women tomorrow.

"Regardless of the limitations of the physical world in which we live, with minds as great as ours, made even greater with the education we've been given at Tech, and will get in college and beyond, the seeming limits of the world we see daily—that's never our reality. What we see directly before us is never our only choice. For in the mind there is power, and a chance to journey, and to come out on the other side in a new territory—one in which we're stronger and better than before. It's through the crossing of mental borders—not just physical borders—that our lives become enriched, and changed forever…"

And this was how the speech went, Kevin avoiding the particulars of his rough adolescence, alchemizing what could have been the leaden weight of a shameful past into a golden cornucopia of hope and metamorphosis. Most of the people in the audience were on their feet by the end, led by Ophelia, who raised her hand in the air as if testifying and shouted, "My boy, my boy, my boy—that is *my* son!"

Kevin looked both pleased and embarrassed. "In case you haven't guessed it yet," he said leaning into the mike, "that's *my* mom."

Clarissa stood, too, videotaping the ceremony. Ophelia claimed, without shame, every bit of that moment, including her son's embarrassment and her own wet eyes. She only wished that Euclin—and even their father—were there. They had had to submit a special letter to obtain two extra tickets, and Euclin's absence after such effort remained particularly unforgivable.

After her son's speech, everything was anticlimactic: Kevin, as class president, receiving the one symbolic diploma for every member of his class (the rest would be distributed later); Kevin accepting the All Tech Award for all-around achievement, athleticism, and service, as well as a special award for being valedictorian; the graduates oath being recited, the Brooklyn Tech alma mater being sung: *Tech Alma Mater, Noble and True, Proudly we arise to salute thee anew…*Four thousand, seven hundred and two ebullient new graduates tossed white carnations into the air.

Seven days later, Clarissa's graduation would pass—attended by family, yes, but barely a footnote in her mother's memory.

Euclin met her mother, Clarissa, and Kevin at the Franklin Street subway station. The restaurant was crowded when they got there, crawling with people, at all of the outdoor tables, at most of the indoor tables, parked at the bar for a mid-day cocktail. They were drinking, smoking, laughing. It was a Sunday. It was a good day for brunch, sunny outside.

Euclin had chosen the Odeon because it was nearby. "My mother is so fussy about any kind of food that she hasn't cooked herself," she'd said to Brent as she'd waited for the elevator to reach their loft. "The Odeon is nice. Simple. Unpretentious," she said. "No need for reservations. Taking them to Montrachet or Bouley would be like going to Mars." Brent had brushed her cheek with his hand and saw her off, saying, "Good luck."

The volume of the crowd, though not exactly surprising, was still daunting to Euclin, who had sincerely believed that they could slide right into prime outdoor seating. Fortunately they were shown to an indoor table, and quickly.

Ophelia was wearing her favorite green silk dress and a colorful cubic zirconia parrot brooch. "But, I say you taking us out someplace nice where I could sit down and consume an expensive meal, yes," her mother said the moment they were seated. "I never see more, oui, the gyul take us out to a diner."

Brent, a golden genie, popped into Euclin's head, mouthing the words *Good luck*. Signaling the waitress, she ordered a whiskey sour immediately. And after popping down a complimentary olive from the center-table bowl, she said, "I wanted to take you someplace where you would feel comfortable."

"Euclin," said Ophelia, "I know the difference between a knife and a fork."

Her whiskey sour arrived and Euclin downed half of it. "You look beautiful, Mum." The alcohol pounded through her veins, unwinding her muscles. They were funhouse versions of each other, Euclin and Ophelia. One wide. One thin. Both dark.

Euclin squeezed her mother's hand. "You really do look beautiful, Mum. And that brooch is so nice—is it new?"

"This old ting." Ophelia peered down at her bosom. "It was a gift from your grandmother."

"Mam?"

"Of course, Mam," snapped Ophelia, clearly irritated by even the vaguest mention of her former in-laws.

Good luck. Switch topics now.

"Did you like the orchids I sent you?"

"When?" asked Ophelia

"On Mother's Day."

"I didn't thank you?" asked Ophelia, almost sounding doubtful. "Yes," she said, recollection slowly registering in her eyes. "My poor old brain is so addled sometimes. Yes, yes. They were lovely. Quite lovely. But they died so fast. Too fast—and no scent. I was surprised that there wasn't a scent. I thought all orchids were scented."

Euclin sipped again. *Good luck.* "I'll keep that in mind next time," she said.

They pored over their menus.

"What's frisée?" asked Clarissa.

"Where?"

"Under appetizers."

"Oh," Euclin said. "A variety of chicory, um, a kind of curly herb they use in fancy salads."

"And what," Clarissa mispronounced, "is Roquefort, and—" she made a face, "what the heck are lardons?"

"Well I'm not sure about lardons, we can ask the waiter that, but Rocquefort is a type of French blue cheese, made from sheep's milk."

Clarissa, looking more frustrated than enlightened, said, "I thought Mom said this was a diner. I don't know what the heck half this stuff is on the menu. They tell you it's salad or they tell you it's eggs, but in between they mix in all this fancy stuff in French."

"A cheeseburger. Hey, Clarissa—look!" Kevin said, excitedly. He pointed to the menu.

"Now *that's* some food I can understand," said Clarissa. "Yo, I'm saying, $8.00 for some stink sheep cheese on some lettuce!" She sucked her teeth. "They could keep that mess."

"Don't forget I'm paying," Euclin reminded softly.

"And since Euclin is paying," interjected Ophelia, "why don't you try something new."

"I don't want something new. I want something that I can eat."

Euclin shrugged. "They're *kids.* It's an acquired taste. There are adults who would spit this stuff out in a minute. In fact, they probably wouldn't even be brave enough to order it. But there's plenty to eat here. As menus go, this one isn't too hard to navigate."

"No hamburger," warned Ophelia, peering over the rim of her glasses. "Choose something else—this isn't McDonald's."

"But it says right there." Clarissa pointed. "Hamburger, cheese-burger, baconburger. Right *there* on the menu."

"This isn't Brooklyn," Ophelia said, unmoved. "Try something new."

"Well, thank you, but I can do my own thinking," said Clarissa.

"You tink is joke I making," Ophelia said, turning to Euclin for combination backup and sympathy, "when I tell you this girl is *completely* out of order."

"Dag, will you leave me alone. You always trying to tell people what to do and what they should and shouldn't be thinking," snorted Clarissa. "Like you think you God, bossing everybody around."

Euclin's eyes became slits, incredulous at the exchange. As a teen-ager, if she had said the things that Clarissa was saying at this table, her mother's hand would have connected so solidly to the side of her face that people would believe it had grown there.

"Oh, suddenly you want to call the Lord's name. I see," said Ophelia. "You invoke him when it suits you. Deny him when it doesn't."

"Well," said Clarissa, "since you seem to think you *are* God most of the time, clearly you don't believe in him, either."

Kevin shook his head. "That made *no* sense."

"Shut up," said Clarissa.

*Unbelievable! What an impudent little…*Euclin didn't linger on the thought too long. But she did know one thing, when she was Clarissa's age, her mother would have had her head and teeth spin-ning on a platter for less. She wanted to say: *Did you not get the memo that the world does not revolve around you?* Was this what it meant to be a teenager? As a species, they were such a curiosity to her now—like she needed to roll them over, and poke them with a stick, in or-der to fully examine them. She and Kevin got along pretty well, but Clarissa remained a dark, brooding mystery—*teenagus enigmaticus. High schoolus terribulus.*

"Fourteen dollars for smoked salmon and a bagel!" Ophelia prac-tically shouted. "In a diner? But what that bagel make with—silver? Gold?"

"Mom, the Odeon isn't a *diner*-diner," Euclin said.

"Well then, why don't they go and sell some more gold bagel and use the money to fix up inside this place. What they charging all that money for? Like somebody embezzling in here, o' what?"

Good luck.

Ophelia, looking around her, continued her rant. "Papa, this is some sort of white people business they have here. Is shabby chic I tink I hear those white people call it. I does read about these things, you know—oh-ho." Ophelia sucked her teeth, then popped another olive into her mouth.

"Dag, I know," Clarissa added, jaw clenched. "Got mad white folks up in here."

Euclin lightly touched the back of her sister's hand, laughing. "Looks like we'll have to get you out of East Flatbush more than twice a year, my love." Euclin remembered her life before Madeira, before she learned to navigate the white world—before white people became flesh and blood for her, not simply curious paper cutouts, Barbie dolls, or characters she'd seen on television.

"Don't worry—I don't think they bite," said Kevin.

"Who?" Clarissa asked.

"The Caucasians—it looks as though most of them have already been fed."

"I think most of them prefer to eat cigarettes anyway," said Euclin. "I've observed them in their natural habitats." Euclin winked, and she and Kevin shared a deep laugh.

"Like that is how you eat, too—cigarettes?" Ophelia said. "I notice how listless you look, and skinny for so. I know when my children are well, and when they are ill—even when I don't see them. Like what-he-name don't like to buy food, o' what?"

"Brent, Mum. His name is Brent."

"If you need food," said Ophelia, "don't be ashamed. We have a set of canned goods at home. Tonight self, Clarissa and I could put together a box for you. Which it is you prefer, kernel corn or creamed?" Ophelia then winked, Euclin and her mother sharing their first laugh of the day. Euclin had almost forgotten the rhythm of her family's ways, the manner in which they often joked, baiting and goading each other—and that what sounded to outsiders like a street brawl was actually love.

"Euclin, I *thought* that was you." A bespectacled pink man had appeared at the edge of their table.

"Roger? How are you?" Euclin said, sucking down her second whiskey sour.

He was a coworker from the record company, and had transported himself and his drink from the bar. "A friend of mine is having a birthday brunch. It's a very small thing. I was facing in this direction and it just kept nagging me. I was like…" He stopped and protracted his neck in a caricature of himself. "Is that Euclin? And sure enough…So what brings you here?"

"A double celebration. A belated Mother's Day and my brother's graduation." She motioned to Kevin. "This is my brother, Kevin. He's headed to Stanford this fall. Kevin, this is Roger. Roger is in charge of the marketing department at Amp."

"Your brother?" Roger tried to look less surprised, but wasn't succeeding. "You both look so…"

"Different," Euclin volunteered, her voice like a turtle's snap. "And yes," she said anticipating the FANQ (Frequently Asked Next Question), "we both have the same mom and dad. My family has a very wide gene pool. That's my sister, Clarissa, and this is my mum."

"You call her mum? That's cute. I'm Roger," he said, shaking hands all around. "Oh yes, this is clearly your mom," he said when he reached Ophelia. "I can definitely see the resemblance."

Euclin was thinking, *Roger—please shut up and get gone.*

"You're quite a good looking bunch," Roger added, still trying to smooth things over. "If anyone in my family looked like that, we would have pimped them off to child stardom and kept the whole family fed."

Shut up, shut up, shut up! All Roger needed, thought Euclin, was to ask if they'd tried the fried chicken special.

"You're too kind," Euclin said, waiting for him to turn and go, lest the *pimp* thing give her mother additional fodder. Roger was a coworker, not a friend, and Euclin was ready to draw the window dressing of privacy back down.

"Well, good seeing you," Roger said.

"And thanks for coming over." Euclin smiled brightly. "Enjoy the party."

"Oh I will," he said, holding up his glass. Then he held up an open palm. "Nice meeting you all."

The remaining trio murmured their farewells.

Roger out of earshot, Kevin laughed. "Well, that was interesting. People just don't seem to know what to make of us." Kevin slouched mischievously against the banquette backing, and tousled his copper curls. "And white folks—well, we just blow their minds. You handled that well, sis." Kevin chuckled again, then smiled admiringly at his sister. Euclin smiled back, and pulled out a cigarette.

When introduced alongside Clarissa and Kevin, her own sister, her own brother, her own blood, Euclin was always mistaken for a cousin—or worse yet, a friend. *You look just like your mom.* That much they'd always get correct. *Duh.* Always a cousin. Always a friend. The whole thing had grown tiring. Her own flesh and blood. Siblings. Why couldn't people recognize the coagulate red that bound them?

Then Ophelia spoke: "Is a funny ting, eh, how you and Clarissa look more like these people than Euclin does—yet she is the one so at ease. So comfortable. White Woman," her mother said, looking directly at her, her smile thin, "you gone, eh? Like you done cross over to that other side—a long time ago."

"You wished me luck, but I had none," said Euclin. "That woman is impossible."

Returned home, she was recounting the afternoon to Brent: the orchids, the hamburger, topped off by bumbling Roger, who, at work or in real life, never knew the appropriate thing to say.

Then she recounted her mother's complaint when her mesclun salad arrived: "Like she must be just gone outside and pick this salad. Is only one set of bush I seeing on this plate." Euclin had been glad that her mother wasn't hip enough to ask her if it was the same mescaline that people took to get high. And she spared Brent the part about having her Black Card revoked—by her own mother. It was too much for him to understand.

"I thought all orchids were scented," she ended. "I mean, Brent, what kind of ting is that to say?"

"What did you just say?"

"I said, what kind of thing is that to say?"

"No, you didn't. You said *ting.* I heard you. Speak it to me." Drawing closer, he cupped her waist with both hands. "Speak to

164

me—with your real tongue."

"Stop being foolish."

He cupped her cheeks, her face. "Your real tongue. Please, I love to hear you. Say it again."

"Ting."

"Louder."

"Ting."

"More."

"Ting."

"More…"

"Ting—papa…mauvaise langue."

Brent pushed his tongue against hers. Underneath its heaviness, Euclin closed her eyes and let the words cease. Kissing him felt like breathing.

Uptown was a parallel universe.

Mouse quickly sprang up, afraid. It was the middle of the night and his father was pummeling him in his bed for no reason. Mouse tried to defend himself, but—as always—found himself incapable. There was a fine line between protecting himself and further escalating his father's ire. How to do this? Mouse had never known how.

"Stop it. What are you doing?" It was Rachel. It was the most that she would say in his defense, hanging back, watching from the hall. There was no one to help him. His father's fist. Black and blue pyrotechnics exploding over and over, welting on the brown of him in the darkness, in the black.

"What are you doing?" Rachel said again. Her words—neither might nor militia behind it—made Mouse feel even more powerless. There was no one to help him. He wished that, for a moment, she would just shut up.

"I'm getting him ready," his father said, wheezing over his shoulder.

Rachel said, "For what?"

"For everything," his father said. "The world will do worse."

CHAPTER SIXTEEN

Upon emerging from the subway at Utica, Mouse and Kevin were engulfed by sound. First, there were the sidewalk cassette vendors with their six-foot-tall speakers, pummeling the air with the latest soca, dancehall, calypso, gospel, mento, or old dub. On the next wave of sound were the brogues and voices, particularly those of the illegal dollar cab drivers, beckoning like carnival barkers to every weary traveler who emerged from the subway:

"Utica, Utica, Kings Plaza, get in."

"Remsen, Remsen, three more for Remsen. Remsen, son?"

"I thought you said you only needed three more people."

"Soon come. Soon come."

"Always one more, two more, always soon come," Kevin said without malice, and let himself be ushered into a minivan with tinted windows. He'd used this driver before, but he doubted the man recognized him. Mouse got in, too, lured by the promise of instant departure, only to find the van empty. The two of them sat in the back of the taxi to wait for more passengers, and laid their heads against the crushed velvet seat, still cradled in the lap of drowsiness.

It was not yet noon, and Kevin had surprised Mouse earlier that morning by showing up in front of his friend's apartment door. Kevin had managed to slip into the building as someone was exiting, avoiding ringing the bell. There had been an urgent knock at the door, and Mouse had opened it, the chain still on, expecting to find the super, come at last to unclog the toilet. Instead Mouse looked as though he had seen a ghost, startled to see his best friend standing before him. As Kevin was preparing to leave for Stanford, things had been so hectic, he and Mouse both thought there might not be time to see each other before he flew out. But Kevin had made the time.

Other passengers began to pile into the van, taking up the seats in front of them. Some were club kids returning from Manhattan discos, but mainly they were the men and women who went to sleep with the sun and rose with the moon: janitors, nurses, night watchmen, au pairs, and domestics come home for the weekend from Long Island and New Jersey to see their families, lovers, and friends.

The van was full. The driver jumped behind the wheel and began to pull off.

"Anyone for Rutland? Anyone before Clarkson? Don't worry, Winthrop," he assured, smiling at Kevin, "Winthrop, m'nah forget you." The driver, remembering him after all, called Kevin by his final destination.

"Rutland," a woman in a white nurse's uniform called out. The driver turned on a religious radio station: A preacher with a bluegrass twang was quoting from Deuteronomy.

Suddenly the whir of sirens, accompanied by flashing lights. Mouse became jumpy, turning to look through the van's rear window.

"Eh, you better move fast, look the police coming. Look, look— make haste nah, man!" The man who issued the warning wore a blue security uniform and an Army-Navy bomber jacket; he had a horseshoe of salt and pepper hair. The taxi driver took off with an unexpected speed, but a bottleneck had already formed: All the other illegal dollar-cab drivers were competing to be the first to escape.

"Don't sweat it," Kevin said, seeing Mouse's face. "The cops are always after them. This kind of thing happens every day."

"Yeah, this happened once before when I was with you," Mouse said, then turned around again and looked through the rear window at the nearing police car. He looked toward the front of the van. A city bus (the chief rival of dollar vans for local customers) was clogging the way, slowly drifting away from the bus stop as though in collusion with the police to help to stall the fleeing chaos. Mouse looked back at the nearing police car: *We gonna have to walk all the way to Kevin's house if they catch us. I hope they don't catch us: I'm tired.* It would take a fourteen-block walk for them to get there.

But, still, there was always a mounting degree of excitement that accompanied each chase, an electric charge dominating the air that reminded Mouse, as Kevin had once pointed out, of the best kind of video game. The people inside the van began to shout out conflicting directions, instructing the driver on how to safely speed off:

"Make a right on Utica."

"No, go down Rochester, turn down a side street. Park quick! Park quick!"

One man uttered a Jamaican curse that started with blood. "Make haste, make haste! They coming, man!"

"So early on a Saturday and they come to trouble people," a grumpy woman in a nurse's uniform said. "Don't want to see people make a honest living. They prefer you go out and peddle drugs or rob someone on the street."

"Woop woop! That's the sound of da police." Kevin laughed. "Woop woop! That's the sound of the beast." Swiveling his body, he peered through the rear window. As the van's speed accelerated, he jerked backward in the seat, ramming his back into Mouse's shoulder.

The driver made a sharp turn down Rochester, alongside the park that was once known by some as Prostitute Alley.

"Here they come," the man with the greying horseshoe warned. "Turn, man, turn, why you so schupid?"

The driver, gripping the wheel, gave the man a look. The police car seemed on the verge of cornering them, then just as quickly sped past the van. It was the green van ahead of them that the police were after. The daily chase between the police and the drivers amounted to a game of mere chance, no different from a lion's infiltration into a wide herd: It is one, and only one, they are after, and focusing in on this one, the patrol cars steel themselves and pounce fast.

The taxi driver gave a nervous laugh. "Lord, m'say m'done for now. M'say 'im get me now. You see that? Lord, Jesus. You see how God is good? Would you believe it, they already give me ticket twice for this week."

"Twice for the week!" said the grumpy woman. She made a twittering noise, using her tongue and teeth, an exotic sound of commiseration. "Is a shame how these police does get on, eh?" Some of the passengers joined in, laughing, exchanging observations, exhaling their fears, some recalling former chases of previous vans.

Several stops later, Kevin moved up and sat in the first row of vacated seats. He handed the driver a dollar bill, his fare. "Mouse, where's your money?" he asked over his shoulder.

"I'll pay when we get there."

As the car idled at a stoplight, the driver adjusted a lenticular Jesus card and a crucifix that dangled from his rearview mirror. Mouse noticed a pocket-sized Bible spread open on the dashboard of the van; he strained to see the scripture it was turned to, but finally gave up.

It was too far ahead for him to read.

Brooklyn dollar cabs were like temples or churches, customized spaces that reflected their drivers' national origins and worldview. The Haitians and the Africans drove ancient Oldsmobiles and Lincoln Town Cars, playing moderate levels of Compas, Juju, Zouk, country music, and Creole talk radio. The drivers from Guyana, Trinidad, Jamaica, Barbados, and the Small Islands were more inclined to customize their vans into signature lairs, ambulatory palaces, marked by automatic sliding doors and plush velour seats, their dashboards and rearview mirrors bearing all manner of trinkets: miniature national flags adorned with fringes; bumper stickers with reclining silhouettes of naked women; pine-tree-shaped air fresheners; religious icons; and dogs with coil necks that wagged their heads as the cars sped along.

On constant lookout for the police, the cab drivers formed a loose federation, communicating with each other over the static of CB radios. And always, in each van, there was noise: wall-to-wall stereos that rocked entire vans with the force of their music, or the subdued politics and commentary of talk radio. On the lowest rungs of the dollar-van strata, however, stood poor and miserly drivers, whose vans suffered from torn upholstery, customer refuse, wrappers, and dirt, their only concern seeming to be sheer survival—making a few dollars, living day to day, avoiding traffic tickets, and fleeing from the police when they could.

"Next corner," Kevin reminded the driver.

"Yuh nah hear me? Winthrop, m'say m'nah forget you. M'know how you stop."

Mouse laughed, at the driver and the quirks of East Flatbush and Brooklyn life. He spent so much time between Brooklyn and Harlem, he felt bi-coastal. With Kevin headed out to the actual West Coast, would that change? Funny, Mouse once thought: *It's like we switching places. Me from Oakland now in New York. Him now headed to Cali.* Mouse sometimes wondered: *Will I still get invited out to dinners at Miss Ophelia's?* He felt genuinely happy for Kevin—but he also felt scared, knowing something would change.

The driver pulled up at the corner of Remsen and Winthrop. Kevin stepped down from the van. Mouse, hunching over inside of the vehicle, gave the driver a ten-dollar bill, then waited for change. He palmed the bills and then pretended to count them outside the van.

"You short-changed me," he said to the driver.

"How much m'give you then?" the driver said, squinting, his arm resting against the headrest of the passenger seat.

"Eight." Mouse held up the fan of singles.

The taxi driver, looking at Mouse with reluctance, reached into his shirt pocket, and peeled off one more bill.

Kevin wasn't looking at Mouse as they walked away. "How much change did he really give you?"

"Nine," said Mouse, nonchalant.

A moment later—like a scratched match—the ugly of memory blazed: Wollman Rink and the silver necklace rose in the flame before him, then, extinguished by shame, withdrew to darkness. Could he blame Kevin for not trusting him? Suddenly Mouse remembered a Bible verse that his grandmother used to quote. *When I would do good, evil is present with me.*

He knew what Kevin was thinking—but he hadn't stolen the chain.

"I'm sorry, man," Mouse said.

"You sure are," said Kevin.

It was late evening now, bordering on midnight. Mouse had polished off one of Miss Ophelia's special meals: curried crabs with dumplings, made especially for Kevin's departure. Kevin was headed west early, spending the remainder of the summer in Big Sur with a girl he had met during Stanford's Admit Weekend the previous fall. Mouse and Kevin had sat in the latter's room since the dinner, satiated. Their bellies, once temporarily obese, had slowly started to go down. The street sounds of a Brooklyn summer night streamed through the fly netting and opened window.

Friends don't stay angry for long.

"You know 'Hound Dog?'"

"Wha…" Mouse exhaled the lungful of smoke. "That song by Elvis?"

"Yeah, Linnaeus told me some lady called Big Mama Thornton sang it first."

Kevin held his hand out for the pipe.

"What you mean sang it first? Before Elvis?"

"Yeah, before anybody."

"So what about it?"

"That makes Elvis a thief."

"Everybody knows that." Mouse looked around the room, crowded with boxes, and half-packed suitcases and carry-on luggage, remembering their own days of petty pilfering, then outright robbing and stealing. He was thinking of how much things, and their lives, had changed.

"But he's my kind of thief," Kevin said. "He knew that good culture, good things, can't be stolen—they belong to everybody. Life belongs to everybody. Life belongs to you and to me." He began to cough. "Knowwhatl'msayin'? Negro, you feel me?"

Mouse sighed, rolled his eyes. "Here we go."

Kevin passed the chalice, the leaves inside, once green, now crackling, burning brown. Mouse put his lips to the pipe, inhaled. The fan was blowing hard, making the incense burn brightly and alternately stirring up and masking the stench. Kevin took the chalice back, and after sucking in as hard as he could, resumed where he'd left off.

"Your old man digs Lynyrd Skynyrd, right?"

"Where is this going?" said Mouse. He'd been trying all night not to think of his father.

"Just answer the question, man. Does he, or doesn't he?"

"Yeah. He does."

"Exactly. That's exactly my point. Then doesn't that mean that "Sweet Home Alabama" belongs to him just as much as to any Confederate-flag-wearing white boy? And doesn't that mean that Vanilla Ice had just as much right to the running man and a high-top fade as Kid n' Play? And," he added, almost triumphantly, "doesn't that mean the Beatles had as much right to the sitar as Freddie Mercury did to rock and roll?"

"N$gga—give me that." Mouse grabbed for the chalice, disgusted. "You old crap-talking Negro. You starting to sound like my father. It's time to put the pipe *down*."

Kevin hugged the chalice tight, like a wino beatbox blaring, dancing with a longneck on a Saturday night. "Nope. You ain't touching this. Hold off and know your place, boy. My uncle gave me that. Now, where was I? Ah yes—the world. I own this world. And not just me, you own this world, too. Can't nobody tell me where to go and what to think when I survey this planet. They crazy? This is *my* world! The day I was born, I heard the alpha and omega tell me that."

"The Alpha who?" said Mouse.

"I can do anything that I want to—I can do anything that I put my mind to," continued Kevin. "And guess what?" Mouse didn't answer, just listened. "The Almighty one told me that, too."

"Ladies and gentlemen…and the crazy-pothead-n$gga-of-the-year award goes to—Kevin Ramtahal." Mouse walked over to Kevin's shelves, picking up book after book and scanning the jacket flaps. "Hey, *Where the Sidewalk Ends*—Shel Silverstein. I remember that. Mrs. Parsalls gave me a copy of that."

"Mrs. Who?"

"Our old landlady, Mrs. Parsalls. The place I used to live with my moms, out in Oakland." Mouse flipped the pages with an extra gentleness. "Shel Silverstein. On the real, yo. That's my n$gga right there."

"What you looking for?"

"Maybe it's not in this one." Mouse said, distracted.

"Let me help you. Which one is it?"

"Alice."

"I don't remember that one." Kevin held the other corner. "*Hector the Collector*, that was my favorite." They looked through the book together.

Kevin pointed. "*Alice*. Here it is." He brought the chalice to his mouth once more, lit it.

"You not scared?" Mouse said, himself looking nervous.

"Scared of what?" Kevin shrugged. "I told you, they're all asleep, and Clarissa's next door—she won't say anything. All right, then, if it makes you feel better…" He turned up the speed on the fan. "Go ahead, son. Read it out loud." Kevin's thumb made a dry scratch against the lighter. "Go 'head, I want to hear it."

> She drank from a bottle called DRINK ME
> And she grew so tall,
> She ate from a plate called TASTE ME
> And down she shrank so small
> And so she changed, while other folks
> Never tried nothin' at all.

"That ain't much." Mouse sucked his teeth and shut the book. *It's funny what stays with you.* "They got much better poems in there," he said. "But all I remembered is that one." Before he had finished, Kevin, fully clad and still wearing sneakers, lay knocked out on his twin bed.

"You asleep?"

"Nah, I just have my eyes closed."

Stoking the leaves with the lighter, Mouse took over the chalice. He inhaled and let go. A white banner swirled from his mouth. He picked up the book again. Pumping it up and down, he weighed it in his hand.

"I feel like I ain't gonna make it, man."

"What?"

"Sometimes…" Mouse's words slowed down. "I feel like I'm one of the ones that ain't gonna make it."

Kevin opened one eye. "What? What you tripping on now?" He reached for the chalice. "Yo, man, here. Pass it."

Mouse handed it over and rubbed his eyes. "I mean…at night… At night, I have dreams. Crazy dreams, man." Then, looking for a segue, a metaphor, anything to clarify his feelings, he said, "One time, I looked at this PBS nature special, about Australia. And they had this one part about kangaroos. About how those tiny little baby kangaroos have to crawl from their mother's womb in order to get to the pouch, crawling all through her fur and across her belly—nothing to help them along, not even their mothers. When they're born, those tiny suckers, they ain't even the size of your thumb, you know. And you know what else? Some of those teeny-tiny little bastards— they don't make it. I feel like that some days—like I'll be one of the ones who don't make it. Man, some days, honest? I don't feel like waking up."

Mouse waited on Kevin, but Kevin, already asleep, said nothing, and Mouse—lunging a little—caught the chalice just in time before it fell on the bedspread or onto the floor, wherever it had been headed as it slowly slid from Kevin's grasp.

CHAPTER SEVENTEEN

The summer was half gone. It was the beginning of July already. Ophelia's garden was particularly fecund that year. With the tree cut down, light had come pouring in, her perennials and annuals grew lavishly.

Kevin's bags were packed. He sat in the air-conditioned living room, waiting for Euclin to drive him to Kennedy.

Euclin came by in the Range Rover. Clarissa and Ophelia, who had been scanning for her arrival from the living room window, came out of the house, lugging the first wave of luggage. Kevin followed. They each made two trips in and out until all the luggage was neatly piled in front of the driveway, behind the dip in the sidewalk where the cars from both adjoining homes entered and left. Euclin played watchman, guarding the Rover.

Her hand on the still-open trunk door, Euclin asked, "That's it?"

"That's it," said Kevin.

Euclin clicked the trunk closed, stepped inside the vehicle, and started the engine. She watched Kevin linger on the sidewalk. He and Clarissa stood talking and laughing, lightly punching each other in the shoulder on occasion, then he leaned over and hugged her. Euclin watched their mother trying to stand strong. At first she was stone-faced, but quickly went from great oak to weeping willow. Unlike with their sister, her brother's verbal exchange with their mother was very brief, almost nothing. They just clung to each other, Ophelia's chest heaving and falling. Minutes seemed to pass as they stood that way. Euclin was surprised that her mother was the first to let go.

Kevin headed for the passenger side and slid in. Euclin rolled down her window so all could wave their final goodbyes. As she pulled out from the driveway, the bedroom curtain in the neighboring house rustled white.

"You see that?" asked Kevin.

"Mrs. Hutchence?" Euclin asked. Like a phantom, she had already disappeared. "She's been like that ever since I was a girl," said Euclin, turning the steering wheel. "Perpetually at that window. All creepy and mysterious."

"I think she's mad at me," said Kevin. "I think she knows I called the cops on Jamal." Euclin could see the sadness on Kevin's face about having just left their mother, and knew he was just filling the void with idle rambling.

"Isn't he in a wheelchair? What could he possibly do?" She flipped her sunglasses up, on her head.

"No, that's Trance. Jamal can walk."

"And steal?" asked Euclin. "Is that what that was all about?"

"Mr. Gary's arcade got robbed. Whoever did it pistol-whipped him unconscious. Now the vision in his left eye is blurred. Word on the street is that Jamal did it."

"Why did you get involved?" Euclin asked, her memory long: *four months on the Barge, two years' exile in Trini.*

"It's just wrong—that's why. We all know Mr. Gary. Mr. Gary was old. Nice. Minded his business. Never bothered anybody. Mr. Gary didn't believe in banks. He was old school—he kept a lot of money in a safe at the store. He had other businesses. A lot of people don't know that. I know because I used to talk to Mr. Gary. After the robbery, all you saw trafficking into that house right there," Kevin said, speaking of the house where Jamal lived, "was new things. New TV, appliances, furniture. What Jamal did was foul—straight up. We knew Mr. Gary our whole lives, ever since we were kids. There wasn't enough evidence to charge Jamal. But *he* knew what he did. And Mrs. Hutchence…You can't tell me that she didn't know or didn't at least wonder where the money came from."

"What makes you think she knows it was you?"

Kevin shrugged. "Pretty obvious. The way she acts now. Runs into her house and hides when she sees me coming, like she doesn't even want to say hello. Sometimes I catch her peeking at me through the curtains."

"Nothing's changed," said Euclin, referring to Mrs. Hutchence's misanthropy. "But it is a shame. I remember Mr. Gary very well. I used to buy my sweets and chips from him, too."

They were already on Kings Highway. The day was so hot, every object outside the Rover shimmered like a mirage. Euclin's fingers fiddled down the radio dial, stopping just short of the left end. She turned up the volume. "Know who this is?"

Kevin smiled. "Of course. Clifford Brown, "September Song," vocals by Ella."

"You've heard of Brownie?" Real pleasure gave a sweet and chewy middle to Euclin's surprise. "I didn't know you knew him."

"Anyone who knows me knows that," Kevin responded. "Anyone."

In that case she was no one. Euclin felt embarrassed, and made a small motion—pulling down the sun visor—to hide her shame. It was as though her brother's lips were moving, but it was her mother's voice coming out. She thought of all the time lost. Of all the missed special occasions. Of all the small, fleeting moments that had scurried by. *But my job is so demanding—and the hours are so unpredictable.* They needed to understand. That was all.

"Decided on your major yet?" Euclin asked.

"Environmental—probably."

"Going to stick to engineering, huh? Heard there's lots of action in Silicon Valley for smart boys like you."

The heat and sun filtered into the car, making Kevin's copper hair and skin glow more than usual. Euclin noticed, and thought for a moment how truly beautiful her brother was. That one day some woman—a truly special woman—would get lucky.

"Working in the Val would be cool, but my motivation is a little more practical," Kevin said. "I think it's Trini still in me. Rio Verde still pulling me."

Euclin bettered the reception, eliminating all static. "How so?"

"When I used to go hunting and camping in the bush with Pa, it was like there were only two colors out there, green and blue: forest, water, sky. Then I'd take the bus to Port of Spain, where everything seemed all beige and grey, overdeveloped, polluted. I always felt like there had to be another color between these extremes, a different way, you know, and I felt like this—I mean, engineering—was a way to figure out what that other way was."

"So civil engineering became your answer."

"What got me thinking about it was my friend, Raven, from Laventille in Trini. Before I came back up and transferred to Tech, he was my best friend at Queens Royal College. I remember, Raven's family was so poor, their life was like..." Kevin laughed, finding the word. "Medieval. But his family was so funny, mad jokes. If they had one piece of meat in the pot when I was there, I knew that they would put it on my plate. And you had to take it. If you didn't, you were reminding them that they were poor—like an insult, like, who are you to pity?"

"I never went up into Laventille. But I remember looking though bus windows," Euclin said, "at those houses in the mountains on their stilts, things leaning to one side, all patchwork, all bric-a-brac."

"I sometimes used to wonder," said Kevin, "if the start of life is a house? If you just have a good house, will you be a different person? Or is there something wired inside each of us when we're born that makes us who we already are, no matter where you put us?"

"You mean as black people?" said Euclin.

"Yes and no. I guess that, too. But what I mean is just as people, humans. Though, honestly, personally, I don't believe in that—you know, in predestination."

"We are what we choose," said Euclin, firmly. "Think about it: You were exiled from America, one of the wealthiest places in the world, and for most of his life, Raven was sentenced to live in one of Trini's poorest. It wasn't your houses that made you. It's the things you chose, you see—or maybe the things that chose you. Do you see what I'm getting at? Your choices, be they bad or good or informed by something inside you, brought you to that common destination. That's how you came to be friends. *Are* you still friends?"

"Nah, we fell out of touch, long time. No falling out or anything. Just distance. We both stopped writing around the same time." Kevin placed his feet on the dashboard, his elbows and arms on his knees, his head in his hands, thinking. Watching him posed that way, seeming to seek answers, Euclin was afraid she could mold him.

And so she attempted.

"You won't lose yourself when you go, you know."

Kevin turned to face her.

"Mom seems to think you lose yourself when you leave, but it's actually the opposite. You will find yourself, Copper.

"I want you to keep a couple things in mind when you start school," she said. "Don't pick your electives by topic. I've found it best, with electives, to choose your courses by professor. Ask around, you'll get the names of all the best ones."

"Classes?"

"Professors," Euclin said impatiently. "Please listen carefully. Study in groups, especially come finals. And always ask all your professors for feedback. Read everything you can get your hands on, you probably won't have that kind of leisure time ever again in your life. Cozy up to foreign students—the truly interesting ones, at least. They will open up a whole world." She laughed. "And places to crash on vacation. And know that everything—I mean everything and everyone—*is your classroom*, all of it, from the campus, to the groundskeepers, to the professors, to the faculty brats. Unplug your mind. Never be myopic in your thinking or point of view. That, according to me, is the Rosetta Stone to learning. But I'm certain there are things that I've missed."

"Is that how you have succeeded?"

"My whole life was trial and error." She laughed again. "But if given the chance, those are the things I would do if I had to repeat it. You will find yourself, Copper. You will." Euclin squeezed her brother's knee, smiled, then let go. "I'm sorry that I've been so busy."

He shrugged. "Nothing new. You're always busy," he said. He hadn't meant it as a jab. Still it hurt.

She asked, "When do you plan on coming back?"

"Mam and Pa are coming up around Labor Day and Mom, she really wants me to fly back home then. I told her it's not practical, but she's already started her campaign to make me feel guilty. I didn't plan on flying back out until Thanksgiving. It's too expensive."

"How long has it been since you've seen Mam and Pa?"

"Three years. Four maybe."

"You should come, then. They may not be around much longer, you know."

Kevin sighed. "You're right. I know. I'll try and do my best to come."

"The ticket's on me, if you do."

Kevin hugged his knees. "Can I ask you something?"

"Sure," said Euclin. "Shoot."

"I met a girl." Euclin smiled so broadly, Kevin paused, startled, and they both laughed. "Her name is Ashley. Ashley Chang," he continued. "She showed me family photos. Her mother's blonde, California born and bred. Her father is Chinese. Ashley and I met during a campus tour last fall."

"A callaloo," Euclin interrupted, commenting on Ashley's being mixed. Every once in a while, Euclin forgot that she was a callaloo, too.

"I have a question. How has it been for you? You know—dating outside of your race."

Euclin smiled wearily. "Well, Brent is his own country," she said. "so he wouldn't really qualify as *the* race. I'm not exactly sure that white people want him representing them, let alone Jewish folks." Euclin laughed. "Angus and I fight about this all the time, but at the end of the day what you're dealing with is an individual. With a human being, you know—both glorious and flawed. I love Brent with all my heart. Honestly, it's really hard for me to picture myself without him." Euclin decided that this was not the time nor place to share her doubts—the complexities of their love that no one else would ever *get*. But there are moments…" Here Euclin paused. "There are moments when you're wishing for something more—molecular. Where the person lying next to you just *gets it*. Where you don't have to open up a history book. But then there are moments that are freeing, *because* they don't get it. *Because* you would have to explain, because this person to whom you've given your heart can make you look at life, at the world, at what you're dealing with and who you are in a *completely* different way. Just learn Ashley, Copper—and love Ashley. And let her learn you. Does that answer your question?"

Euclin was not even sure that she had answers to her own questions.

It was the same day, but evening now. Dusk blended into the sky, streaking the firmament above Central Park West with coral. Euclin felt a badge coming her way: She'd taken the day off from Amp to be a do-gooder, and lent a hand to both Kevin and Angus.

Euclin helped Angus sort through the crate of Negrobilia that he'd gone to collect from Patricia, his recent fiancé. There were Aunt Jemima cookie jars, Banania table settings, salt and pepper shakers of bug-eyed pickaninnies munching on slices of melon. She held up a grinning Uncle Ben bin for storing rice. "Don't most people just leave behind a razor and a toothbrush?" she asked. "A stack of CDs, or an extra pair of drawers?" She'd chosen the word drawers over underwear to get him to laugh, and he did.

"After flea market shopping on Sundays, we'd always bring our finds, both hers and mine, back to her place then we'd go out for dinner. Though..." Angus paused. "Most of the markets were closer to my place than hers; but it seemed to make sense at the time." He laughed. "Yes, it seemed to make sense then."

"Did she give you any trouble when you went to pick up your stuff?"

"As we walked to the elevator, I asked her if we could be friends, at least. She said that would not be possible." Angus laughed. "No, not feasible—that was her exact choice of words."

"Was she crying? Diplomatic?"

"Clinical. But you could see the pain." Angus laughed again. "Crying? Actually, no—never. Not my Pat. But flesh is not wood, and eyes remain windows."

"As a woman," said Euclin, "I feel for her, but as a person, a friend, I think you were brave."

Angus palmed the skin on his scalp. His body still smelled of Raymond's cologne. "Selfish, "he said. "not brave. I had this woman eyeballing China patterns and picking out handmade cotton stationery from some ancient paper mill on Italy's Amalfi coast—rarefied, lovely wedding things from places I had never even heard of." Angus, moving to the window, stared out at the western half of Central Park.

"No, no, brave, Angus," Euclin said coming up behind him, touching his elbow.

"Not selfish."

Angus asked again, "Why brave? Why do you insist on brave? That's a strange choice of words."

"Because you put it all on the line for happiness, for Raymond," she said, referring to Angus's new lover, "even knowing that as you won, you would lose."

"You mean lose relationships?"

"Patricia. Some family, I guess."

"I haven't told my family yet, my father. I still have them."

"Will you ever tell them?"

"Someday, of course. But not over the phone. I'd want to fly out to Cleveland. I can just hear the good Reverend now, after choking on a mouthful of my Gram's smothered chicken at Sunday dinner. He'll throw the book. My biggest fear is that things might get physical. My father is not a violent man—but I don't know how he will take it. How does it go? Ah, yes..." Angus held a piece of his collar in either hand, his elbows stiff and authoritative like some colonial orator: "Do you know that the wicked will not inherit the kingdom of God? Do not be deceived: Neither the sexually immoral nor idolaters nor adulterers nor male prostitutes nor homosexual offenders nor thieves nor the greedy nor drunkards nor slanderers nor swindlers will inherit the kingdom of God."

"Well, you have plenty of company," Euclin said, trying to make things light.

"I've heard it from the pulpit so many times," said Angus. "Baldwin was a preacher's son, you know."

"I know, and a boy preacher himself," said Euclin. "But some people's parents surprise them—support them in small, unexpected ways."

"I already know the outcome. I know my folks. Who I choose to be becomes them. That's the problem, Euclin. You just don't understand."

"Thanksgiving will be hard," said Euclin, not knowing what else to say, and feeling foolish. She wished she had his power. She wished that she could make such tough choices—on family, on love. But here she stood. Still.

Angus said, "Sure. This Thanksgiving I can probably get by without a barrage of questioning. They'll probably give me an extra helping of sweet potato pie to help me soothe the pain of my breakup. But by the third Thanksgiving of double pie helpings, the questions will come. There has to be a point of revelation, you know. There has to be a point of reckoning.

"You have to understand my origins. We're one of Cleveland's finest old colored families, the descendants of free men and women of color—not slaves—on both sides. Doctors, lawyers, preachers, and politicians all the way up until the present. I might as well set fire to the house. Once the ashes clear and they've salvaged the silverware, they'd still find more forgiveness for arson than for that kind of announcement."

"This town makes you move fast," Euclin said. "That's the thing."

Angus held up a Golliwog doll, weighing his words before answering.

"It makes you grow older, too. You take love where you find it, Euclin. You take it. You don't ask."

CHAPTER EIGHTEEN

It was two days before Labor Day—the latter being the single most important day in all of West Indian Brooklyn. Two days later, by nightfall, Eastern Parkway would be littered with a shantytown of makeshift shacks erected by vendors preparing to purvey their wares at the upcoming West Indian-American Day Carnival, which seemed—outside of Trinidad, New Orleans, and Brazil—to be the largest party in the world.

Ophelia was jubilant, Kevin—her Kev-vy—had come home after all. He had surprised her by coming back for a brief stay before school, instead of waiting for Thanksgiving. Not telling her in advance, he'd snuck back into town, taking the A train from Kennedy, and had shown up at the family's front doorstep. Ophelia's head and heart had taken several minutes to recover. Kevin had said, hugging his mother, "Euclin paid for my ticket." Mouse, come down from Harlem, would be staying the entire long weekend.

Ophelia first headed down to the crossroads of Utica and Church Avenues, humming, and swaying, and shopping in the best of moods. Then she headed back up the hill on Utica, in the opposite direction, to complete her purchases. On Utica she planned to get firm Julie mangoes, fresh pigeon peas, red sorrel blossoms, pommecytheres (a fruit called June plums by Jamaicans) and live blue crabs.

It was largely thanks to the Korean merchants that these items had become so accessible, so plentiful—no longer scattered or covert. Prior to the coming of the Koreans around the time of Reagan, homesick West Indians often employed illegal means to obtain their favorite foods, relying on the generosity, boldness and guile of relatives and friends who had traveled home to the Islands, or their own boldness and guile when they traveled.

They lied. Mainly, this was how they did it. When U.S. customs officers, with probing hands and probing eyes, asked questions about illegal and undeclared foods…they lied. They lied about the bhaji and the barbadeen bush, the star apples, the stewed wild meats and the cleverly hidden ackee bundled up in pants and short-sleeved shirts, or lovingly rolled into the centers of their sleeping clothes, like the sweet fillings of rugelach.

They lied, these West Indians, both brash and meek, both unbelievers and Christians. They lied about the pickled, the preserved, the raw and the cooked, bound by twine and wrapped in wax- and newspaper, transported in the hulls of carry-on bags and over-stuffed suitcases. They lied. Wanting so desperately to bring back a piece of home to where they were now, living in New York's cold, mortared hardness, they lied. And when these West Indians looked into the eyes of each customs officer, their wanting—so strong—transformed each lie to truth.

Some delicacies remained unobtainable in New York, and still could only be had by smuggling. But now there was so much of the Islands in Brooklyn, so much of the Islands to be seen in the bustling shopping districts on Utica, Nostrand, and Flatbush Avenues. Enough of the Islands left over to spoil, grow mold and grow soft—there was so much abundance—much to the amazement of Caribbean immigrants, old and new, who felt as though they had never boarded a plane and left home.

Utica Avenue, in particular, stood as the gateway to Crown Heights and East Flatbush. It was a place where Arabs, Pakistanis, Koreans, and the Caribbeans themselves came to set up shop, selling their skills and their wares. It was a place where ambitious Caribbean men and women opened up accounting and dental practices, bakeries, travel agencies, beauty salons, and medical offices. It was also the starting place from which older, knife-faced Caribbean women began their journeys—intent on elbowing their way through the world.

It was a place where one could buy gold tooth caps with diamond studs, and large nameplates made of Guyanese gold. And it was a place where Rastafarians pedaled their bikes uphill, their locks piled high into red, gold, and green tams that puffed out like portobello mushrooms. Utica Avenue was a place where the bells of the Catholic Church rang out on one hour, and the muezzin cried out from the mosque on another.

And, in the summertime, it was a place where the young Jamaican glitter-gyuls—in their marriage of English punk and Island

Yardie—signaled the changing of the seasons with their microscopic shorts, metallic lipsticks and their preternatural synthetic hair, in gleaming blondes and reds and blues as vivid as the leaves of the upcoming fall.

The Hasidim were there, too. Crown Heights was Chabad Lubavitch World Headquarters. Bumper stickers and banners proudly declared and commanded: *Welcome Moshiach. Do a Mitzvah! Moshiach is coming.* In their Chabad Lubavitch Mitzvah tank, which also became the menorah mobile (come Chanukah), they drove up and down Eastern Parkway, all around Crown Heights. There were pictures of Rebbe Schneerson everywhere, and there would continue to be, even long after he had died. They largely kept to themselves, but their presence overlapped that of the West Indians. They were part of the fabric, too.

But the children—those of the West Indian immigrants—were curious, and did not keep to themselves. And their parents—here one must pity them—were befuddled by the results. Their children, having slipped from the cage of West Indian Brooklyn, returned unrecognizable: goths, strippers, club kids, queers, globetrotters newly returned from London and Milan, eating kimchee, holding the hands of white boys and Japanese women.

As Ophelia let herself into the house and began to unpack her wares, she thought of the things about America that remained alien to her: most of all, her own children.

What did these children know of wanting? They did not know what it meant to be without shoes, or to have to use gazette paper (or, as the Americans called it, newspaper) in lieu of toilet tissue. These American children did not know how frightening it could be to enter an outhouse that might be filled with scorpions or snakes. Ophelia recalled her terror: looking into the hole, seeing nothing but blackness at night, and in the day, feces and worms. Even as a child, she could not hide her revulsion of the night-soil men, no matter how kind, who used to go down into their outhouse hole and scrape it clean.

Nor, back then, did they even have beds as one understands them today, much less linens to cover them. Instead they lay down each night on coconut fiber stuffed into cheap mattress ticking. And there were no electric lights, only flambeaus—pitch oil bottles, with torn rags fashioned into wicks—that one leaned to the side so the kerosene could keep it lit. Yet another memory brought revulsion: bed bugs that exploded under the pressure of your fingertips, drenching your hand with your own stolen blood.

These American children did not know what it was like to walk to church in potato sack dresses or short pants cut from used policemen's uniforms. The shame one felt was indelible, no matter how smartly one's mother had washed, refurbished, camouflaged, and adorned those secondhand garments.

Nor did these American children know how it felt not to eat rice with meat, but only rice *flavored* with meat because the actual meat was reserved for the adults, no, for one's father, since one's mother ate whatever the children ate, which was little when times were hard. No, these American children, they simply did not know.

Before placing them into the freezer, Ophelia studied the packs of ribs she had purchased for the family barbecue. Ophelia weighed their solidness in her hand. *Meat—good meat.* These children simply did not know.

"I don't want waffles," Clarissa said, pushing away the uneaten contents of her plate. "These are from yesterday. I want hot bake." The children had come down late for breakfast.

Sighing a little, Ophelia lifted the picked-over plate from Clarissa's setting, stepped on the foot pedal, and scraped the food into the trash. She took a lump of dough from the fridge and removed it from a mixing bowl. The evening before, she had combined flour and yeast for fried bake, letting it rise overnight. Dusting fresh flour onto a cutting board, she began to knead the dough with one fist.

Kevin came down from the upstairs bathroom, still rubbing his hair with a towel. Spending his days in the California sun, he had gone from copper to bronze. And his curls were as messy and sea-beaten as the Pacific surf that he and Ashley entered with their boards almost daily. Hearing his brisk walk on the stairs, then seeing him enter the kitchen from the hall, Ophelia was shameless in her mirth; nothing that weekend seemed capable of dimming her pleasure at the sight of her son.

Just then, Mouse emerged from Kevin's shadow. Kevin sat down to the table, fixed himself a plate of eggs and waffles.

"I changed my mind," said Clarissa, grown greedy as she watched Kevin eat with gusto. "I want waffles *and* bake."

"Wait a minute here. How the two of you going to have bake *and* waffles?"

"We're hungry," said Clarissa. "The waffles are a snack while we wait for the bake."

Ophelia shook her head. "I will never understand you children, yes. If you want more waffles, you best get up and get them from the fridge yourself." Pinching and molding out individual cakes with her fingers, she eased the bits of dough into a waiting skillet, its exterior darkened by age, its inside hot and bubbling with oil.

"Mom, under what conditions was Clarissa conceived? I mean, look at her eat. Look—she's a beast. Look how she's massacring that poor little waffle."

"I was conceived and born under the same conditions as you, moron."

"OK, have mercy on the syrup," said Mouse. "Give it here."

"Clarissa, Kevin—please stop it. Stop it now!"

"All right, Mom," Kevin promised. "Me hear you."

Clarissa, Kevin, and Mouse soon ran out of waffles and took pulpy swallows of orange juice, waiting for the first batch of bake to come from the flames. All three were skylarking—as Ophelia would call it—joking and laughing, their interaction devoid of any of the tension that sometimes stunted exchanges between Clarissa and Kevin, and made her wonder if they had come from separate wombs. Mouse completed them—less friend than triplet. Their laughter grew so loud at times, Ophelia winced. And even then she smiled.

She checked the underside of the dough with her spatula. Mouse and Clarissa were talking now. Secretly, she listened, trying to decipher their slang, their youthful argot. She snatched at fragments—trying, through intuition, through reasoning, to make a composite from the steady stream of unintelligible words that floated by her, one following the other, just short of her reach.

But the words were piling up, mounting, one by one, like bricks, until a great foreign edifice seemed to stand between herself and these children who sat in her kitchen.

"...how was I supposed to know that he was rolling with the Bush Mobb, yo?" Mouse was saying. "He just look like a regular n— Excuse me, my bad.. I mean, I mean he just looked like regular folk to me." Mouse shrugged his shoulders, then drained the remaining juice from his glass. Ophelia peered directly across at them, still at the stove.

Laying her palms on the table, Clarissa sat erect in her chair. "But you was crazy illin' though, I'm sayin'. I know how to handle myself. You don't know what he could have been carrying. Yeah, he was sweatin' me, yeah, he was foul, but you just can't be stepping to people like that. I'm sayin', nowadays, people be acting *mad* ill. People just be acting crazy, yo."

"Nah, man," Mouse laughed, lightly brushing the air with his hand. "I knew he was just talking junk. Word is bond. I *had* to roll up on him like that. I *had* to. Ain't nobody gonna disrespect none of my peeps and I'm just gonna sit there. Come on now, Clarissa, how that look? Yo, buss it. I know I be messing with you sometimes, but we like family. We tight like this—"

Ophelia watched as Mouse interlaced both of his hands.

"I'm not gonna stand there and let nobody roll up on you like that. Come on now, that ain't right, and that just ain't me. It was Columbus Day, our day off, and there he was, standing right in the middle of our fun. What was I supposed to do?" Mouse turned to Kevin for affirmation.

Ophelia gripped the spatula.

Something happen months before. That Columbus Day party. Something happen. But the children, they here—they safe. Where was Euclin when this ting gone on? Why Clarissa didn't tell me as soon as she get home? What it is? Look how many months pass. And nobody tell me. What it is that happen?

At the table's center, Ophelia lay down a china plate filled with steaming bake. "Clarissa, what it is that you two talking about?"

"Nothing, Mom. Remember when Euclin invited us to that party last fall? Wait, it was Columbus Day, right? Well, we was just talking about this guy who was acting all stupid, trying to flirt with me." Clarissa laughed. "Relax, Mom. Why you look so worried? You all tense. Take it easy."

"You tink is funny, eh? You tink is joke? I have a right to be worried. Don't tell me to relax. So many months gone by and you never even tell me. Euclin never tell me."

Kevin shrugged. "She probably didn't want you to worry, that's why," Clarissa continued, "Look at how jumpy you are right now

187

and all we was doing is talking. Mom, really—you're making *me* tense. Relax—please."

"Don't tell me to relax! And is more than that that gone on, not just boys and flirting."

Ophelia sensed the half-truth. She often wondered about the things that her children kept from her. *Where do they go? What do they do when they not home here with me, Lord? When I can't see them, what it is that these two children does do?* Kevin had changed after going to Trinidad. He had changed, and she trusted him now. But she sometimes resented being shut out by their private language, the street talk that she could not understand. They were like her Haitian and Jamaican coworkers, talking in the nursing home cafeteria: huddling in their corner, shutting everyone out with their French Creole or their Yardie patois.

Yet Ophelia knew that there would always be things they kept from her. She knew that there would always be half-truths. And she knew this because when she had been young, she once had kept secrets, too.

"Which one all-yuh want: salt fish or fry ham to go with your bake?"

"Ham, please, Mrs. Ramtahal," said Mouse.

"I want salt fish," said Kevin. "We have any left over from yesterday?"

Ophelia went to the fridge. Digging deep, past the overflow of newly bought goods for the family barbecue, she took out a chilled bowl of codfish garnished with olive oil, tomatoes, and onions. She placed it on the kitchen table, next to the bake. Returning to the stove, she came back several minutes later with a platter of fried ham, green peppers, and onions.

Ophelia watched as Mouse buttered a hot piece of bake, rivulets of gold melting over the bumps of its hand-kneaded surface. Pridefully, Ophelia viewed the open pleasure on his face as he chewed.

"Mrs. Ramtahal, you know what this tastes like? It tastes like…a cloud."

"Listen to you, you cheeseball—*It tastes like a cloud*," Kevin mocked.

"Shut up. It do."

Ophelia did not like Mouse when she first met him. He smelled of the streets, which made her leery. At the time, Kevin was already slipping away from her, into thuggery and theft. But each time he returned from working with Linnaeus at the parlor, and spun out tales of his afternoon, Mouse's name was always in the middle. Leery, yes, but she could not ignore him. Over the years, he had become as much a part of Kevin as her son's own arms and legs.

At last, Ophelia met the great Mouse: small, ashy, uncombed hair, and hand-me-down clothing. What was so great, she could not see. All she knew was Kevin was crazy in love with him. So Ophelia searched hard to see what her son saw, surveying every inch of this polite but scruffy boy, his hair thick and knotted. Clearly there was something more to him than what her eyes beheld, and Ophelia tried her best to see, accept, and love whatever it was that had mesmerized Kevin.

"Mom, Clarissa stinks, and she's sitting to the table with civilized people."

Clarissa raised her hand and shoved one armpit near Kevin's face, still chewing her bake. "That close enough for you?"

"Move, you gorilla. Look at you—you're funking up the place!"

"Kevin, wait a minute." Ophelia's recollection: "When you came home yesterday morning, I hope you didn't sit on any of the bed linens in those nasty set of subway clothes you were wearing. And did you tuck away your suitcase?"

"No, Mom. I did not, Mom. Yes, Mom, I did. And why are you asking me this one day later, Mom?" With each word, Kevin lolled his head from side to side in exasperation. Pained by this show of mockery, Ophelia laid the spatula against a metal trivet on the stove, turning her face from her son.

Too American. This was her diagnosis.

Too American, Ophelia would conclude, trying to make sense of her children, their intractability and foreignness. Too American, Ophelia would conclude, as though pinpointing the very disease that was eating away at her children's respect and civility.

All the relatives, flown up from Trinidad, came that night. Some were staying at the house. Soca and calypso were blaring throughout the Ramtahal's wedge of East Flatbush: from the backyards, porches, and cars of neighbors behind and in front, everyone preparing for Labor Day. And in the kitchen—everywhere—there was the smell of food. And Clarissa, on a high stool, sat in the middle of everything.

Tanty Merle was kneading ghee and flour, one batch with chick-peas for roti, the other without for buss-up shot ("It's buss-up shot, like burst-up shirt," Tanty Merle said, confirming the one thing about the ragged, delicious flatbread that Clarissa already knew.) Her Tanty kneaded out each lump of dough with a rolling pin, then with her hands set them down, one at a time, on the cast-iron tawa, which had been brushed with oil. She turned up the flame and the dough started roasting. Clarissa was waiting for her to turn her back so she could steal a pinch of buss-up shot.

Behind her, set out on the table, were the wild meats that Tanty Lily had slipped past customs. It was these things that her rela-tives dug out of their suitcases—particularly the wild meats—that Clarissa was wary of: the manicou that was really stewed opossum; the succulent cured tatou that turned out to be one unlucky armadil-lo; and the delicious plate of seasoned agouti that was essentially an oversized South American jungle rat. Squirrels, snakes; her relatives with their iron stomachs seemed to find anything with four legs—or no legs—fair game.

But it was the breads and desserts that predominated, and held Clarissa's attention: black cake smelling of rum, sweetbread, and marble cake with rainbow swirls. Clarissa always found it strange that when Americans said marble cake, they were talking about a lump of black and white sponge, when the marble cake made by her family's hands always exploded with color.

Tanty Merle was pounding out the last of the roti. Her skin was cream-brown with flecks of gold, like the cups of cassava and ginger stirred and baked into Christmas pone. Clarissa, sitting on her stool, imagined that there was a time in her mother's life, perhaps even when Euclin was a girl, when Trinidad was like this: freshly picked and killed foods and a flurry of kitchen activity. Her American Trinidad had been an abridged experience: hot currant rolls and heavy-dough bread on Sundays from Allan's Bakery; curried goat and roti nesting in plastic bags from West Indian takeouts; strange, dark foods smuggled in unlabeled condiment jars—absent, the faces that went with the hands that had made them.

Earlier, in the living room, which now smelled of life, Clarissa remembered poring over aged amber photographs of people with ac-cents so much like her mother's, and so unlike her own. There were white spaces along the edges of those photographs, perhaps, for her, a space waiting. Kevin was never asked to help slice the brown edges off bread, or to help carry trays, or to find the bamboo coasters in the dining room hutch. But on this night, Clarissa did not fret about it. She was in the company of these women who made wonderful, delicious things, who took dough and water and sugar and rice and a stray spice here and there and made such incredible edibles with a flick of the wrist, or simply with the pressure of brown hands capped by fingertips the color of scorched cream.

While her mother and the women continued with their brazen talk and market-woman's laughter, she volunteered to knead more dough for the next day's batches of buss-up shot and roti. "No, is so you do it," her mother said, Ophelia cheerfully sticking the heel of her palm into the dough, her dark hand atop Clarissa's pale one. "So. You knead it so."

Clarissa did as her mother told her, vigorously leaning into the dough as expertly as she could. She tried to put the energy she had seen the women around her inject in their cooking—and in doing so, Clarissa began to feel as though she were one of them. A woman now—no longer a girl or a child. "You see this one here?" said Ophelia. "I don't know what to do with this one here. Clarissa there only talking talk about cutting she hair again."

Through various forms of threat and manipulation, her mother had kept her from cutting her hair for six months, and dark-brown ringlets now hung past Clarissa's ears in the halo of a soft bob.

Tanty Lily said, "But she have such good hair."

Tanty Merle said, "She have Spanish hair like she father."

"Don't say that! My hair is not like his!" It was the little black girl, hard as a black pearl deep inside her, who spoke.

"Clarissa, behave!" her mother said. In all this time, Clarissa had not bothered to tell them about all the girls in school who teased her, all the girls who walked behind her in the hall and called out, "Hey, white girl!" or made her *have* to get ugly in the stairwells or the yard after school. All that trouble. To look like her father and be considered more white than black within a black world made her hair a territory to which everyone felt they had a claim—in cutting her hair, Clarissa seized control.

"Babygirl, you don't listen to Felee," Verlee cooed. She stroked her niece's cheek. "Don't even take she on. Long or short, you wear your hair as you please. You hear me?"

"That big horse. That hard-back ting. Is she you calling babygirl?" Ophelia kneaded her fingers into Clarissa's neck. "That's right, eh, love. This is *my* babygirl." Her mother, stooping, kissed Clarissa's forehead. Things grew pleasant again.

Inside they were all flag women, these women in her mother's kitchen, not just on holidays, but 365 days of the year: wildly blaring their whistles, walking and wining and waving their flags without ever losing track of the beat. When their men went after younger flesh, more tender to a fondling hand, they were still waving their flags these women, knowing that life will—and must—go on. And in the same way that too much rum and Guinness made the men talk too loudly and too much out on the porch, an excess of food and beer made these women in her family begin to gossip as they worked.

"Watch she, nah," said Tanty Merle, chucking her chin, capping her lips over the mouth of her Carib. "You eh notice how Feelie only glowing bright, bright so, like some sort of teenager?"

"Is that Yankee man have she bright, bright so. He shining up she kettle."

"Yes," Verlee piped in. "That Yankee man stirring up she pot well good."

Making her way from the table to the stove, Ophelia did not respond immediately to the saucy talk about Linnaeus. Instead, beneath the clean, red linen of her summer dress, she let her massive hips sway as she placed a tear of roti topped with curried potatoes and chicken into her mouth.

"Don't you know there are many uses for an old pot," Ophelia said. "We old pots know *exactly* how to sit on the flame."

The singsong pirouettes of the women's voices transformed into scandalous laughter, until a dull, angry thump rocked the kitchen floor.

It was Mam, Clarissa's grandmother. "All-yuh stop with all-yuh slackness!" Mam tightened her grip on her cane. "And look at Lily—Lily with she both breasts tumbling out like two big, black melongene."

Lily sucked her teeth. "What?" she said, adjusting her bra, "You tink we didn't see when Verlee slip you that half glass of Coke and Old Oak, o' what?"

Pouring Mam another half glass of Coke and rum, Lily slid a

peace offering across the wood-top table. "Why stop at a half glass." She winked. "That bottle of Old Oak still good and full, and Pastor Neville ent here."

Mam tightened her grip on her cane, her parched-corn face turned pommerac red.

But it was all in good fun. Into the break of morning, Clarissa listening so attentively, she did not notice the call of her own sleep. The women gossiped, and drank, and worked:

Remember how all through she pregnancy Mincy Gonzalez tend herd and she daughter born looking like goat each one had a nice pair of legs and a big, big head of hair but Lord them Vancee girls ugly for so I used to feel shame just to watch she stepping out in hot pants and them schupid little set of gyuls they tell you plain they don't want no part of school all they want is man Clarissa forget them boys all they have to offer is what in they pants when she catch she self she do so but how long Margie dead I does say to myself look how Margie just stop so and dead mouth open and tori jump out Lily pass me another Carib, oui.

Clarissa's heavy head, laden with curls, bobbed up, down, up, down, then down, and her eyes shut.

When Labor Day arrived the next morning, the day sped forward like a time-lapse film; the sun rising just as soon as the moon is setting, birds zipping through the sky, cars whizzing by as silver-red streaks of light, monuments rising and falling as clouds plow across the sky and the whole world spins an ugly, ugly eddy.

Noon.

"The ribs are almost ready," Clarissa announced. Ophelia watched as she fashioned a fleshy megaphone with her hands, then shouted again. "Mom said the ribs are almost ready."

Extended family and neighbors crowded the yard. Some of them, as though pitching tents, had staked their corners from as early as 11:00 that morning. Accents wove together. The older West Indian men stood out in their fancy, embroidered guayaberas, a combination jacket and shirt to which Trinidadians referred as shirt jacks. Their African-American counterparts, like Linnaeus, wore polos and T-shirts, dutifully tucked into the waists of their shorts. Both sets of men favored dress caps.

The elder women ran the continuum from demure to whorish. Island grandmothers, in their floral house frocks, sucked their teeth and whispered about their elderly peers who dared to walk by wearing sandals and shorts: "But look at she, nah. Like she trying to play young gyul o' what?" Spandex was a staple for nearly all the middle-aged, heavy women: stretched out in unitards and tube tops, and, in the form of capris, topped by artfully shredded T-shirts, airbrushed or tie-dyed and complemented by dangling beads. Their weight did not seem to trouble the highly appreciative, touchy-feely, sweet-talking Island men, the descendants of kings for whom a fat wife was a treasure.

Those among the younger generation were dressed almost identically, boys and girls favoring the same hip-hop bagginess and ragamuffin, name-brand dishevelment. Occasionally, among the girls (junior versions of their moms), some parroted the ready-for-action, maximum exposure of women in videos. Scattered between the barbecue crowd were a handful of newly arrived West Indian immigrants who, still not fully acclimated, distinguished themselves from the rest of the group in distinct but unintentional ways (by wearing Cross Colours, for instance). And everywhere there was gold: capping teeth, replacing teeth, on wrists, on fingers, on ankles, in earlobes, and—laced with beads of jet—hooked around the pudgy arms of infants. The jet was meant to protect beloved children from *maljo*, the evil eye.

There was dancing, laughter, and foreign phrases fluttering about the yard like exotic butterflies. Ophelia returned with a fresh foil tray laden with buss-up shot and roti skins. The moment it touched the buffet, Mouse took a large serving immediately, accompanied by a big helping of curry.

"But eh-eh, look how Mouse tearing up that roti like he navel string bury in Trinidad," Lily said, reaching for another plate of food. "Go ahead nah, boy, eat up as much as you want. I see you like we Trini food too bad."

Linnaeus, in good spirits from rum and shandys, added, "Seem like no matter what you put down, that boy is always there, ready to devour it."

"You tink I don't see," said Verlee, "how that boy consume food. Before you could say Jack Sprat could eat no fat, his wife could eat no lean, he plate clean and the boy disappear."

All of them laughed, Mouse, too.

A blithe Ophelia massaged the back of Mouse's neck with her hand, "Go ahead boy, you can eat the whole table today if you so desire. Mister Mouse, today, you can do as you please." The skin on Mouse's neck yielded and warmed to her touch, like the nape of a puppy nipped between its mother's jaws in order that she might carry him.

A little while later, Kevin came to his mother, catching her alone in a quiet nook under the porch. "This is what they mean when they say fête!"

"Yes," Ophelia agreed, "but some of these people don't know what it means when you say party done and is time to go home. And is the same blasted ones year after year. Come midnight, I *know* who and how it will be."

"Mom," asked Kevin, turning from the guests, "do you remember when I told you that, financially, it made no sense for me to pay all that money to come home for such a short while? And do you remember what you said to me? You said, 'The cost doesn't matter. It's your presence that does.'"

Ophelia, condensing two half-empty bottles of barbecue sauce said, "Yes, and what about it?"

"Well," he admitted. "You were right. And I was wrong. I'm glad I came. It's like Euclin said, who knows how much longer Mam and Pa will be around? I'm glad she paid for my ticket."

Ophelia was both startled and pleased to hear that Euclin had said this, although Euclin's own absence at family gatherings was a hurtful void.

"For the first time in my life, I'm actually glad you nagged me." Kevin laughed. "I'm having a really great time."

"Who it is you calling nag?" Ophelia asked, smiling.

Kevin, kissing his mother, answered, "You. And without your nagging and your caring how and where I ended up, I would have stayed, you know…" Kevin paused. "The same." A quiet moment passed between them. Kevin looked sheepish. It was the closest he had ever come to apologizing for all the grief and worry she had borne.

She remembered Kevin's final time in juvie, just before she shipped him off to Trinidad: all the little black and brown boys in their orange prison jumpsuits, looking like astronauts who had never had a chance to leave the ground. *These American children are a ting onto themselves*, Ophelia thought, watching him depart. So full of surprises. So full of bewildering possibilities.

"Gather round, gather round," she called to everyone in the yard. On her initiative, cups and bottles of rum and beer were being passed round, the aromatic smell of champagne cola for the children filling the air.

"Kevin, come here." Ophelia drew her son close to her side and began: "We are grateful and blessed to have Kevin here with us today, even though it is only for a short while. And I would like to propose a toast in his honor—that we lift our glasses to the wonderful young man who now stands here before us. For those of you who have known Kevin from baby through the many phases of his life, I can happily say that now that Kevin is going to university, I think my ulcer gone down. And maybe," she crooked an index finger, "maybe I can throw away my medicine now." Everyone laughed, and Ophelia, beaming, drew Kevin close and returned the kiss he had given her.

"To Kevin," she held her glass high.

"To Kevin," everyone toasted.

"And what about Clarissa? She will be starting college, too," someone said.

"And oh, yes, to Clarissa."

"Clarissa," said all.

It's funny how quickly life changes from helium to heavy. All you have to do is take a step. Which is what Ophelia did, away from the grill where she had been finishing broiling a rack of ribs, getting ready to leave the grill to her brother, Niles. Ophelia fanned herself with a dishtowel. "This cross making hot on my chest here, dangling over this grill." She removed the hot crucifix from her flesh, put it down on the slats of wood that fashioned a shelf on the grill, and dashed into the house for more Matouk's pepper sauce.

"Mom's cross." Clarissa, passing the grill, picked it up. "Who found it?"

"I did," Kevin confessed. "Don't say a word—Mouse had it."

"What!"

"It was an accident. Keep your voice down."

"What, like it accidentally jumped in his pocket?"

"Pretty much."

"Stop being stupid, Kev. Tell me what really went down."

Kevin shrugged. "Just like I said, pretty much. When he took a shower, he left his clothes in the bathroom. Then, when he went back to ball up his stuff and put it in his duffle bag, the clothes and the chain somehow got mixed up into one."

"Somehow." Clarissa snorted. "And you stupid enough to believe him?"

"Yeah. As a matter of fact, I am."

"Of course you would, he's your boy."

"Nah, for real though. He don't steal no more." Kevin shrugged again. "I know him, C. Mouse wouldn't do that, and definitely not from our house—and not from Mom."

But Clarissa was distracted. "Look at that."

"What?"

"Up in that tree. That big, black crow. It's so ugly."

Just then, Ophelia's heavy walk shook the metal stairs above. Clarissa looked up at her mother—but Ophelia's great oak face didn't reveal any hint of what she had overheard, let on the truth. A thief. All this time, all these years. She'd been housing and feeding a thief.

Yes, Ophelia did not like Mouse when she first met him. He smelled of the streets. Now she knew that, as most mothers are, she had been right all along.

And the day sped forward, clouds plowing across the sky.

Ophelia sat in one of the extra folding chairs she had rented for the barbecue—her first chance to sit down. As she took it easy, her body grew warm, not only from the sun, but at the thought of her man, her children, her present.

The backyard's gas-powered grill had become Nile's station since Ophelia transferred it over. The apron he wore ("World's Greatest Dad") ornamented his aspiring paunch. Starting from that morning, by the time noon struck, Niles had downed three Caribs. Now, half past noon, he was in the midst of imbibing another. The more Niles drank, the more batches of chicken he burned. Sitting down for his meal, he found that the best pieces of meat had already been taken.

Picking off charred flesh from what was left, he found that two nibbles met bone.

Using her fingernail, Verlee jimmied a charred, hardened fragment of meat that had long forfeited its right to be called chicken from the gap between her left canine and premolar. "Bobo," she said, calling Niles by the name he used in his former life as Rastafarian playboy, "what it is that you was doing in that bathroom upstairs for so long? Like you take a good smoke o' what?"

"Verlee, stop with your blame nonsense!" he said. "If not for me, at least respect the children."

She banged a blackened chicken thigh against the arm of her chair. "Like I say is charcoal I here eating, man—not fowl!" Ophelia laughed.

Soon, Niles was banished to the front porch, where there was no raw meat or fire. And he seemed quite happy to go, as most of the men from the party had congregated there by now.

Clarissa sat on the wall that divided their porch from that of the row house next door. Despite the summer heat, the brick wall felt cool and pleasant against her legs. The men of her family, sitting on the edges of folding chairs webbed with bright nylon slats, standing, drinking beers and stout, some sitting on the wall next to her, were talking *ole talk* with the neighbors, men from the Small Islands, men from the South. Kevin, sitting on the lid of the beer cooler, was cracking and eating unshelled peanuts like an old woman. Mouse sat on the porch's front wall, directly behind him, his body set at a right angle from Clarissa.

Their Antiguan neighbor, Barima, was talking about a recent debacle that he had had at a mechanic's shop; there were times when the car had continued accelerating even when he had his foot on the brake, so he had gone to get it fixed. But before he could continue, somebody called for the clarification of race.

"What was he?" It was Tanty Lily's husband, Shelby who had asked.

Everyone knew right away what he meant by that.

Clarissa had observed, helped along by Ophelia's frequently grumbled complaints, that the American obsession with race made establishing color foremost on the conversational agenda: Black?

White? The listeners ask. As though there are no others.

"Black, a Caribbean fella," said Barima, "I forget which island, though. Now, I tell this fella I have a family reunion to go to," prefaced Barima, beginning his tale in earnest. "I tell him that we driving down to Virginia, and I will need to have the car ready by Friday morn. So I call up the mister, Vernon is his name, and I go, 'Vernon, is the car ready?'

"Vernon say, 'Yes, man, it is ready.'

"I say, 'Vernon, you sure?'

"Vernon say, 'I'm sure.'

"All right then." Barima cocked one finger, signaling the kicker to come. "I get there, my family patiently waiting at home with the luggage, mind you, next thing Vernon tell me he notice something in the exhaust, and he's got a couple more steps to take. You know, we didn't leave New York until two a.m. the next morning, the same day as the reunion itself. Man, when I tell you…" Here Barima sucked his teeth.

"Is the business new?" offered Linnaeus. "Maybe he still hasn't worked out the kinks." Linnaeus, still eating, was salvaging what meat he could rescue from a batch of drumsticks that Niles had burned.

"Kinks!" Barima sucked his teeth again. "I have been going to Vernon for *ten* years now—and he has had that business for more. The only kinks that that Vernon needs to work out are the ones growing out of his head." This drew a round of laughter from the men, along with some back and thigh slapping.

"You people are not easy, you know," said Kingfish, a mechanic himself, who hailed from St. Vincent. "Man, the sort of stories I could tell you."

"Well, did you tell him?" Linnaeus asked Barima.

Barima sniffed, "Tell him what?"

"Have you ever told him that his service is lousy, and if he doesn't improve, you and your wallet are headed elsewhere to someone who will get it right—and there's a very good chance that that person on the other side of the counter won't likely look like either of you?"

"What are you, a politician, o' what?"

"An undertaker," said Linnaeus.

"Man," (more teeth sucking), "I'm a working man. I don't have time for all that."

"Why do we give up on each other so easily," said Linnaeus. It was a statement, no question mark on the end.

"Because we do each other wrong," said Barima. "I told him that I had to have the car the day before. What was so hard to understand about that?"

"Me, I ask," said Linnaeus. "I don't pretend to be a mind reader. I ask my clients what they think about my staff and me because I'm not afraid to hear what they have to say. That's how, in my time, I've come to know and bury generations. The trick to our success at McBride's is that we know how to handle the living as well as the dead."

"Like is a one-man chamber of commerce we have here, o' what," quipped Shorty from Barbados, a motorman for the MTA.

Linnaeus turned to face him. "Have you ever worked with a black mechanic?"

"Once," Shorty said scornfully, fishing through the cooler for another beer. "And once was enough."

"Do you even hear yourself talking?"

"I see," said Barima. "I see I was wrong. You're a mortician who wants to get into politics."

Clarissa had heard this talk many times before: about the Indians, the Jews, the Chinese. As though blacks had created *nothing*. The talk at every gathering invariably turned to black failure, with angry polemics about the areas where other races had surged ahead, while black people had failed—and failed miserably.

Kevin finally said, "There is not a doggone thing wrong with black people except misplaced priorities."

"Priorities, college boy? Is curse black people curse, I telling yuh!" Barima shouted. "*That* is what I know."

"That frame of mind is dangerous," said Linnaeus. "I have seen a different truth, a Southern truth. My great-grandfather was a businessman, too, a businessman who began to encroach on another man's territory—a white man's territory. Then he had the nerve, my great-grandpap, to be looking to expand, asking around about buying a sawmill. The Klan threw a rock with a calling card attached to it through his drawing room window."

"The politician back again I see," said Barima.

Linnaeus ignored him. He wiped the tip of his nose with his handkerchief, and steadied his plate. "It all started with the Black

200

Codes, you know."

Clarissa said, "I don't understand. What are the Black Codes?

"One thing it meant," said Linnaeus. "is that apprenticeship laws forced black children to work for planters—without pay, without even giving their parents a say in it. We couldn't rent land in rural or urban areas, either, and the vagrancy laws were so vague that any black person who couldn't prove that he or she was working for somebody white risked being fined. Want to know what those Codes did? They chopped off our feet before we could even toddle out the gates of slavery.

"What?" he said, looking at Barima specifically. "You think I'm of that bootstrap, elephant-riding camp that blames us for our own sorrow? That it's just that some of us didn't want to move forward? No! There was a collective historical reality—called slavery, emancipation, racism, colonialism—on both sides of the ocean," said Linnaeus. "You West Indians had things different than we did. You had a specific number of sugarcane tasks to chop, then once it was chopped, the rest of the day was your own. Here in the U. S. of A., you had to work from sunup to sundown. It's hard to call one brand of slavery superior to another, but, from what I've read, in the Caribbean—freedom?—our ancestors were given more."

"But," asked Mouse, "how could a slave be free?"

"Sharp," said Linnaeus. "Massa gave out rations to our ancestors here and in the Islands, but in the West Indies, those little plots of land to grow their own gardens and feed themselves were the best gifts that slavery ever gave them. Those little plots meant autonomy."

"So are you saying that we West Indians had slavery *better* then?" asked Niles, his smile thin. The rum he'd recently drunk had grown teeth and a tongue, and Clarissa felt a brawl coming on. "You're saying that the scars from the cat o' nine tails my great-great grandmother had tattooed into her back, that those scars did not mean anything? So you're saying that we had slavery better then?"

"You know I'm not saying that, brother," replied Linnaeus. "And of course your grandmother's scars meant something. But you didn't know the Klan," said Linnaeus. "You knew humiliation, yes, but not horror."

Niles said, "Do you have any idea what they used to do to us—to our ancestors—down there? The most barbaric thing I heard of was how they'd tie each limb of a captured brother to four different, flexible trees, then cut the rope and his arms and legs would be ripped from their sockets, his body torn to pieces. The seeds of that terror were planted into the walls of black women's wombs like seeds that you drop into the black earth. You want to talk about humiliation, let's also talk about colonialism and institutional racism."

"But at least you got something to show in the end for your misery," argued Linnaeus. "Now those Islands are yours."

But Clarissa kept on thinking. She couldn't help it. For, at that moment, a chill had migrated up her spine and crystallized around her heart as she visualized a whip marking the backs of each man, woman, and child in the amber family photographs that lined the piano. And Clarissa wondered why she was hearing this story for the first time, why no one had taken the time to tell her this story of her great-great-grandmother before. And as Clarissa kept on thinking, a hate-filled black speck grew into a seed in her heart, and planted itself beneath the pale diamonds of frost that had framed her discovery.

Long past the day it was planted, as the seed grew, she would begin to see topics such as the ones that the men had discussed more clearly. For instance: It had become a rite of passage, she would observe, for (all) immigrants to immediately scale one rung up the American social ladder by standing on the backs of African-Americans. They said to themselves: *Sure our accents sound funny—but at least we are not black. Yes, our clothes are hand-me-downs and out of fashion—but at least we are not black. True, I survive off welfare and food stamps, for now—but at least I am not black. In my own country, I would not be ranked among the brightest or the best, but here I can be* ANYTHING, *because at least I am not black.*

And black immigrants—Caribbeans, Africans, Latinos—in their hearts and heads were immigrants first. They said to themselves: *Sure our accents sound funny—but at least we are not* AMERICAN *blacks. Yes, our clothes are hand-me-downs and out of fashion—but at least we are not* AMERICAN *blacks. True, I survive off welfare and food stamps, for now—but at least I am not an* AMERICAN *black. In my own country, I would not be ranked among the brightest or the best, but here I can be* ANYTHING, *because at least I am not an* AMERICAN *black.*

Until, one evening, after the sun has set, still just a boy, you wander into the wrong neighborhood in search of a used car, clutching an umbrella—no more than that—and end up dead, shot twice in the heart by a snarling mob.

Until your football accidentally bounces off a patrol car, next thing—you are gripped in an illegal chokehold and are slowly dying.

Until forty-one bullets ring out in the dawn.

Until the handle of a bathroom plunger ends up in a place it has no right to be.

And then came another rite of passage as you understand, under the pale diamonds of frost: You are just black, just plain black—no longer innocents, no longer immigrants. Your armor is gone, and you are dragged headfirst into the eternal American fracas called race.

Yes, Clarissa had heard the talk many times before: About how the Indians, the Jews, the Chinese had worked smart and worked hard to become successful. As though Blacks had created *nothing*.

Tanty Lily sliced open a five-gallon bag of ice cubes with a paring knife and emptied it into the cooler. "There is no curse," she said. "It's about not having a sense of who you are, *that's* what keeps you downtrodden. No sense of where you came from, or where you are going."

"The curse is the way that we treat each other and ourselves," added Linnaeus. "The curse is denying that our African past is the keystone to building our future."

"You want to hear the truth?" Tanty Merle laughed, and hoisted a Carib to her lips. "Our house lay right next door to Mr. Ho's shop. And when I tell yuh in truth, them Chinee children stay at home, study book, and mind shop. That was life for them Chinee children. Of course you go be bright and get ahead if only book is your friend."

Pa replied, both a question and a dare: "Then why the black boy can't make book he friend, *too?*"

"What, you think all black people blame schupid, o' what?" schupsed Tanty Merle. "Just look at Kevin. Yes, just look at Kevin. You need look no further than this porch."

Several heads nodded approvingly, admiringly, everyone looking to Kevin.

And Clarissa burned inside, longing to be called bright, intelligent just once. She wanted—just once in her life—to be admired and marveled at for something other than beauty. She wanted—just once in her life—to be someone's star.

"Sure we have our bright ones, but not enough," said Barima. "Especially not in this generation."

"If we're shabby at business," Linnaeus was insisting, "it's because we put the cart before the horse. The Civil Rights movement focused too much energy on political reform and far too little on economic empowerment." Several of the other men tried to join into the verbal fray, voice their opinion: "But listen nah, but listen nah…" They jockeyed to be heard. Their voices sounded like barking.

In a tree near the porch, two crows had descended onto a branch.

"Let's head up to the Parkway," Mouse said. "And pick up Addie."

"Yeah, it's getting late," said Kevin. "We'll only catch the tail end of the parade. We should tell Mom." He turned to Clarissa.

"No," Clarissa said, still thinking of the day, and the many ways that she had been rendered invisible. Clarissa felt no desire to converse at length with anyone else. Not even their Mom. She was also reeling from the confusion she now felt, as the black seed dissolved the pale diamonds of frost that had once covered it, its bitterness beginning to liquefy—and mingle with her blood. Clarissa just felt angry—and she didn't know why. "No need to tell her. Let's just go," she said.

Euclin, in a cab, was fighting the old superstition: When your ears ring, someone is speaking your business—calling your name.

And they probably were talking about her, wondering why she hadn't come to the barbecue. The answer was simple and selfish. At the barbecue there would be questions—bothersome ones, and too many of them, about her job and her love life. It would be a gathering of people who knew nothing about the concept of personal space. About stepping over the line. Or that there even was one.

It was after the first and only time that she'd brought Brent home that her mother had taken to calling her White Woman. Even four years of Madeira and the accompanying tilt to the lilt in her voice had not inspired such vitriol. In her mother's mouth, White Woman became a slur. Shorthand for the foreign—the soulless, the *other.*

And forget about using Angus as a diversion. If she dared bring *him* home, already she knew the first question that they would pose: "You and Brent mash up o' what?"

"No, we're still together."

Then Angus, being brawny, brainy, beautiful, and black—and very much not her boyfriend—would be flooded with queries both overt and sly about the whereabouts of his girlfriend or about his conjugal status. Immediately, the mental calculating, matchmaking with daughters, friends and friends of friends would begin. And how could she explain that recently, Angus had taken a fancy to men? Why spend the afternoon dodging questions and spinning lies when all she wanted were the simple things: some shade, buss-up shot with curry, and barbecue?

The answer was to opt out. Euclin had found her solution. Cowardly? No, brilliant. By not being present, there would be no questions, and nothing to explain.

Angus sat in the taxi's back seat beside her. From the Upper West Side they were headed downtown to Chelsea to pick up Raymond, Angus' boyfriend, and Raymond's friends Kiki and Cocoa, fraternal-twin drag queens. The quintet would then go to that year's Wigstock celebration in the East Village at Tompkins Square Park.

"Do you really think it will be that easy?" Angus said. "Just not show up?"

"No. Of course not. Such is my life, a delusional mixture of deflection and denial. The first thing Mum'll do is complain about how skinny I am, then she'll try to fatten me up for the slaughter." Euclin pinched the flesh on her wrist, then said haughtily, "As if I don't eat. Don't I eat, Gus?"

"Sometimes. But when you do, it's with relish—which keeps me from worrying about you those times when you do not. You know how our people be," Angus quipped. "We like us some biiiiig women: When you're riding a bike, you know…You want some handles that you can hold onto."

Euclin laughed and slapped his hand. "Nasty!" She joked, "Why everything got to be so doggone scandalous with you?"

Just then, Euclin's cell phone rang.

"We spoke too soon," she said. Her mother's number had appeared in the phone's caller ID window as she lifted it out of her LV tote.

"Who is it?" asked Angus.

Euclin replied, "The inquisition."

Angus smiled. "Your mom?"

Euclin nodded.

The phone continued ringing.

"Aren't you going to pick it up?"

Lethargically, she began to go through the motions.

Angus laughed. "Easy now, if you're nice to her, I'm sure she'll be nice back."

"Hello?"

The voice on the other line said, "Hi. It's me."

"Kevin?" This confused Euclin initially, until she remembered the ticket. "Baby—you're here! Kev." Euclin laughed, then confided. "I thought you were Mum—I almost didn't pick up the phone." Then she whispered: "You know how *that* goes."

Kevin laughed; her keeper of secrets.

"I borrowed the cellphone you gave her," Kevin said. "Clarissa, Mouse, Addie and I are on our way to the Parkway." In the background she heard the other three yelling *Hiiiii!*, followed by giggles, hollering, and hooting. Kevin said, "You should have come to the barbecue—you would have had fun. Mom's been really, really mellow this entire time. I guess she's just happy to see me. The day I came, I purposely rang the bell, instead of using my key. You should have seen her face when she came to answer the door—and there I was."

Euclin laughed. "Listen to you, just loving you some drama!" Then she asked, "So how is Cali, my love—what is your new life made of?"

"Hiking, swimming, surfing, long drives, brunches—a girl. The one I told you about. I've been calling this summer with Ashley and her family my Cali taste test, then it's on to Palo Alto. School starts when I get back."

But stuck on one groove in the story, Euclin teased, "Her again! I thought you were out there for a pre-semester summer program."

"No, no, I decided not to do that. That's the whole point—I told you that. I flew out there early to hang with Ashley."

She hadn't asked enough questions on the way to the airport. She liked the fact that he had found someone, but already he was placing this girl before school. This Ashley began to worry her a little. Driving Kevin to Kennedy, Euclin had thought that he was headed directly to Stanford. There was a seven-year difference between them. What was going on in that head of his? Would he take her advice? Euclin loved her brother—no, make that adored him. But what did she really know about him?

"Forgive me for being such a poor listener the first time round," she said.

206

"Don't sweat it," said Kevin. "Like I said before, her mother's blonde, from Cali. Her father's Chinese—from the Mainland. They met when he came to study at Berkeley, and he never went back. He's a geneticist. She's a visual artist, and a biophysics dropout. They're the coolest parents in the world. Really laid back." Kevin continued, "They have a weekend house out in Big Sur. That's where we're staying. We've gone camping, driven down to Carmel, visited the aquarium at Monterey. They're thinking about moving to their house in Big Sur for good."

"Where are they now?"

"Marin County—which is not too shabby, either."

"I know." Euclin was nodding, though her brother couldn't see her, adding, "Well, that was fast." By this she meant the girl.

Kevin said, "Sometimes that's how things happen. Ashley, she's good for me. Leaving New York has been good for me, too."

"That's awesome," said Euclin. "I must see you before you go. I know—maybe you can come by and hang with me and the Bush Mobb while we're in the studio. Tomorrow we're laying down some tracks. I'll call you in the morning, and let you know what time—and give you the address."

Kevin said, "Cool. I'd love that."

Then they said their goodbyes, and Kevin was gone.

A small sunburst of wonder popped in her voice as Euclin, leaning back in the seat, turned to Angus. "He's so incredible, my brother. So focused now, so different. Such a good, sweet kid."

"What a happy little girl she is. So full of jokes and chat," Mam fawned and cooed. "Look how bright she is, spilling out laughter." Mam, Ophelia, Verlee, Lily, and Merle were all fussing over Niles's and Cordelia's baby daughter, Indigo, whom Mam was dandling on her knee. With her angular features and her long ballerina's limbs, this beautiful child, at four years old, was a pecan-colored replica of Euclin.

"You don't see how she does follow she daddy around like a tail." Ophelia laughed, plucking her niece from her mother's lap. "Euclin used to do the same thing. Anytime Cecil had to leave the house, you talk about bawl. 'No daddy, no, no daddy, don't go! And Euclin throw she self around he leg until the man can't move." Ophelia, kissing Indigo, set her down on the floor, smoothing the creases in her toddler's halter and shorts.

"And I could see exactly why Indigo love she daddy so," said Merle, confirming with Verlee, "And you ent fine she looking like Niles in print?"

"But I also fine she resemble the mother and she have a bit for the grandmother," added Lily. Like many Trinidadians, she used the word fine in lieu of find.

To which Verlee responded, "You fine?"

"No, is Euclin she favor," said Ophelia. "You don't see."

Just then, Ansel, Lily's eight-year-old son, and the son of another guest, came barreling across the yard, playing tag and roughhousing. Indigo, caught up in their playtime tempest, lost her footing in her petite sandals and fell on the flagstone floor.

"WAAAAAAH!"

"You have no home training!" Mam called out angrily. "No *brought-upcy.*" Standing up, she coaxed the still crying Indigo into the bony but welcoming crook of her lap.

"We're just playing," Ansel said. "Why don't you leave me alone!"

"Who you tink you talking to!" Lily grew fangs and began pounding away, clouting him about the ears, head, and shoulders. "Like you lose your mind, o' what? How you could answer granny back so?"

"Come again, nah. Is back chat you want to back chat!" Mam, vindicated by Lily, stood up and shook her fist like a cudgel. "Come. Meh hand still straight, you know."

Merle, sucking on a piece of pickled pig from the souse bowl lazily egged her on. *And the ghost of the overseer's whip went down.*

Linnaeus shook his head and picked up Indigo.

"Today it's like they're wired for defiance," observed Ophelia.

Niles came and took Indigo. "I don't believe in hitting children. I believe in talking to them. We grew up thinking that these children need to be hit, just as we were. It's a legacy of slavery, you know. No," he said, his scorn evident. There was also real pain in his voice.

Linneaus added, "They're reasonable, intelligent little human beings who know—or can be taught—the difference between right and wrong."

"Slavery, slavery, slavery. Everything is the black man and slavery. What I tell you, Bobo," Verlee joked, calling her brother again by his

Rastafarian name. "Is kill you killing the people mood. Come nah, lewwe go dance!"

So Verlee put "Nani Wine" on the turntable, and all began to dance. This was the way it was at family gatherings: seventy-year-olds dancing with two-year-olds. Women dancing with women. Siblings thrashing about on the floor, locked in lewd and questionable embraces. It was a ritual, a way of life, a form of expression, a West Indian way of loving, and nearly everyone in the yard was singing "Nani Wine," their voices seeming to rise as high as the day's hidden stars.

"But how, when Verlee live alone and I have three children, you could give us both the exact same ting?" Ophelia was haggling over the equal amounts of food and goods from home that she and Verlee had been given.

Mam was doling out the spoils from her suitcase: one bottle of Kuchela; one bottle of amchar; five packs of channa; three packs of kurma; and half a black cake each.

"Is three of you, Feelie," countered Mam. "Is three children I have, and each of you get the same."

In truth, they didn't. Ophelia had always found it curious that, in the division of the spoils, Niles was always off busy somewhere, never present, which had led Ophelia to wonder if Niles was getting things—surplus helpings or extra special little things—denied to herself and Verlee. Now, Mam raked through her suitcase, revealing the yellow of a barbadeen bushel. Barbadeen, when squeezed through muslin, made a liquid that when swizzled with evaporated milk and sugar became a delicious, creamy beverage. Nowhere in Brooklyn had Verlee or Ophelia ever found it. Verlee caught sight of the barbadeen, too, and their collective oohs and aaahs lit up the guest bedroom like kindling.

"Mum, pass that barbadeen here, nah!" said an excited Ophelia. She just wanted to touch it.

"That, we will get to that later." And like an animated cast-iron bank swallowing a quarter, the barbadeen bushel had disappeared with a flick of their mother's thin wrist. Why, Ophelia wondered, did each visit by her parents embark with joy then shipwreck on the lingering sense of someone having been cheated? Ophelia knew why: because she—with her three kids and Verlee with none—never really got the same. And Niles—with his two children—got more than both of them. This was serious business.

And this was why, as children, Ophelia always carried herself in direct opposition to Verlee. When Verlee shimmied up Mr. Syril's mango tree in her best Sunday garb, Ophelia stood chastely on the ground. When Verlee was bad and grey, Ophelia was golden. When Verlee threw away her books and went to chip chip behind band after band for Carnival, Ophelia studied harder, excelled.

Still, it was Verlee and Niles on whom her mother had always doted, had always adored.

Much later, Ophelia was coming downstairs with the watermelon that Kevin had requested a whole half hour before. It was not a big one because all the big ones at the Pathmark were gone. The melon was round, almost cranial.

What she did not know was that because it had taken a while before she'd gotten around to retrieving it, Kevin, Clarissa, and Mouse had grown tired of waiting out on the porch for the melon slices and left to meet up with Addie.

What she did not know was that one of the younger children had left a toy on the porch stairs, a toy she did not see. And with this, Ophelia's foot went back, twisted just enough to lose her balance, and the watermelon she was carrying went forward, flying through the air. Up, up, up, then down. It landed on the hard flagstones in the yard, and all that was left was the softness of red, large, bright pulpy fragments.

"Look at that, I ent even self see that toy, you know," said Ophelia. There was an air of incredulity in her voice, not anger at the waste, but surprise and a little sadness. Ophelia, bending down, picked up the hollow fragments of gourd. With the sheets of floral-patterned paper towel she scooped up soft hunks of the melon's spoiled red insides and trashed them.

It was at that moment, suddenly, that something dawned on her.

It was in fact at the final phase of the cleanup, when Ophelia was about to move past the point of using paper towel—at the point where she was about to rise from her knees and wash away the last bits of sticky red, whose sweetness had already begun to attract flies—that this thing dawned on her.

"Where is Kevin? Did Kevin leave?"

Ophelia asked again, "Where is Kevin?"

"Kevin? Kevin gone long time," Verlee said. "Clarissa, Mouse, too."

And Ophelia got up from on her knees. There was something in the air. There was something in her.

CHAPTER NINETEEN

All of we is one. Labor Day in Brooklyn was a day of unity, not of balkanization among the West Indians of the various islands. All the prejudices that kept the older generations apart dissolved in the close embrace of wining and song. *All of we is one:* The Barbadians who sound like they are chewing their food, the Jamaicans who swallow their h's, the Trinidadians who always sound like a flock of scattering, high-pitched birds. The Islanders, who found themselves marked from their Brooklyn peers by their various scars from mango-tree climbing, were their parents' children today: Trinidadian, Bajan, Haitian, Jamaican, Guyanese, Small Island—too many to name— are all proud to be Caribbean, and for one day, abandon the grind of pretending to be American. Religion didn't matter, either; skinny lit- tle church girls abandoned their Payless heels for the shortest shorts, whistles, and sneakers. And as the day advanced, the bacchanalian spirit endowed the revelers with a superhuman strength, squeezing out the day's last juices; as long as there was a truck with twenty-foot speakers two feet ahead, they were willing to walk, wine, and jump into infinity.

Kevin, Clarissa, Addie, and Mouse were passing someone's front garden. Two rows of sunflowers, with their drooping necks, yellow curls, and sad, black faces watched them go by. Kevin, Clarissa, and Mouse were now waiting, loitering in the parking lot of a Wendy's restaurant. Addie was changing in the bathroom inside. When she emerged, finally, there was an astonished silence between the three. They were marveling at shorts that sliced her brown buttocks into perfect melon wedges, her white halter with red polka dots, her black gladiator sandals seductively snaking up dewy calves. Mouse and Kevin, for a moment, seemed to regard Addie in a different light. Clarissa noticed. Clarissa, herself, was dressed modestly in knee- length shorts and a T-shirt silk-screened with a Trinidad flag, overlaid with a steel drum and two mallets. Kevin and Mouse seemed to consider for a moment—Addie—then remembered the things that were important to her, the kind of girl that she was.

They all walked down the street, cars honking from all directions, strange men calling out to her. Addie called back to them, laughed, moved into the group's inner sanctum, closer to her friends. Clarissa wanted to protect her friend. Mouse and Kevin kept walking—their once-attentive gazes now focused on other things.

On the day of the parade, starting from Empire Boulevard, no cars were allowed to climb up the hilly part of Utica Avenue that leads up to Eastern Parkway. Eastern Parkway, where all were headed, had been under construction for more years than were countable. Yet even with new benches, new trees, pseudo-Victorian streetlights, and the new slate-grey tiles that smoothed the sidewalks, the Parkway, with its daily waltz of illegal dollar cabs and its hustle and bustle, felt as though little had changed.

There was chaos when Kevin, Clarissa, Addie, and Mouse reached the top of the hill. People selling whistles and neon necklaces. Cans of soda for a dollar. Baby carriages. Jerk chicken broiling inside of oil-drum barbecues. The police, ubiquitous and blue, were a counterpoint to the Island women who made a hobby of teasing them. The women gyrated within an inch of the officers' bodies, making them squirm and blush. At one stop, a man dressed as Neptune was egging on a policeman who was trapped between two women, one lithe, the other corpulent, both agile, both pretty. Neptune called out to the trio and stamped his triton on the asphalt for emphasis: "Do the ting, man. *That* is it man—do the ting!" Drinking sloppily from a disposable cup, Neptune danced in a happy circle, the sweat and beer dripping down his beard, swinging like the tentacles of some exotic fish.

The Parkway was a seventy-two-pack meltdown of color, a mile and a half of national flags, head dresses, glitter, and spears, the revelers bound together in a heaving, lascivious unity that began at J'ouvert. J'ouvert, a French expression for early morning, is a precursor parade in which people chip—take short, lazy steps in time to the steel drum bands—or run half-naked through the streets, their bodies caked in mud. The mud is meant to obliterate differences of class and race among those chipping. *Égalité! Fraternité!* Cocooned in mud, *all of we is one.*

Flanking the action on the main road, the downtown and uptown service roads of Eastern Parkway had become alleyways of confusion and pleasure. The crowd was *jumping up* past the brownstones, car-wash, pharmacy, synagogues, prewar apartment complexes, churches, park benches, and pseudo-Victorian streetlights. Perched atop moving flatbed trucks, oversized speakers blared calypso, soca and reggae, as plainclothes merrymakers danced alongside, blowing whistles and waving flags and colored bandanas. They did a line dance, commanded by the DJ who was spinning from the back of the flatbed. There were dancers on the trucks as well, but they hardly had room to move, and most were less colorful than the dancers below.

The trucks, with their savage tires, were massive, and there was always the threat of being crushed. Nearly every year someone got killed that way. Pushed by accident, pushed on purpose, gone under running from a fight. One year a man said goodbye to the people he loved, then dipped his body under the wheel. And always there was the threat of fight, a stampede: resulting in the screaming and crushing of thousands.

But overall, year after year, it was pleasant. And, year after year— larger, swollen—the crowds returned. Kevin, Clarissa, Addie and Mouse walked and danced down Eastern Parkway. A man swung by in an undulating bolero and suit made entirely of white plastic forks. Sheathed in iridescent green sequins, a cocoa-skinned woman—Medusa for the day—tugged at the strings on her arms, causing the snakes on her head to menace the crowd. Avoiding the powder and mud bandits, the four friends slipped into a band, and did not let each other go. They wined in unison, interlinked bodies forming one body—legs upon legs upon legs closely moving together like the body of a centipede, then like that of a millipede as strangers joined the line.

Along the way, they stopped to eat again. Kevin and Clarissa were chewing on sugarcane; after sucking out all the sweet liquid, the stalk was airy on the tongue and as fibrous as sawdust. Mouse was sucking on a mango, and the bright yellow threads were stuck in his teeth. Yet walking made them tired and thirsty, so mainly they drank water and sodas.

The weather was two-faced this time of year, hot in the morning, cool in the evening, all without warning, delineating the absolute end of summer and its warm nights and warm days. From this point on, there would be mixed weather, ending with winter's cold bite on both cheeks.

The girls, a threesome, were dressed as mermaids with flowing blonde and black weaves and clamshell brassieres. In the sun, their flesh glistened, moist, plentiful.

"Choice," said Kevin.

"Prime rib, son. Now *that*," said Mouse, "is what I call scrum-dil-ly-umptious, kid." Mouse made sure he said this loud enough for the girls to hear.

"No doubt," said Kevin, smiling.

Unlike Addie, there was no friendship, no history. Mouse and Kevin ogled until they were filled. The girls in the band and their flatbed truck advanced at a crawl down the Parkway. They turned and waved at Kevin and Mouse with shy smiles, then, farther away, turned again with a look of longing. Mouse and Kevin laughed that knowing boy's laugh, slapped hands at their luck.

Mouse said, "That was just edible."

"No diggity," laughed Kevin.

Up came Addie, sucking her teeth. "That wasn't even their hair."

She had been wronged a half-hour before, and since that time, had not stopped pouting. A marauding group of dirty boys had surrounded her, wining, groping. Lost in a wave of T-shirts, low-slung jeans, and nimble hands Addie's voice had bubbled out from their center as though she were drowning, "Get off me. Get off me. Mouse! Kevin! N$gga, I said to get off!"

When they saw Kevin approaching, the wolf pack had gone as quickly as they had come, laughing and whooping. Mouse didn't move.

Addie crossed her arms around her chest. "Why didn't you help me!"

"I was coming," said Kevin.

"Well, you didn't come soon enough." Addie's clothes were twisted, her hair flattened and frayed, her lip gloss a smear.

"That's what you get for dressing like a slut," said Mouse.

"I can dress however I please!" snapped Addie, and cursed him.

"I'm here to have fun, not be your bodyguard. Prepare to be leaving here in rags once all these dogs are done sniffing and pawing you. That wasn't the end of it. I know."

"Shut it!" Addie pounded Mouse's chest with her fists. "Shut your face."

Mouse just laughed. "Go put some clothes on."

"Yo, man, chill," said Kevin. "Cut it. Addie—here." Removing his nylon jacket, Kevin tied it around Addie's waist. He patted the knot. There. "I think you'd better keep that on."

Addie smiled. "Thanks, Kev."

"Girls don't know nothing," Mouse said. "You lucky Kevin's here."

"We girls know not to be boys, and that's the only thing we *need* to know," said Addie.

"Holla!" Clarissa, smiling, slapped Addie a high five, then stuck out her tongue at Kevin and Mouse.

Addie pulled out her compact and repaired the damage to her lip gloss.

Clarissa flung herself on Kevin's back. "I want a piggy back ride. Come on, give me a piggy back ride, boy!"

"What the…Get off me, you big-legged thing!"

"Aw, come on, twin. There's something going on up there. I want to see. Please, pleaaase, I want to see!"

"All right already—whatever."

Clarissa scaled her brother's back. Helping her to balance, Kevin adjusted his weight. The truth was that there was nothing to see. Clarissa had simply had an urge that Kevin's back, Kevin's shoulders, was the place she needed to be. And here she sat still, mussing his hair, smelling his peppermint shampoo. And there she remained for as long as she could, until her brother could no longer carry her.

The man said the picture would cost seven.

"A single picture?" Clarissa was talking. The price, like the cost of everything else on the Parkway that day, had been inflated.

"So—you want to take the picture?" They hadn't realized that they were taking a long time to decide.

"Yeah, sure," Clarissa said. She motioned the rest toward her. Kevin linked arms with her. She laid her head against Kevin's left shoulder, prepared to lift it just in time for the flash. Mouse crouched in front, ghetto style, one elbow on his knee, his knuckles propping his chin. Addie held two fingers up behind Mouse's head, gamely flexing one leg.

The man moved back, pointing his Polaroid. He dropped the camera, dissatisfied. "Too wide a shot," he said. The camera hung over his heart. Gesticulating, he suggested that they shift poses, altering the scene.

They settled for simplicity in the end, arms around each other's waists and shoulders.

The man pulled out the Polaroid shot, disposing the wrapping. Kevin, Addie, and Mouse congregated over the still-warm photograph, waiting for themselves to materialize out of the tiny fog. Clarissa was paying the man.

"I ran out of change," said the man. He beckoned, crooking a finger, took back the picture. "I'll hold onto this," he said. He gave Clarissa back the twenty. "Here. Hold on, I'll make change from what I have. I'll be back."

They waited.

Waited.

Waited.

"We can't stand around forever," Addie said.

"Just give him one more minute," Clarissa said.

"Aw, just come on," said Mouse.

They moved on, Clarissa lagging, looking back, searching for the man's face in the crowd.

"He's not coming back. Come on," said Kevin.

"I was just hoping…Just wait a minute, y'all." Clarissa scanned the crowd a final time, pushed her hands in the pockets of her shorts, then caught up with the others, walking quickly.

She had really wanted that picture—felt like she needed that picture before Kevin left New York.

The parade was winding down.

Squeezing out the last of the day's juices, they followed a merry band of Haitians, Compas rocking from their flatbed truck. For miles they followed the Haitians and their van as they rounded street corners, unquestioning, turning off to destinations unknown.

Suddenly the music stopped. The crowd dispersed. The police had created a roadblock. Kevin, Clarissa, Addie, and Mouse wandered idly through unfamiliar back streets, passing other people from the Carnival.

"It's getting late. I want to go home," said Kevin.

"Don't be such a sourpuss," Clarissa said, sweeping her palm through his hair. "Come nah, old man, the parade done, but the day isn't over."

"I heard about a party down near your Aunt Verlee's house," said Addie.

"I'm down. I don't want to go home," said Mouse.

"Shoot. You *know* I don't want to go home!" said Addie.

They stood at an impasse. Their eyes, not their mouths said it: *Kevin?*

"I'm tired, yo." He looked twisted, pressured, bronzed, and beaten from the heat. He scraped his sneaker against the curb. Beige gum came off the bottom.

Clarissa said, "Labor Day won't come again until next year."

Mouse put his hand on Kevin's shoulder. "N$gga, when I'm pumped like this, you know I don't want to go home. What say you?"

"OK, OK," said Kevin. "I'll go."

They took the subway as far as they could, jumped into a dollar cab, then walked the rest of the way. When they arrived, the party that they were looking for was nowhere to be found.

They looked forlorn.

They looked sweaty.

They looked pitiful.

They looked like most West Indians do when the parade is over, but Labor Day still had hours to go.

In Trinidad, the end was definitive, merciful: When midnight struck, it was Ash Wednesday, and everyone fell to their knees. But this was New York, and every man and woman was his or her own cathedral, had his or her own calling, and made his or her own rules.

What do you do when the party is still trapped inside of you?

What do you do when, even though your body's still, your heart is still *jumping up?*

If you hear music, you follow. And if you are in Trinidad—and the time is nearing midnight—you do not walk, you run.

"We don't even know these people," said Kevin.

There were at least a hundred people at the backyard party, hanging out on the porch, leaning against cars, spilling drinks, spilling out onto the sidewalk.

"Don't be so sour. You hear that bass?" said Addie. Grabbing his arm, she led the way.

The music took up residence inside them. Their postures improved. The night air dried their sweat. Mouse, hungry again, boldly stood in line and got a free plate of food. He came back with three Guinness Stouts balanced in the crook of his arm. Kevin and Addie each took one.

"Reach into my pocket, Rissa," he said, one hand balancing the plate, the other importing a chicken breast to his lips.

"You nasty, I'm not reaching in there."

"Yo, will you stop acting dumb? Reach in. I got something for you."

Cagily, she slid her hand in. Shrieking, she recoiled. "Eeew, what you got in there that's so cold!"

Addie, proxy, stuck her hand in. "It's a soda, silly." She wedged the cold metal against Clarissa's chest. "How sweet—here, Minnie Mouse. He remembered that you don't drink."

Clarissa thanked him, and gulped it down, grape bubbles fizzing into her nostrils.

Just as the crowd completed the happy frenzy of the Donkey Dance, the signature wine that accompanied the United Sister's soca song of the same name, the DJ put on Super Cat's "Cabin Stabbin." Men tightly drew their partners around the waist; women flexed and grew feisty; hands went up in mock gun salutes—bow-bow-bow—index fingers pointed up.

What is the meaning of Cabin Stabbin?

What do you do when the party is still trapped inside of you?
When the right song comes on,

> you
>> lose
>>> your
>>>> mind.

"Awwwwww sh—!"

The streetlights flicked on. It was officially evening.

Mouse grabbed Clarissa. They cut a path through the driveway that served as the dance floor. Suddenly, they were the center of everything.

With so many bodies, the yard was a steam bath. Clarissa and Mouse lifted their sticky T-shirts from their skin, as their flesh began to ooze sweat. They started their dance as a freestyle, arms barely touching. Soon they were doing a slow dancehall *grind*—same as everybody else—but the gulf between their bodies made it look like an instructor's demonstration, not the real thing.

"Come here, girl. No time to act stupid," Mouse said, grabbing her by the waist. Clarissa did not decline. Bodies suctioned, they began to grind lovely.

What do you do when the party is still trapped inside of you?

The dance, not who you're dancing with, becomes supreme. On the Parkway, your desire to dance is so strong, so insatiable, it is only after the dance is over that you turn around and see, all this time, that it was an ugly man rubbing his bulging front on your backside. But you wanted to dance, so what do you care? When he leaves, you make a mental note: *Ugly men dance good.*

What do you do when the party is still trapped inside of you?

In an infernal backyard, Super Cat on, you let a boy whom you've loathed for half your life put his arm around your waist, rub his pelvic bone against you, chafing the meat of your thigh. And suddenly, you take note of things that you have never noticed before. His body's lean muscularity, for instance.

A wind lanced the night, and in that cool summer air, Clarissa could not help but inhale his good smell. It unnerved her, so she let go, saying, "Excuse me, Mouse, I gotta pee."

On her way to find a place to relieve herself, she wondered: *Is it possible for sweat to smell like peaches?*

Mouse watched Clarissa go. He was thinking, *She dance mad good.* He wondered why she only wore long shorts and jeans. He watched her, standing in one place, coolly scanning her surroundings. She crossed the street, looked around again before crouching between two cars. Mouse looked away, to let her be.

Next to him, a dread wearing a red, gold, and green tank top was puffing away.

"Yo, man, you got smokes?" Mouse said.

"Done, man. I all out." He held up an empty Newport pack, grinned at Mouse, crushing the cardboard in one fist.

Mouse recognized the accent. He sounded like Clarissa and Kevin's Uncle Niles. Then he recognized something else—someone else. It was the guy he'd gotten into a fight with at the Blakk Rukus party the previous Columbus Day. Mouse's face became a snarl, and they locked eyes. Now the guy had a friend—the kind of guy who made other men cross the street to avoid trouble. Mouse's face darkened even further. *I'm not scared of them. LayQuan. Yeah, that was that kid's name.* LayQuan held up his Heineken, stared Mouse square in the eye and smirked. Then he and his friend disappeared.

Mouse, seeking out Kevin, found him free-styling with a reed-thin girl, pure Brooklyn: The girl's earrings were large and gold, her hair stained maroon, her legs unshaven. A diamond-studded gold cap beamed brilliantly, like a lighthouse, from her front tooth. The girl kept leaning forward and talking to Kevin, talking his ear off. The girl was all teeth. Clearly envied by all the other girls, she looked enthralled to be by his side. Kevin just looked trapped. Mouse laughed to himself, and thought, *I woulda done ditched that chickenhead. That n$gga way too nice.*

Kevin and the gold-toothed girl were no longer alone.

The girl was yelling at the newcomer, "Blocker, why you don't go home and cool yourself. I ask you if you want to come, and you tell me no. Now you come here to bother me. Get the freak off of me!" The boy named Blocker grabbed the girl's elbow. In the fray, the girl hurled her Heineken bottle at him but missed. The bottle hit the house's aluminum siding, spraying glass.

"Hey, ease up. Don't handle her like that man," said Kevin.

"Back off, pretty boy. This is between me and her," said the boy, cursing. "Yo, I said to back off!"

The boy and the girl began to wrestle. The boy slapped the girl. Kevin made a move like he was about to intervene, do something. The girl left. The guy stayed. The boy, for the rest of the night, kept eyeballing Kevin.

Mouse sidled up to Kevin and whispered, somewhat breathless from having made his way through the crowd: "Remember that n$gga named LayQuan I jacked up at that Columbus Day party we was at for Blakk Rukus? That guy, Blocker—I saw him before. He was just with him."

"Let's get out of here," Kevin said.

"I'm not afraid of that punk," Mouse said, boldly looking in the direction of the boy that the girl had called Blocker. "He's not going to spoil my fun."

Blocker stared back. "You got an eye problem, man?"

Mouse replied, "Maybe I do." Mouse's anger grew tall, like a bear rising up on hind paws.

A mild shoving match quickly ensued between them. Mouse shoved him hard. Blocker nearly fell to the ground, but regained his balance—just in time.

Angrily, he cursed Mouse. "N$gga, you a dead man!" he said, pointing one jittery finger as another one of his friends pulled him away.

"Oh, am I?" Mouse said, "So why you leaving then? So why you leaving then?" Mouse, still standing tall on hind paws, hurled every expletive he could think of.

Blocker wiped off the dust from his clothes and left with his friend.

"Man, I knew he was just talking junk. See how I knocked him down like a bowling pin. I knew that n$gga was fronting."

The crowd was dancing again.

"Nah, man, I'm ready to bounce," said Kevin.

"Don't worry 'bout him, man, let's just wait till Clarissa comes back, see what she and Addie want to do." Mouse grabbed Addie, and they began dancing. But in the middle of their dance, Mouse felt the heavy thing again. It was so sudden, Mouse failed to recognize it at first, until…

the gunfire
      lit up
         the sky.

"What you say? Say something now," screamed Blocker, his finger still cocked on the trigger. Then…

Kevin went down.

Everyone started running, shoving and trampling each other. One of the speakers toppled to the floor, weakening the power of the music. Some of the partygoers only ran as far as the other side of the street, then stood and watched.

"Clarissa."

"Addie."

"Kevin."

"Mouse." Blindly, they looked for each other.

Finally, Mouse saw Kevin. Blood was flowing from his mouth. Kevin was on the ground, still. Mouse's first instinct was to pick him up, to force him to stand. Placing his hand at the back of Kevin's head, Mouse tried to cradle him, attempted to lift him. But he could not.

Why can I not lift him? Why can—I—not—lift him?

Chunks of blood and grey matter marred his copper curls, and the back of Kevin's head fell apart in Mouse's hands.

He watched what was once Kevin's head fall to the ground in large and small pieces.

"Copper…Copper! Oh, God, Copper…" Mouse wailed, head back, rocking to and fro on crouched legs.

The leering silence of the moment is all that is left.

Everyone dispersed from the yard. Some people crossed the street but stood and watched, shameless. Some people started home. As the crowd parted, Clarissa finally made her way through the confusion, back into the yard. At the sound of her scream, Mouse looked up.

Clarissa's body convulsed as she shook her head: in awe, in shock, in foolishness—at everything they'd chosen that could not be undone.

She lifted her right hand crookedly, touching the ether of air. "The crow," she said, "I saw it on top of the tree. We should never have come. I should have *known* that we should never have come here…"

Addie, leaden, just dropped to her knees.

Mouse was still holding Kevin's neck, which felt weightless now, sickeningly light in his left palm. And all he could do to keep from looking down again was to keep looking up at Clarissa, who was standing with her right hand still raised, touching the ether of air that would not touch her back. Anesthetized.

There was something in the air.

There was something in her.

CHAPTER TWENTY

They were all gathered together after the funeral—but where was Mouse?

Even in the fog of her grief and despair, suddenly Ophelia knew she was right.

She had always had a bad feeling about that boy, and in his absence a new, and unsettling, awareness washed over her beneath the darkness of the parlor awning: Although the details had yet to be revealed, she was now sure that Mouse was the cause of Kevin's murder. Or at least behind it in some way.

Cecil placed his arms around her waist and embraced her. As he did so, a full five inches shorter than Ophelia was, he pressed his chest into her abdomen, the way he used to when they were one; the way they had on the night they conceived Euclin, and, later, Clarissa and Kevin. But in this embrace she was still hearing his final words to her: "What man go want you? What man go want a big, black, ugly woman like you? What man go want a hard-foot woman like you?" As he had shouted this, the veins bulged in his neck, thick and rigid as cables. Now her body was rigid, her arms at her sides, and when he broke their embrace, the air of relief slipped from her mouth.

Two hours before, at the start of the funeral ceremony, Cecil had taken his place on the right of the front pew where she sat, preceded by his new wife, Consuela. He had no right to be there—and every right to be. Ophelia needed him there in spite of the past. They were both in pain. She could see it in his eyes. But she also knew that she and he both were too full of bitterness and pride to share the burden of their grief. She knew that she would mourn just as they had lived for the past eleven years since the separation, then divorce: selfishly and apart. No one grieves like a mother grieves. The Mother's Day that Cecil left her, Kevin and Clarissa were only six. For eleven years of Kevin's life, Cecil had been absent. For eleven years of Kevin's life she had been father and mother both.

When Kevin won his first karate match, who was there? His first trip to Disney World, who was there? Who had taken him to the hospital when, for a fifth-grade art project, he had used one of his father's old razor blades instead of school-box scissors; who, who, *who* was there? And after missing more than one half of his son's life—the last thing they had made in their final years of marriage that could ever universally be called love—all he did was saunter into the funeral parlor and take his place on the right of the pew so that Ophelia would be forced to gaze upon him, and think about what Kevin would have looked like as a middle-aged man.

She had brought Kevin back from Trinidad reformed, but America had stalked her son again, chewed him up, and eaten him. Now, just as she had feared—no, in fact, had known—the day had come when she was forced to wear black. It wasn't supposed to be this way. The black she expected to wear and should have worn was for the other Kevin. The moment he had flown to California, in her mind, she had laid a helping of white mothballs against that black dress and shelved it. Now she had shaken out the creases of that dress and put it on—for this? No. Not for this. It was not supposed to be for this. His death was supposed to have been the price of badness. Not goodness. For badness. Isn't *that* the way it was supposed to be?

People were still queuing up to view the open coffin holding her son, laid out in the grey herringbone suit he had worn to his graduation. *So many people.* His new girlfriend, Ophelia kept forgetting—*What is that child's name?*—and her mother had flown in from California. His old girlfriend had flown in from DC. People had come up from Brooklyn to Linnaeus' parlor in Harlem, where the service was being held. People had come from Jersey, Long Island, Queens, Georgia, Florida, Canada. The relatives from Trinidad had extended their stays. But it wearied Ophelia. As they turned from the open coffin, she'd grown fatigued by the looks that people gave her. Looks of contempt, outrage, accusation, nausea, disgust.

She could hear them whispering in the rows of pews behind her:

"Why? Why did she do that?"

"How could she?"

She wanted to speak. To answer them. And she would, soon.

Linnaeus and his assistant emerged from the wings and closed the upper half of the casket. The service and the eulogies were about to begin. This is the way they were seated on the pew: Cecil, Consuela, Brent, Euclin, Ophelia, Clarissa, Addie, and Mam and Pa. Pa needed the aisle space for his wheelchair and oxygen tank—the news of Kevin's death had caused his collapse at the family barbecue. Ophelia turned around, wondering where Mouse was. Euclin squeezed her hand, not letting go. Had it not been for the cream color of their palms, their plum hands cupped so tightly together would have been indistinguishable.

She looked at the coffin again, knowing that one day it would be closed forever. And at this thought, the pit of her stomach went cold. And she could feel it: her sorrow, started as a chilly lump of snow, massing into an avalanche. She could not breathe. But she was walking. Living. How was that possible?

All rose at the preacher's command.

The room sang:

> *Abide with me; fast falls the even tide, the darkness*
> *Deepens; Lord with me abide: when other helpers*
> *Fall, and comforts flee, help of the*
> *helpless, O abide with me!*
>
> *Swift to its close ebbs out life's little day; Earth's joys grow*
> *Dim, its glories pass away; change and decay in*
> *All around I see: O Thou who changes not abide with me!*

And then, like a twig, Ophelia's mind snapped. And this was when Ophelia started to live in fragments. This was when she started living among the dead, the ancestors in the sepia living-room photos gathered, encircling her.

Now Niles stood at the podium.

When he, Cordelia, Kissey-Ann, and Indigo came in and sat in the pew behind them, alongside Tyler and Angus, Ophelia smelled rum on her brother's breath. And when he had opened his mouth to kiss them in greeting, the scent had rushed out like a flambeau.

He was talking.

Ophelia heard the words black-on-black, love, murder, and nephew tumble from her brother's mouth. She tried her best to hear him, but could not breathe. But she was living. How was that possible? There should have been two oxygen tanks in that center aisle.

"Some of these children come out of the wombs like gourds…" Niles said. "Outside, their skins are drawn and hard, inside there is nothing but emptiness. But why is there emptiness? There's something in me. I can feel for you. And you can feel for me." Niles pointed to the audience. "What is it that keeps these children from feeling what you and I feel? After all, didn't an encounter between a sperm and an egg conceive us—all of us!—in the very same way?"

The minister placed a stern hand on the podium. Niles apologized to the audience for taking so long, then put his hand over his heart. "But I know that these children *can* feel…That there is something in these children, too, and we—Feelie…" he said, singling her out, entreating his sister directly, "Feelie, we must find it. Lord, God, Feelie, please help me find it."

And the minister's stern, strong hand caught Niles by the shoulder just as his knees gave way. Linnaeus and his assistant, Habeas, helped lead him back to the pew.

Many took to the podium: Euclin, Linnaeus, Kevin's former and most recent girlfriends, some of Kevin's other friends, but none of them had figured as prominently in Kevin's life as Mouse. They stood at the podium, these minor leaguers, heads down, hands in their pockets, muttering words that only rendered part of her son, not the whole. Only Mouse—not even Ophelia—could have given the whole. Kerchief and pocketbook in her lap, she turned and scanned the room, still wondering where he was. Later on, days after the viewing, she would learn that some of these other friends had talked about finding the perpetrator, getting revenge. But where was Mouse?

A white-gloved hand appeared before her. Linnaeus led her from pew to podium. It was her turn. It was her time. Ophelia collected herself.

Standing at the lectern, she began:

"I have heard talking in front of me, to the back of me, on all sides. And I wish to talk to this talking. The reason that I had an open casket is because I want all the world to see what they did to my son." Ophelia pointed to the closed casket, where her son lay beneath, his head poorly patched together, only partly reconstructed. Linnaeus had done the best that he could, and suggested a closed-casket ceremony. Ophelia had refused.

"I want all the world to see what they did to my son," she continued from the lectern, "the holes from which his life and all his life's memories came spilling out onto pavement. The way in which someone had stolen and spilled to the ground all the tings about my son that were irreplaceable.

"You know what I heard as I sat in that pew? 'What a horror. How disrespectful. What a shame. It does not even look like him. How could she do this?' My son was taken from me, stolen from me, ripped from me, and you dare to ask *me* how could I do this? You tink I care what you tink. You tink I care for propriety—that I have time for etiquette? That I have the patience to pity you for your squeamishness?

"I want the world to see what they did to my son. I want the world to see him like this. This is *my* son. And the shame and the vengeance is on the head of his killer!"

Ophelia refused all help as she dismounted the podium, past the metal casket where, before the service started, her lips so warm had pressed against his cheeks so cold. She returned to her place on the pew, where it started all over again as the minister took to the podium, the world vaulting at her in fragments. This was what she heard:

We travel by faith, not by sight.

All death has a purpose. We don't know what it is, but it does.

Current times make life such a business of bewilderment. What we call death is a movement to another existence.

Faith will see you through.

God always takes the good ones first.

Sometimes God plucks the prettiest flowers in the field and draws them nearer to himself.

The ultimate purpose of death is to glorify the goodness of God.

These were the only words she latched onto in full, when the minister read from Psalm 90:

> *You turn men back to dust, saying*
> *"Return to dust O sons of men."*
>
> *For a thousand years in your sight*
> *are like a day that has just gone by.*

Pa got up as the minister stopped speaking, the tubes from the oxygen tank pulling him downward, but he resisted. "The old are meant to precede the young," he announced, "not the other way around. Is that not how it is meant to be? Then if that is how the world is meant to be, why are so many young men leaving us before their fathers and grandfathers?" He said it loudly, as they placed him in his chair to wheel him to the front of the chapel, nearer to the casket where he would make his own speech, the final speech, as he had requested. Pa lingered before the closed coffin and stared at the lid. His head and shoulders slumped. Soon the queue for the final viewing would begin to form again.

As she received her father's eulogy in fragments, large and small pieces, Ophelia, realized why she could not breathe: She was drowning.

The rain had followed them into the house. And with it came a dampness that brought out the true smell of things and of people, as though those supernal droplets had stirred the dusty and the hidden to life.

Take Mrs. Hutchence, for instance. Ophelia had been surprised to find her with a cupful of punch, downstairs at the wake mingling with the rest of the mourners. But the false potion of sympathy and concern that her neighbor had swabbed behind her ears washed away at the top of the stairs: Ophelia caught her in the act of entering her son's bedroom. When she called out, "Lucy," Mrs. Hutchence's first name, the woman had jumped and taken her hand from the doorknob.

"Oh, I'm so sorry," she said with a shame-filled insincerity. "I thought this was the bathroom."

But now Ophelia smelled the stench of her intentions. She had always mistrusted this woman, had always seen the jealous way this woman had eyed her children, as though comparing them to the rotten fruit of her own sons.

"Well, it's not the bathroom. You need to find the right door," said Ophelia, upon her now. Physically Ophelia dwarfed this woman; with a single hand she could have crushed her like a moth. She had never known that kind of violence dwelled inside of her. Her patience was thinning, her anger rising. She was growing tired of the wake, of having so many people around her. Someone had once warned her of the phenomenon of false mourners: "Some come to give you comfort. Others only come to see how you live." Mrs. Hutchence excused herself, and not ten minutes later she was gone.

Downstairs, the drumming started. People, singing, dancing, carrying on, rum and beer passing from hand to hand as though the barbecue had never ended.

And they sang—

> *I went to the rock for a hiding place, and the*
> *rock cried out, I'm a hiding, too…*

And they sang—

> *One by one. Two by two. Three by three. Jesus*
> *called them by their number…*

And they sang—

> *Jordan river so chilly and cold, it chills*
> *my body, but not my soul…*

And they sang and they drank, and they drank and they sang. Ophelia wanted to throw these people out of her house. Shout: Have respect for the dead! But this was the way, in Trinidad, that they had always mourned. She was still experiencing the world in fragments, large and small pieces. And this scared Ophelia, this not being herself. And in her mind Ophelia heard herself saying: *Is toutoulbé I turning. But look at me…I turning toutoulbé!* Ophelia couldn't remember the word she was seeking, the American equivalent.

And then she did: the Creole word she'd used translated as stupid, but *crazy* was what she meant. Ophelia knew she had to snatch the fragments, construct a complete exterior, to keep people from knowing, to keep from falling apart like a cake in the rain.

Was she even here on Earth? She felt as though her words were controlled by the hidden hand of some unseen, but powerful ventriloquist.

But where was Mouse?

As they had all gathered together after the funeral, under the parlor awning, Ophelia had come to a conclusion—but there was still a part of her that did not want this as truth. That did not want to be right. She had pressed Clarissa with the same questions directly after the funeral, and now again at the wake: "Are you sure that someone called to tell him what day and time it was? That the service would be at the parlor? That we would travel back to Brooklyn for the wake? Someone did reach him, you sure? You sure he get the message? You sure?" Ophelia rubbed her chain, feeling the points of the cross digging into the calloused flesh of her palms.

He had always smelled of the streets, that boy. There was no turning back in her mind: Now she knew for certain.

In the midst of her grief, Ophelia wasn't seeking *the* truth, but scripting *her* truth, based on the substance of things seen—even though it was a warped truth that would define and frame her relationship and interaction with Mouse forever.

But why Kevin—why not Mouse? That dirty, scruffy boy. This was not the first time she would think this about Mouse. From that day forward, her life and his forever would braid together in life, in death, in grief. Forever enmeshed, held together by Kevin's copper thread.

CHAPTER TWENTY-ONE

Drained from the funeral and the wake two days before, Clarissa sat in her room, at the edge of her bed, her fingertips pressing into the piping of her bedspread. It was girlish and ruffled, not the sort of thing she liked, but she had agreed to place it on her bed to please her mother as they prepared the house for the wake and the crush of guests. Clarissa listened to her mother's and sister's voices as Euclin helped order Ophelia's suitcase, her tickets, her passport, her life, in a way that made sense in anticipation of her trip down to Trinidad.

For Ophelia had decided that she didn't want Kevin to be buried in America.

Euclin was there to drive their mother to the airport, Clarissa accompanying them.

Ophelia was the only one who would be flying with the body to Trinidad. She and he were going back home. Linnaeus, who would be joining her later, was coming in on a flight the next morning. The beauty of Linnaeus was that he knew when to pull back, when to take to the wings and give her space. When they reunited, they would take Kevin's body to the family plot in the Rio Verde countryside; and after they flew back to New York, Mam and Pa would make sure that the plot did not become overgrown.

Ophelia had deflected Cecil's overtures at attending the final burial service. There would be no more sharing. She had already done enough of it at the parlor and the wake. And Clarissa's freshman semester at City College had already begun, so Ophelia would not let her travel down to Trinidad with her, either.

"You're in college—not just a big girl, but a woman now. You must stay," Ophelia insisted. "The first weeks' classes are very important." Ophelia then showed her all the precooked meals she had stored in the freezer. While she was gone, Clarissa was to spend the weekend with Euclin; and during the week, when she stayed at the house alone, Verlee and Niles would come by to check on her.

"At least let me go for the drive to the airport," Clarissa implored, and took part of the day off from school to see her mother off.

In the car, they talked about perfunctory things like the best way to get to the BWIA airline terminal, but otherwise their trip was chaperoned by silence.

As the skycap took her luggage, Ophelia thought of Cecil, of how he had come and left. And she wondered if their feelings were synchronized at that moment, if he was grieving in Venezuela, or if in the arms of his new bride his life had already gone on.

Linnaeus was flying down to meet her because they weren't able to book their flights together, and Ophelia was secretly relieved at the solitude this glitch afforded her.

The coroner's office hadn't even let her see Kevin. They had taken a Polaroid of his corpse and brought the picture out for her to ID him.

Ophelia sat buckled in her seat, waiting for the plane to taxi down the runway, to exit JFK and New York.

They had taken the picture at an angle that had hidden the missing part of his head. Had this been intentional?

It was Linnaeus who had told her the extent and the truth of Kevin's condition, once his body had arrived at the parlor. Not one, but two bullets had entered his head, shattering his skull. One bullet had exited through his right eye.

The initial report that she'd been given said that he had died from multiple wounds to the head, but it hadn't yet settled into her conscience, her bones, that Kevin was not whole, was not breathing. *They show pictures*, Linnaeus had explained on the drive home, *to keep people from grabbing*. He said your first instinct is to grab when you see the one you love, the one you kissed, or the one you birthed. A picture de-escalates the drama, keeps it two-dimensional, avoiding the touching, the wailing, the clinging, the messiness of it all.

Other people don't know what it's like to lose a child, Ophelia thought, and looked down through her window at a receding New York. This kind of grief was a scenario that she had imagined as she read other people's stories in the paper. But she never thought it would happen to her. She was a fool to assume the danger over. Fool, fool, fool. And she was the one who had done it. He had wanted to stay in California to be with his new girlfriend and her family, to meet the new friends that now he never would. All he'd wanted was to bury his head in his books. But she, so controlling, had forced him. She had coerced him to his death and he came running. And before he was gone, he had thanked her for the call.

How strange.

Ophelia felt the cold metal of irony bury itself in her spleen. All she had known for the past eighteen years was how to be a mother to three children, once the twins came. Now she had to learn how to be a new creature: a mother of three but mother to two. Ophelia closed her eyes and crossed her arms on her chest. Before her, her very future, once premised on the elements of a clear past, lay diffused, spread out on the floor like spilled milk. Useless.

Now they were undoing their seat buckles for the stopover in Barbados. The seatbelts went clink, clink, clink in layered unison. Backs, legs, and derrières rose from the nubby upholstery of airline seating and made an eager, rubbing sound. And overhead compartments made an open-sesame *thunk*, followed by the sounds of passengers retrieving carry-on luggage and fall outerwear. Hidden underneath that gear in Kennedy were poplin capris, straw totes, sandals, flip-flops, and so much skin, glorious skin; they were wheeling out their epidermises, these tourists, by the truckful. There was supposed to be something inviting about this; after all, for them, it was a vacation.

Ophelia moved out to the waiting area and read her travel Bible, waiting for her connecting flight. Next to her a woman was showing her a pretty pair of coral earrings she had bought in Duty Free, trying to strike up a conversation. She was mildly freckled, the woman, fleshy, redheaded, and beautiful. Affable. A Midwestern aura.

"My husband is Trinidadian, Afro-Trinidadian," the woman said. "It's my very first time down there. My husband warned me that there is far too much concrete, and that it's not as pristine as Tobago. Is that true?"

Ophelia nodded. "The countryside where I grew up is much prettier," she said, feeling put upon to make conversation.

The woman did all the talking after this, until she'd exhausted her interest in her own world and had gotten round to Ophelia's.

"And what are you here for?"

Ophelia replied, "I am here to bury my son. His coffin is in the belly of the plane."

The woman's laugh lines froze, suspended and unnatural. "Oh, I'm so sorry..." she said. "I'm so very, very sorry." The attempt at condolence came out limp and laggardly.

Ophelia had neither patience nor pity for squeamishness. She had no comfort to give. Citing the ladies room she rose and walked away.

She hid in the bathroom and wept until the connecting plane arrived for departure. This was the first of many such encounters—another reason why, in the months to come, though Clarissa would mock and officially christen her crazy, Ophelia would begin to use her house as a citadel to hide from life and earnest people. Few knew how to talk to the bereft, speaking to her not as though she was simply a person with a loss, but as though she, too, numbered among the dead. As though she were the one who had died, whose presence among the living was an anomaly. As though she, Ophelia, were some kind of dressed and jeweled mummy who had fooled the world into counting her among the living by simply speaking and breathing. A talking mummy, or a leper. Kevin's death had made her all of these things.

Her next flight landed at Piarco Airport. Ophelia was finally home. Barbados, Trinidad, Tobago. This was a vacation for everyone else. The passengers descended from the plane directly onto the runway, into the open air.

Ophelia stood on the airport's stretch of asphalt and pressed her hand against her hat to keep it from blowing away. She wanted to move, but couldn't. So many times she had touched down in Piarco. So many times she had walked down this tarmac. Yet, suddenly, she did not know in which direction to move forward, in which direction to turn.

What next?

www.ingramcontent.com/pod-product-compliance
Lightning Source LLC
Chambersburg PA
CBHW030806020726
47499CB00006B/1789

* 9 780099 613601 *